D0872090

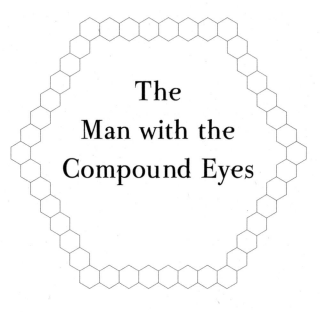

# The
# Man with the
# Compound Eyes

# The Man with the Compound Eyes

## Wu Ming-Yi

Translated from the Chinese
by Darryl Sterk

Pantheon Books
New York

Translation copyright © 2013 by Darryl Sterk

Grateful acknowledgment is made to Special Rider Music to reprint lyrics from "A Hard Rain's A-Gonna Fall" by Bob Dylan, copyright © 1963 by Warner Bros. Inc., copyright renewed 1991 by Special Rider Music. Reprinted by permission of Special Rider Music.

Library of Congress Cataloging-in-Publication Data
Wu Ming-Yi [date]
[Fu yan ren. English.]
The man with the compound eyes : a novel / Wu Ming-Yi ;
Translated from the Chinese by Darryl Sterk.
pages   cm.
Originally published in Taiwan as Fuyanren by Fudan Press in 2011.
ISBN 978-0-307-90796-7 (hardback) ISBN 978-0-307-90797-4 (eBook)
1. Islands—Fiction. 2. Families—Fiction. 3. Missing persons—Fiction.
I. Sterk, Darryl, translator. II. Title.
PL2966.U825F82513 2014     895.13'52—dc23     2013042177

www.pantheonbooks.com

Jacket illustration by Brendan Monroe
Jacket design by Peter Mendelsund

Printed in the United States of America
First United States Edition

2  4  6  8  9  7  5  3  1

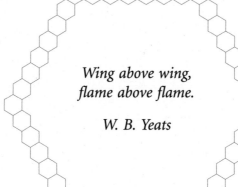

*Wing above wing,*
*flame above flame.*

W. B. Yeats

I

# I. The Cave

The trickling of water through the fissures in the subterranean rock was suddenly drowned out when the mountain made an immense but also somehow distant sound.

Everyone fell silent.

Then Jung-hsiang Li shouted. That sure wasn't groundwater surging. Wasn't loose rocks shifting or bedrock bursting, either. And it obviously wasn't a vocal echo. It sounded more like when something bumps into a flawless glass vessel—from somewhere within the glass you hear a spider's web begin to spread before the cracks appear. The sound vanished straightaway, and the only thing the people in the cave and the control room could hear was the huff of each other's breathing and the hiss of the radios.

Detlef Boldt heaved a huge sigh of relief and asked, "Did . . . did you all hear that sound just now?" speaking in English with a heavy German accent. Nobody replied, not because they hadn't heard it, but because they didn't know how to describe it. Then the electrical system cut out, and deep in the mountain the cave went black. It was too dark to see a thing. There it was again. It was as if some colossal being was marching through the mountain, either toward them or away.

"Shhhh! Stay quiet!" Jung-hsiang Li deliberately kept his voice down, lest the sound waves induce vibrations in the rock walls and cause another collapse. But actually everyone had quieted down already.

# 2. Atile'i's Last Night

The people of Wayo Wayo thought the whole world was but a single island.

The island was situated in the midst of an immense ocean, far from any continent. As far as island memory reached, the white man had once visited the island, but nobody had ever left and brought back news of another land. In the beginning, people believed, there was nothing but a shoreless sea, until Kabang (the word for "God" in the Wayo Wayoan language) created the island for them to live on, as if placing a small, hollow clamshell in a tub of water. The island followed the tides, floating around in the ocean, which was a source of sustenance for the people. But some of the ocean's spawn were the avatars of Kabang. The *asamu,* for instance, was a black-and-white fish sent to spy on people, and to test them. For this reason, it was counted among the creatures that could not be eaten.

"If you are so careless as to eat an *asamu,* you will grow a ring of scales around your navel, a ring of scales that you could never finish peeling off your whole life long." Leaning on a whalerib staff, the Sea Sage hobbled over and sat under a tree every day at dusk to tell the little ones all the stories of the sea. He talked until the sun dipped below the waves. He talked until the boys became youths, and until the youths endured the rite of passage and became men. His speech carried the smell of the sea, and there was salt on his every breath.

"So what if we grow scales?" one boy asked. The children here all had enormous eyes, like the eyes of a nocturnal animal.

"Oh my child, people can't grow scales, just like a sea turtle can't sleep with its belly to the sky."

Another day, the Earth Sage took the children to the field in the hollow, to the place where the *akaba* grew. One of the only starchy plants on the island, the luxuriant *akaba*, a word that meant "shaped like the palm of a hand," seemed to raise innumerable hands in supplication to the sky. The island was small and the people lacked farming tools, so pebbles were piled around the plots, to keep the soil moist and to serve as a windbreak. "You must love the land, my children, and ring it in with your love. For the land is the most precious thing on this island. It is like rain, like the heart of a woman." The Earth Sage showed the children how to arrange the rocks. His skin was dry like cracked mud, and his back was arched like an earthen mound. "In all the world, the only things worth trusting in are the land, the sea and Kabang, my children."

At the southeast corner of the island was a coral lagoon, a good place to catch fish with thrownets or to collect clams. To the northeast, at a distance of ten husks (ten throws of a coconut husk) there was a cay, a coral reef that was fully exposed at ebb tide. This was where the seabirds flocked. The Wayo Wayoans hunted the birds with *gawana*. To make a *gawana*, they tied branches into a tool that had the virtues of club and spear, with one end blunt and the other end sharpened to a point; then they passed a rope of saltgrass through a hole in the blunt end and tied one end into a noose. Armed with a *gawana*, a fisherman would row his *talawaka* near the cay and let the ocean current carry him along, pretending to ignore the birds as he prayed to Kabang. When he drifted within range he would hurl his *gawana*. Blessed by Kabang, the noose would slip, just so, over a seabird's neck, and a deft flick of the wrist would impale the bird on the pointy end. Blood would trickle down from the point, as if the *gawana* itself had suffered a mortal wound. The only resistance the albatross, the booby, the pelican, the petrel and the seagull could put up was proliferation. When the birds stopped in spring to build nests, people would feast on eggs, wearing cruel and satisfied smiles on their faces.

As on any island, there was never enough fresh water on Wayo Wayo. The only sources were rain and a lake at the center of the island. Consisting mainly of fish and fowl, the diet was salty, giving the people a thin and dark appearance and often leaving them constipated. At dawn they would squat over pit latrines, facing away from the sea, often getting teary-eyed from the strain.

The island was so small that most people could set out after breakfast, walk all the way around and return not long after lunch. For the same reason, people were accustomed to a rough parlance of "facing the sea" or "facing away" to orient themselves, and the only way to face away was to face the hillock at the center of the island. People talked facing the sea and ate facing away. They conducted rituals facing the sea, and made love facing away, so as not to offend Kabang. There were no chiefs among the people, only "elders," the wisest of whom were called "old men of the sea." The front door of the home of a family in which an old man of the sea had lived faced the shore. Adorned with shells and carvings, Wayo Wayoan houses looked like capsized canoes. They stuck fish skin to the walls, and the whole community would gather round and build a coral fence out in front to block the wind. The islanders could neither walk to a place where the sea could not be heard nor have a conversation in which the sea was not mentioned. In the morning, they greeted each other, "Are you going to sea?" At noon they asked, "Shall we test our luck at sea?" And at night, even if the weather had been too rough to go fishing today, they exhorted one another, "You must remember me a story of the sea." As a rule, the Wayo Wayo went fishing every day. Fishermen who met on shore would yell, "Don't let the *mona'e* steal your name!" *Mona'e* meant wave. When people bumped into one another, one would ask, "So how's the weather at sea?" Even if a gale was blowing, the other had to reply, "Very fair." The tonality of the Wayo Wayoan language was sharp and sonorous, like birdsong, with each utterance ending in a light trill and a plop, like a hungry seabird that swiftly dives and breaks the waves in search of prey.

Occasionally, the people went hungry, the weather was too rough, or two of the villages would come into conflict; but no matter how he spent his days, everyone was skilled at telling diverse stories of the sea. People told tales at meals, when they met, at rituals, and when making love. They even told them in their sleep. A complete record had never been made, but many years later anthropologists might know that the islanders had the greatest number of sea sagas of any people on Earth. "Let me tell you a story of the sea" was on the tip of everyone's tongue. They did not ask how old people were, but simply grew tall like trees and stuck out their organs of increase like flowers. Like the obstinate clam they just passed the time. Like a sea turtle each islander died with the curl of a smile at the corner of his mouth. They were all old souls, older than they appeared, and because they spent their lives staring at the sea they all had melancholy miens and tended to get cataracts and go blind in old age. When they were ready to go, old folks would ask the youngsters by the bed, "What's the weather out at sea like now?" People believed that dying while gazing at the sea was the grace of Kabang. Their lifelong dream was to arrive at the moment of death with an image of the ocean in the ocean of the mind.

When a boy was born, his father would select a tree for him and carve a notch for each resurrection of the moon. When there were a hundred and eighty notches, the boy had to build a *talawaka* of his very own. Years before, the anthropologist S. Percy Smith had described the *talawaka* as a "canoe." Actually, it was more like a grass boat. The island was too small to have enough trees with trunks thick enough to be made into canoes. Students of anthropological history smile at Smith's mistake, but nobody would laugh at him, as anyone who saw a *talawaka* would assume it was a dugout canoe. A *talawaka* was made by weaving sticks, rattan stems and three or four different kinds of silver grass together to form a frame and applying three coatings of plant pulp. Peat from the bog was used to plug any remaining cracks, and the craft was waterproofed with sap. A finished *talawaka* really did look like a finely finished canoe made by hollowing out the trunk of a sturdy tree.

The finest and sturdiest *talawaka* on the island was made by a youth named Atile'i. Atile'i's face had the typical traits of his people: a flat nose, profound eyes, shining skin, a sad, slouching spine and arrow-like limbs.

"Atile'i, don't sit there, the sea fiends will see you!" hollered a passing elder upon seeing Atile'i sitting by the shore.

*　*　*

Once, like everyone else, Atile'i thought that the whole world was but a single island drifting on the sea like a hollow clamshell in a tub of water.

Having learned the art of *talawaka* construction from his father, Atile'i was praised as the most skilled *talawaka*-maker among the island youth, even more skilled than his elder brother Nale'ida. Though young, Atile'i had the physique of a fish and could catch three ghostheads on a single breath. Every girl on the island pined for Atile'i and hoped that one day he would waylay her, throw her over his shoulder and carry her off into a clump of grass. Three full moons later, she would discreetly inform Atile'i that she was with child. Then she would go home, act normal, and wait for Atile'i to arrive with a whalebone knife and a marriage proposal. Maybe that's what the most beautiful girl on the island, Rasula, was hoping for, too.

"Atile'i has the fate of a second son. What good is a second son who can dive? Atile'i is destined for the Sea God, not for Wayo Wayo." Atile'i's mother often complained in this vein, and people would nod knowingly, understanding that raising an outstanding second son was the most painful thing in the world for any parent. Atile'i's mother grumbled day and night, her thick lips trembling, as if the more she bemoaned her son's fate the greater his chance of avoiding it might be.

Unless an eldest son died young, the second son seldom married and went on to become an "old man of the sea." Upon reaching his one hundred and eightieth full moon, he would be sent out to sea on a mission of no return. He could take no more than ten days' worth of water and was not allowed to look back. Hence the saying, "Let's just wait until your second son returns," which simply meant, "Perish the thought."

With flashing eyelashes and sparkling skin, covered in crystals of salt, Atile'i looked like the son of the Sea God. Tomorrow he would brave the waves in his *talawaka*. He climbed the highest reef-rock on the island and gazed down at the distant swells, at the white creases in the fabric of the sea. The seabirds flying along the shore reminded him of Rasula, who was as nimble as the shadow of a bird in flight. And like a shore pounded by the waves for many eons, his heart, he felt, was about to break.

According to custom, Atile'i's admirers laid ambush at dusk. Atile'i had only to wander past a clump of grass and some young maiden would accost him. Every time he hoped the girl in the grass would be Rasula, but Rasula never appeared. Atile'i made love over and over again to the girls in the grass, for this was the last chance he had to father a child and leave some small part of himself behind on the island. In fact, as a matter of propriety and morality, he could not refuse their propositions: the girls of Wayo Wayo could ambush a second son on the night before he went to sea. Atile'i broke his back making love to the girls in the thickets, taking no pleasure, intent only on nearing Rasula's place before dawn. He had a feeling he would meet her there. Each girl along the way sensed that once inside her Atile'i was in a rush to leave. Hurt, they all asked, "Atile'i, why don't you love me?"

"You know that people can't pit their hearts against the sea."

Atile'i finally made it with pale fishbelly dawn on the horizon. A pair of hands appeared from inside the grass and lightly drew him in. Shivering like a seabird ducking beside a boulder to dodge a flash of lightning, Atile'i could barely get an erection, not because he was exhausted but because the look in Rasula's eyes was like a jellyfish's sting.

"Atile'i, why don't you love me?"

"Who says I don't love you? But you know no man can pit his heart against the sea."

They cuddled for a long while. Eyes closed, Atile'i felt like he was hanging in thin air, gazing down upon the open ocean. He gradually became aroused, tried to force himself to forget that soon he would go to sea, wanting only to feel the warmth inside Rasula's body. At dawn, the villagers would all go down to the shore to see Atile'i off. Except for the Sea Sage and the Earth Sage, nobody would have noticed that all through the night departed spirits of second sons had been coming home. They all wanted to ride with the youth whose skin sparkled like the son of the Sea as he piloted the *talawaka* he had fashioned himself, carrying a "speaking flute," a final gift from Rasula, as he rowed away to the fate he shared with them, each one, the fate of every Wayo Wayoan second son.

# 3. Alice's Last Night

Alice Shih got up early one morning and decided to kill herself.

Actually, she had mostly made all the necessary preparations. Or perhaps one should say now nothing stood in her way: there wasn't anything she wanted to leave anybody, and she did not have much of an estate. She was simply someone who wanted to die.

But Alice was an obstinate person. She cared about all the people she cared about. There weren't many left, her son Toto and the students who had entrusted her with their hopes and dreams. Once Alice had known what she would need. Now nothing was clear.

Alice had tendered her resignation, returned her faculty ID. She could finally let out a big sigh of relief: now the torment of this life would end and she could try her luck in the next. Alice had gone to grad school to pursue her dream of becoming a writer. She had sailed into this faculty position after getting her Ph.D. With her delicate appearance and sensitive disposition she seemed in Taiwan's conservative society typecast for the role of the writer. A lot of people envied her; after all, for a literary person, this was the smoothest road one could possibly take. Only Alice knew the truth: that becoming a good writer was no longer the issue, that she simply had no time to write. Stifled by administrative duties, she had not had a breath of fresh, literary air these past few years. Oftentimes it was already sunrise before she was ready to leave the office.

She decided to give away all the books and things in her office to her students. Trying not to get all emotional, she treated each of the students she had mentored to a meal as a way of saying goodbye. Sitting in the dreadful campus cafeteria, she observed the different expressions in their eyes.

"So young," she thought.

These kids imagined they were on the way to some mysterious destination, but there wasn't really anything where they were going, just an empty space like a basement, a place that was heaped with junk. She tried to keep a glimmer of sympathy in her eyes, to let her students think that she was still listening and interested in what they had to say. But Alice was just a shell through which air was blowing, all words like stones being tossed into an empty house that didn't even have windows. The only thoughts that flickered through her mind were memories of Toto and possible ways of ending her life.

On second thought, that seemed a bit unnecessary. The sea was right on her doorstep, wasn't it?

Alice had not bid farewell to practically any of her colleagues. She was afraid she might reveal the knots of revulsion toward the world that life had tied in her soul. Driving through town, Alice felt things looked about the same as when she first came here over ten years before, but she was struck by the sense that this was no longer the land of gorges and villages that had drawn her here. Halfway down the east coast, separated from the overdeveloped west by the Central Mountain Range, Haven had once seemed a refuge. But now the huge leaves, the clouds that would gather all of a sudden, the corrugated iron roofs, the dry creek beds she would see along the road every couple of miles, and the vulgar billboards—all the things she had at first found so endearing—were gradually withering, growing unreal, losing their hold on her. She remembered her first year in Haven: then the bush and the vegetation came quite close to the road, as if neither the terrain nor the wild animals feared the sight of man. Now the new highway had pushed nature far away.

Originally, Alice reflected, this place had belonged to the aborigines. Then it belonged to the Japanese, the Han people, and the tourists. Who did it belong to now? Maybe to those city folks who bought homesteads, elected that slimeball of a mayor, and got the new highway approved. After the highway went through, the seashore and the hills were soon covered with exotic edifices, not one of them authentic, pretty much as if a global village theme park had been built there as a joke. There were fallow fields and empty houses everywhere, and the fat cats who owned these eyesores usually only appeared on holidays. Folks in the local cultural scene liked to gush about how Haven was the true "pure land," among other cheap clichés of native identity, while Alice often felt that except for some houses belonging to the aboriginal people or buildings from the Japanese era, now maintained as tourist attractions, the artificial environment had been intended to spite the natural landscape.

Which reminded her of this one conference coffee break when her colleague Professor Wang started spouting off about how sticky the soil in Haven was, how "stuck-on-Haven" he felt, and not for the first time. What a disingenuous comment! Alice couldn't help telling him, right to his face, "Don't you mean stuck-in-Haven? There's fake farmhouses and fake B&Bs all over the place; even the trees in the yards of these places are fake. Don't you think? These houses! Ug. What's so great about it if all it does is cause phonies like that to stick around?"

Professor Wang was at a loss for words. For a moment he forgot to wear the mantle of the senior faculty member. With his drooping eyelids, gray hair and greasy appearance, he looked more like a businessman than like an academic. Honestly, there were times when Alice could not tell the difference. Professor Wang eventually managed, "If you say so, then what should it really be like?"

What was it really like? Alice ruminated on the drive home.

It was April. Everywhere was a sluggish, damp smell in the air, like the smell of sex. Alice was driving south. To the right was the Central Mountain Range, a national icon. Occasionally—no, more like every day—Alice recalled the way Toto had looked standing up on the car seat, gazing at the mountains with his head sticking up through the sunroof. He wore a camouflage hat, like a little soldier. Sometimes her memory would dress him in a windbreaker, sometimes not. Sometimes he would be waving, but not always. She imagined that Toto must have left the foot-sized indentation in the car seat that day. That was the last impression she had of her husband and son.

Dahu was the first person she called for help after Thom and Toto went missing. Dahu was Thom's climbing buddy. A member of the local rescue team, he knew these hills like the back of his hand.

"It's all Thom's fault!" She was frantic.

"Don't worry. If they're up there, I'll find them," Dahu reassured her.

Thom Jakobsen was from Denmark, a country without any true mountains. He was a flatlander who became a climbing fanatic soon after arriving in Taiwan. After finishing all the local trails with Dahu, he went abroad to train himself in traditional alpine climbing techniques. He wanted to prepare for an ascent on a mountain of over seven thousand meters, three thousand meters higher than the highest peak in Taiwan. Taiwan became a place he only visited on occasion. Alice, feeling herself getting older day by day, was almost no longer able to handle not knowing if or when Thom would return. But even when he was by her side his expression would wander far away.

Maybe that was why lately Alice tended to think first of Toto, then of Dahu, and only then of Thom. No, she hardly ever thought of Thom. He thought he knew everything there was to know about mountains, forgetting there were none back where he was from. And how could he? How could he take their son climbing and not bring him back? What if he had gotten sick that day or forgotten to charge the battery or even slept in a bit longer? Everything would have turned out different, Alice often thought.

"Don't worry, we're only going insect hunting! I won't take him anywhere dangerous. We'll be fine. Everyone knows the route we're going on." Thom had tried to reassure her but she heard a hint of impatience in his voice.

Most people could not believe that at ten years old Toto was already a skilled rock climber and mountaineer who knew more about alpine forests than the average forestry graduate. Alice understood Toto belonged to the mountains and tried not to stand in his way. Maybe Dahu was right that fate is fate, and that when the time comes, fate can fly like the shaft that finds the wild boar.

Dahu was a close friend of Alice and Thom's. He was many things: a taxi driver, a mountaineer, an amateur sculptor, a forest conservationist and a volunteer for some east-coast NGOs. He had a typically stocky Bunun build. He also had a charming gleam in his eyes; best not gaze right at him or you might think he has fallen in love with you, or that you have gone and fallen for him.

A few years before, his wife had abandoned him, leaving behind their daughter Umav and a note. She just wrote how much money she had withdrawn from the account and what she had taken from the house as well as the words THESE ARE MINE, without offering an explanation. Like a relinquished pet, Umav was just another item on that list of possessions left behind for Dahu. At first, Dahu would send Umav to stay at Alice's place for a few days at a time. He had the best of intentions, but the truth was he had no idea how to cheer up his daughter, and Umav and Alice only ended up making each other even more depressed. Alice would realize she had not said anything to Umav all afternoon. The girl would have spent the whole time looking bleakly out to sea, clipping and unclipping her bangs, unable to get her hair right. So Alice bluntly asked Dahu not to bring his daughter over anymore. Later, after the rescue mission failed to find any trace of Thom and Toto, she also stopped answering his regular sympathy calls.

Alice resolved to wall herself in. The only thing she looked forward to was sleep. Though sleep was just closing her eyes, at times she could see more clearly then. In the beginning she made a point of meditating before bed so that Toto would visit her in her dreams. Later she tried not to dream about Toto, only to discover that not dreaming about him was more painful than dreaming about him. Better to dream of him and bear the pain of waking up and realizing he was gone. Now and then, lying awake late at night, she would pick up the flashlight and tread into Toto's room to check on a boy who was not there, wanting to see whether his breathing was regular. Memory confronted her like a boxer whose power punches were too quick to dodge. Sometimes Alice wished she still felt lust; as anyone who has once been young will know, desire is the best antidepressant in the world, dulling the force of memory and keeping a person in the present. But the Thom who appeared in her dreams no longer offered her desire. Holding a climbing ax in his right hand, he would hack away at his left hand as it morphed into a mountain wall. He never said a single word. Each time she tried to grasp the meaning of a dream, she would call the police to see if there was any news. "I'm sorry, Professor Shih. If we hear anything, you'll be the first to know." The police had gone from whole-hearted to halfhearted, as if taking her calls had become a matter of routine. Once in a while there was even a hint of disgust in the voice on the other end of the line. "It's that woman again. She's just not gonna leave us alone," Alice imagined the policeman saying to his partners after hanging up the phone.

This April it had been constantly raining and unseasonably warm. There were supine beetles everywhere under the campus streetlights at night. Now there was a scarab inside the car. Alice rolled down the windows, but it could not find a way out. It just kept smacking against the windshield, its blue forewings faintly glowing.

These past few months, Alice discovered how dependent on Toto she had become. It was only for his sake that she had bothered to eat breakfast and keep a regular bedtime and learn how to cook. Alice had also learned to be more careful, since her safety was her child's safety. Anytime he went out, she had to worry that some goddamn drunk driver might smash his warm young face into the sidewalk, or that his classmates might bully him, or even his teachers, as people who spend a lot of time around children can sometimes be shockingly cruel. Alice remembered the girl with the dirty uniform she and her classmates used to gang up on. They taunted her day in, day out. They would splatter her dirty clothes to make them even dirtier, as if to show how clean their own clothes were by comparison.

Alice passed a bridge over a floodplain to the left. The bridge had been washed out a few years before. The new bridge had been built higher up in the hills, almost three kilometers further inland. A burst of honking forced Alice's attention back onto the road.

A few minutes later, the car rounded a stretch of coastline, formerly the most famous in Haven. Years before, a developer had gone in, shoveled away part of the mountain, filled it in, firmed it up and built an amusement park. And then, with the full backing of that mayor who was knee deep in corruption charges, the developer kept right on digging away at the mountain wall on the other side of the site. But a major earthquake over nine years ago had caused the foundations of most of the facilities to shift, rendering the rides inoperable. The company filed for bankruptcy to avoid having to pay compensation. What with the rising sea level and the encroaching shoreline, the uncleared cable-car pylons and Ferris wheel looked stranded now. To one side, on a boulder that must originally have been part of the mountain, sat an angler, his boat roped to a pylon. Alice kept driving along the New Coastal Highway, until finally her own distinctive abode came into view in the distance, as sunlight sprayed down on the land through a light rain. Despite the drizzle this was the best weather in weeks.

Her house was by the sea. But since when had the sea gotten that close?

Alice opened the door, which now served no meaningful purpose, and looked around at the last of her possessions: the sofa, the mural Thom and she had collaborated on, the Michele De Lucchi chandelier, and the dried-up house plants. She and Thom had selected everything together. The hollow in the pillow, the facecloth in the bathroom and the storybooks on the shelf all bore the marks of Toto's presence. Making a final inspection, Alice realized she had not figured out what to do about the aquarium. It would just be too cruel to leave the poor fish to wait, bewildered, helpless and speechless, for death once she died first. Sitting on the sofa, she remembered a student of hers named Mitch who really liked keeping fish. But she no longer had a cell, and she had cut the phone line. She mulled it over and decided she would just have to make one last trip to the university to arrange for Mitch to get the plants and fish. Of course, Mitch could take all the equipment if he wanted. Alice got back in the car. Thank God there was still about thirty kilometers of juice in the battery.

Alice called Mitch from the department office. Mitch soon arrived with a girl by his side. They all got into Alice's car. Mitch had an athletic build but appeared nebbish, a bit of a doormat. A lit major, he seemed a classic case of passion without talent. Mitch introduced his girlfriend as Jessie. The girl had a mischievous look in her eyes, a sweet smile and extremely fair skin, and was covered in accessories, but her appearance was about the same as any young woman walking down the street. Jessie was wearing a pair of skinny jeans. She said she had taken two courses from Alice, and though Alice had no particular impression of her, the girl seemed somehow familiar. The car was silent and stuffy the whole way back; Jessie and Mitch pretended to take in the scenery along the way to avoid having to talk to Alice.

The three of them treaded in mutely through the back garden. When Alice opened the door, Mitch gasped with surprise, crouched in front of the aquarium and asked, "Hey, isn't that a shovelnose minnow?"

"That's right." Those fish had been raised by a friend of Dahu's to be reintroduced into the wild. He had given Toto the ones he didn't release.

"Wow! You don't find these in the wild anymore. Can I see what's in the cabinet?"

"Sure."

Mitch opened the cabinet below the tank. Thrilled, he said, "It even has a cooler and a pH control! Awesome!"

"It's all yours." Mitch's exclamations were getting on Alice's nerves.

Mitch could hardly believe his ears. He confirmed she was serious and called a classmate. Soon three big strong boys arrived in an SUV and bustled the equipment into the back. Alice noticed Jessie quietly glancing at the digital photo frames hanging on the walls and at the spines of the books on the shelf.

"If you see a book you like please feel free."

"Uh . . . for real?"

"A few books won't make any difference." In the end Jessie only took a collection of short stories by Isak Dinesen in the original. Head cocked, Alice asked, "You read Danish?"

"Oh no, it's just, um, for a memento. Danish looks really neat."

Before getting in the SUV Jessie came over and asked: "Professor Shih, will I see you around campus?"

"Probably not."

"I was just wondering if I could send you stuff I write? I'd totally understand if it's not okay."

Alice had nodded, then shaken her head. Now, without any emotion, she remembered who the girl was.

After Mitch and Jessie left, Alice wandered into Toto's room and flopped onto the bed, which once had that familiar smell. Now Alice did not have to worry about the fish dying, only about how she would die, which somehow did not seem to matter as much. She stared up at the map on the ceiling of the hikes Thom had taken Toto on. They had drawn it together. Often she'd be cooking while they were in here hatching secret plans. Mountain climbing was always their thing, and all these years, no matter how hard Thom tried to convince her, she just would not go. She would not go to church, either.

"Sometimes in life you should be able to say no," Alice thought.

Alice would never forget her first climbing experience. More a hill than a mountain, the Emperor's Hall was located in the rocky country to the southeast of Taipei. At the time intercollegiate coed socials were popular, and Alice got dragged along to one by a classmate. Never a sporty person, she was all right for the first half of the climb, but once she went past a little temple she had to pull herself along with a rope and clamber over roots, until she made it to this ridge where there was nothing to hold onto. People kept encouraging her, and at the time Alice was too timid to refuse. She carried on for another few minutes and then broke out in a cold sweat and suffered a panic attack. She did not scream to get some gallant boy to help her along, as a typical girl might have done. The tears just started falling. Why of all places did they have to come here? One boy offered his arm but she refused. The fellow looked polite but was actually empty-headed (as she had discovered riding on the back of his motorbike). Instead, she made her own way back down, half-walking and half-crouching. She had never gone hiking since.

The map had intersecting red and blue routes labeled with different colored flags. She did not know what the colors meant and could only try to imagine the alpine vistas Thom and Toto had seen. Who knows how much time they spent on it or what was going through their heads when they were drawing it? She followed the routes with her eyes. Although she never went climbing, she had often looked at the map and planned treks with Toto, as if playing a game. She knew the map just as well as Toto and Thom, but for some reason she had always had a funny feeling that a few routes were not drawn quite right, though she could not say why. Alice kept staring until her eyes glazed over. It started getting dark outside, and the routes on the ceiling gradually withdrew into shadow. Alice pictured Toto sitting on his high stool or standing on Thom's shoulders as he traced out a route, until finally she lost track of time and sank into a deep sleep.

Sometime later that night there was a strong earthquake, strong enough to reawaken people's childhood memories. At first, she was still half-asleep; after all, she had been living in earthquake-prone Haven for quite a while now and had felt worse than this. But when the earth was still shaking over a minute later, and the tremor was getting stronger and stronger, Alice sat up in bed automatically, instinctively wanting to take shelter or flee the house. How ironic! Why should a person who is ready to die care how it happens? Alice lay back down and seemed to hear a great dull roaring coming from somewhere, as if the mountain itself was about to move. She recalled that huge earthquake that hit when she was in elementary school. No one in her family was killed, but her school had collapsed, and a science teacher who really liked her named Miss Lin as well as a boy who sat next to her in class, often gave her treats and wore spectacles had both been crushed to death. After school the day before, he had walked with her in the student procession and given her five silkworms. Five days after, maybe as a result of eating mulberry leaves that had not been cleaned properly, the silkworms all produced mushy black poops and died, their bodies all shriveled up. Those were the two most intimate memories she had of the event. An earthquake does not have to kill you to induce mortal terror; it is enough that it can take away something dear to you, leaving nothing but a shriveled skin behind.

The rumbling sound lasted several minutes before the world fell silent again. Alice was so tired she fell right back to sleep. It was not yet light out when she awoke to the inexorable rhythm of the waves. She got up, looked out the window, and found herself standing on a remote island in the midst of an immense ocean, as frothy waves rolled relentlessly across the distance toward the shore.

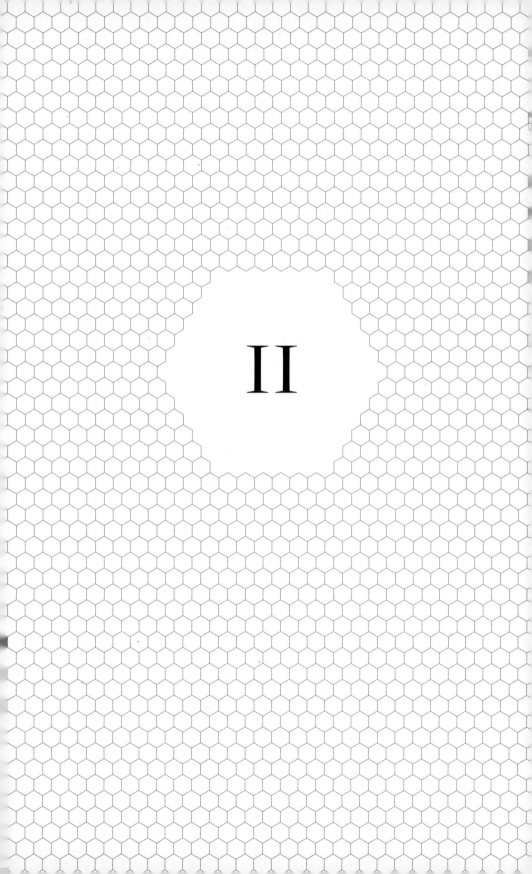

II

# 4. Atile'i's Island

The fog seemed to emanate from the ocean deep. It permeated everything, as all-pervasive as Kabang Himself. For a moment Atile'i wondered whether he was underwater. He might as well rest his oars, for what was the point of rowing in such a great fog? Seven days from Wayo Wayo, he was convinced that oars were useless in the open ocean. No wonder the islanders had established an invisible boundary around the fishing grounds, for any man who crossed it might never return. Not to mention the fact that his provisions of food and fresh water had run out. Though in spirit he had given up hope that his fate would be any different from any other second son, he had not despaired in the flesh. That's when he started trying to drink seawater.

Near midnight it started to rain. The rain and the fog blurred the boundary between sea and sky. In the rain Atile'i assumed he had gone through the Sea Gate. Legend had it that at the extremity of rain and fog there was a gate in the sea, beyond which lay the True Isle, the abode of Kabang and all the other aquatic deities, the island of which Wayo Wayo was but a shadow. Usually this True Isle was hidden beneath the sea, only to rise above the waves at certain fateful hours.

Atile'i sought shelter under the palm-leaf awning he had made especially for his *talawaka*, but it was dripping wet underneath, not much drier than out in the open. He murmured, "A mighty fish has fled, a mighty fish has fled." In the Wayo Wayo language this meant: Forget it, forget it. Though he had not said it out loud, Atile'i had already blasphemed in his heart: when he wondered whether, out here on the ocean, the ocean was greater than God. How could any god rule the sea? The sea itself was God.

At dawn, Atile'i realized his *talawaka* was sinking. Vainly but out of necessity, he bailed the water out, and only abandoned ship when it was almost submerged. Atile'i was a first-rate swimmer among the youth of Wayo Wayo, his legs as supple as a fishtail, his arms slicing through the water like fins, but in the open ocean even a jellyfish has more wherewithal than a man, even a man like Atile'i. Atile'i was swimming hard. No thoughts remained, not even the thought of quitting. Atile'i was like an ant that stumbles into a puddle and flails around, fighting for its life, knowing neither hope nor despair.

Though he had sinned against Kabang in his mind, Atile'i still prayed to Him with the words of his mouth. "O Kabang," he chanted, "the only one who could dry up the sea, if You would forsake me, please let my corpse turn into coral and drift homeward for Rasula to find." Atile'i lost consciousness as soon as his prayer was complete.

Atile'i woke to find that he was still floating at sea. He seemed to remember a dream, in which he had almost made it onto an island. On the edge of this island stood a group of youths with sad eyes, fins growing where arms should have been, and blotchy bodies, as if they had spent their whole lives rolling around on a reef. When Atile'i's *talawaka* was upon them, a gray-haired youth addressed him, saying, "A little bluefin tuna told us just the other day that you would arrive and join our tribe." The other youths started singing a mournful song, as if a wave of melancholy had just swept in. It was a song the islanders often sang when they went to sea, and Atile'i could not help singing along.

*If the ocean waves come on,*
*We'll block them with our song*
*But if a storm begins to blow*
*Alas, fair maiden, you must know*

*That into tuna, we might grow*
*That into tuna, we might grow*

Their youthful voices were like stars consoling the darkness, like mournful raindrops showering the sea. Then a one-eyed youth said, "Listen, his voice is different from ours. It's different, like he'll be beached on an island of his own." At this a wave hit, Atile'i lost his balance and out of dreamland fell.

After coming to his senses, Atile'i found he really was beached on an island. Apparently boundless, the island was made not of mud but of a multihued mishmash of strange stuff, and there was a weird smell hanging in the air. The sun was now out. The waves had taken all Atile'i's garments and ornaments, leaving him almost naked, but what bothered him most was the loss of the bottle of *kiki'a* wine Rasula had given him. The thought of Rasula's *kiki'a* wine made him very dry of the mouth. Thankfully, but bizarrely, he had not lost the "speaking flute," which he had been clutching in his hand when he fell unconscious. This must be the afterlife, Atile'i thought. He walked all over the island, discovering that most parts of it were none too firm. Some spots were quite spongy, like traps. Sometimes you could sink to a depth of several grown men or so before rising up again.

A round object caught Atile'i's attention. If he turned it toward the sun it shone with a dazzling rainbow light, but if he held it toward himself, Atile'i saw a tawny, mottled, lacerated face. Could something so hard be made of water? he wondered. Otherwise how could it reflect my appearance?

Atile'i soon discovered that there were many sorts of colored bags all over the island. They were different from the burlap bags of Wayo Wayo in that they could hold water, though with some of them the water whooshed out as soon as you picked them up, leaving mussels, sea stars and other odds and ends high and dry. There were bags like this on Wayo Wayo, too. The elders said the white man had left them behind, but the past few years you often found them floating in the sea as well. The islanders used them to hold water, and they were more resistant than rock to the ravages of time. He pried open a few of the mussels and ate them raw. He even tried drinking some of the water inside. It had a stench, but no doubt it was fresh. Atile'i was so grateful he almost started to cry. With water he could live.

Atile'i kept exploring the island until noon. He found shrimp and fish wedged between various objects, scarfing things as he went along. Before he knew it, it was sunset. He had picked up lots of sodden, ripped articles, apparently of clothing, but everything was so soft, not at all like the woven hemp raiment he was accustomed to. Still, one seemed to be able to wear them once they were dry. He also discovered some bottles, which he started collecting because they were so buoyant and brightly colored. He assumed they might come in handy if he made a boat or something like that.

"This must be the land of death, and who knows what one might need here?" He piled up the bottles and other curiosities and prayed that the sea would not turn to rain, so that tomorrow the sun could lift the damp and dry everything out.

When night really fell, Atile'i figured he must still be alive, because of an old saying about the netherworld: half the year the sun shines bright, and half the year is ruled by night. The rhythm of time on this island felt the same as on Wayo Wayo; it sure didn't seem like half a year had passed. Night in the middle of the ocean was not total darkness, as people generally imagine. The starlight and moonlight would drop through the clouds, and wondrous glowing lights would suddenly appear, sometimes so blinding a person could not get any sleep. Entranced by the spectacle, Atile'i sat on the edge of the island and brooded over an uncertain future.

When the moon started to get low in the sky, Atile'i had a feeling he was not alone. Suddenly, all around him, stood the youths who had appeared in his dream. Wearing enigmatic smiles, they observed him in his distress. Atile'i made the Wayo Wayoan gesture of goodwill, turning his palms up with his figures slightly curved. He was about to question them when a youth with a gash from his left shoulder to his abdomen pre-empted him, saying: "You guess right, we are spirits not men. All the spirits of the second sons of Wayo Wayo are here."

"You've been expecting me?"

"Yes."

"I should have known this was the netherworld. Or is this Midway Isle?"

"May the sea bless you. In all honesty, we don't know where we are.

We've been all over, but we never knew there was such an island. It drifted here not long ago," said the gray-haired youth from the dream.

"So, are you going to take me with you?"

"No. We're not angels of death. We've been waiting for you to join us, but since you're still alive, all we can do for now is wait," said the youth with the huge gash.

"Even after they die, the second sons of Wayo Wayo can never leave the sea," said the gray-haired youth, and the others all echoed their agreement.

The spirits of the second sons were not lying: this was the first time they'd found this island. "Several days ago we agreed to meet over at Petrel Ridge and get ready to greet the next member of our company: you. That was the first time we noticed the edge of this floating island on which you've landed. The day of your leave-taking, we all hastened back to Wayo Wayo to hear the elders sing the psalm of farewell, praise Kabang's wisdom and celebrate the island's riches, your bravery and Rasula's beauty. Every day, when we incarnate, transform into our sperm whale avatars at daybreak, we tagged alongside your boat, until it sank. You mustn't blame us. We are the dead, the spirits of the second sons, duty-bound to observe what happens without offering help or doing harm. We never expected that you would show the strength of a fish, that you just would not die. We've followed you all this way, and we saw a current carry you onto this island," said the gray-haired one, who seemed to be the leader.

Another thickset youth with a toothless mouth like a yawning cavity added, "We saw right away how strange this island was, and guessed it might be a trap set by Kabang, or a trial."

"But then we noticed something else," the gray-haired youth said.

"What was that?"

"That this island was moving. That it might float beyond the range of the spirits of Wayo Wayo."

"*Beyond* the range of the spirits of Wayo Wayo?"

"That's correct: there is an invisible line we cannot pass."

"You mean that if I'm still alive when this island crosses the line then *you won't stay by my side*?"

"May the sea bless you. If you die out there, your spirit will drift forlorn on an infinite sea."

"So I can only join you if I go and drown myself now?"

"Don't ever do that. Anyone from Wayo Wayo who commits suicide will turn into a jellyfish. Jellyfish can't recognize one another. You don't really want to become a jellyfish, do you?"

Atile'i had no wish to become a jellyfish. But now the spirits of the second sons were out of ideas. They waited with Atile'i for dawn. Actually, to the spirits, dawn no longer had any meaning, it was merely the time when, at the first light of day, they would dive into the water and turn into sperm whales. At night, after regaining their ghostly forms, they would wander on the sea, singing, zoning out, waiting for the arrival of the next second son. The sperm whales into which the spirits transformed during the day were pretty much the same as actual sperm whales. The only difference was that the sperm whale avatars wept.

Atile'i could only wait until the island silently crossed the borderline and left the spirits of the second sons behind at a speed that was hard to grasp and which neither wind nor rain, tide nor dream, could change. When thrice the moon and the sun had traded places, the spirits of the second sons could barely make out the edge of the island when they emerged above the surface. "Atile'i! Atile'i!" they shouted, but their shouts changed into flying fish, leaping over the water and plopping into the waves.

"Now it's just me." It took Atile'i two alternations of sun and moon to face the fact that he would have to bestir himself to survive. He tried catching fish, collecting rainwater, and weaving warm clothes out of various things he found here and there on the island. But though he was an expert fisherman, Atile'i was no good at weaving. When he draped himself with the garments he'd pieced together, he looked like a gaudy bird.

Several days after picking up a kind of flexible club, Atile'i had the bright idea of grinding one end into a point and attaching something else he'd found, which was also elastic. In doing so, he had made himself a spear gun. He used the same method to make himself a *gawana*. Made out of different materials, it was more resilient and springy than the ones on

Wayo Wayo. There was also a kind of ball that was harder than the pit of a fruit but bouncy, which could be hurled out beyond a *gawana*'s striking distance at birds in flight. Atile'i learned the hurling stance for the ball from a book he had found. There were colorful pictures in the book, and finely printed "words." (Though people on Wayo Wayo did not have writing, the Sea Sage and Earth Sage still had many "books.") Inside the book he found a picture of a man with the same brown skin as himself. Atile'i thought his stance was perfect, and the man's hurling hand was aglow.

Evening was the best time to catch waterfowl and sea turtles with his custom *gawana*. At first he could only stun the turtles, yank out their heads and suck blood from their necks. Then one day he found a shiny knife on the other side of the island. It was the sharpest knife he had ever seen. (They only had stone knives on Wayo Wayo). With it, he could dine on turtle meat, which was like sea cucumber but firmer. Sometimes a turtle would keep flapping its flippers after he had sliced its abdomen open, as if it was still underwater.

But later Atile'i saw there were actually lots of dead sea turtles around the island. When he butchered them, he often found indigestible objects in their stomachs. "Did the sea turtles die from eating a piece of the island?" Atile'i wondered. Except for the water he collected, he had better avoid ingesting anything on the island.

When Atile'i started diving more often, he realized that "the island under the island" was even more immense than the island itself. It was almost like an underwater maze, "so big as to be another kind of sea." Atile'i could not think of a better way to describe it. To him, anything big could be compared to the sea. The subaquatic flotsam was a tangled mess, but a large wave could disturb its ad hoc order. Given that the island was translucent and in a constant state of change, it was no wonder Atile'i tended to get a bit lost at first when he went diving. He tried to move anything that might come in handy up onto the island. In no time he had quite the collection. Some things were useful, others just interesting. Atile'i gathered things that were weird or captivating. It was the same on Wayo Wayo, where everyone collected shells to decorate the dawn-facing side of the house. At first Atile'i hung these fancy things on his own "decorative wall," but as the sun rose from a different direction every day there was no way to keep it facing the sun. The island seemed to be turning.

A while later, Atile'i started to collect thin little boxes with pictures on them. The briny seawater had not yet rotted away some of the pictures, and you could see naked female bodies in them. The girls gazed at him so tenderly, exposing their pale white breasts the likes of which Atile'i had never seen before. It went without saying that Rasula was a match for any of them. She half resembled them, but the rest of her was of the island. Anyway, by this point the sight of any nude female body seemed sufficient to cause Atile'i's penis to swell and incline him to *kawalulu,* which he did, thinking of Rasula. He often thought maybe this was a kind of love.

Atile'i also collected "books." He had seen "books" at the Earth Sage's place, but they were few and far between, and had to be kept in transparent bags to keep them from getting ripped or rotten. The Earth Sage's "books" were allegedly left behind by the white man. The Earth Sage said the white man called the marks in the books "writing." The islanders did not have writing, nor did they think that the world had to be remembered in written form. They thought that life was a kind of resonance between story and song, and that was good enough for them.

Atile'i considered anything with writing to be a book, no matter what symbols it contained, illustrated or not, a single page or a thick stack. The symbols varied from book to book, but there seemed to be a hidden pattern. Perhaps because he had no way of knowing who established the pattern or what its provenance was, Atile'i felt a strange reverence for those marks. There were a few things on the island Atile'i had no trouble understanding, like tree trunks, fish carcasses and stones, but most things came from a world outside of his experience and beyond his knowledge. The marks in the books were the most amazing thing he'd seen, though, because they clearly came in different varieties. Why had the white man, or some other kind of islander, created something that seemed so *utterly useless*? As he stared at those marks, his body felt hot. He noticed a slight trembling.

"May the sea bless you, for Kabang has His reason," he murmured, and stacked the books in a certain place, but the stack got heavier and heavier, and some of the books ended up sinking back down into the sea.

At first Atile'i depended on the novelty of his collections to sustain his deteriorating psyche, but anyone who has dwelt long in solitude must be aware that the gap between moments can seem like a yawning chasm that no one can cross by mind alone. Atile'i now tried to fill it with remembrance. Having suffered great physical torment at sea, he relied on his aversion to jellyfish to keep from killing himself. The only thing keeping him pathetically alive, was memory. He recollected his last night on Wayo Wayo to relieve himself of desire, the words of his father and the elders to understand the sea, and the island songs to know the ways of love.

Atile'i had almost forgotten in which direction Wayo Wayo lay.

If a Wayo Wayoan encountered a rough current or some other hardship while out at sea, he would close his eyes, raise his head and stretch his spine, for it was said that the man of rich experience could "smell" the direction in which Wayo Wayo lay. At first Atile'i could still catch a whiff of the island's powerful aroma through the stench of the sea and rain, but seven songs later and only the thinnest filament of scent remained. After another seven songs he could only roughly guess that Wayo Wayo was somewhere toward the sunset. Alas, like all Wayo Wayoans, Atile'i knew that the sun sets in a different place every evening, so that was not the exact direction in which Wayo Wayo was to be found.

The past few days, Atile'i had seen all manner of ocean scenery. He had never experienced such weird weather in all his life: one moment it was scorching, the next minute freezing, and the sky could turn from fair to foul before a single fish was hooked. Sometimes night came suddenly, and sometimes darkness would rudely descend on the afternoon. One minute the stars would be shining, and the next moment the sun would rise with a blinding light. One time he saw nine cyclones appear at once above the sea, with thunder chasing the lightning through the clouds. The clouds seemed to grow spidery legs that reached downward to the sea, and as soon as they touched the water up a vortex sprang. A storm followed hot on the heels of the twisters, and Atile'i kept praying to Kabang to just take him away and let that be the end of him. When the sky cleared, Atile'i was surprised to find a long shadow lying like a ribbon on the sea. He swam over to take a closer look. The ribbon was composed of butterflies' corpses, which had floated here from who knows where. There were so many of them, and they stretched out so far, that he was reminded of his own interminable odyssey. Oh, when would it end?

Atile'i was losing any notion of dusk and dawn or noon and night, and he gave up trying to tell direction by observing the heights of the moon and the morningstar. He let himself go like a fallen leaf, like a dead fish floating on the sea. Hungry, he ate. Tired, he slept. For a while he even thought that Wayo Wayo was just a poignant fantasy, a story he had made up. But Atile'i had to admit he wanted desperately to see his island home again, that any ghost would do. Atile'i would holler at the sea whenever he sighted the shadow of a whale, for he knew that the spirits of the second sons turned into sperm whales by day. Even the north-migrating eagles were sad to hear him this way. It would be so nice if Rasula and her mother Saliya were here, Atile'i thought. In all the island, only their voices had the power to summon Masimaga'o ("a whale with a body like the sea" in the Wayo Wayoan language), whose posture in the water allowed the Sea Sage to divine the future. Wouldn't you know it, one day a pair of Masimaga'o really did appear after Atile'i had finished singing. They "joined tails" near the island and knocked a hole in the weakest part. When they surfaced their bodies were covered in colorful objects, like idols ready for some religious rite.

Once, Atile'i speared a sailfish swimming by the island and got dragged into the water when it swam off. Just when he was about to let go and give up, the speed of the dive caused him to black out. His head told his hand to let go, but his hand held on tight. By this time the wounded sailfish had swum into the island maze, sometimes rising to the surface, sometimes sinking among the sundry oddities of the island. Atile'i could only pray, "O Kabang, the only one who can dry the sea, even if you have forsaken me, please let my corpse turn into coral and drift homeward for Rasula to find."

The fish tried and tried but could not find the way out of the underwater island. It had gotten all scraped up, and its head was covered in clutter. Badly wounded now, it was losing strength, giving Atile'i, who was still clutching the spear, the chance to flip the fish over, grab onto a corner of the island and find a pocket of air. He realized an instinctive need to see the light of day again. He only ate a single piece of sailfish before stashing the rest of it there. The next day all of it had vanished. Even the bones were gone.

Alone, not knowing when he would be able to go back to Wayo Wayo, Atile'i thought he would need a place that could withstand the wind and rain. He found a sheet of highly water-resistant blue cloth and draped it over a lattice of flexible yet sturdy rods to make himself a little makeshift shelter. It was soon wrecked by a storm, so Atile'i resolved to build himself a small house. Of course it wouldn't be able to withstand a real storm. (Nothing in this world could, right?) But at least it would not be quite so flimsy as the shelter. "A weak house makes a weak man," as the Wayo Wayoan proverb put it. Atile'i used whatever rain would not rot, nor seawater erode, in the construction of his house. It would drift with the ocean currents, maybe someday all the way back to Wayo Wayo. Even if by that time he was dead and gone, his house might still be there, bringing back news of what had befallen him at sea.

Now that he was seriously considering building a house, Atile'i discovered that the island was actually rich in rot-resistant materials. Atile'i used the metal rods from the shelter and whale jaws and ribs for the beams, with the kind of club he had used to make the spear for the columns. Then he secured the frame with a colorful material that would not rip no matter how hard you yanked on it. At first he built a structure with space inside for three people to lie down in, and as the sun and moon kept trading places the house was taking shape. Atile'i also built a storage shed, as well as a place to store water, which he called the sakaloma, meaning "a well on the sea." Made of things available around the island, the house blended in with its surroundings when you looked at it from a distance, as if purposefully camouflaged. Looking at the house he had built with his own two hands, Atile'i felt himself truly rich.

But Atile'i had also noticed a lot of other dead sea creatures around the island, guessing they must have eaten part of the island just like the turtle. The island sometimes looked like a giant floating cage—a shadowy incantation, a rootless place, the cemetery of all creation. Aside from a few species of seabird that made nests and laid eggs on the island from time to time, nothing else could survive there. Creatures that died from eating bits of the island eventually became part of the island. Atile'i thought he too might end up becoming part of the island. So this is what hell was like, he thought. So this is the land of death.

In the distance Atile'i had seen mighty ships far bigger than a *talawaka*, and frighteningly noisy iron birds. He remembered the Earth Sage had spoken of "the birds of hell and the ghost ships of the white man."

Atile'i knew nothing of the worlds inhabited by other men. He heard that when the Wayo Wayo islanders first saw the white man they had said, "Have you come here along a road through the sky?"

A rainbow was a road through the sky. The Earth Sage said, "Only spirits are light enough to cross it." Atile'i sometimes saw rainbows in the distance, wondering what he would do if he ran into a white man. How should he talk to him? Could a white man take me back to Wayo Wayo? Atile'i remembered another of the Earth Sage's offhand remarks: "The white man may come and the white man may go, but we will live by the law of Wayo Wayo. We don't need the white man. The gifts he left us are harmful, ill-gotten gains. There's just this useless watch, a couple of books, and a few children like Rasula." The Earth Sage sighed and said, "But there may come a day when the other men who live upon the earth cause Wayo Wayo to vanish. You never know."

The other men who live upon the earth . . . Everyone had probably forgotten him. But that couldn't be the whole truth, for Atile'i was well aware that everyone on Wayo Wayo knew he had gone to sea. They were just intent on forgetting him, trying not to remember. The thought made Atile'i feel that death would be easier. It was like he had been imprisoned in a world so much larger than the only one he had ever known, like a terrible silent punishment had been imposed upon him. But why? Was this the will of the omnipotent Kabang, the fate of second sons?

The pain only eased when he discovered a kind of twig he could use to draw pictures in a "book." Actually, he had found many such twigs. He used them to poke around on the island or in the tongue-and-groove work in his house, and was amazed that one of them left marks on certain things. Day after day, the greatest foe Atile'i faced was silence. There was nobody on the island to greet him, nobody to praise his swimming technique, nobody to wrestle, and nobody to compete in diving with. But at least with this kind of twig he could draw what he saw and thought.

Quietly combing the island for twigs, Atile'i found ones of different sizes and colors, though some stopped drawing as soon as you started using them. He also discovered that there were many materials you could draw on besides books, including his own skin. One day on a whim he started to draw the sights and sounds of the island on his calves, thighs, belly, chest, shoulders, neck and face, as far along his back as he could reach, and even on the soles of his feet. He layered drawing upon drawing like a palimpsest. When the drawings came off in the rain, Atile'i drew new ones.

This morning Atile'i was racing around the island. From a distance he did not look like Atile'i anymore. He looked more like some other kind of being, like a ghost perhaps, or maybe like a god.

# 5. Alice's House

Toto was born the third year after Alice and Thom met. Guess you could say he was an accident, or that it was fate. She and Thom had never thought of having a child. They did not think it possible, psychologically or physically, and a child was not a part of either's life plan. Thom and Alice disagreed on a lot of things, but they both felt that bringing a child into this world was a kind of punishment, a form of suffering.

Preparations for Alice and Thom's house had been finalized when they found out Toto was on the way, but it wasn't too late to calculate his future into the design. Thom had drafted the plans himself. The exterior was based mainly on Erik Gunnar Asplund's three-in-one Summer House, with some adaptations. Thom added a second story to the cabin on the right-hand side, and raised the ceilings in the two blocks in the main wing. The original Summer House was a cosy cottage lying low in the forest; Thom's design looked rather different. The structure also had to be different, because Asplund, building on a fjord, hadn't had to worry about the resolute tides and wayward winds of the western Pacific.

The summer they met, Alice and Thom went traveling together from Denmark to Sweden. The third day in Stockholm, they made a special trip to see the City Library, another of Asplund's creations. As soon as she walked in the library Alice gasped with surprise. It seemed as if the shelves had been arranged to the lovely rhythm of Claude Debussy's Quartet for Winds, level upon level, floor upon floor, as if they led all the way up to heaven. This was the most beautiful "book repository" Alice had ever seen.

Haven County had beautiful scenery, but except for some heritage sites the cultural landscape was horrendous. The new train station was ghastly, the library nearby even more so. Alice remembered the Taipei municipal government had built a nice library in Pei-tou, but that was just a container without too much in the way of content. Asplund, by contrast, had grasped the true meaning of a library. Though the circular wall of books seemed to weigh down on you like history, it was not overbearing or oppressive. With the little open windows around the rotunda above letting in rays of sunlight, Alice had the sense she was participating in some sort of religious rite as she stood on tiptoe to reach up for a book on the top shelf. Her hands trembling, Alice felt like a handmaiden of light and like the lady of the books.

Alice especially liked the Story Room. It seemed to have the power to turn back time. It was on the ground floor, in a children's corner inside the library. When you walked in, it was like a fairy kingdom in a mountain cave. There were murals of scenes from Swedish folktales on the walls, with the reader's chair (which seemed to give whoever sat in it the ability to tell magical stories) in the center of the room. Children were sitting on the crescent benches on either side of the chair, or right on the floor in front. Warm light shone on the murals, making it seem as if the slightest breeze would start the elves talking. The children's eyes were gleaming as they listened to the story. For the first time in her life, Alice thought that maybe it wouldn't be so bad if she had a child of her own.

"Only in places like this have spirits ever appeared," Alice said.

Realizing Alice was under Asplund's spell, Thom had an idea. "Any plans for tomorrow? Want to visit another building by the same architect? It's a private residence, though, not a public building."

"We had plans, but they just changed."

The next day they set off from the campground, rode the bus for almost two hours, and walked for over ten minutes from the bus stop until they reached a path through the woods. It was summer. The sunlight sprinkled down through the leaves, dappling the path, like a sign. The ambience made Alice feel so much younger, especially with Thom there. She felt like a maiden who could weave a new life for herself with thread spun from her lover's smile.

At the end of the forest was a trail winding leisurely up a hill. It was quite a long hike, but the view was so beautiful that one did not feel the least bit tired. At the top a meadow opened up: to the left, obdurate, unyielding, a crag; to the right, a famous fjord; and straight ahead the Summer House. Though the owner was not in, they could still look on politely from afar. But Alice would often remember that moment in later years. It was as if she had witnessed something, not just a house but daily life itself.

"Will I ever live in a house like that?" Alice asked, a bit slyly and flirtatiously.

"Of course," replied Thom, matter-of-factly. For a moment Alice did not quite feel like herself; usually she would never speak in such a way to such a visibly younger man.

And now the only consolation Alice had was this house in the sea. She remembered how they met. In retrospect, it was her romantic nature making mischief. That summer, after finally completing her infinitely tedious Ph.D. in literature and sending off an application for a job she thought she had no hope of getting, she packed a tent, a camera and a laptop and took a trip to Europe. Alice actually intended to write a book about her travels, *Tales of a Lady Wayfarer* perhaps, and launch her literary career. Maybe it would be a best-seller and she would not have to enter the academy.

Her first stop after landing in Copenhagen was the Charlottenlund Fort Campground on the outskirts of town. The campground really gave you a sense of history. There was a big old cannon covered in waterproof camouflage tarpaulins. There was even a stable. Alice had planned to make this her base for a weeklong visit in Copenhagen. One evening she missed the last bus and had to walk all the way back through the sparsely populated suburbs. Alice felt a bit fazed. Worse, she took a wrong turn, and had to walk across a forest park to get back to the campground. Much bigger than a typical "park," it was more like the Black Forest (it actually was a black forest). The trees might be centuries old or even a millennium or more, and there were fallen logs blocking the path, which was none too visible in the first place. The forest park was a different world in the evening. There were no dog-walkers or joggers anymore. The only thing she could hear was the hooting of the owls. Just as she was starting to get really anxious, there was a pale beam of light in the distance, and a crackling sound.

Alice was instinctively suspicious of anyone she might meet in a situation like this. Her heart started racing involuntarily. She was anxious to find a place to hide out of sight of the path, not expecting how incredibly quickly the figure would approach. A tall, bearded man, with a slightly juvenile look came riding along on his bike, stopping by her side.

"Hi."

"Hi," Alice managed.

"Going to the campground?"

"Yeah."

"Hop on, I'll give you a lift."

"I'm all right."

"Don't be scared. Look, this is my staff ID. I saw you yesterday. You're staying at Charlottenlund Fort Campground, aren't you? I work there. You'll be frightened walking alone, and soon it'll be dark. You can trust me. The forest recognizes my bicycle." Actually, Alice knew that around this time of year it would not get dark until after nine. But her heart was still racing, which made it hard for her to judge why she felt at a loss—was she nervous, or was there some other reason? She glanced at his bicycle, a road bike without a rear rack.

"On this? How will you give me a lift?"

The man took a detachable rack out of his backpack, mounted it on the seat post, and said: "You couldn't be more than a hundred pounds; this thing can bear a person of a hundred and forty. No problem."

So, wearing his backpack over his chest, the man gave Alice and her luggage a ride. Sitting on the rack, Alice rested her hands lightly on the man's firm waist. Her heart hadn't slowed a bit. The two of them hung out after they made it back to the camp, talking until dark. The man got a guitar out of his tent and sang songs for her, songs she had grown up listening to. They did not retire to their respective tents until it was too dark to see the windmill generator in the distance.

As she got to know Thom (a common Danish name, as she later discovered) a bit better, she learned that, after all, the beard was deceptive: she actually was a bit older than him, by three years. But in terms of life experience it was the other way around. He had cycled all over Africa. He had navigated a sailboat across the Atlantic and drifted onto some deserted island after the boat broke down. He had trained in Baji-style kung fu. He had run across the Sahara with an ultramarathon team. And he had participated in an interesting sleep experiment, which revisited the research done at Midnight Cave in Texas in 1972 by revising certain experimental conditions. He had spent six full months thirty meters underground.

"What's it like underground?"

"What's it like underground? Well, it was actually more like spending time inside a living being."

Thom was widely experienced and adventurous. Solving problems and taking up challenges was his idea of fun. These were personal qualities generally lacking in the men from the island Alice had grown up on. It all made her a bit giddy. Especially since Thom had such gentle, sparkling eyes.

"You've done so many things! What's next?"

"Mountain climbing. Not in Denmark, though. Denmark is a country without mountains. I'm training in professional rock climbing three days a week in Germany. I'm working here to save up for my climbing gear."

Not understanding a word of Danish, Alice could only communicate with him in English. Neither was using his or her mother tongue, so they always seemed a bit hesitant. But the language they were speaking was beside the point. Her mind would always wander when she talked to him, even recalling lines of poetry: "For shade to shade will come too drowsily." Oh no, Alice thought, this isn't good.

Thom was also attracted to this petite, scatterbrained woman who would sometimes launch into Mandarin without warning. He ditched his next plan, to go canoeing up a fjord. Meeting Alice was as exciting and unpredictable as any wilderness adventure, and possibly more dangerous. Thom offered to serve as Alice's tour guide. He carried his tent, she carried hers, and they went backpacking together, both feeling excitable and frolicsome, like kids. Three weeks later, Alice had made a tour of northern Europe and returned to Copenhagen to catch her flight. Originally Thom was just going to see her off, but at the airport she was pulling her luggage and he was pulling his, and just as she was about to board the plane he made a last-minute decision to go with her to *terra incognita* Taiwan, just to see what it was like. The flight Alice was taking was already full, so Thom had to take the next flight. Instead of going home, Alice waited all day in the airport in Taipei for his connecting flight to arrive from Bangkok. The moment they found each other at the arrival gate that evening, the question hanging over their hearts was answered, the doubt in their minds dispelled.

Alice got home to find her mailbox full, and among the mail was a letter informing her that her application for the teaching position had been accepted. So without any second thought Alice immediately started getting ready to move to Haven. She recalled why this was the only university she had applied to. Her romantic tendency had been acting up again: one half of her wanted to live by the ocean, while the other half wanted to rekindle her dream of being a writer. To do so she thought she should choose to live somewhere that seemed far from the crowd but was actually at a suitable distance for people watching. The week before Alice hastened to Haven, Thom had already gotten in touch with an alpine club and gone on an expedition to Great Snow Mountain. After he got back to Taipei and heard Alice talk about Haven this and Haven that, he decided to move there with her and see how it went.

At first they lived in the faculty housing on campus, but because they weren't legally married they could only be assigned a cramped single's residence. Living quarters designed by public agencies in Taiwan are generally uninhabitable. The condensation was so bad in summer that when the air cooled at dusk even the duvet cover would get damp. A flatlander on a hilly island, Thom went climbing everywhere, and started practicing rock climbing with some local friends. Although Thom had started too late in life to become a true mountaineer, his attitude seemed to be: see how high you can go.

"This place is really humid, not like Scandinavia."

"Tell me about it. It's a tropical island. Hey, don't you need to worry about money?"

"That piece I sent back to Denmark has been published in a travel magazine. For now I'm all right. Do you really think I would've come all the way here just to sponge off you?" Thom winked his right eye. Alice had discovered that he did this when he was not being completely honest with her, so she did not ask to have a look at the magazine or inquire further into his financial situation or family background.

Wasn't it great? You don't have to know a person's family to be able to live with him, Alice thought, as Thom enthused about his newfound passion for rock climbing: "Up on a cliff, you can only see part of the sky. You feel your paltry strength through your feet and you thrust your fingers into the clefts in the rock, but you can't share anything you see or smell with anyone. You ever had that feeling? You can hear your heart beating, you sense your breathing is getting labored, and if you're really several thousand meters up on a cliff you know you could die at any time. That's the feeling." Thom's eyes were shining now. "Like you might be one moment away from a vision of God."

Alice looked into his eyes, which had always charmed her so, and still did. But somehow the qualities that had attracted Alice to Thom in the first place were now her biggest worry.

As the days went by, Alice became more and more anxious that this sexy guy might up and leave her at any time. She wanted to let go of him, but a certain expression of his—melancholy, profound yet innocent—was just so appealing. She almost felt that the rot in this humid residence had seeped into her heart. She did not know what to do.

Alice had spent a long time researching a local writer named Kee and become close friends with his much younger wife. Kee's second wife fell in love with him during an interview (but that's a story for another day). She had short hair, spoke slowly and liked to wear sandals. Though not exactly beautiful, she had a certain fresh quality. She was especially fond of the fiction of Paul Auster. Love causes people to make strange judgments, including to try to rise above sex across a thirty-year age gap and the difficulties involved in any marriage. People who thought they were having a platonic affair were shocked when the old fellow divorced his wife to marry her. Friends thought that either Kee would end up leaving behind a young widow and a pile of manuscripts or his second wife would eventually get tired of living in seclusion with the old man and awaken from the literary spell he had cast on her. Nobody guessed that Kee's young wife would leave the world one step ahead of him.

Kee's wife was swept away by a huge wave that appeared out of nowhere one day when they were at the beach for a walk. Reportedly, there had been a fairly powerful deep sea earthquake the previous day, resulting in a localized tidal wave. Kee was in the temporary public washroom put up by the local tourist bureau when the water sloshed in and flooded the place up to knee level. He looked out the window only to see his young wife on the distant strand get tripped up by the sudden wave and taken silently away.

Because there were no eyewitnesses, the police closed the case after an investigation of nearly two weeks, concluding it was an accident. They never expected that Kee would commit suicide the next day, and in a manner that was at once nothing special and highly unusual. He had sealed the doors and windows and started burning his manuscripts and letters. He succumbed due to inhalation of the smoke and fumes of his own writing.

Kee's only son Wenyang was indignant when his father left his mother for a much younger woman. They had a falling-out, and Wenyang took his mother to Taipei to run a sporting goods business. Wenyang and Alice had a discussion after his father's death, and he decided to sell off the estate.

"I don't want anything, not the house, not the land. Professor Shih, all decisions concerning the publication of the collected works are at your discretion. Just as long as the royalties and the proceeds of the sale of the house are transferred to my mother." He left the writer's ex-wife's account with Alice. Actually disposing of Kee's library would be the easy part. She just had to convince the university to assign an office for it. A real estate agent could sell the house in Haven, and Alice herself had fallen in love with the wooded shoreline lot where Kee occasionally went but on which he had only built a tiny thatched cottage. She transferred all the money in her "faculty rate" bank account to Kee's ex-wife.

That is how Alice got the chance to read the diary entry Kee had made the day before he committed suicide. In the entry, he described the appearance of the wave: "At first sight it wasn't just a wave crashing in so much as the sea itself surging up, silently and suddenly. Before I got a good look at it, it had returned whence it came. It did not make any sound. It merely confiscated a few things. That's all it did."

Thom was away in Chamonix on an international winter expedition to Mont Blanc the whole time. He suddenly turned up in the kitchen of their residence one morning several weeks later and started making breakfast.

"Hi."

"Hi."

"Bacon omelette with onions?"

"Sure." Alice was used to reunions like this. She pretended she didn't mind, enraged at herself for being so weak. Thom told her about his adventure while they were eating. This time he had almost gone snow blind. (She suspected that he had taken off his snow goggles on purpose to pay homage to Michel-Gabriel Paccard, who became the first man to climb Mont Blanc in 1786. Thom was always replicating the "near-death experiences" of adventurers like Paccard). Alice started to segue toward the topic of home architecture.

"So when are you going to take me to Chamonix?"

"Anytime you want."

"Are the houses nice?"

"Only you are fit to live in the houses I saw there."

"Do you still remember the Summer House?" She cut to the chase.

"Sure. A charming little cabin." He lightly kissed the ketchup away from the edge of her mouth.

"I want to build a house like that."

"You do?"

"I've bought some land."

"You've bought some land? You mean you've bought a piece of land to build a house on?"

The land was quite close to the ocean, by a coastal copse. The shoreline here was rocky for the most part, with only a thin layer of topsoil. Although it was registered as farmland, you would not be able to grow much. Alice read through Kee's manuscripts, still no wiser as to why he had bought this property in the first place. Standing at the edge of the lot, Thom started letting his steps guide him toward the sea. Then he tore off his clothes and jumped in naked. It was like he had been separated from a lover for too long and needed to give her a big hug and some sweet loving to celebrate the reunion. Standing mutely in the middle of the lot, Alice watched his curly sandy locks bob up and down in the water, like a keepsake she might lose at any time. He came back up on shore, gave her a big kiss, and said: "Let's build a house like the Summer House."

Thom borrowed a stack of architecture books from the library and started doing research. He almost never went climbing. Alice had total faith in him. Though he was no genius he had drive, and could finish anything he started if he was willing to put his heart into it. But could she really keep a man like this?

Thom said, "The exterior can be like the Summer House, but the whole concept has to be different. I want to build a house that suits these surroundings." He rotated the house slightly. The side of Asplund's Summer House that had faced a Scandinavian fjord now faced the Pacific Ocean, but at a thirty-degree angle in order to deflect the stiff ocean breeze. Also, sunlight reflecting directly off the water might bother people instead of creating the kind of comfortable atmosphere that would make them want to take their time getting out of bed in the morning, and a thirty-degree turn would illuminate every corner of the house, affording ample but not glaring light. Thom raised the ceiling in the attic of the right-hand cabin by a meter so that the window would have a full view of the Pacific.

Listening to Thom's explanation, Alice started imagining herself writing at the window. She said she wanted to call it the Sea Window. Thom also explained the rationale for keeping the little cross passages between the cabins in Asplund's original design: each would be granted a certain semidetached independence while maintaining a friendly rapport. "You'll live in the right-hand cabin. The one on the left will be mine. I've moved it back slightly so I'll have a view of the sea, too." That sense of distance appealed to her.

For the main cabin, Thom put various plants inside and out, so when you looked in from the outside you'd see a charming tropical living room. Rather sneakily, Thom went and stayed in all the B&Bs up and down the coast. With total self-confidence, he reported back to Alice, "I think many people who build houses don't understand that people 'live' in their houses. Particularly in Taiwan, where you have people building places just to serve as B&Bs, because most guests will only 'stay for a night.' A house you really live in for ten or twenty years is different. I want to build a home we can live in for a long, long time." This last declaration made Alice fall madly in love with him all over again.

Given the warm climate in eastern Taiwan, there was no reason to keep the famous fireplaces in the original Asplund design. Thom found the fake fireplaces in many B&Bs in Taiwan silly and pretentious. But under Alice's guidance he became quite enamored with Taiwan's once ubiquitous rural "hearth culture," and added a traditional stove room to the modern kitchen.

"We'll really be able to use it. Only a house in which you can make authentic local cuisine is a true home."

Thom spent another full year on the electrical system. He compared many different brands of solar panel. He adjusted the angles and covered the tops of the sloping eaves with panels, creating a solar awning for each of the three porches, under which a person could cool off, meditate or take a nap. He also went online, ordered a small desalination machine from a German firm and designed a salt-and-fresh dual-plumbing system. He planted salt-tolerant local plants like the pongam oil tree and the white-bloom mangrove, spacing them out outside the line of sight of the windows.

He even calculated the growth rates so the shade of the mature trees would not fall on the solar panels fifty years hence.

A year and a half later, Thom had finished the graphic design, the 3D mock-up, and the blueprints for the electrical and plumbing systems. Alice had been watching and listening to him put the little house together, her heart faintly trembling the whole time. She had a sense of reckless bliss, a bit like turning on the tap and watching water come pouring out.

Before construction began, Alice pledged all her assets to secure a big loan from the bank. Building the house allowed her to extricate herself from her stuffy, unimaginative academic life and let her orient herself toward a specific goal. Then the day they started digging the foundation, Alice went to the hospital because she felt nauseous. The doctor recommended that she take a pregnancy test.

Alice would later say that Toto and the Sea House were the same age, which was basically true. Thom's attitude toward Toto's impending arrival was about the same as any father's. He was thrilled. He added a place for Toto in both the left-hand and right-hand cabins, so both mum and dad would have time alone with him.

Toto was conceived before building began, and born before construction was complete. He was three months old when Alice finished planting the garden. She put Toto under the eaves and started planting herbs around the house for butterflies to eat. She had an acquaintance named Ming, a colleague at the university, who had written some literary essays about butterflies. Alice asked him to list species that would be appropriate for a coastal property and teach her how to plant them.

Thom loosened up the dirt road that had been packed hard by the bulldozer, and planted a windbreak on both sides to create a tree-lined path down to the shore.

But there was a series of strong typhoons the year the house was finished, and the foundation of the coastal highway, which had already been rebuilt ten meters inland from the old road, started to scour. Not long thereafter a whole stretch of road collapsed unexpectedly, and the Bureau of Public Works had no choice but to retreat another thirty meters and build a new "coastal" highway at a slightly higher elevation, drilling through a few mountainsides to do it. In the aftermath of the Great Flood that struck Taiwan on 8 August 2009, whether or how much of the island would be underwater ten years hence became a hot-button issue. But to many folks, this was still "outside the realm of possibility." Alice thought that the lives the flood had taken would only give the survivors a fool's confidence that there was no disaster people could not handle. Some folks shrugged it off by anthropomorphizing the disaster and running off at the mouth about the "cruelty" and "inhumanity" of nature.

After hearing Alice's thoughts on the matter, Thom would occasionally promote his own Danish viewpoint, that, "Actually, nature isn't cruel at all. At least, it isn't especially cruel to human beings. Nature doesn't fight back, either, because nothing without conscious intent can 'fight back.' Nature is just doing what it should, that's all. If the sea will rise then let it rise. When the time comes we'll move house and all will be well. If we don't move in time the worst that'll happen is that the sea will serve for our watery tomb, and we will become fish food. Not so bad if you think of it that way, is it?"

"Not so bad?"

At first Alice found it hard to understand what exactly Thom was saying. After all, she had invested everything she had in this property, and she had even gone into debt. But gradually she seemed to understand. In the end she just had to get on with her life, fleeing when it was time to flee, fighting when it was time to fight, and dying like a meadowlark when it was her time.

For the past year the sea had been like a random memory. In no time it had arrived on her doorstep, and since Christmas last year, she'd been forced to give up on getting in through the front door at high tide. Twice a day, Alice was put under temporary house arrest before being released a couple of hours later. At high tide, the sea would skirt the drainage ditch, encircling the house. When it receded it would leave various things behind at the back door: dead porcupine fish, driftwood in fantastic shapes, part of the hull of a ship, whalebones, ripped clothing, et cetera. The next day at low tide Alice would open the door and have to step over various dead things before she could get out of the house.

The local government had informed Alice that she was living in a dangerous building and should vacate and move somewhere else. But Alice was adamant that, "If the house collapses due to flooding I'll take responsibility. Please don't encroach upon my freedom: I've got a legal right to live here." A tabloid magazine even published a story about a lady professor living a cloistered life in a solar house on the beach. The only thing that story had going for it was that it included some of Thom's architectural ingenuity, including those swiveling solar panels that followed the sun across the sky.

Dahu, Thom and Alice's Bunun friend, who was originally from Taitung in southern Taiwan, and Hafay, the Pangcah owner of a local bar, tried several times to get Alice to consider moving, but eventually they gave up.

"Your head really is as hard as a boar tooth," Dahu said.

"You said it. That's the way I am." Alice sat in her house and looked out at the misty sea, as if she was sitting inside the body of some living organism. This little house was so nice. In all her life, she had never had such a wonderful time as in the past few years. It had been so wonderful that it seemed like a perfectly smooth glass globe, or like a holly plant without a single brown leaf. It was all a bit too perfect, a little too good to be true.

In the end she never wrote at the Sea Window. She would just sit there quietly. The sea had no memory, but you could still say that it remembered things: the waves and the stones all bore the traces of time. Sometimes she despised it for all the memories and the pain it brought her. Sometimes, out of futility, she believed in it and depended on it, like a fish facing a baitless hook, knowing full well it's going to hurt but going after it anyway.

Alice lay there quietly, sensing the moonlight on her eyelids and the tide rolling in on her eardrums, like glass shattering somewhere far away. Outside the raindrops were falling big as stars, cloaking the earth in a humid, restless and surging air.

Even though the weather bureau had predicted the possibility of a big quake within the year, many people had a sense of despair, a feeling that "it's finally here," when an earthquake struck this evening. During the quake every inch of the house was moaning and groaning, but Alice was ready to let it bury everything and have done. She had no urge to flee at first. Only later when the quake intensified did she feel an instinctive desire to find shelter. Remembering her suicide plan, she couldn't help a grim smile. The house Thom had designed and built was stronger than she had imagined: aside from a slight skew in the beams, it was fine, just refusing to collapse. At high tide the next morning, the water had not only surrounded the house but also reached almost all the way up to the highway. Looking down from the road, the house appeared to be floating on the sea.

Alice walked over to the window and looked out. The sea had flooded the house, reaching halfway up the first story. The waves beat against the walls, sprayed her face. She walked back to the stairwell and saw a lake down below. There were fish swimming over the red tile floor she and Thom had laid together. It was like being dropped into a huge aquarium. A bit dizzy, she reached out to steady herself, resting her hand on the rosewood picture frame hanging on the wall by the stairs. On one side of the frame they had stuck birthprints of Toto's tiny feet, marks she used to remind herself of hope, pain and determination. But Alice found that now, inexplicably, her desolation seemed to have hidden itself away, like the blue sky that was always disappearing above the island. Alice felt this might be a sign she was already dead. Thinking about it this way, it no longer mattered whether she sought to kill herself or not.

Under the combined onslaught of grief, ocean waves and the shuddering of the wave-battered and wind-lashed house, Alice almost lost her balance a couple of times. She stuck her head out the window for a breath of fresh air and noticed a shivering black shadow on a piece of driftwood right outside the window.

It seemed to be a kitten. No, not just seemed. It *really was* a kitten, looking at her with sad eyes. Very peculiarly, one of its eyes was blue, the other brown.

Alice leaned out the window and lifted the quavering kitten in. It was so scared it could not even manage a threat display. All it did was curl up softly in her arms.

"*Ohiyo,*" she said to the kitten. She remembered that morning when she'd said good morning in Japanese to Thom and Toto just for fun. Toto so looked like a miniature adult in his climbing gear. Soaking wet, the kitten was still shaking, like a beating heart. She almost felt like the earthquake wasn't over yet.

She picked up a towel to dry off the kitten, found a cardboard box as a temporary shelter, and gave it some biscuits to eat. The cat did not eat, only looked at her anxiously. How big had the quake been? And how many casualties had it caused? Alice had no way of knowing. Her ability to reason had returned, but without a television, a cell phone or traffic noise she felt all alone on a deserted island at the end of the world. All she could do was focus her attention on this kitten. It—she—was dry now, and, seeming to realize that the worst had passed, had gone to sleep out of sheer exhaustion, tucking her soft forepaws into her belly and curling up into a fluffy fur ball. Her hind paws would jerk a bit from time to time, as if a dream had slipped in through a crack somewhere and entered her body.

Suddenly there was another burst of roaring. Might be an aftershock. Alice's body had regained the ability to react. She automatically grabbed the box in which the kitten was sleeping, intent on finding a place to hide.

Only a few minutes earlier Alice had still been hoping to die, but now, in the flesh at least, she needed to stay alive.

III

# 6. Hafay's Seventh Sisid

No doubt it was because of Hafay that the Seventh Sisid was so well known along the coast. Was it true that Hafay was no longer beautiful? No, you couldn't say so. The most you could say was that she had put on a bit of weight over the past few years. More precisely, even with a bit of extra flesh she still had her radiant moments. It's just that her beauty was no longer quite so easy to see.

And to tell the truth, although Hafay's cooking was distinctive, always making use of wild greens commonly seen in Pangcah cuisine, opinions were mixed about how the meals tasted. There was less disagreement about the drink menu. Who could say a bad word about Hafay's brews? The only thing for the tourists to buy was millet wine or plum wine in tall colored bottles and cardboard containers. But if you asked Hafay, she'd say that's not millet wine at all, it's a box of chocolates. If you asked the customers at the Seventh Sisid, they would say it's not millet wine at all, it's monkey piss. Millet wine is supposed to be put in jugs and drunk out of the bowl that you've just finished eating with. How can you call it millet wine if it's packaged up like this? The millet wine at the Seventh Sisid had a fragrant grassy sweetness, with dregs that hadn't been completely filtered out floating in it. It went down smooth and had a kick. It was wholesome and fierce, and seemed to radiate light and heat once it got into your belly.

Besides millet wine, the Seventh Sisid had another attractive feature, its windows, or perhaps one should say its ocean views. The house was built on *omah*, uncultivated coastal land, out of bamboo, crape myrtle and Formosan michelia, as well as slate from the local hills. There were windows on all four sides, and from almost every window you could observe the constant waves of the Pacific from a different angle. The decor had mostly been donated by local aboriginal artists. But if you asked Hafay which artist did what, she would say, "What do you mean, 'artist'? They were just people with nothing better to do who left these things here to pay for their meals. Artist my ass!"

Customers had carved messages all over the tabletops. There was also quite a lot of verse by third-rate poets, some of it incredibly kitschy, some of it passable, just barely, and some of it was obviously plagiarized. More idiosyncratically, each table had a plate of betel nut. If nobody chewed it, Hafay wouldn't bother replacing it, so if you happen to pay the Seventh Sisid a visit, whatever you do: don't try the betel nut.

Aside from such details, to most customers the space itself was nothing out of the ordinary. But somehow Hafay shuttling back and forth, her figure nicely plump, lent the place a wonderful ambience, and even the thin film of sand on the floor somehow made people feel at ease. For regulars, indulging in a drunk monologue with Hafay there to listen was almost a healing ritual. The best part about talking to Hafay was that she would never judge the sudden sadness that overcomes people after they've imbibed. She never got involved, but those long-lashed eyes of hers made you feel nobody could understand your private sorrow better than Hafay.

But seriously, everyone found it a little hard to believe that Hafay could keep the place going all by herself. There must be elves sneaking in at night to help her prepare the food and take care of all the chores.

Sometimes Hafay would start singing after hearing customers mumble and grumble. Strange to say, Hafay couldn't speak Taiwanese or English, but she seemed to be able to sing songs in any language. Nobody ever asked how she had learned to sing them, because few people really remembered the songs she sang. Her voice infused people with the essence of a song. It would turn into a windblown seed: you never knew where in your heart the seed would fall, nor when it would sprout. Customers would be back in Taipei, riding on the subway, and Hafay's voice would just start playing in their minds and drown out the subway noise. Then the other passengers would see someone look out the window, eyes welling with tears. But Hafay did not sing very often, and if someone made a request or sat at the bar and said:

"Hafay, sing us a song."

Well, then she would reply, "Why don't I give you a hundred bucks and *you* sing a song for me?" Nobody who asked Hafay for a song ever heard her sing again.

The client base of the Seventh Sisid was simple, mostly friends from the village, tourists from the local B&Bs, and students and teachers from the U of D. Hafay tried not to bother remembering customers referred by the local B&Bs, but she would give a warm welcome to passersby.

Hafay did not herself run a B&B, not because she was on her own or because she did not need the money, but mainly because she felt the B&Bs here weren't what B&Bs were supposed to be like. They were mostly little inns operated by pretentious people from Taipei. Most people who chose to stay in such places were boring, run-of-the-mill. The vulgar and garrulous greatly outnumbered the pleasant and engaging. There were middle-class families who would not tell their noisy kids to shut up and big clans who wanted to spend the whole evening singing karaoke. Then there were couples who had just started seeing each other. They would come for a holiday but end up locking themselves in the room and spending the whole day in bed. Of course, there were also quite a few middle-aged couples. Some hoped a vacation would rekindle the flame, others were just having an affair, and Hafay could tell which was which at a glance.

Another reason why Hafay did not operate a B&B was because she hated having her picture taken with customers. At first she would let them, but then some of them would post the pictures on the internet, and a few would even send them to Hafay. It disgusted and irritated her to see herself posing with a bunch of people she'd known for all of an hour or two. Forgetful Hafay usually wouldn't be able to remember who they were. So Hafay often told regulars who encouraged her to open a B&B that, "Hey, I'm not cut out for it. Neither are most people who run B&Bs, mind you, but the difference is, I know I'm not and they don't."

To be honest, Hafay did not really care for some of the professors and students from the university, especially students who would come around to do fieldwork for some silly class project. Hafay knew that the only reason old-timers in the village were willing to tell stories to these university people was because loneliness had overwhelmed them, left them longing for the good old days, not because of any highfalutin notions like cultural heritage or anything of the sort. It was loneliness that made their stories flow like water from an open tap. Hafay often thought that if she ever wrote a thesis, she would argue that the true source of culture is loneliness.

Alice was a regular customer, that was for sure. The past year she had been coming to the Seventh Sisid once in a while all by herself, but always at dawn when the place was empty. Very few customers knew that the Seventh Sisid never closed. Maybe it'd be better to say that Hafay would always leave a little door open on the sea-facing side. Regulars could stick their hand through the hole in the door, undo the latch, come in and pour themselves a glass of wine or brew a pot of coffee anytime they wanted. Of course the café would be closed. Outside opening hours, Hafay might be out and about or in her room sleeping, but the Second Rule of the Seventh Sisid was, "Please make yourself at home: for the purpose of a Pangcah house is to entertain friends." The First Rule of the Seventh Sisid was, "Help yourself to the wine." Hafay thought that anyone who didn't know the door was always open for regulars and tried to force his way in was a thief.

The reason why Alice became a regular was simple: it was less than a five-minute walk from the Seaside House to the Seventh Sisid. At first Alice came alone; later she and Thom often came together, always sitting at the table to the far left that everyone called the Lighthouse. They called it that because Hafay had put a teardrop lamp on the table, supposedly positioning it so that sometimes even distant ships could see it at night, if the weather was clear.

Alice liked to order *salama* coffee, while Thom always had millet wine. Thom was never stingy with his time, helping folks in the nearby villages, mostly old people, fix this and that around the house. He was a forthright and intelligent fellow. Hafay thought that he might well be the first Dane to be able to speak Pangcah. So when Toto was born everyone living along the coast was happy for them. Having no time for Taiwanese child-rearing taboos, Thom was taking Toto everywhere less than half a year after he was born. Toto had the most beautiful blue eyes. But they had a hidden depth that made the boy look at once innocent and aged.

After Thom went missing, Alice would still sometimes come alone to the Seventh Sisid, but she always came when no other customers were around. Every time, she would sit at her usual seat at the Lighthouse and gaze out to sea. One time it was really late at night. Alice did not even turn on the light, maybe for fear of waking Hafay. From her room, Hafay saw Alice pour coffee cold from the pot and drink it looking out the window toward the Seaside House. No, now that the sea had risen the name had changed: it was now called the Sea House.

Hafay knew that Alice had stepped into a kind of spirit trap. For the time being she was only watching, figuring out a way to get her out. She knew that at a time like this she could not try forcing it open or she would only end up tearing Alice apart.

Hafay eventually decided to put on her nightgown and go out and have a drink with Alice. She quietly made a fresh pot of coffee. They did not even make eye contact in the darkness. Hafay brought out a candle holder a friend had carved out of a piece of driftwood and lit a candle, giving the two of them something to stare at. Hafay had a funny feeling that *kawas* was near, which she found reassuring. The two of them faced the firelight, and the sea. Finally Alice said, "Hafay, I'm sorry, I've barged in again to steal another cup of coffee."

"Barge in any time you like. Whatever you see here is yours."

Alice's spirit had left her body. She was just sitting there, living off lingering warmth. The day she cooled off completely might be the beginning of a new life, or the end of everything. It was like the millet: it might ripen or wither, depending. Hafay could tell that was where Alice was at. She could just tell.

"Hafay, I don't mean to be nosy, but do you have family somewhere?" Alice turned her cup around in her hands. "If you don't feel like talking about it, forget I asked."

"Yeah, I had parents, and I loved a fellah once. I often thought about having a kid, no matter who the father was."

Alice was looking out to sea, and Hafay too. They both knew that sometimes it's better not to look right in someone's eyes. "Hey, you know no one's alone in this world. Don't look at me now: when I was young I weighed all of a hundred pounds, and all male eyes would veer my way whenever I walked on by. But now time's passed, and I've lost everything I had, 'cept I've gained a few extra pounds." Hafay laughed cheerfully. Her laughter was contagious, and Alice even managed a laugh in return, just to be sociable.

"But you've got this restaurant."

Hafay nodded. Yes, figuratively speaking, the Seventh Sisid had given Hafay a skeleton on which to hang her thoughts and memories.

The two of them were drinking *salama* coffee, a fusion of Brazilian beans with a dash of sorghum, and certain fragrant herbs picked wild in the hills. The typical customer didn't pay too much attention to it at first sip, not expecting to be drawn farther and farther, sip by sip, into the *salama* trap. Customers would smell the aroma left in the cup after the last swallow, a melange of rainforest, dusk and the burnt smell after a forest fire, and from then on would drink nothing but *salama* at the Seventh Sisid, almost without exception. Alice put the cup under her nose and her face opened up, like a window that had always been shut but was now letting in a bit of light.

Hafay was still gazing out to sea when a gecko stopped on the glass. A glimmer appeared in her eyes. As if awakening from a long dream, she started to sing.

*Long long ago Nakaw and Sra came down from Mount Cilangasan*
*to found Kiwit, the place where the Pangcah began,*
*for each of Nakaw's children was the founder of a clan:*

*Tapang Masra settled by a river in the north*
*    by the coast, in Ciwidian.*
*Tomay Masra erected two stones that have stood henceforth*

*in the valley, in Sapat.*
*Calaw Panay stayed right at home*
*    and lived her days in Kiwit.*
*Karo Korol went off to roam*
*    and made it up to Tafalong.*

*Proud children of Mother Nakaw and Father Sra we'll always be.*
*Just scent the wind and trace the stream and face the sea,*
*and you'll find growing there the scattered seeds of Pangcah posterity.*

As Alice did not understand a word of Pangcah, all she could do was follow the notes and let images appear in her mind: mountains, trees, leaves and wind blowing through a valley. There was a small film of water around the coffee cups on the table.

Hafay did not see Alice for a while after the quake. It was not that Hafay never "saw" Alice, just that they never talked face to face. Looking out the window, Hafay could often tell whether Alice was home or not. There were signs. If the second-floor window was left open, for instance, Hafay knew Alice hadn't gone out. Early one morning, as the seawater lapped around the house leaving water marks on the walls, Hafay saw Alice lean out the window, jump down onto the first in a series of stools, then onto the second stool and the third, wobbling like a seabird trying to stop on the ocean in a stiff gale. Alice got home at dusk, carrying various bags, large and small, only to find that all the stools had gotten bowled over by the waves and drifted off. Wanting to go over and ask if Alice needed any help, Hafay remembered that Alice never wanted help, so she just watched. Alice dragged a board over, put her bags on it and pushed it slowly toward the window. After leaping through the window, she hoisted the bags in one by one.

Was a house like this still habitable? Hafay wondered.

She was even more curious about the change that seemed to have come over Alice. Several nights before, Alice had almost reminded her of a meadowlark in the depths of despair, but now from a distance she looked somewhat different. Hafay could not say how, but it seemed that Alice was out of the woods, at least for now. People around you can tell whether you have the will to live, and you can bet that someone who dies without warning has no one around her who cares. At this thought, Hafay felt like talking to someone, but there had not been a single customer in the Seventh Sisid all day. Hafay started to sing a little song to comfort herself, making up the words as she went along. The song was about a young Pangcah maiden named Hafay.

Maybe her voice carried, for soon after she started singing, Hafay saw Alice open the window, hold out a tiny black-and-white kitten, and wave at her.

*Ohiyo.* Reading Alice's lips, Hafay seemed to see her say *Ohiyo,* but she could not be sure.

# 7. Alice's Ohiyo

Dahu waded over and knocked at Alice's door the morning after the earthquake. He breathed a sigh of relief when Alice stuck her head out of the second-floor window. His daughter Umav waved from where she was standing, up on the road.

"Thank God you're all right. I came two times already first thing this morning, but I didn't see you. I noticed your car was gone, so I assumed everything was all right, but couldn't stop worrying, so I came back to check up on you."

"Was it serious? The earthquake, I mean."

"Well, it wasn't that strong, but it did a lot of damage. Many coastal areas in Tai-tung got flooded, maybe because of land subsidence. They've been talking about resettling my home village for a decade now, and this time we might really have to move. The weather bureau says that this isn't the Big Quake the seismologists have been predicting, but it might be another foreshock, a kind of omen. This time only a couple dozen people were injured, with two or three casualties."

Alice wanted to grieve for the victims but couldn't feel anything. Over the last ten years, there had been more and more earthquakes and floods. Sometimes all of a sudden a drizzle so faint nobody would think to bring an umbrella would turn into a downpour. Or three typhoons would hit one after another out of season. Lots of river trekking spots had been buried in landslides, and access roads outside levees had themselves become watercourses. Fishermen said that what with the new seaside embankments and concrete wave-dispersal tetrapods all around the island, even the coastal currents had become erratic, and the water temperature had changed, too, all year round. But we've got to get used to it, right? Alice thought.

"Are you coming up? You can get in through the window. Can Umav climb up?"

"Hah, the door won't open anymore? Do you want to stay at my place . . . ? I mean, it'd be safer."

"I'm fine. The house is still here. I'd rather stay."

"All right then." Dahu knew Alice too well. She had made up her mind, and nothing he could say would make any difference. "So? Anything I can do?"

Alice thought for a second and said, "Well, if you go into town, could you pick me up some groceries?"

"No problem."

Right then, the cat started meowing.

"What's that?"

"A kitten. With a black-and-white coat. I took her in on the morning of the earthquake."

"Is it all right?"

"She's fine. Wait a sec." Alice disappeared, soon reappearing at the window holding a frail kitten with a black-and-white coloring and a black head, as if it'd donned a black mask. She waved at Umav with the kitten's right forepaw and said, "Look, Umav! Say hi, Ohiyo."

Umav exclaimed, "Oh, it's a kitty!" Any child, no matter how shy, turns into a different person when she sees an animal. Umav couldn't help herself.

"Wow, her eyes are different colors!"

"Yeah, they're different colors, like different kinds of weather: one side's fair, the other foul. If you do go into town, Dahu, would you get me a bag of cat food? Umav, you can come play with her anytime."

"Can do. I'm taking Umav to see the doctor, but we'll come back for a visit. Umav, say goodbye to Auntie Shih and the kitten."

Umav waved and asked, "Are we really coming back?"

"Sure." Back up on the road, holding Umav's hand, Dahu thought he'd better ask again. "You know an earthquake could strike any time, and come summer there'll be typhoons. This house isn't safe anymore. You have to think about moving to our village."

Alice assumed the water would recede after a while, but it didn't. That afternoon, Dahu brought over various canned foods, and Umav played happily with Ohiyo for the longest time. Now it was Dahu and Alice who couldn't think of anything to say, and didn't know what to do. They just looked quietly on at the kitten and the girl.

"Auntie Shih, do different colored eyes see the world the same way?"

Alice shrugged. The question was beyond her. "Is there anyone who sees exactly the same thing out of either eye?"

Umav looked to be giving this question serious thought.

Over the next few days, Alice could only go out to get water when the tide was out, wearing her rubber boots. To get out at high tide as well, she arranged a row of stools from tall to short, so when she wanted to go out she could lean out the window and step onto the first stool, then hop onto the second, then the third, and so on. On a windless day, Alice's reflection must have seemed like a seabird flying past to underwater creatures. The problem was that the waves would bowl the stools over, and she would have to arrange them all over again when she got back. One day she discovered that the stools were not falling over anymore, because someone had put iron bases on and spiked them to rocks on the seabed. Dahu must have come and done it while she was out.

Actually, Thom had noticed several years before that the sea was getting closer and closer. When the house was being built, he measured and the closest the high water line came was 28.75 meters. A year later the sea seemed to have eroded a bit of the shoreline. Thom started measuring every month. He said, "The sea'll be here sooner or later, but at this rate we'll be long dead and gone by the time it floods the house."

The water table along the shore had gotten salted up, rendering it undrinkable, so folks had to buy bottled water now. Several years before the government had offered DOW (deep ocean water) subsidies, which had to be pumped up through huge pipes and then desalinated. Some residents installed not inexpensive minidesalinators in their own houses. Unable to abide state support for corporations that exploited nature without ever giving anything back, Alice stubbornly refused to have anything to do with DOW. For one thing, these were the same corporations that had made a fortune on concrete and quarrying investments. For another, from the start they canvassed a bunch of experts to endorse DOW by declaring it would have zero impact on coastal ecology, but gradually the muckrakers started exposing problems. Some experts suspected that DOW extraction had disturbed the deep ocean water profile, leading to subtle changes in salt concentration, convection and even the sand in the seabed. And fishermen thought the fish had left for the same reason. But nobody dared say for certain what the consequences would be, of course, because the complex interdependency of any ecological system is beyond human imagining.

Thom and Toto had been gone a long time, but until the earthquake Alice kept up the family custom of going to draw water from the creek every once in a while. They had discovered this creek when Alice's colleague Ming had taken them to photograph Moltrechti's tree frogs at night. Though it wasn't too far from the newly built Seaview Hotel, the place was off the beaten track.

While scrambling down into a ravine to get a shot, Ming said, "Whoever designed this hotel had dreadful taste, don't you think? European buildings aren't like this, are they, Thom? I sometimes think it's really a shame that Taiwanese children vacation in tasteless holiday resorts like this. They'll turn into tasteless adolescents and then adults. There are such interesting creatures right next door but nobody notices."

"You're too much of a pessimist," Alice said.

"I'm not a pessimist, I'm a misanthrope."

"Just as long as you're aware of it."

"But I completely agree with you on the terrible taste of the hotel," Thom said.

So what if it was in poor taste? Didn't the customers keep coming all the same? Alice thought Ming was acting like someone with an anxiety disorder. He was so negative about everything, and writing made him even more uptight. It had been a few years since his last novel, and he had writer's block. She knew he'd gotten stuck, that he paid too much attention to the opinions of a handful of readers who criticized the fictional worlds he'd created. And he got overly worked up about the current literary scene. To Alice the only thing to do was wait. Good novelists were like escape artists, able to get themselves out of any bind, while a bad writer would get so stuck underwater that no one could save him.

The next day, Thom and Alice camped out in the clearing by the creek. Without Ming there it was a lot quieter. They drank tea made with water from the creek and looked up at the stars that studded the night sky, thrilling to the sight. The dust storms from China were getting more and more frequent the past couple of years, and even the relatively clear skies above eastern Taiwan were now filled with haze. They hadn't seen such a clear starry night sky here in a long time. It was so touching, as if the universe were still watching over the planet, benignly and tolerantly.

"This is the best tea I've ever had in my whole life," Thom said.

"So I'll be coming here a lot to get creekwater for tea?"

"It's too far."

"Is not."

"Is too."

"Is not." Thom smiled and let the matter drop. Alice smiled too. Later, every so often, Thom would come here himself and bring back water from the creek.

Actually, there's nowhere in all the world that's truly far, or near. Alice realized there was a contradiction in her sudden epiphany.

These past few days, Alice and the cat had been forging a subtle mutual trust to help each other through these difficult times. The cat began to be comfortable going to sleep in front of Alice with her underbelly exposed. Alice decided to take her to the vet for a thorough checkup. Six out of ten homes in cities around the island had been without power since the earthquake. Only residential areas with solar or wind power had been spared. Though the power supply was gradually being restored, Alice had to search in town for quite a while before she found an animal hospital with backup power.

"It's a strong, healthy cat. And it's really special that her eyes are different colors. That's rare. I've never seen it in a stray," the young vet said, before giving Ohiyo her vaccinations.

"Things could be worse, but lots of houses collapsed in the earthquake. Is yours holding up all right, miss?"

"It's fine." Alice was not young anymore, but men who did not notice the lines around her throat almost always assumed she was twenty-something, thirty at the most, maybe because she had remained slim and liked to wear plain white T-shirts. Sometimes she looked like a graduate student from a distance. Alice had never been proud of looking twenty when she was past forty. It was a fact that nobody could ever change.

Alice was originally planning to leave the cat there and let someone else adopt it, but when the nurse at the registration counter asked her the cat's name, she blurted out, "I call her Ohiyo." The nurse looked a bit doubtful, but still got her to write it out on the chart, not knowing which Chinese characters to use for the three syllables in the Japanese word. When Alice was writing the name out she somehow felt like giving it a try, to see whether she and Ohiyo could get along living under the same roof. She kept repeating "Ohiyo," and the puny kitten lifted her head out of the box, as if responding to her name. She kept looking up anxiously, as if Alice was the only one she trusted in these strange surroundings. Every time Alice murmured "Ohiyo," her little tail would quiver. Something noncorporeal came over Alice, shaking her long silent, suicidal heart back to life.

After the cat got its shots, Alice bought kitty litter, a litter box, some veterinary formula, and even a play stick. The cat might never understand why she would belong to someone and have a name once an ID chip was implanted. And Alice could not understand why on earth she was investing in new "property" for the sake of this tiny living thing when she had obviously spent the past little while getting rid of most of her own possessions.

Leaving the animal hospital, she saw a follow-up on the earthquake on the TV news. As Dahu had said, seismologists suspected this was not simply an energy release. The next report was news to Alice, though: a huge Trash Vortex in the Pacific Ocean was breaking up, and a big chunk of it was headed for the coast right near where she lived. Watching the aerial footage of the vortex, Alice could not believe her eyes. She could not believe her ears, either, when the report, drawing on an international news media source, adopted a tragicomic tone, declaring that in the vortex, almost everyone would be able to find almost everything he'd ever thrown away in his entire life.

When she got back home, Alice went into Toto's bedroom to look for the *Illustrated Encyclopedia of Cats*. Soon after Toto was born he was diagnosed with growth retardation. As a little boy he often got a mysterious cramping. There was no problem with his intelligence, but he seldom spoke in complete sentences until he reached three years of age. He was unable to express himself in Mandarin, English or Danish, except occasionally to call Mummy and Daddy. For him, speaking was like trying to force something too large for the passage up through his throat. They took him to a number of specialists. For the most part the doctors said that there was nothing wrong with Toto's speech organs; most probably he suffered from some unknown brain disorder. Or maybe there were psychosomatic factors. They were certain there hadn't been any postnatal trauma. And Alice and Thom had been model parents, absolutely, almost never leaving Toto alone and certainly never fighting in front of him. So what psychosomatic factors could there have been? Of course, it wasn't as if Toto could not speak at all. In fact, sometimes he said the most amazing things. One time when he was climbing with Thom he caught a rare stag beetle, a female alpine yellowfoot. He took care of it for a while, and made a specimen of it when it died. One day over breakfast, Thom and Alice heard Toto say, into the feeding box, "I can't see what you can see anymore."

Not especially linguistically inclined, Toto had amazing visual acuity. Alice remembered one time when they went out for spaghetti, Toto picked up the menu pencil and started tracing Thom's climbing routes on the paper table cover. For the longest time Alice and Thom did not realize it was a route map. Finally, while they were sipping seafood bisque, Thom exclaimed "Hey isn't that the Nenggao Traverse?" The two of them were so happy they cried. They would not let the server take away the dirty cover. They took it home and framed it. It was still hanging on the wall in Toto's room.

From six years of age, Toto often tagged along with Thom on his hikes, but maybe because he was still just a kid he was not as crazy about climbing as his dad. Even so he had marathon endurance, and mental fortitude to match. It seemed all he wanted to do was check the climbing routes he'd seen in different books, and take his field guides along so he could identify insects. Sometimes he'd sit in his room and read the field guides all day long. Toto could do realistic pencil sketches of insects, with every branch of each antenna clearly differentiated, even at life size. Thom and Alice bought as many field guides for him as they could. There were shelves of them, hundreds in all, in several different languages (Thom bought some Danish ones). There were ordinary insect, bird, starfish and spider guides, and special guides to footprints, mammal excrement, tree bark, dragonfly and damselfly wings, fern spores, and so on and so forth.

Though Alice wasn't so passionate about field guides, she always thought they were amazing things. A field guide seemed different from a work of literature. There's no spoor to guide you when you take a walk in the fictional woods, and repetition is a sin. While natural science seems to have developed through humanity's gift for identification, and then using our reason to create principles for the classification of the myriad creatures of the world, placing special emphasis on certain subtle anatomical unities when discriminating kinds. Alice intuited that there was something poetic in the field guides, and if you read them carefully you could identify the principles by virtue of which human beings understood the world as well as some hints about human nature. Maybe someday Toto might become a certain kind of poet. Did he not deliver some poetic-sounding lines to these insects?

To Alice it seemed that the bigger Toto got the more species he recognized, that every time they went out he got a little taller and more mature. He was starting to explore the world in all its amazing intricacy and extreme regularity. Alice would read the same books as Toto and remember the same insects. Whenever she had a question she would e-mail Ming. Apparently a lonely fellow, Ming always gave her a quick reply. The only thing she couldn't manage was mountain climbing. She could climb the hills around town to get water, but she had a phobia of mountains above a certain height.

Alice would never forget an accident Toto had in grade two. He got bitten by a snake one day while playing in the bushes. Not knowing what kind of snake it was, they took Toto to several hospitals to inject him with various antidotes, none of them at all effective. Toto was in a coma for nearly a week. Alice prayed with all her might to all the gods she'd ever heard of, until finally he woke up. She sometimes felt that Toto had really died that time. For a long time, Alice would not let him take part in any outdoor activities, but for a boy like Toto this was just a form of torture. Even more importantly, Thom didn't approve: he thought that no matter how dangerous it might be Toto should try to survive in the wild as much as possible.

Alice was flipping through the *Illustrated Cat Encyclopedia,* imagining Toto was still by her side listening to her explanation. The classification system this encyclopedia used was really interesting: you cross-referenced the length of the coat and the shape of the face. Alice kept turning the pages but could not find a cat that resembled Ohiyo. Was it because she was too young, and her distinguishing features had not appeared yet? "It's just an ordinary cute little black-and-white 'mee-kuh-ssi,'" said the nurse— a Mandarin approximation of the English word "mix." Which just meant it was a crossbreed. But as far as Alice knew, housecats were all one species. After all, couldn't any couple of housecats mate and produce a litter of mixes? It seemed people only divided cats into breeds as a way of investigating the cat world or establishing a ranking system for the cats. The logic of the system was human, while the cats had their own logic and pecking order and played by their own rules.

So were inferences about nature really concerned with the laws of nature? Or merely human laws?

Alas, but this was the kind of linguistic vortex into which Alice's literary training was always causing her to slip. Before she knew it, she had spent the whole afternoon leafing through the *Illustrated Encyclopedia of Cats* and almost all the other field guides on the shelves. Now she got the feeling that the world was composed more like a field guide than she had realized. Maybe she had gotten it wrong as a young woman in assuming the world was full of random occurrences. Maybe the world was neatly and intricately arranged, and everything was actually a twist of fate.

The next day, Alice stayed home watching Ohiyo. She'd never thought that you could get so engrossed just observing the various activities of a cat: Ohiyo asleep on the bookshelf, eyelids heavy, limbs dangling; Ohiyo padding near a leaf beetle that had flown in the window; Ohiyo with her huge round eyes open wide gazing attentively at Alice.

"So adorable." Alice sighed. Everything had to change when you raised a cat. It was just like having a child. That evening Alice went to sleep with Ohiyo under her arm. Ohiyo was purring, dreaming about who knows what. But later that night, Alice had a dream of her own.

Just a month before, unable to go on alone like this, Alice had traveled to Japan for a course of "dream grabber" therapy. The dream grabber was a technology developed several years before by a team led by Professor Yukiyasu Kamitani, director of the Computational Neuroscience Lab at the International Advanced Telecommunications Research Institute. They used MRI to record people's dreams. At first they could only display brain activity as simple geometrical shapes, but gradually they were able to image the data in the dream waves. The images weren't photographic or videographic. They were more like the enigmatic patterns on a television screen when there is no signal. But the therapy was not available to just anyone off the street. It was a medical treatment, so you needed a referral from a medical specialist. Kamitani had done the research hoping to counteract the dream interpretation shows that flooded the airwaves and the internet, not anticipating that after he started offering his service the television and internet producers would copy him and add "dream grabber" shows of their own. All Kamitani could do was lobby for legislation controlling the use of such images. But the situation was already a mess. After all, in this day and age everyone needs something to grab hold of.

It was Reiko Matsusaka who had introduced Alice to the therapy. She was a translator and professor at a women's university in Tokyo. Years earlier, Alice and Reiko had collaborated on the translation of one of Ming's novels into Japanese. Both young scholars with a fervent passion for literature, the two of them had become online friends, meeting to discuss the intricacies of Chinese–Japanese translation. For instance, Reiko couldn't understand the idiomatic Taiwanese expression "make-it-big-truck," so Alice explained how Taiwanese people bought small trucks in the hopes of striking it rich and even asked the author how many cubic feet the engine would have and what model it might be on her behalf. Alice also guessed at the particulars of the male characters in the novel, because Reiko told her there were several different ways for a Japanese man to say "I." It was so much more complicated than in Chinese.

Reiko gave Alice a Skype call after learning of her situation from a fellow scholar. At first Alice refused even to consider the therapy, but then something Reiko said changed her mind. "The dream grabber won't solve your problems for you, but it seems that quite a number of people discover little clues or issues that make life worth living again."

Despite years of correspondence, Alice's trip to Tokyo was the first time they met in the flesh. Reiko had a round face, a medium build and a very Japanese smile. A bit eccentric, she wore a pair of glasses with molded plastic frames (though for all Alice could tell they could be expensive handmade spectacles) along with a pair of rather sexy fishnet stockings. To Alice the outfit seemed extremely mismatched. Surprisingly few scholars floating around in fishnets, are there?

The therapy was supposed to take a whole week. On the first day a session with a psychologist was scheduled. That evening, Alice stayed at the clinic, which was just like being in a five-star hotel, except with brain-wave detectors in the pillows and the mattress. The second and third days it was just like being on vacation. She revisited Yoyogi Park and the Ueno Zoo. She also wanted to go back to the Tamagawa Zoo, where she had taken Toto, but unfortunately they were closed for some animal escape drill. On the fourth day Alice's dreamscape data from the first three nights was compiled.

Alice regretted coming as soon as she saw her dreamscape. The doctor and technicians could not decipher the dots and lines on the screen, but Alice could. That is the way memory works: often you're the only one who can recognize what something means. The dreamscape viewing was supposed to be followed by a session with an experienced counselor, but

Alice simply said farewell to Reiko and caught a flight back to Taiwan instead. Reiko did not particularly ask Alice why she was leaving so suddenly when she saw her off at the airport. Alice just noticed she had changed into a pair of extremely eye-catching purple pantyhose.

Alice woke up from the dream they'd recorded in the clinic in Tokyo. Still half asleep, she saw from the clock over the bed that it was about four in the morning. Ohiyo was sound asleep. Do cats ever need a lot of sleep! Ohiyo was sleeping by a digital album she had knocked over. Alice did not have to look to know it was the album beginning with one of Toto's baby pictures. Alice tried stretching out her hand to get at it without waking Ohiyo but could not get at it. She could only play the images she knew only too well in her mind's eye. It occurred to her that Toto might just be sealed off in a deathless world somewhere, that he might be alive as if in a photograph, in a place death could never enter. Was Toto somewhere like that, carrying his specimen case as he searched for something he had never seen before?

IV

# 8. Rasula, Rasula, Will You Really Go to Sea?

Before Atile'i went to sea, Rasula prepared a bottle of fine *kiki'a* wine, a local delicacy women and children made by letting the rhizome of a certain tuber ferment in their mouths into a viscid liquor. The process sometimes required three days of chewing. The taste of the wine varied with the smell and composition of the saliva of the person who chewed it. The mellow wine from Rasula's mouth had been the toast of the island since she was a girl. Mixed with the starch of the tuber, her saliva produced an aroma men found captivating. Instead of making you drunk, it tended to induce the most indescribable palpitations. Some men who had drunk it even claimed that their futures had flashed before their eyes.

After Atile'i had shot his seed, Rasula took out the wine she'd chewed for him and advised him to sip her wine slowly so as to remember her smell, the look in her eyes, the warmth of her nether parts.

But where was Atile'i now?

The men of the island all desired Rasula but none dared make a move on her. Nobody knew who her father was. Her *Yina* (the Wayo Wayoan word for mother) Saliya's weaving was the best on the island, but, lacking the protection of a husband, Saliya had no way to obtain an allotment of land, and women were not allowed to go to sea. The only way she could get land, fish and other forms of upkeep was to do public service in the village. Mainly, she wove saltgrass sandals for the islanders. Rasula would often help Saliya pick vines in the woods and collect saltgrass by the shore: the vines were for the sole, the saltgrass for the upper. Saliya's weaving talents were not limited to sandals; she could also make fishnets, nets that not even the Ima Ima fish, the strongest fish that swam in the waters around the island, could escape. Saliya might well have woven enough nets over the years to cover the entire island.

Men would often take a detour past Saliya's house after a hard day of fishing and help with repairs around the house, maybe leaving a fish or two, or maybe a sea cucumber or a tasty octopus. It was only after she had her first period that Rasula realized that they were actually there for her mother's hands, not only for the sandals, the fishnets or out of a desire to tell stories. Rasula had heard their tributes to her mother's hands:

> They revive the dry grass.
> They can calm a fierce squall.

When Saliya was young she was as beautiful as Rasula, or even more lovely, because Saliya had a pure, Wayo Wayoan beauty. *Saliya* in Wayo Wayoan meant "a spine with a graceful delphine arc." As a maiden, she could simply sit at the seashore facing away from the village with her hair hanging down her back and it was enough to make the island's heart break.

Rasula's favorite activities were watching seagulls bearing the moon aloft and collecting freshly molted crab shells, but now she was like a seabird with wounded wings, gazing at the sea but unable to leave the island. Saliya could totally understand what Rasula was feeling. She quietly regarded her child, suspecting that another little spark of life had appeared within her soul. Being unable to spend a lifetime with the man she loved was the fate of many a Wayo Wayoan woman, but to bear his child was the grace of Kabang. This was because the child might be a boy, and a boy could help them start a new family.

One day when mother and daughter were sitting in the doorway weaving sandals, Rasula suddenly struck up a conversation.

"Yina, why aren't women allowed to go to sea?"

"This is the rule of the ancestors, the law of nature. Women can only go to the seashore to collect shellfish. But you must never forget that shellfish with spines are not to be touched."

"Why did they make this rule, and what if one breaks it?"

"Oh, my dear Nana (the Wayo Wayoan word for daughter), you well know that a girl who breaks this rule would turn into a spiny urchin which none would dare approach."

"Have you actually ever seen someone change into a spiny urchin?"

"There are urchins everywhere."

"No, Yina, I mean have you ever seen a real live person turn into an urchin?"

"No, Nana, and neither has anyone else, for she would sink into the sea before the change comes upon her."

"Yina, I don't believe you." Rasula heaved a long sigh, with a faraway look in her eye. Saliya looked at Rasula and in her heart answered her sigh, thinking: It wasn't my wish for you to have such a pair of pearly eyes, daughter of mine.

"Yina, I don't believe you. I want to build a *talawaka* of my own."

"What? No, you can't. A *talawaka* is not for a woman to own."

"I want to *build* a *talawaka*."

Saliya knew that when Rasula had made up her mind she was as irretrievable as a stone sunk to the bottom of the sea, and so she said nothing more.

When a man made a *talawaka,* Rasula would stand off to the side and quietly observe. Sometimes when she was chatting with Nale'ida she would ask lots of questions about the techniques of *talawaka* construction. She knew that Nale'ida was deeply in love with her, and that if she had conceived Atile'i's child Nale'ida would be obliged as Atile'i's older brother to care for her. This was another Wayo Wayoan custom. But she did not love Nale'ida back. Atile'i and Nale'ida were like *Yigasa* (the sun) and *Nalusa* (the moon). She loved Atile'i's sunny disposition, not Nale'ida's lunar nature. There was nothing she could do about how she felt, for no one can pit her heart against the sea. She let Nale'ida visit her at dusk simply because she wanted to listen to him tell stories of the sea and tell her more about the principles of navigation.

But you had to give him credit: Nale'ida, who looked like Atile'i except for his nose, talked a lot of sense. "The sea cannot be taught. You learn it with your life," he said. But even though Nale'ida loved Rasula the way a fisherman loves an enormous fish, he still did not dare break the taboo against lady guests riding in a *talawaka*.

Without telling anyone, Rasula began gathering and preparing the building materials on her own. She cleared a place in the woods a fair distance from her house, keeping the unformed, fetal *talawaka* covered during the day, coming only at night to work on it in secret. Weaving was no trouble, as she had inherited Saliya's nimble hands; moving the bigger branches out of the woods was harder, though she could do it with a bit more patience and a few bruises on her arms and legs. Rasula's *talawaka* was taking shape. She used a file made from a sea urchin to do the finishing work and carve an image of the seafaring Atile'i on the hull.

The island was small, but Rasula did everything with the utmost secrecy, so almost everyone remained ignorant of her seafaring scheme. Nale'ida was blinded by love, the other men who visited the house by burning lust. The only one who knew, her mother Saliya, chose silence, believing that Rasula would quit. Saliya could tell Rasula was pregnant from her posture and smell, and assumed that when she discovered the soul of a little Atile'i inside her she would give up as a matter of course.

Thrice the moon died and thrice it came back up to life. Early next morning, Rasula burrowed under the covers and to her mother said: "Yina, tomorrow I'm going out to sea."

"Going out to sea?"

"Yes. My *talawaka* is ready. I've heard many stories of the sea. Atile'i was my teacher, and Nale'ida, too, has taught me well, so even though I've never gone to sea I know its ways. Now all I need is your blessing, and nourishment for the trip, that I may find Atile'i safe and sound."

"Atile'i's dead and gone, Nana."

"He is not dead. I know. I feel it."

"Nana, do you realize there's a little soul in your body? Atile'i is in your belly."

"Yina, I know. I want to show Atile'i the Atile'i growing inside me."

"Nana, do you know where Atile'i is?"

"I know that he is somewhere on the sea."

"The sea is too big, Nana. You are dooming yourself and the Atile'i in your belly to death."

"You know, Yina, that living on this loveless island is about the same as death."

"You think I do not love you, Nana?"

Rasula did not cry. She was like a sinking ship, getting heavier and heavier. The water was pouring in, not flowing out.

"Forgive me, Yina, forgive me."

Saliya could've gotten the villagers to stop Rasula, but she did not. She knew that restraining her daughter would merely cause her to wither away before her eyes. Let be, let be, Kabang must have arranged for Rasula to die at sea, her tomb an ocean wave.

Saliya gave up on persuasion. She helped Rasula push the *talawaka* all the way to the seashore at midnight the next day. As she pushed, Saliya felt her soul sinking into the sand. The two of them were shocked to see someone standing on the shore in the moonlight.

It was the Sea Sage. Obviously, there was nothing about the sea that the Sea Sage did not know. He had been watching the situation unfold, just letting it run its course. He walked over and helped Rasula and Saliya push the *talawaka* into the sea. He performed *Mana,* a ritual blessing, by sticking the skull of a great fish onto the prow. A *talawaka* that had not received *Mana* would go blind in the sea and mistake itself for a fish. Moving swiftly along, it would suddenly sink beneath the waves and actually turn into a fish, never to float to the surface again.

"Kabang has spoken: the fish will always return." Not even the Sea Sage had the words to comfort Saliya. All he could manage was this old island proverb.

Pregnant and untrained in the operation of a *talawaka,* Rasula was unable to pit herself against the wind. Nor could she "feel the direction of the wind with the testicles," as Atile'i had put it. She stopped trying to steer and yielded her heart up to Kabang, her body to the *mona'e,* to the waves of the sea. Maybe because she'd received the Sea Sage's blessing, the sea remained calm for three days in a row, like a preternaturally flat inland plain. But this was the first time Rasula had come face to face with the sea itself, and she did not know where to turn: where in such a vast, shoreless expanse should she look for Atile'i? Her search had gotten her powerfully motivated, and terribly lost. It had become an obsession, an irresistible idea, and it would bury her. The "sea rations" of dried fruit, dried fish, coconut and cooked breadfruit were running out, and the water in the seaweed skin was almost gone. Rasula had an oyster-shell hook, but fishing was not as easy as she had imagined.

And where was Atile'i now?

Rasula enjoyed three days of fine weather, but only three. Then the weather broke, and swells appeared out of nowhere. The spirits of the second sons of Wayo Wayo wanted to reveal themselves, to warn Rasula and tell her to row left, but not being a second son she could neither see the spirits nor hear their voices. All the spirits could do was turn into sperm whales and swim alongside her *talawaka,* inadvertently raising even bigger waves.

But not even the spirits of the second sons of Wayo Wayo knew that these waves would beach this island maiden on the shores of another island. At first glance, this other island looked about the same as the one on which Atile'i had landed. Very luckily, the island had a crescent-shaped promontory, creating a safe haven for Rasula. Her *talawaka* wedged in, stopped and moved no more. Rasula fell into a coma, like going to sleep.

Little did Rasula know that Saliya had cried nonstop for a week after she left. She cried blood in the end, until finally, at dusk of the seventh day, she fell down on the beach, like a little shell, like an oar that didn't belong to any man. Saliya's spine was still as beautiful as a dolphin's when the men discovered her body, and almost all the island men attended her funeral. In their hearts, they were all truly sadder to lose Saliya than they would have been at the passing of their own wives.

Another thing not even the spirits of the second sons knew was that the island onto which they saw Rasula step, which looked about the same as Atile'i's island (both being compounded of countless bits of strange stuff), was not the same island at all. In fact, Rasula's island was headed in the opposite direction.

# 9. Hafay, Hafay, We're Going Downstream

I sometimes think I've come full circle and ended up back at the shore.

When I was all of eleven months old, Ina (which means mother in Pangcah) brought me along when she left the village and went into town to find work. Ina's man abandoned her and nobody knew where he went. But there wasn't much work in town, so soon Ina took me to Taipei. At first she had a part-time job as a babysitter. Later she did a bit of everything, from nursing drooling old folks in the hospital to waving signboard ads for presale apartments. But don't underestimate how much it costs to care for even a little kid. It's really a lot of money. In the end Ina had no choice but to find work in a karaoke hostess bar. The customers were all old geezers, and she didn't do much with them besides eating peanuts, drinking beer and chatting. Some fellows would touch her hands, tits and ass on the sly, but that's about it. Later Ina started living with this guy called Old Liao. Old Liao was always getting drunk and using her as a punching bag. By that time I'd already started elementary and I remember more of what happened. We were living by a creek. There wasn't too much water in the creek. Sounds strange, doesn't it? Yup, at that time we were living by a creek without much water in it.

I'd left my home village when I was less than a year old, so I had no idea what village life was like. Every time Ina mentioned something about the village I drew a total blank. I don't know why, but Ina never had any plans to take me back to the village at that time. Sometimes I'd hear her talk about a creek by the village, and that because the water in that creek was muddy they called it Makota'ay. Pale silverflowers bloomed all along the creek we lived by in Taipei. Ina said that if you ignored the buildings in the distance it looked just like home. So I would often squint and try to see the view of the silverflowers without the buildings behind, thinking to myself maybe this was what home looked like.

One time, Ina had an idea to pick silvergrass hearts and cook up some broth for me to drink. She said she'd done the same thing right after I was born when she wasn't producing enough milk. She picked silvergrass hearts growing near Makota'ay to make me soup as a substitute. At the time I was still so small and hadn't grown a memory yet. But somehow the moment I drank the broth Ina made with silvergrass by the creek in Taipei it tasted different, not like home. You won't believe that I would remember the taste of soup I drank when I was a year old. But I did remember, I really did.

Old Liao made the house we lived in at that time out of scrap formwork. Old Liao was a truck driver and did heavy labor. When he wasn't working he'd go wait under the bridge and see if anyone was hiring. He was the sort of guy who would work if there was work to do, but of course most days there wasn't. Ina said that she met him working at the hostess bar. In my impression, Old Liao was fairly polite when he wasn't drinking. He was skinny and small, not the heavy labor type. But after he hit the booze he would get out of hand and hit Ina over every little thing.

At the time I could not understand why Ina would never fight back. She could've taken him on: we Pangcah women are pretty tough, you know. Why'd she let him hit her like that? And what was even more of a mystery was why she would get up before dawn the next morning and cook up a meal for him like nothing had happened. It wasn't like Ina couldn't support me on her own. Why did she have to shack up with a guy like that?

In those days if there was something I didn't understand I'd run off and sit on this big rock near the mouth of that creek, the place where it flows into the river, and sing. I'd sing songs Ina taught me, songs I heard on TV, songs from CDs classmates lent me, songs from the karaoke. I'm real good at remembering the words, even words I don't understand. I'm not trying to brag or anything, but everyone said I sang real nice, so nice that my voice would make the millet sprout. But the folks living in the temporary tribal village in Taipei didn't plant millet. The only thing growing on the creek bed was silvergrass, and you didn't have to tend silvergrass. It grew rampant, and you could never cut it all down.

In elementary I used to get up real early, because I liked to take the long way to school. I guess I left the house at around five in the morning. I didn't have a watch, so I didn't know exactly what time it was. I would draw a watch on my wrist with a pen, setting the time to 6:10. I thought I had a kind of magic power: when my classmates asked me what time it was I was always amazingly accurate. I was incredible, I'm telling you. Time seemed to live somewhere inside me, walking around, back and forth, back and forth inside my body.

I used to like watching this tall dark boy from the class next to mine play basketball. His name was Spider. He had really long arms and legs, and his movements were kind of comical. But on the court he was so into it, so svelte. To this day I find men with that kind of intent expression irresistible. Doesn't matter if a guy is fat or thin, tall or short, rich or poor, just as long as he knits his brows when he can't figure things out and stays focused on what he's doing: that's my kind of guy. I often watched Spider until about 6:10 in the evening, because 6:30 was the latest his dad would let him come home.

When I felt it was almost 6:10, I'd pretend to look at my watch, and Spider would leave the court, sloppily wiping away the sweat with his shirt. We took the same route part of the way home. Spider would push his bike a ways behind me, never beside me. I would stop at the fork in the road, and Spider would push his bike past, smile awkwardly at me, say see you tomorrow and go home. I'd have been waiting all day long to spend this time with him, waiting for this moment when he would smile and say see you tomorrow.

Ina always worked until five in the morning, came home and made breakfast for me before going to sleep. She liked to ask me what time I'd gotten home the previous evening and I'd always say 6:10. Sometimes I'd save the money Ina had left me for dinner and spend it on whitening creams, because I thought my skin was too dark. I would eat dinner at one of the neighbors' instead. Our neighbors were real nice to me. They'd come and invite me over to eat. That's what it was like. The kids in the neighborhood would run around eating at different houses. I remember that year a rumor went round that they were paving a riverside bike path or something and that the village might be torn down. Quite a number of outsiders came to our village, saying they wanted to help us fight the government.

There was one villager called Dafeng who was really active in the village. He was the "city chief" we elected. I remember one time he got up on the stage and held the microphone and proclaimed, "Urban renewal is all about renewing us out of house and home, isn't that right?" Everyone standing in front of the stage said, "Right!" Then he said, "But we're not really afraid of any bulldozer. It's the man behind the wheel that makes it run, right?"

"Right!"

"So it's the man that scares us, no matter whether he says he's here to protect us or to tear our houses down. Because he never tells you why, because his Han Chinese why doesn't mean the same thing as our aboriginal why, right?"

Everyone below shouted, "Right!" I still remember his words. Sometimes protesters would come and hold vigils and tell me to go up onstage and sing. When I sang the songs Ina'd taught me, everyone would start crying, young and old, their tears dripping down like rain.

Several times the government really did cut the water and power and tear down houses in the village. Eventually some folks moved into the "projects" the government built. It seemed to me that all those protests never did a bit of good. The government was so big, and we were so small. But sometimes they couldn't do anything about us. We'd wait until the bulldozers and backhoes had left and go back and rebuild using waste formwork, election posters, corrugated fiberboard, iron sheets and driftwood. Those houses weren't much to look at, but you could live in them just the same. The folks who lived in them came from many different tribal villages, not all of them Pangcah. Ina said there were many people like her, who'd run off not really knowing where they were going and stumbled into Taipei without enough money to buy a bus ticket home. Ina said, "Those guys want us to move somewhere else, but where are we supposed to move? We couldn't get used to living in those suffocating apartments in the projects, and some of those Han Chinese landlords would call us 'savages' and look down on us." Old Liao helped Ina rebuild the house in no time flat. That's the only reason I can think of why Ina couldn't bear to leave him.

One time not long after everyone'd moved back to the village by the creek to rebuild, Old Liao came home drunk and started smacking Ina around. He picked up the *Sea of Words* dictionary I'd left on the table and started hitting Ina with it on the head and shoulders. Maybe because Ina scraped against something on the wall and started bleeding, her hair was all stuck together and crimson. I was so mad I started kicking Old Liao. The *Sea of Words* was a gift from a teacher after I'd done well on a test. My teacher had said to the class, "When Wu Chun-hua grows up maybe she can be a teacher." Well, Old Liao went and smacked me on the face with that dictionary. He was so nasty, you know? My head really hurt. It even left a scar. See? It's faint but you can still see it. At the time, I thought the reason why it hurt so much was because Chinese characters were so hard to understand. And now when I sing, I still can't hear my voice on my right side too good. That night was the first time I'd ever heard Ina cry. The sound of her weeping merged with the sound of the creek outside, like two rivers surging around in my heart.

Ina often told me, "Sometimes I wish I could pretend that the creek we're living by is Makota'ay, but it isn't really, only seems like it." I thought a creek wasn't a good place to live by, because if you couldn't sleep at night you'd hear the trees and rocks cry. The wind echoed the sound back and forth across the creek, as if it meant to make people's hearts ache.

That night I kept tossing and turning, couldn't get to sleep. The next morning I got up real early, before it was light out, and sat on my rock and started singing. I'd probably sang three songs before the sun made its way up. All of a sudden there was a swarm of golden dragonflies over the creek. It was a kind of dragonfly as looks like a butterfly. Usually you only see them alone or in pairs, if you see them at all, but that morning there was a whole swarm of them, like they were going to school or a meeting or something. If I close my eyes I can still see every eye in the swarm. Dragonflies have green eyes, and I sometimes wonder whether the world looks green through dragonfly eyes.

I'll never forget what happened when I was walking to school that morning. Spider swooped in out of nowhere and said, "Hi, it's almost time for class." Then he slowed down and walked his bike behind me, talking with me as we went. When we were almost at the gate, he pulled even with me and then half-rode, half-ran past me, saying, "You sang real nice just now." Then he vanished into the bike lot behind the school in a cloud of dust. He pedaled standing up, his shoulders swinging to and fro like he was about to take off. It was the first time he'd ever said, "You sing real nice." I felt like a bird about to fly away.

That afternoon it started raining, a huge downpour, like someone was hurtling stones down at the iron roofs of our shacks. Ina opened the window and looked out, and the sky was darker than night. At around three in the morning, Old Liao made a trip back to see us. Looking gloomy, he told Ina: "Take Hafay to an inn. Ride the scooter. Here's five hundred bucks. Get your things ready. When you find a place to stay call me and I'll be right over."

"What's wrong?" Ina asked him.

"I don't know yet. The rain's been torrential. I'm scared there's gonna be a flood. I just heard them saying on the radio that it won't let up, so I came back right away. I think you'd better go stay somewhere else for now," said Old Liao.

"We'll wait for you and go together," Ina said.

"No, my buddy Moe will give me a ride on his motorcycle. You go first."

By the time the rain was falling the hardest Ina and I were already safe in an inn downtown. That inn still used thermoses from fifty years ago! Still in soaking-wet clothes, we turned on the TV news. The news kept jumping around. We saw our village and a flood coming. Our village was jumping on the screen.

It was still raining the next day. Ina took me back to the village on Old Liao's scooter. No, I shouldn't say back to the village, because the village was gone. It'd turned into a huge mud puddle. The rain had even broken through the embankment to the right, flooding the basements of all the new high-rises in the area. The water still hadn't receded. Water doesn't care if you're aboriginal or Han. The police had cordoned off the area, not allowing anyone in. It poured and poured. It was so heavy that the search and rescue team could only get into the full swing on the third day of the storm. They were pulling corpse after corpse out of the sand and mud and from between the rocks, body after body, battered and wrecked; many had broken bones, and some were twisted beyond recognition—you couldn't even tell that was a person. I walked along with Ina. She covered my eyes with her hand, but I kept my eyes open and through the spaces in her fingers I saw a body all swollen up and wearing Spider's clothing. A section of that body's legs had snapped; it had gotten real short. But the shoulders were still intact, and though I'd never leaned my head on those shoulders I knew them so well. It was like my blood had turned to ice, like vermin were eating my heart from the inside. I cried and cried, without making any sound.

The rain didn't let up. Villagers remember it rained for all of ten days. And in all that time Ina did not cry a single tear. She kept walking along the creek, telling me: "Hafay, Hafay, we're going downstream."

She was stubborn as a wild boar, checking more carefully than the search and rescue team in the cracks in the rocks of the creek and in the flat places. She helped the team find three bodies, but all corpses, no survivors. It seemed like everyone who'd stayed in the village that day became a corpse, but Old Liao was nowhere to be found. Ina said maybe he'd drifted somewhere else because he wasn't from the village. She kept walking and walking, and I followed her until I was nearly out of breath. I told her, "I don't want to walk no more, I don't want to walk no more," so Ina borrowed a tent from the search and rescue team and let me sleep inside. She went out again and kept walking, and it was real late before she came back to sleep. Early the next morning she got up and told me again, "Hafay, Hafay, we're going downstream."

I remember it was the evening of the fifteenth day after the rain stopped. Ina woke up in the middle of the night and went outside. I felt her get up, so I woke up too. I could vaguely hear her talking to someone, but who would there be to talk to so late at night in a place like this? I got up the courage to crawl over to a corner where the flap was raised enough for me to peek out. I saw someone standing in front of Ina. It was a man. That man was big and tall, and though I couldn't see him clearly I felt he must be a young man, but he also seemed kind of middle-aged and youthful at the same time. He was just like a shadow, one moment big, the next moment small. I heard them, and they seemed to be talking about something. For a moment his eyes met mine, and those eyes were . . . how shall I put it? Ah, it's hard to say. It was like a tiger, a butterfly, a tree and a cloud looking at you all at once. *Aiya,* I know it sounds crazy.

I immediately rolled back to my spot and pretended to be asleep, but that man's eyes filled my head. Ina came back in, crying for the first time in weeks. I sat up and asked her what was the matter. She said, "*Kawas* has spoken. Come with me." *Kawas* in the Pangcah language means ancestral spirit. Ina said, "I know where he is."

Ina held my hand as we waded into the creek up to our waists and then leaped up onto a big rock, and from that rock onto another. The moon wasn't too bright that night, but it was bright enough to see the rocks. If someone had seen us we would have looked like a pair of ghosts. Ina was sure-footed in the dark, and it was as if she had a flying squirrel's eyes, no deliberation, no hesitation.

Around about sunrise, Ina stood on a boulder, peered into a deep, dark pool and dove in. I was stunned. Her black hair spread out on the surface of the pool and then plunged, like it was a living creature. The hem of her skirt flared out underwater, like a white flower. I stood on the rock, crying. Suddenly I felt a chill: it was raining again, and the raindrops were flowing along my neck and down my back. But come to think of it, the creek was totally quiet while she was under. I don't know how much time had passed when the white flower of my Ina's dress was gathered into the murky depths and her black hair floated back up to the surface. Ina opened her eyes and, gasping for breath, said, "I . . . saw . . . Old Liao's . . . face." Ina told me to tell the rescue team where we were with the walkie-talkie they'd given us. They were there in no time. Ina told them where to look and they pulled Old Liao's corpse up. He'd gotten trapped deep down in a crack in the rocks. His body was all swollen up, like a big wild boar.

"What time is it?" Ina asked. She'd forgotten I didn't have a watch.

The watch I'd drawn on my wrist said 6:10, so I told her 6:10. I'll never forget the gray sky that morning, like there was a mist over the river valley . . . And even now, telling you the story, I feel like I can't see too clearly, seriously. I thought it was mist, but actually it was sand. The sun appeared as soon as the rain stopped, and the earth had turned to sand. I took it for mist, but if you walked through it would scratch your face. Ina walked up the shore without speaking. I found it hard to keep up, and for a time I couldn't see her at all. I felt like I was the only one left in the whole entire world.

Alice finished her cup of coffee. She looked at Hafay and suddenly felt that she finally understood some things in some of the novels she'd read. Hafay walked to the bar, poured Alice another cup, then thought better of it. She took the cup back and said, "It's not good for you to drink so much coffee. You need a glass of wine."

Hafay's teasing got a wry smile out of Alice.

Hafay said, "Sometimes I think Ina didn't take anything with her when she left the village because she thought it was safer to bring nothing, not even love. That was the first time I understood how you can still love a person who beats you up all the time." Maybe Hafay said this not to Alice but to herself, as a conclusion she'd reached about her Ina as she remembered her.

Alice nodded, not because she agreed with what Hafay had just said but rather because of something that had just occurred to her, a new conception of life: that life doesn't allow you any preconceptions. Most of the time you just have to accept what life throws at you, kind of like walking into a restaurant where the owner dictates what you're having for dinner. Looking down, Alice saw Hafay's feet, for the very first time. Hafay usually wore sneakers or boots, but not when she was woken out of bed in the middle of the night. Now she was wearing slippers that exposed her toes. Her big toes seemed to be split in two, giving each foot an extra little big toe, a size smaller than a regular big toe. Alice looked away to avoid awkwardness, only to find the window covered in moths, moths of all different colors, many of them with eyespots of different shapes and sizes on their wings. It was as if they were staring at something.

Right then, she could almost see something out on the ocean, something approaching the coast, heading their way.

# 10. Dahu, Dahu, Which Way to Now?

"You guys couldn't even put a bend in my dick! What kind of search and rescue team are you?" Dahu caught up with Black Bear and took the lead again. Dahu was used to cracking harmless jokes with the younger members of the search party. They were used to it, too. They knew Dahu mostly resorted to humor when the search seemed hopeless, when they needed a burst of laughter to lift their spirits and boost morale. Now was such a time.

Black Bear was in charge of orienteering and tracking, but now he had the expression of the hunted, not the hunter. Dahu knew he'd lost confidence. In the mountains, confidence is sometimes more important than endurance, and if you lose it in your mind your body will feel it immediately. Your limbs will start quitting, and the mountain will know you're faltering. And that's when it gets dangerous. So Dahu quietly walked on ahead, replacing Black Bear in the pole position. He patted Black Bear on the shoulder and motioned for him to fall back and rest a bit.

You couldn't blame Black Bear or anyone else, though, because this was the sixth day of the search, and so far they'd found nothing, no sign of Thom or Toto on any of the trails in the area. That was the strangest part. All Dahu needed was the slightest trace, the tiniest clue, and he was sure he'd be able to tell which way they'd gone.

"Dahu, which way to now?" asked Black Bear. Dahu didn't have an answer. He could have told them which way the sambar buck they had seen twelve hours earlier had gone. Why not now? How come he had no idea where to look? Dahu almost lost patience with himself, but experience told him to stay calm, because getting upset would only affect his judgment. The only possibility Dahu could think of was that Thom might somehow have stepped off a cliff. But there should be something left behind on the dense tree canopy below, or some sign of stress from a fall: he'd be able to tell if there were any broken branches, because the color was different. But there wasn't anything, no sign at all, and another search party had gone through the valley without finding a thing.

"Is it possible that they didn't even take this route?" asked Machete, another team member.

"Who knows? Maybe it's got something to do with all that rain. Shit, was it ever heavy," Dahu said.

The helicopter had nothing positive to report. Thom's transmitter seemed to have failed completely. There had been no signal for nine days, and the initial signal was from along the route Thom had registered. Then they'd lost it. Dahu thought a device failure was unlikely, because seasoned climbers like Thom would bring more than one. Besides, today's transmitters run on solar power, and with the current technology the odds against a multiple device failure were astronomical.

Of course it wasn't impossible. But Dahu couldn't help wondering whether this was the tragic outcome that that series of bad omens had augured. Or if the worst was yet to come.

When Dahu got the call to form an alpine search and rescue team the silvergrass had just bloomed: Bunun people consider this a bad time to undertake a long journey. Besides, when Dahu called Alice right before he left, he heard his daughter Umav sneeze over the phone. There was another *suhaisus hazam,* another bad sign, when he got outside: a flock of *has-has* birds (Japanese white-eyes) flying left. It was like the coincidence of almost all possible bad signs. Yet over the past few years Dahu had begun to doubt whether *masamu* (taboos) had to be adhered to. After all, a taboo that applied when the *has-has* fly left didn't make any sense. There were flocks of *has-has* flying all around in the mountains, and as they tend to dart around in flocks, flying left is commonplace. "And what day and age are we living in, anyway?" Dahu asked himself. If they canceled the original plan because of a taboo like this, wouldn't it be a bit too . . . ? Dahu harshly censored the irreverent word that had appeared in his mind. After all he was a Bunun, and disbelieving in the taboos was in itself a great taboo, not to mention his disrespectful language. If his father were here he would surely tell him that even though he had a master's degree in forest ecology he still had to respect the mountain spirits.

"Without the mountain what forest would there be for you to study? The forest is for us to hunt in and revere, not for us to research," Dahu could imagine his father saying in that booming voice of his.

But as this was a matter of life and death, Dahu set out anyway. Even if something unfortunate should happen to him, doing his duty was more important than respecting the taboos, especially considering his duty on this trip was to Thom . . . Or maybe he was doing this for Alice. Dahu hollered for Moon and Stone to get on his motorcycle, one sitting on the gas tank up front, the other on the seat behind. Moon and Stone were black Formosan mountain mutts. With a crescent streak on her chest, Moon looked a bit like a Formosan black bear, often called a moon bear, while Stone had a lopsided mouth, because the first time he'd gone hunting his lip had gotten torn by the tusk of a wild boar. No matter how much bigger or stronger the quarry was, Stone would always stand his ground when attacked, never giving an inch. Moon and Stone were Dahu's loyal companions of the alpine forest grove. But now they too were going in circles in the mountains. Occasionally the two of them would raise their heads, as if the scent of the target they were tracking had floated up into the sky.

Sometimes a person does not know where to go, or how he has ended up where he is. Dahu remembered how he'd decided to move here to Haven over ten years ago. It was all on account of Millet. Dahu had just graduated with a master's in forest ecology from a respected public university, which was a rare event in the village he came from. Actually, it was unprecedented. "Grad school for the forest, eh? What about fishing?

Is there a master's degree for 'shooting the gun,' too?" Dahu's friends all made fun of him. At the time aboriginal people tended to do native language-related or sociological topics for their degrees, but Dahu was only interested in the forest.

Dahu soon decided he should finish his mandatory military service before starting anything new. One time he and a few fellows from his company got sent into Haven on an errand and started drinking. Then they up and decided to visit one of the "gentlemen's spas" in front of the train station for a "special massage." They knew they didn't really need a massage. What they really needed was what the sign euphemistically referred to as an "essential oil detox." Dahu noticed his heart was beating faster than usual as he was walking up the dimly lit stairwell, maybe because he was drunk. The stairwell led to a dark hallway with doors that opened on little partitioned rooms. He was with two buddies, and each of them got his own room. About ten minutes later, a girl knocked on the door. "Will I do?" Dahu nodded, without actually having gotten a good look at her.

His friends had explained the general procedure over drinks. "The 'beautician' will give you an essential oil massage for about half an hour to an hour, then she'll tell you to turn over. She'll dim the light. This is when you get the 'special therapy.' When the time comes, don't be too shy. Just enjoy yourself, eh."

Lying facedown on the massage table, Dahu was looking through the breathing hole at the toes peeking out of the girl's high heels. They were exquisite, almost like they'd been specially created. Dahu's pulse hadn't slowed a bit. He felt like a sambar deer with a hunter hot on his heels. The girl asked him where he was from, what he did for a living, her manner businesslike, but her voice was so soft he felt he was walking through a pathless wood. While they were chatting, Dahu found out the girl was from Tai-tung, just like him.

But during the "special therapy," Dahu was so nervous he could not get fully erect. Her back turned, the girl was pumping him up and down with her hand, but Dahu had not ejaculated by the time the bell rang. He hadn't even touched her. He'd just been looking up at her waist-length hair. From this angle she looked quite young, maybe as young as twenty. But when they got talking about how old they were, the girl was upfront about her age: she was already twenty-eight.

"Baby face."

"Yeah, baby face."

"Uh, what's your name?"

"I'm Millet, Number eight. I do hope to have the opportunity to serve you again soon." Like a memorized line of a customer-service girl at a telecom company, Dahu thought. This was the first time he'd gotten a good look at her. She had a short purple dress on and quite a few bracelets on her arms. She looked just like a typical young woman on the streets of Taipei. She had a roundish face, not too fleshy. Her nose was somehow stubborn looking. From her skin color, she didn't look much like an aborigine, but her eyes sure did. Before leaving, Dahu was still peeking down at her toes, which appeared even more bashful now, as if they were sorry they'd walked in. What pretty toes! thought Dahu.

From then on Dahu often drove to Haven on his own. He would go in with his head lowered and tell the manager, "Number eight, Millet." Gradually the two of them were getting familiar, and sometimes Millet would go out with Dahu for a midnight snack. She'd complain to him if she had a bad customer. She told him some fellows would demand a discount if they hadn't been able to "shoot." "The matchmaker can't promise a son, am I right?" said Millet in not very correct Taiwanese as she got out a cigarette. "There ain't no sure things in life." Her skin was a lot lighter now, maybe from working indoors for so long.

Millet usually did the night shift from eight till six and caught up on sleep during the day. Dahu originally planned to apply for a position in a research institute and study the Bunun relationship to the forest, but later he decided to return to his home village for a stint as a substitute elementary teacher. Who'd have thought he'd up and decide to move to Haven and drive a taxi, just to be able to see Millet more often? It made perfect sense for him to go pick Millet up after work, waiting at the entrance of the spa at six every morning.

At first Millet refused to go to bed with him. All the senior girls had warned her never to fall for a customer. "Unless you're sure it's just a fling, just don't go to bed with him. If you do, you can wail and moan all you want, but all you gonna hear is I-told-you-so," said Ling, an older girl who'd taken Millet under her wing. Ling had gone into the business to raise her two kids after the sudden death of her husband due to a drug overdose. She would turn the light down while servicing customers, and would never look at them.

But as the days wore on, Millet couldn't help letting Dahu into her heart. He was a good listener, never groped her, and came almost every day to pick her up after work. Millet gave Dahu her cell number and a key to her studio apartment near the spa. The past few years of Millet's life had been spent helping her mother pay back her father's debts. She divided her time between her apartment and the "office." Sometimes Dahu would bring home lunch and quietly watch Millet while she caught up on sleep. Dahu felt that Millet, false eyelashes removed, became herself again, the girl with the nearly perfect, seeming freshly sprouted toes, the only part of Millet he'd been able to see through the breathing hole in the massage table.

Dahu drove the taxi, but he still missed the mountains, so he started to meet some other climbing enthusiasts and joined a search and rescue team. When there was an emergency in the mountains, Dahu would drive the taxi up and participate in the rescue operation. With his rich knowledge of mountains and forests, Dahu soon had quite a reputation. He helped avert a number of alpine tragedies. There were people from all walks of life on the team: tour guides, junior high school teachers, and a steak vendor and tonic hawker from the night market. Once the call to assemble went out, they would all drop whatever they were doing and gather to form the team. In their leisure time, they became climbing buddies. Many of them were mountaineering legends in their own right. Some were Han Chinese, some aboriginal—Pangcah and Amis, Bunun, Sakizaya and Truku. They shared a love for the mountains. None of them was willing to give up the mountains for all the money in the world.

Dahu missed those days with Millet so much that he didn't dare let himself get sentimental, or he might start ruining or revising those fragile and dangerous memories. Dahu missed Millet so bad, but he tried hard to forget, not wanting to get the present tangled up in the past.

Night fell and still no sign. The mountain Thom had registered to climb wasn't that difficult, but it linked up with a few peaks that were actually a lot more treacherous than many famous climbs. The "famous climbs" were all well-traveled, had a continuous stream of hikers on them. The spot you set out from was often not too far from the summit. The essence of the experience, finding a new route up the mountain, had been lost, and all that remained was hiking, sheer physical exercise. These mountains weren't like that. They remained mysterious, intuitive, like true mountains. Dahu often thought that when you start climbing a true mountain, common sense no longer applies. Anomalies always cropped up on the rescue missions he went on. There was this one time when several students got trapped on Nanhu Mountain. The rescue team kept finding discarded clothes along the path at a time when the temperature in the mountains was close to freezing. A young rescuer asked: "Could it be a distress signal?"

"Not necessarily. There are lots of recorded instances in Taiwan and abroad of lost climbers found without much clothing left on. Hypothermia gives people hot flashes. I don't think it's a distress signal. I think it's a sign that they're lost, that they've lost any sense of direction and are no longer in their right minds. We have to hurry." Dahu was right. When they found the students, they were almost unconscious and nearly naked.

Dahu sometimes went on international search and rescue trainings. Friends he met on these affairs had told him that when people are lost and haven't seen a single soul for days on end, many will deliberately avoid rescue personnel because they can't tell the difference between fantasy, illusion and reality anymore. Some retained their physical vitality but would not respond when called. Some would even hide like startled beasts. So on the current mission, sometimes Dahu called out their names, while at other times he just kept quiet, watching for signs. He asked the other searchers to keep it down as well. Not a few times he had the feeling *something was out there*, but it was always fleeting.

Several days later the rescue team returned with nothing to show for its efforts, not even a corpse. This was a heavy blow for both Dahu and Alice. The hardest thing for Dahu to bear was the look of disappointment in Alice's eyes. For a month after the incident, team after team of volunteers had gone into the mountains without making any progress. How was it possible? Dahu just didn't get it. The paper described it as an unsolved mystery. After all, all the usual alpine tragedy involved was people dying in the mountains: there was always a body. But this time it was like looking for clouds that have turned to rain and fallen on a river, something impossible to identify or trace.

As often happens in such enigmas, the search and rescue operations trailed off. The world was like an unimaginably immense machine that wouldn't stop working because a few people went missing. But on account of his lingering suspicions and his promise to Alice, Dahu decided to go into the mountains one last time. This time he had a new route he wanted to try, and some new ideas.

Not all aboriginal groups in Taiwan live in the mountains, but the Bunun are certainly a mountain people. Dahu, a second son, inherited his uncle's name. "Dahu" means soapnut, a shrub that is plain and resilient, pretty close to Dahu's own temperament. But no matter how tough he was, it was hard for him to face Umav by himself. He remembered how unstable Millet had become after conceiving Umav. No longer able to work at the spa, her income of a hundred thousand NT dollars a month suddenly dried up. But in this town, the only pleasure in life for a young woman like Millet was dolling herself up. Besides, like many masseuses, Millet had started using drugs while she was in the business. Dahu tried to force her to quit several times, but though Millet seemed dependent on Dahu's tenderness and reliability, she still felt that there had to be more to life than this. She would take it out on Dahu, and Dahu would only face her with an attitude of resignation. Millet could not stand herself like this. She needed to forget herself, and the only way to do that was to keep buying drugs on the sly from a customer.

As for himself, Dahu wasn't too strong, either, yet he was unwilling to appear weak. All he did was drive longer hours to avoid conflict. One day he came home to discover the scooter gone, and when he opened the door he heard Umav sobbing in her crib, but no one else was there. Then Dahu saw the note Millet had left. She hadn't written much, just, *I'm going to Taipei. Take good care of Umav.* It should have been easy to find her, but he did not go looking. Instead, he bought a safety seat at the Carrefour and kept driving the taxi. He put Umav in the passenger seat and talked to her as he worked.

Umav's eyes would light up like the eyes of a sambar deer when she listened to her father's stories, but the moment a story ended her eyes would turn to stone. After Umav fell asleep, her tiny bosom would rise and fall, but sometimes the rhythm of her breathing would change and she would wake up and burst out crying. Though still an infant, she seemed to know some things. She was like a wounded bird. Every day Dahu worried about the world his daughter would have to face when she grew up, because he knew that for a wounded bird in a real forest death was inevitable.

Dahu walked solitary along the path, then started wandering off. The way ahead got less and less distinct until finally it was just an animal trail. Dahu knew he had entered the "alpine interior." It was a far cry from the mountain paths packed firm by many feet, mountain paths with ropes climbers have tied and plastic markers they've left behind. Moon and Stone kept running in and out of the woods. They would bark to let their master know where the target was. There was nothing more important to a Bunun man than choosing keen and brave Formosan mountain mutts. They were your companions in loneliness, not just hunting dogs. Father had told him to pay close attention to a dog's eyes and tail: if the tail doesn't perk up the dog is craven, and if the eyes don't sparkle it's not intelligent. Either that or it can't calm down. A dog that doesn't stay calm can't really see danger in the forest.

Moving fast through the forest was Dahu's forte. He often joked with friends that for a Bunun man growing taller than five foot eight is a disability, because if you're too tall you can't shuttle easily through the trees. Moon and Stone were one step ahead of him. They had discovered a water source, a stream in the wilderness that made a silvery sound, like it was talking to you. Dahu got out his portable cooking stove and made a pot of tea. Dahu took in the view and drank the tea and seemed to forget for a while the troubles that he had brought up the mountain with him. It wasn't quiet, though. It never was in the mountains, especially near water. Dahu had discovered that many creatures would sing their own unique songs with uninhibited delight when they found water.

One time Father told him a story while they were out hunting. One of the main reasons why he liked going hunting with Father was that he was a good storyteller. Seeing him with the gun slung across his back, telling stories while they checked the traps along the route made Dahu happier than anything. They were resting by a stream and Father said, "Dahu, did you know that in the olden days streams never used to talk?"

"Why did they start talking so much later on?"

"Well, life was actually really hard in the old village deep in the mountains. People were too busy hunting and planting. They didn't like to dance much, actually, but sometimes they sang. Nobody recorded their songs, though. One day a boy and a girl went up the mountain to do some work. In fact, they'd been secretly in love for a long time. They felt so happy to have the chance to go into the mountains together that they started taking turns singing songs they made up themselves. Well, they came to a stream, and over that stream was a log bridge. It was real narrow, but they still tried to cross it together. Unfortunately, maybe the boy wasn't paying enough attention or maybe the girl wasn't paying enough attention. Probably thinking about something else, eh? Whatever the reason, while they were crossing the girl fell off the log. The boy tried to save her, and he fell into the stream, too."

"Did they die?"

"It wasn't like dying, Dahu. You must understand that sometimes people aren't alive, but it doesn't necessarily mean they've died. That's the way it was for this couple, and they became the voice of the stream."

People aren't alive, but it doesn't necessarily mean they've died? Dahu didn't get it.

"Folks say that from then on, the stream would always make a whispering sound. Listen, doesn't it sound nice? Later, when Bunun people hunted or worked on the land, they would sometimes, often or always listen to the sound of the stream for a long time. Later some Bunun folks imitated that sound, and that's how *pisus-lig* (harmony) came to be."

Dahu's father was a good singer and hunter, but a failure in life on the plains. He often got depressed, lost control of himself, and got into fights with guys at the factory over little things. So on holidays he liked to take the gun and face the wild boar up in the mountains and reminisce about the glory and the terror of the Bunun hunters of old. Dahu would always remember the look in his father's eyes the first time he took him on a group hunting expedition. The dogs were tracking the prey, and Father was directing the hunters to form a ring around it. Dahu's sweat kept dripping into his eyes, so much he could barely see the path. He had to rely more on hearing and intuition to scramble to his own position. There were gunshots all around him, which sounded like birds above the forest, flying, circling and sometimes leaving without a backward glance.

Dahu wanted to sing, but there wasn't anyone to sing along with him, and after a few phrases the feeling just wasn't right. He took out some jerky for Moon and Stone and picked some watercress for himself to raise his spirits. He washed it down with tea. In the forest, Moon and Stone were family. He thought it over and decided he should make camp a bit higher this evening. There shouldn't be any danger of a landslide at the place he had in mind, and it was close to water. He looked over at Moon and Stone and said, "Oh forget it, let's have a good night's sleep and keep looking tomorrow. Even the moon needs to take a rest. Isn't that right?"

Dahu looked up at the sky, the stars and the trees, thinking of the time when a village elder had told him, "You must often speak to the sky, the stars, the clouds and the forest, because they may be avatars of *Dihanin* (the host of spirits). If you don't speak to them, *Hanito* (evil spirits) will descend upon you when you're alone." Dahu wanted to speak to them but did not know what to say.

Nearby there was the dog-like barking of a muntjac and the buzzing and chirping of a chorus of insects. Some drab owlet moths appeared out of nowhere and started crawling around on his night light. A while later Dahu discovered that more moths had gathered, lots of them. Some were giant moths like the ones he'd often seen as a child. He'd heard a climbing buddy who knew a lot about insects call them emperor moths. There was another pale turquoise-colored moth with a long beautiful tail called an Indian Luna. And there were still other moths with eyespots on their wings, like innumerable eyes staring at him. Moths like that were usually giant silkworm moths. They don't fly around much, just stick quietly to tree trunks, like they're part of the bark.

Suddenly Dahu felt faint, far-off shadows drawing slowly near. He looked up, hoping to see more clearly, only to find it was raining. Every thread of rain was glowing, as if the moon itself had turned to rain, like the moon was falling all around him.

(

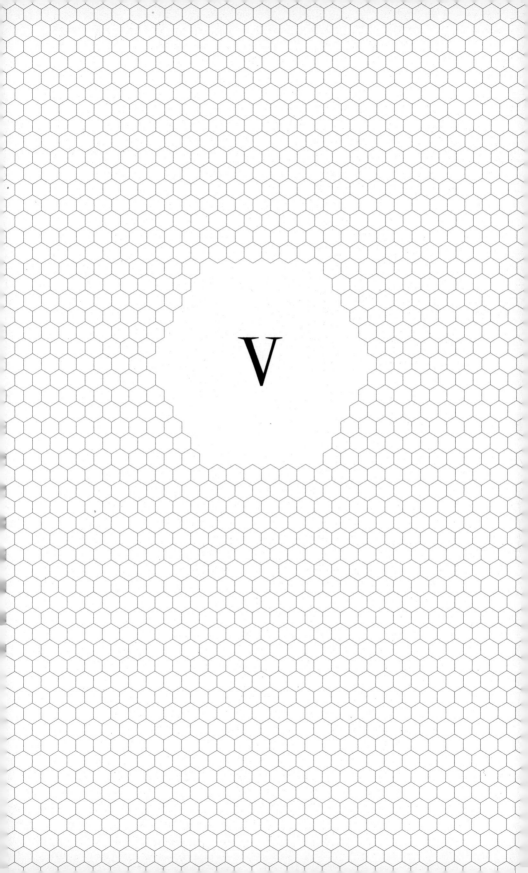

V

# II. The Vortex on the Sea

Hafay always felt her best cleaning up the Seventh Sisid first thing in the morning. The aromatic melange of seawater outside and sea-grass mats and wooden chairs inside was reminiscent of the smell of cookies, and this rather childish odor allowed Hafay to forget her cares for a while.

On the first Sunday in July, Hafay saw a couple of new faces in the Seventh Sisid. A man and a woman came in right when Hafay opened, sat at the Lighthouse table, set up a camera, and didn't move the whole morning. The man wore a cameraman's vest that was literally covered in pockets and a huge backpack; he was big and strong, and had dark skin, a buzz cut, and single-fold eyelids. He looked like the kind of guy who likes working out and pays attention to detail. The woman was skinny, and with heavy eye makeup that made her face seem a bit unreal. And she was wearing silver high heels, in a place like this! She seemed made for TV. Well, I guess, Hafay admitted grudgingly, she is beautiful, but just barely.

The woman had turned on her tablet right after sitting down and had been staring at the screen ever since, like she wanted to avoid looking at her partner. He had set up a telescope and a professional video camera, with a sticker deliberately covering the brand name. Hafay only needed one look to know they were definitely not there for the bird-watching. A few friends of hers who often went bird-watching had mentioned that, what with upstream factories diverting water into their weirs and discharging waste into the river, over the past few years the fish population at the estuary had collapsed and the birding had even gone to hell at the river mouth. Besides, looking out from the Lighthouse today there weren't any birds at all, only a gray expanse.

"Here on holidays?"

"No, we're here on business. Our job today is watching the sea," the man said.

"Well, I've been here watching the sea for many years now, and it's really not a simple thing. Please take your time," Hafay joked. Maybe they were here to do a story on Alice's house. The past couple of years really quite a few of these media people had made the trip. She turned on the stereo and put in a CD from a long time ago. It was the aboriginal singer Panai's song "Maybe Someday." Panai was really popular with young people at the time, and one time Hafay heard Panai sing live at the seashore. It was so intense. To Hafay it seemed that though Panai was trying to be laid-back when she sang this song, there was this heavy vibe, as if maybe someday would never come.

> *Maybe someday, you too will want to leave this bustling town behind.*
> *Maybe someday, you too will want to see that childhood place you*
>     *keep in mind,*
> *"a place like Heaven," Mama would say . . . maybe someday.*

The man ordered the daily special. Hafay called today's special Three Hearts, because she made it out of screwpine hearts, silvergrass hearts and shellflower hearts. She had gathered the vegetables the day before. For the main course you could choose wild boar shank or steamed fish. The man came over to the cashier and presented his name card. As she expected, he was a videojournalist for some TV channel, and the woman was an on-location correspondent.

"You can call me Han."

"My name's Lily," said the woman with the heavy eye makeup, long false lashes and turquoise eyes.

"What are you reporting on? We do not want the attention."

"Hey, don't get us wrong, ma'am. This is a great restaurant, and it'd be perfect for a feature. But we're not working on a fine dining piece right at this time. We're mainly here because we heard that this is where the trash island might hit."

"The *what* island?"

"It's been all over the news. It's not really an island. I should call it the Trash Vortex. Ah, you don't seem to have a TV here."

"Nope." Television was one of the many things Hafay disliked, and she did not subscribe to a newspaper, either.

Lily batted her false eyelashes and started to explain: "Some thirty years ago, scientists discovered ocean currents had been carrying people's garbage into a huge floating trash dump. Hard to imagine, isn't it? It's just so fascinating: this heap of trash is floating this way, and the whole world is watching. You've got to help us, ma'am."

"What do you want me to do?" Hafay couldn't understand what was so fascinating about it.

"Let us shoot from here. You've got a great view. And when the time comes we'd like to interview you and get you to share your thoughts."

"Sorry, I don't do TV." Hafay waved her hand dismissively. "Will there be other reporters showing up?" she asked anxiously.

By the afternoon, all the local inns and B&Bs were full of reporters. There were even quite a few foreign correspondents. Every so often helicopters and paragliders would fly by. Journalists of all shapes, sizes and colors covered the beach; some were even setting up tents. But except for Han and Lily, Hafay refused to serve any of them. She wished Han and Lily would leave, too, if possible, but she wouldn't kick them out. She'd only turn away new customers. Han and Lily were thrilled when they heard about the house rule. "This way we'll get exclusive footage. These days, no matter what the story, everyone interviews the same people and even gets the same camera angles. It really kills us when we can't get anything unique."

Then Lily, who was still holding the tablet so she could stay online with the news studio in Taipei and the helicopter flying overhead, said, "The news copter has flown out on the open ocean and surveyed the edge of the vortex, but the tidal currents near the shore have been so strong lately; they've been pushing the trash offshore. So we really don't know when it's going to hit. The experts we consulted with predicted that once the low pressure system forming over Luzon starts moving north the airflows will cause the edge of the vortex to fragment. Part of it might spread to Japan, and another part may get sent here."

"Go up in the helicopter and you'll get the shots you want," Hafay said.

"Sure, we've got aerial footage already, but the wind's been too strong the past few days. And it costs a lot to fuel the news copter, so we can't run it all the time. What we really want to capture is the moment when the vortex hits the shore, and then get local reactions to the incident," Han said. "Oh yeah, is there a boat in the area we could charter?"

"Maybe Ah Lung can take you out. I'll give you his number." Ah Lung was a local fellow who made wood sculptures and fished at the shore.

Hafay took in the familiar stretch of sea, but try as she might she couldn't understand what Lily and Han were talking about. It was like when she couldn't understand an arithmetic problem as a girl. All those things we tossed out assuming the tide would take them away and the ocean would digest them were now floating slowly back?

"Is there anyone living in that house over there?" Lily pointed at the only house in the line of sight of the Lighthouse. Hafay didn't have to look to know that they meant Alice's place.

"Sure is."


Alice was getting used to things she just couldn't understand coming in with the tide.

Finding Ohiyo was like opening a door and letting in a ray of light. Every morning, she would wake up to the sound of Ohiyo's meowing, and after pouring her food she'd sit at her writing desk by the Sea Window and zone out, or scribble whatever came to mind, without any particular aim. She wrote in a notebook rather than use a computer. She was not writing so much as performing a kind of ritual to the ocean, as if praying to it and beseeching it. Ohiyo's appearance seemed to have given her faith that if serendipity had brought Ohiyo to her, then maybe it had delivered Toto to something else, maybe something that had ended up taking him in. This possibility dispelled her suicidal thoughts, at least for now.

At first, she was thinking of letting someone more suitable adopt Ohiyo, or taking her to the animal shelter. But every time she put her in the pet carrier she had bought from the vet she couldn't help letting her out and stroking her head as she licked her hands with her flickering tongue. Ohiyo, seeming to understand that this person who was petting her needed her, would sit shamelessly on Alice's lap while she was writing or, even more brazenly, right on top of her notebook, and there was no way she was moving. The little lass knew Alice could not bear to push her away. All Alice could do was try to keep writing, or stare blankly out to sea. The sea was not the same color as when she was a girl. It was a bit darker and grayer now, rarely glowing with its own light. It was like some despairing middle-aged woman one occasionally runs into on the street, who's been married awhile and has now started to put on weight.

Sometimes Alice would think and think or write and write and end up falling asleep at her desk. At some point Ohiyo would always give herself a shake and spring out the window. Alice would worry she was gone for good, but she discovered Ohiyo had figured out the stunt of hopping from stool to stool to reach the shore. She'd also learned to swim. Watching through the backdoor window, Alice saw Ohiyo squeeze headlong into a thicket of grass. She didn't know whether it was a coincidence, but the most solitude she could stand before getting suicidal was two or three hours, and just when Alice's thoughts tended in that direction Ohiyo would make a nimble entrance. Her meowing was just the thing to ward off Alice's thoughts of leaving the world, as if someone had deliberately bolted the invisible gate that led toward the land of death.

For the longest time after entering the academy Alice used a computer to increase her productivity. When speech recognition became popular later on Alice followed suit. So it felt kind of awkward when she went back to writing by hand, and there were lots of characters she'd forgotten how to write. Editing was even more of a problem, because now she couldn't just click undo. Sometimes she'd be on the last line and make a mistake and have to crumple up the page and start over. But Alice liked this feeling: the characters had to settle in her mind a bit longer before they could take shape on the paper, stroke by stroke, like stalks of grass rustling out of the ground until she cut them down with the mower and waited for them to grow again. No matter how hard she tried, Alice could not remember why she used to like writing fiction when she was younger. Maybe the feeling was gone never to return, like all the migratory birds that had stopped visiting the island. Observing herself slowly turning into a word machine these past few years, Alice had become extremely short-tempered, and took it out on the scholarly articles she was asked to review. You draw a salary for producing this kind of garbage? The nerve! she always thought. Eventually, Alice got a reputation in the academic world for being unfathomably harsh. "Don't send her articles," people would whisper. Soon she was isolated, the way a vicious fish might be put in a Plexiglas separation chamber in an aquarium.

A few days before, Alice had gone to a new bookstore in town to get the right notebook. The prevalence of computers did not seem to have decreased the number of notebooks on the market. Lots of people still enjoyed having a booklet close at hand, jotting things in it when they felt like it. The store had a large selection. Alice took a liking to a notebook with a blue cover without any lettering. But the "paper" inside felt really neat to the touch. The clerk explained, "It's made in Germany. It's really cool. You can also buy a vial of this correction fluid. It's an organic plant-extract, and you use it wherever you want to erase and rewrite. It erases just like that, no sweat. The paper is made out of hemp fiber but has the texture of traditional paper."

"Amazing, fake paper that's just like the real thing."

"No, no, miss, this is real paper."

Well, the clerk was right. Maybe she'd fallen into a kind of intellectual trap. She'd started with a preconceived notion of paper and regarded anything that seemed "like paper" as fake paper or a replacement for paper. She felt that the whole world seemed to be of the same composition as this paper, but she could not say how, at least not until she got home and another thought occurred to her. About a dozen years before, people had started promoting "green living" or "slow living," and so forth, but this was just the latest fad. The people of this island basically pursued whatever was popular, not because it was significant but because it was "the latest." Saying "this is the latest" to Taiwanese people was like casting a spell on them, or like playing the melody of a magic flute that made whosoever heard it follow along. And this paper seemed to provide temporary repose to all such newfangled notions. But it was not a digital repose. It was writing out one stroke at a time the characters that appeared really necessary, worth preserving for all eternity.

"Yes, I guess it is, in that sense."

Alice bought a stack of notebooks in one go. Sitting by the Sea Window, she would write poems in the shape of a mouse's tail, in imitation of *Alice in Wonderland*. Sometimes she'd draw Ohiyo fast asleep, or copy out Toto's insect notes: highland red-belly swallowtail butterfly (Mount Li), Chinese hairstreak (Mount Ninety-Two in Nantou County), jewel beetle (Plum Mountain in Chiayi County), midnight luster stag beetle (Mystery Lake), moon-gazer stag beetle (Lala Mountain) . . . Alice discovered that insects sometimes had very charming names. They got more and more familiar until she pretty much had them all memorized. Now it was like her mind contained a forest, a mountain.

Today Alice would try writing fiction again. For a while, she thought she could keep writing stories on this paper. She would finish one, erase it and write another, over and over again. One day a reader might think he was reading a single story when he was actually reading countless stories. But right at this moment, all she had in her mind was an opening:

*Nobody has ever seen the forest she now beholds, like a forest in a novel that has grown into a real wood.*

That was as far as she had gotten. Didn't matter, though, because in any case she was no longer writing with a particular end in mind. Besides, maybe a single sentence could be considered a complete story. She put down her pen and poked her head out the window, wanting to enjoy the nice weather, only to discover a bunch of people setting up tents on the beach all the way from her house to the Seventh Sisid, some even pointing cameras right at her place. She couldn't believe her eyes. When the cameras noticed the lady of the house sticking her head out, it was like they'd found a new quarry: all of them turned toward her as if they were synchronized.

Alice was momentarily dazzled, by the hue of the sun and the glare off the water. The light turned into a kind of strange vibration. It confined her, confused her. Her chest was ready to burst; something inside her yearned to escape. Then, in the midst of a mind glitch, she suddenly dove out the window, like a dolphin.

These days wherever Dahu went, he would think of the scene that day in the mountains: a gorge shrouded in a milky mist, a young man appearing out of nowhere like rain.

Could someone really "go back" to the mountains? Dahu was watching Umav, who was unclipping her hair to check whether her bangs were even with rapt, undivided attention.

They were eating at the Old Shandong Noodle House. A regular patron, Dahu ordered the usual: a plate of noodles and a bowl of meatball soup. And Umav had beef dumpling soup. Though Umav had Bunun features, her skin was extremely fair. Aboriginal kids like Umav had been born and raised in the city. The TV they watched and the kids they met mixed fashions and lifestyle trends from Taiwan, the United States, Japan, Korea and a few other countries; they learned their fashion sense and way of life from the internet. Dahu wondered whether Umav's generation was a new breed of Bunun. Umav reclipped her hair and started jamming away at the air keyboard on the edge of the table. Dahu waited for a pause in her performance before asking: "What's the tune?"

"'The Happy Blacksmith.'"

"Oh, 'The Happy Blacksmith.'"

A few years before, Dahu had followed the latest trend in children's education and sent Umav for piano lessons. This appeared to be her favorite activity. But Dahu was utterly ignorant. He did not know who had composed "The Happy Blacksmith" or what the notes were. Since he'd never met a blacksmith in his entire life, he wondered why the blacksmith would be happy instead of sad. Come to think of it, the blacksmiths in some of the movies he'd seen all looked pretty glum, at least when they were striking the iron. Anyway, maybe there weren't any blacksmiths left at all anymore.

On TV, the beautiful anchorwoman was reporting on an incredible news story in a broadcaster's standard Mandarin. The volume was turned way up, but the speaker seemed to be broken and the sound kept breaking up. All you could make out from the spluttering speaker was words like "trash," "island," and "Pacific." The anchorwoman's voice was strident and shrill. For some reason TV stations today seemed to favor such loud news anchors.

The Old Shandong Noodle House was a greasy spoon, but Dahu found this kind of restaurant had the tastiest side dishes. The proprietor wasn't from Shandong at all. He was a local, born and bred in Haven. He changed the name after his son married a girl from Shandong. After she arrived Dahu thought the taste of the dumplings changed, and later he realized it was the skin that had changed, not the filling.

Dahu got the remote control, turned it down a bit, spread out the greasy newspaper on the table and found that the report he'd just seen on TV was front-page news. The headline read, COAST IN CRISIS! TRASH VORTEX ABOUT TO ENGULF TAIWAN.

[staff report] Taiwan is about to be sucked into the Trash Vortex! In 1997, the oceanographer Charles J. Moore was the first to discover that a vast tract of the north Pacific was strewn with plastic trash, forming what can be described as the world's largest garbage dump. Others have called it the Plastic Continent or the Trash Vortex. The vortex had been kept in place by swirling underwater currents, typically ranging from 500 nautical miles off the coast of California all the way to Japan.

Moore has described how he discovered the vortex one year while en route to the start of the Transpac sailing race from Los Angeles to Hawaii. It was the day before the big race and without realizing he steered his craft into the "North Pacific Gyre." He thought he had stumbled into some kind of alternate dimension. In the gyre the ocean circulates slowly because of little wind and extreme high pressure systems. Usually sailors avoid it. Moore was astonished to find himself surrounded by rubbish. His ship plowed through the stuff day after day, taking about a week to reach the other side. At the time Moore believed there was over a hundred million tons of flotsam circulating in the north Pacific, divided into eastern and western garbage patches in orbit around Hawaii. That was in 1997. Now it's even more massive, totaling at least two hundred million tons.

Mr. Moore, the heir to a family fortune from the oil industry, subsequently sold his business interests and became an environmental activist. He launched the Algalita Marine Research Institute. To him, containing the Trash Vortex had the same symbolic significance as humanity's efforts to combat global warming. And he was willing to lead the fight. Marcus Eriksen, the former research director at Algalita, says that historically the trash entering the North Pacific Gyre has biodegraded. But modern plastics and composites are so durable that intact items thrown away half a century ago can still be found in the Trash Vortex today. A number of charitable foundations have reserved funding for scientists analyzing its composition or searching for a solvent that would "obliterate" the garbage, but the search has proven elusive, because any solvent that can dissolve plastic would release toxic chemicals into the water, potentially hastening ocean death in and around the vortex.

Based on scientific analysis, about a fifth of the trash is from ships and oil rigs, while the rest has been dumped into the ocean by Pacific Rim nations. Because the confetti of plastic rubbish is translucent and lies just below the water's surface, it is not detectable in satellite photographs. It can only be seen passing along the hull of a ship. The tiny plastic pellets of which the vortex is composed act like chemical sponges, absorbing hazardous chemicals like hydrocarbons and DDT, which then enter the food chain. People have also discovered lighters, toothbrushes and plastic syringes in the stomachs of the dead seabirds and sea turtles that mistook these things for food. Dr. Eriksen said that what goes into the ocean goes into these animals and onto your dinner plate. It's that simple.

The Algalita Marine Research Institute went bankrupt after over a decade of operation, but the Trash Vortex is still floating around in the ocean. It has now fragmented into several parts, one of which is headed west across the north Pacific. Taiwan lies right in its path. Several years ago, the Ministry of Environmental Resources and the US government discussed the possibility of skimming or turning the vortex in the event of an emergency, but the job was simply too big, and even if it had been possible to sweep it up, nobody knew where the waste should be buried. At the present juncture, the Kuroshio current is pushing part of the vortex toward Taiwan. The Ministry has put out an evacuation advisory notice for east-coast residents, because nobody knows what harmful substances the nonbiodegradable waste in the vortex might contain.

This is unbelievable, Dahu thought. He told Umav, "There's a trash island floating this way."

"What trash island?"

"It's made of stuff like this," said Dahu, yanking at the plastic tablecloth. "We keep throwing this kind of thing in the ocean. Gradually a heap of garbage formed, and when it got big enough it turned into an island."

"Are my slippers on the island?"

"Possibly."

"What about your binoculars?"

"Probably."

"What about Mummy's headband?"

Dahu didn't reply. Umav found a headband somewhere when she was very small. He knew it was Millet's as soon as he saw it. It was a little thing he had forgotten to throw out, maybe on purpose. Umav asked him whether it was Mummy's, and he shook his head. Umav said it was, and he said it wasn't. "Yes it *is*," she said, and put it away before he had a chance to reply. But it had floated off somewhere in the flood. Dahu thought Umav had forgotten all about it.

At the mention of his binoculars Dahu recalled again what had happened that day.

After taking Alice for a hike along the rescue route, Dahu had a sudden intuition about another route he could try. He went up alone, only to suffer a string of bad luck. What bugged him the most was the loss of his trusty binoculars, which had been with him through thick and thin for over a decade, until they fell into the creek in a moment of carelessness while he was arranging things in his backpack. They were brand-name binoculars he'd bought back in his student days, eating nothing but instant noodles for months in order to save up the money. Because they'd fallen right against the base of the cliff, it appeared he would never retrieve them. In a huff, Dahu decided to call it a day. He took out a betel leaf he had picked at the foot of the mountain and folded up the two ends. Then he used his Swiss army knife, first to poke a hole in each end of the leaf, then to sharpen the end of a strip of bamboo, which he passed through the holes in the leaf to make an improvised platter. He had picked arrow bamboo shoots on the way up. Now he prepared them one by one: you pinched the tip and swiveled the base around to remove a vertical strip down the sheath, then the whole sheath would just come off. He wanted to make a soup.

Just as he was about to build the fire, he seemed to see a human form walking toward the edge of the gorge.

Usually in a situation like this Moon and Stone would give chase, but that evening the two dogs didn't move a muscle, like they hadn't noticed anything. Dahu shouted and it was like they'd suddenly realized what was going on. Dahu went after him, but he did not run, afraid that if the fellow was a mountain climber, Dahu might frighten him and cause an accident. Instead, he tried talking to him: "Hey there, what's up? I'm just up here hunting. Care to join me for a drink? I've got some fine tea with me, and there's wine as well."

He and his dogs tried to approach the man, but the man kept his distance. Apparently he was of medium build, but he also seemed to be a muscular young man. Dahu was ready to give up, thinking it was just some guy, probably someone in the habit of coming up alone just like him. Why not leave him alone? But when Dahu stopped, he was certain he *sensed* the man waving at him. Before Dahu had a chance to react, Moon and Stone went after him. Dahu had to follow along.

The chase proceeded in a tacit, single-file arrangement: the man, Stone, Moon, with Dahu pulling up the rear. It carried on for about half an hour before the man ducked under a bush. Dahu, about a dozen meters behind, could barely make out the man's movements in the faint moonlight. Dahu reached the bush, hesitated for a second, then crouched down and went in. Up ahead, Moon and Stone were barking like crazy, like they'd suddenly seen something. It started raining harder and harder, with the raindrops pattering down on the tree canopy above. Dahu hastily put on his water-resistant jacket.

The space under the bush was too low even for a Bunun. Dahu was crouching so much he had to prop himself up with his hands. He was almost crawling part of the way. Finally he was able to stand up straight, right when a dark cloud hid the moon from view. Dahu groped around in the darkness and found that he had arrived beneath a huge rocky outcrop. Moon and Stone had run off somewhere, so Dahu felt along with his hand to see whether the path ahead was level or not. It turned out not to be: there was a pit right in front of him, as wide as a man's outstretched arms. To one side was the huge root of a cypress tree, and the tree shade made it even harder to see the pit, which looked deep, even bottomless, in the darkness. Momentarily unable to keep his breathing regular, he got some rain up his nose and coughed so hard his chest hurt. Had that man lured him here to show him this pit?

Dahu called for Moon and Stone and soon they appeared. Dahu decided to go back to camp to get spikes, a rappeling rope and a headlamp: he had to see what was down there.

"Dad, look!" Umav said, pulling Dahu back to reality. She was pointing at the TV. Dahu looked up and hey, wasn't that at the Seventh Sisid? Dahu could tell immediately: that was the view looking out from the Lighthouse.

The shot started panning across Alice's house, stopping for a few seconds. Then a head appeared through the window. That was Alice.

Seemingly before she'd had time to react, Alice in the shot jumped out of the window and dropped into the sea. There was barely any splash to be seen on the screen. It was like a perfectly executed dive by a trained dolphin.

Atile'i sang to calculate the time he had been away from Wayo Wayo. According to the Sea Sage, in the olden days the islanders wrote a song for every star, and because the stars were just too many in the sky nobody could truly learn all the island songs. Someone who said he had sung a new song was surely a liar, for the islanders assumed that the song already existed and had suddenly been recollected. All songs on the island of Wayo Wayo were old songs, which is the reason why you sometimes start crying when you hear an unfamiliar island melody.

These days Atile'i had been singing one island song from the moment the sun was born to the moment it passed away. He kept singing until he couldn't remember how many songs he had sung, nor did he know which songs his parents and people in the village had taught him and which he had improvised. The songs he sang went on and on, like the sea itself. While he was singing, Atile'i often thought that all would be well if Rasula were here: she would harmonize with his melody, and then together they would sing a new song. He didn't notice at first, but he had started pinching his throat so he could sing Rasula's part. When the song ended the sound of the sea breeze made him feel like an empty cave, or like a translucent shell some crab had shed and left behind on the beach.

At the same time, Atile'i noticed that his body was changing: his gums often bled and his joints ached, too. He could not swim as smoothly as before. Sometimes he even felt dizzy, like he was back on land. (Never had Atile'i felt dizzy at sea).

Several days later Atile'i discovered a suppurating wound on his left leg, right over the spot where he had drawn the island of Wayo Wayo. He took this to be a bad sign. Lately the weather had been getting warmer, so warm that he could no longer escape the torrid midday heat by hiding out in his "house." Worse, the whole island emitted a blinding glare and exuded a horrible rotten stench that blended with the raw smell of the ocean. Atile'i kept vomiting, and his body became weaker and weaker. Atile'i also noticed a huge increase in the number of insects on the island, with flies and mosquitos everywhere, and the currents had become erratic, too.

Was the island approaching another world?

Atile'i had learned long ago from the Sea Sage that there was another world besides Wayo Wayo, and the past couple of days the idea that he was approaching this other world had been occurring to him. He tried to suppress the thought while anticipating the possibility that he was approaching the place whence the white man came, the place whither the hell bird and the ghost ship hastened. The problem was, did Kabang still rule over this other world? Atile'i didn't have the slightest idea, and there was nobody he could ask. So when he discovered people visiting the island every so often, no matter how far away they were, he chose to dive and wait it out beneath the island. He had dug lots of "wells" all around the island that went all the way down to the sea, so that he could take cover at a moment's notice. Yet once in a while Atile'i still imagined himself getting trapped and taken away by another race of man: the idea of this happening had him in its clutches, like a sickness.

Lately the hell bird and the ghost ship had been appearing far too often! He saw them almost every day. Several times while underwater Atile'i had even encountered "men" tightly clad from head to toe in black attire. Atile'i did not know if they'd seen him. He just looked for a place to hide. He was much better at swimming than they were, but because they held glowing things in their hands that darted hither and thither like slithery sea snakes, he suspected they might have caught a glimpse of him. Are they looking for me? That's impossible, for in all the world, only men of Wayo Wayo know that I exist, right? No, Kabang also knows, and so does the ocean, Atile'i thought.

Today was the peak of Atile'i's unease. He was burning up, almost too weak to stand. He intuited that he had been spotted by a hell bird with a single wing on its head. The hell bird raised swirling squalls all over, until it actually stopped in the northwest, which Atile'i knew to be one of the island's firmest spots. It was about a day-and-night's journey on foot. Although it was quite far from Atile'i's hideout, he knew he might be discovered very soon. He was not surprised the next day to hear noises coming from that direction. He summoned his last ounce of strength, picked up his spear gun, and uncovered the "land lane" near his house that led all the way down to the sea. He dove right on in.

Right then it started hailing. Great chunks of hail knocked fish leaping out of the water senseless, and in no time the ocean was covered with stunned or lifeless fish. Atile'i was floating in a seething sea of lifeless fish, as if he himself had transformed into an enormous fish.

# 12. Another Island

This was a summer the islanders would never forget. It all started one gloomy morning at the cusp of dawn when hail began falling to the south of Haven. Woken out of the deepest dreams, people walked outside or stood by their windows and looked out, bewildered at a seemingly shrunken world. Lit by the streetlamps, shooting hunks of hail pounded the seashore, glowing like mini-asteroids with a silver-blue light. Although the sound of the hail battering the corrugated iron roofs, the asphalt road, the stone steps by the beach, the streetlamps and the cars parked by the side of the road must have been deafening, somehow people's memories of the scene that morning were like silent movies: nobody recalled hearing a thing.

The hail immediately blasted several holes in the roof of the Seventh Sisid, and the first ray of dawn beamed down onto Hafay's coffee pot, as though the light had shattered it. Many of the reporters in the press contingent camped out on the beach were hurt. Arrangements had been made for senior correspondents to stay in a five-star hotel in town, so most of the reporters on the beach were relatively young; but one senior reporter fond of gesticulating on camera like she was playing mah-jong had somehow failed to make it back to the five-star hotel the night before. Still in the same outfit, she was stunned by a piece of hail the moment she stepped out of the tent and was immediately rushed to hospital. The incident later became tabloid fodder. Once squawky, she reportedly became unusually quiet, soft-spoken and lucid after the incident, and was soon relieved of her regular duties.

The teams at the beach were reporting live while dodging chunks of hail, so that the scenes the nationwide audience saw that morning were somewhat chaotic, with shaky video and reporters holding various objects over their heads for protection. Many viewers found the morning news at once shocking and hilarious.

The hailstorm stopped as soon as it had started, but because of the hail everyone missed the moment they'd all been waiting for, when the Trash Vortex hit the shore in several giant waves. The hail was also the reason why everyone scrambled up onto the road and escaped the deluge. For in the moments after the hail stopped, the storm clouds kept changing shape, with white, lead-hued and purplish-gray clouds gathering into a magnificent soaring thunderhead. It was a cloud like a floating myth, like an overwrought line of epic verse. When they remembered it later on, many coastal aboriginal villagers said they had never seen a cloud formation like that before, that it was more impressive than the vibrant sky on the eve of a typhoon. The cameramen were shooting this astounding sight, and all the while the monster wave was rolling toward the shore in the faint light of dawn. Many thought the wave explained why they did not seem to remember hearing anything during the hailstorm: though its source was near, the sound of the hail was nothing compared to the sonic force augured by the wave. That wave spoke with a cosmic voice, as if the risen moon had been silently storing up sound ever since time began and now let it out, all at once, in one great burst. By the time people figured out that the sound was coming from the sea, the wave was already upon them.

It had been exhilarating for the news crews to report live on the hail. So when the great wave finally hit the shore and swept away everything in sight, they were all momentarily transfixed, as if their feet were shackled to the road.

At first Lily and Han were thrilled to be able to capture the moment when the hail was coming through the ceiling of the Seventh Sisid, but Hafay felt something wasn't right when she looked out to sea. She rushed the two reporters up to the attic to safety. Her keen Pangcah intuition was soon proven right when the wave sloshed in, as if suddenly raising the height of the sea. It almost dragged the Seventh Sisid into the ocean when it receded. Knowing the wave would not just let it go at that, Hafay told Han to carry Lily, who was bawling hysterically, up to the road. Han dropped everything but his camera and tore up the beach with Lily on his back.

Grabbing the photo on the counter of her and Ina on the way out, Hafay evacuated just before the wall facing the Sea House fell. Everything else— her herbal medicine jars, her coffee stash, the cask in which she brewed millet wine, her mattress, a stack of letter paper and a stone she had brought back from the shore of that creek in Taipei—spilled out on the sand. As if in response, the Sea House itself half-collapsed, and all its contents—photos of Toto, the books on the shelf, Ohiyo's little cardboard box, Thom's climbing ropes, Alice's first, self-published book of poetic juvenilia, and some old clothes she hadn't had time to toss in the donation bin—got dumped onto the beach and mixed together with a hodgepodge of smelly plastic refuse that the wave had strewn upon the shore. It was as if all the world's garbage had been collected here.

The wave only produced one or two crests before it subsided and allowed the beach to reappear. But buried in a grotesque agglomeration of junk, the beach was radically altered, giving people the misapprehension they had landed on a distant planet. Han reached the road, consigned Lily to the care of a group of onlookers from a nearby aboriginal village, and immediately started shooting the uncanny scene. In a shot near Alice's Sea House, he noticed a dead bird and zoomed in for a close-up: it was a rare Chinese egret. Once an avid bird-watcher, he had personal reasons for holding the shot longer than the average videojournalist would have. He held it until a sodden black-and-white cat scrambled out through a crack in a fallen wall and scurried across the frame from left to right.

Alice was not in the shot of the Sea House. She'd regained consciousness in a hospital bed just in time to witness the live feed of this scene on television. She only hesitated a few seconds before pushing aside a young nurse who had just come in and, like someone who's just seen something, rushing toward the front entrance.

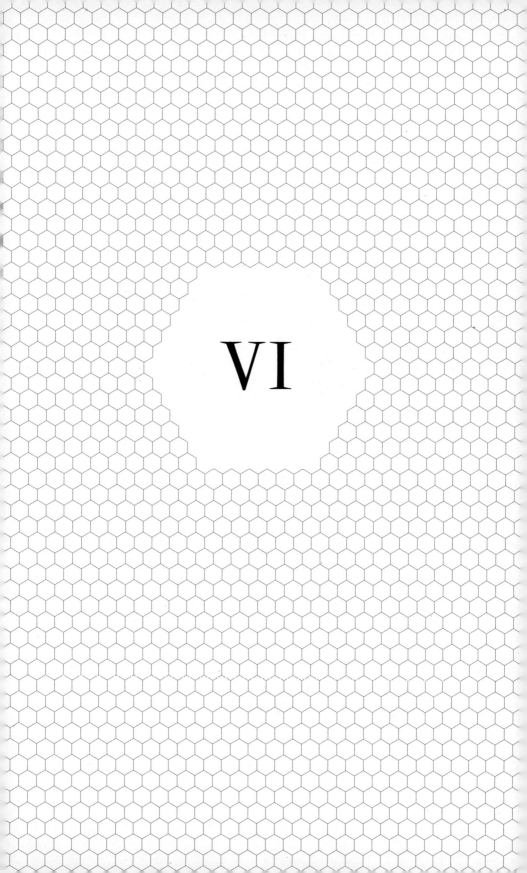

VI

# 13. Atile'i

Walking along the mountain path, Alice had been thinking she smelled something. How to describe it? That smell mingled the warmth of sunlight, the invasiveness of seawater, the stink of raw fish and the harshness of musk. It was an odd amalgam of contradictory odors that could never go together.

Alice now knew it was the youth's smell. It was so strong that she seemed to be able to smell him even when he wasn't by her side. Now Ohiyo was trying to squirm her way out of Alice's embrace. Alice held her close, afraid she'd run off if put down, and walked a bit slower. Cats are really soft little creatures. Holding her reminded Alice of this one time in kindergarten when she had found a black kitten walking home from school. She took care of it for three days without telling anyone. When she got home on the third day, the kitten was gone, but nobody in her family, not her mum, dad or elder brother, would admit to tossing it out. Alice refused to eat; it got so serious that she fainted and had to be sent to the hospital to get an IV. She only started eating rice gruel again one evening when she discovered her mother in tears by the hospital bed praying for intercession of the Bodhisattva Guanyin. The kitten never did come back. From then on, whenever she saw a black cat on the street, she would think it was the one that had walked off or gotten thrown out.

She and the youth finally made it within sight of the Seaside House. He saw a crowd of people around when they were still a ways off, and motioned for Alice to look. Those were reporters and people who were there to clear the beach. Alice hesitated, then walked up a nearby rise and found where her conspicuous yellow car was parked.

"Looks as if Dahu charged the battery for me," Alice said to herself.

She took a deep breath. So many fateful events in such a short time! As if something had been pushing her from behind. The path was slippery. A drizzle was falling, so faint it was barely visible to the naked eye. A flock of Japanese white-eyes flew by Alice and the youth up ahead from the right.

Alice tried to recall exactly what had happened that day when the cameras focused on her window. It wasn't out of anger, nor was she trying to escape. Still less was she really trying to end her life. She'd been waiting for Ohiyo to get back from her walk, and it is very important to stay alive when you have a reason to wait. Maybe she just temporarily lost control of her own body.

Alice had always been like this. Similar things had happened to her a few times in university. One time her date had stood her up on Valentine's Day. Befuddled, she paid the bill and bumped into the French window on the way out, startling everyone in the café. Back home, still not in her right mind, she had left the gas on, giving her family an awful fright. Her extreme reaction was just too much for her boyfriend, who soon proposed breaking up. Her mother remembered that as a girl Alice had gotten on really well with her maternal grandmother, so she decided to let Alice go stay with her grandmother for a while.

Alice never found out why her boyfriend had not kept the date. She could not even recall what he looked like. It was living in the fishing village she remembered. She could just close her eyes and the images would appear in her mind, gliding toward her: the village street; at the end of the street the temple to the sea goddess Matsu, built facing the sea; the mudflats crisscrossed with ruts from the buffalo carts, and the raw ocean breeze . . . Was this vision the earliest reason for her later insistence on living by the seashore?

When her mother took her home as a girl, Grandma would often take Alice oyster picking. She'd pick the oysters off the racks, put them in hempen sacks, then load the sacks onto the water buffalo cart one by one. The cart felt totally different on the mud: it was like rolling over something extremely soft, something living. Only long after did Alice realize that it felt really similar walking on the forest floor.

When Alice visited that time in university, some petrochemical firm had already moved in and reclaimed land for a refinery in another little village to the south. Life changed after the plant was finished: Grandma's oyster field silted up more and more every year, occasionally an oily film slicked the ocean, and the sky was always hazy. Grandma had to drag the water buffalo into the icy sea every few days to check the racks or pick oysters. Oyster picking is toil, and the winter wind off the ocean is chill, but sitting in the cart laden with oysters on the way back, with the wheels leaving much deeper tracks in the mud, you had such a steady, satisfied feeling. After picking the oysters, Grandma would spend the whole afternoon sitting on a chair "shucking" them. Those tough-looking oysters were actually soft inside. In a few short months Alice got used to oyster soup, oyster omelette, oyster crisp, mud crab and yam greens planted in the backyard. The days passed, and at some point so did her boyfriend's face.

Alice thought later maybe her personality changed in some subtle way during those days she spent at Grandma's place. When she went back after her break, her classmates all felt she was different.

The year Thom and Alice started building the Seaside House, Alice's brother called to inform her of Grandma's death.

"What did she die of?"

"Of old age."

"Of old age," Alice said, as if reciting. Actually Grandma had suffered from lung and kidney disease for more than a decade. Most of the people in the village left the world on this account. So one holiday, Alice and Thom made a trip back to the fishing village on the other side of the island. Driving through, they could hardly see any open gates. There didn't seem to be anyone there. From the seashore they saw that another petrochemical plant had been built to the north. Alice vaguely remembered protests against the plant over quite a number of years, but it got built in the end.

Lots of bird-watchers used to visit the shore, huddling behind their telescopes as if anticipating the advent of some great change in their lives. But later, according to Ming, after the petrochemical plants, even the birds had changed direction.

The plants needed workers, not old people. One time when Alice went back for a visit, Grandma launched into a litany of the conditions the neighbors were suffering from. Usually a reserved person, Grandma just would not stop talking that day, like she was afraid she'd never get another chance. Alice listened, feeling that those old folks who'd left the world before Grandma had probably died of loneliness, and that loneliness had led to the other symptoms.

Thom stood on the strand. Mostly buried in the sand, the oyster rack only reached his calf. Grandma's house, the water buffalo shed and the empty oyster racks seemed like an assemblage of monuments without anything to commemorate. And without anybody to maintain them, the bracken and the sandy muck were gradually encroaching.

Thom said, "Seems like it was once a charming little fishing village. Now all you could do here is film a period flick."

Alice gave him a cold stare and said, "Actually, it's been plundered." Maybe because she'd been standing in the mud too long, her feet were quite stuck when it came time to leave. Thom had to help pull her out. Watching the distant smokestacks belch black smoke, Alice suddenly recalled the tabi booties with the separate big toe that Grandma always wore to keep her feet from sinking into the mud.

Alice felt her head hit something when she dove into the ocean that day. Her arms and legs went instantly numb; the water was frigid. Then everything went black. The first thing that crossed her mind after waking up in hospital was Ohiyo. The devastated shoreline was playing on the TV news, and wouldn't you know it there was Ohiyo.

"She must be looking for me. She has to be. Ohiyo is trying to find me!" Alice removed the IV: ouch! She'd always hated getting shots, and if she was awake and the doctor said she needed a shot she would definitely make a scene. Alice ran a bit, deliberately making a detour to give the nurse she'd just bumped into the slip. When she got to the entrance, she pretended to be going out for a stroll just like a regular patient. Luckily she was wearing her own T-shirt, just not the one she had been wearing when she had jumped out the window.

Dahu must have brought it for me. He knows I do not like to wear hospital gowns, Alice thought. She had jumped into a taxi before panicking when she realized she had no money on her. She sure hoped Dahu would be at the Sea House when she got there. But when the driver saw the mess on the shore he didn't even ask her to pay.

"You live here, ma'am? You can't live here anymore. The houses have all been flooded. Forget the fare, it's on me."

"No, I insist. I just don't have money on me is all." Alice took down his license and phone number and promised, "I'll send it to you tomorrow!"

Moon and Stone were the first to see her there, and their barking caught the attention of Dahu and a few police officers. Dahu came right over. His shirt was extremely wrinkled, and he had obvious bags under his eyes. He looked like he'd had an unfortunate life. There were people there, maybe the police or from some disaster relief agency, cordoning off the Sea House with a ring of a yellow tape.

Dahu said, "They've just cleared a spot for the things that fell out of the Sea House. Anything that could be salvaged is there. I was watching." He did not ask what Alice was doing there, why she wasn't in hospital. Alice wasn't surprised, because that was the way he'd always been. Dahu! Don't you know women like a guy to take charge sometimes?

There was a rotten odor in the air Alice had never smelled before. Maybe it was seaweed mixed with the things that had been washed up on shore by the wave.

"Have you seen Ohiyo?"

Dahu shook his head. Alice wondered whether that meant he'd forgotten about Ohiyo or that he really hadn't seen her. The coastal villagers were all gathered on the beach talking. Several people waved at her, but from that far off it was hard to say if they were unhappy, in low spirits or what. Whatever they were feeling, they seemed prepared for the worst.

Actually, when the ocean started rising a couple of years ago, the only residents on this stretch of shore who had not moved uphill were the owners of the Sea House and the Seventh Sisid, so there were very few homes left. Everyone was trying to get as far away from the ocean as possible, like it was the plague. Not that it was necessarily any safer in the hills. When they were building the big seaside amusement park and hotel, for instance, they ended up loosening the dip slope of the mountain, and now there were several spots where the shoulder of the highway would always subside after a heavy rain. As Dahu had put it, "The mountains here seem like they might trip and fall at any moment."

Alice walked over by the Sea House. The coastguard and a few of the cops kept coming over to ask her questions, but she ignored them, speaking only to Dahu. "Is Hafay all right?"

"She's fine, staying at my place for the time being. You're welcome to come over, too."

Alice fell silent, then said, "Dahu, can you do me a favor?"

"Sure."

"I need you to help me charge the car and park it around here for me. Can you do that? Then I'll come and drive it away?"

"Sure, but you need to tell me where you're going."

"Um, okay, but some other time, I promise. Are our friends around here all doing all right?"

"They're all well. But everyone's worried that the sudden hail and the wave are bad signs."

Bad signs. There had been enough bad signs. Too many. So many that they no longer counted. Alice picked up a blue backpack she'd bought with Thom in Oslo and started packing things she might need. Crossing the cordon, Alice found the home first-aid kit by the Sea House—only one wall had collapsed. Luckily she also found her wallet and cards, which she'd put in a drawer. The sleeping mat she had just bought for Ohiyo and the waterproof hard drive containing photographs of Toto were there, too. She kept picking things up, feeling like here was her life, scattered all over the place. On the verge of tears, she hurried to speak to try to distract herself.

"What happened? Where'd all those things come from?"

"From the sea. The Trash Vortex brought all of it. You remember all those news reports about the Trash Vortex? Plastic refuse thrown away around the world drifting around with the ocean currents, gradually gathering together, until eventually . . ."

"Oh, that. I remember that. That was big news. Didn't the government say it would do something about it?"

"You believe the government?" Then, seeming to remember something, Dahu slapped himself on the thigh and said, "Is Ohiyo the black-and-white cat you found?"

"Yeah, I thought you remembered."

"*Aiya,* when you suddenly appeared I was so relieved that my mind relaxed for a while there. I didn't realize what you were asking. There's a camera guy who apparently got footage of her."

"Right, I saw it in the hospital. It was on the news."

"I'll go find him. He was staying at Hafay's before the wave. I know what he looks like," Dahu said, running off into the crowd.

Alice looked off toward the Seventh Sisid. Perched on a rock, it seemed left out in the cold. It was half a lifetime of labor, Hafay's heart and soul. It was as much part of Hafay as the Sea House was of Alice.

Alice had almost finished packing by the time Dahu returned with a tall man with a buzz cut. They nodded and exchanged greetings, then the man flipped open the monitor on his camera. In the footage, Ohiyo was walking along the refuse-strewn beach and mewling, apparently quite distraught. This was the clip that they had played on the television news. The next part had not gotten airtime: Ohiyo hopping from the beach up onto the road, walking in the direction of the path to the stream where Alice often went to draw water. At the end of the clip Ohiyo disappeared into a thicket of grass.

"I'm a cat person, and this kind of footage is compelling, so I tracked it awhile. It looks like it went that way."

"Thanks. Dahu, I'm off to find Ohiyo."

"I'll go with you."

"No, I'm fine by myself, and they need you here. If you can, help me tidy up the stuff that fell out of my house. And take good care of Hafay.

See if our friends here need any help. *Aiya*, what am I saying? You're already doing these things."

"All right. But you have to tell me where you're going to be. I can't just let you go like this."

A cop wanted to stop her from leaving, so she looked over imploringly at Dahu.

Dahu came up with a plan. "Here, you take this," he said, getting out his cell phone to give to Alice. Then he did all the talking for her, saying, "It's all right. Let her go. Nothing's going to happen to her. Look, she's fine. I'll make sure she goes to the station to report her losses." The policemen all knew Dahu. This one just waved her on, not wanting to argue.

Dahu turned to Alice and said, "You have to answer when I call, all right?" Alice nodded and jogged off. Moon and Stone kept following her.

"Go back! Back! Back to the shore," said Alice, shooing them away.

Alice walked up the path to the stream hollering, "Ohiyo! Ohiyo!" It was getting dark out, had started drizzling. She slipped the waterproof cover onto her backpack, and put on her raincoat. The path was really slippery, but Alice had walked it a million times. All she could think about was finding Ohiyo as soon as possible, as it would get cold at night and something might happen to her. Alice kept calling Ohiyo, Ohiyo, until she rounded the bend and saw that a huge section of the side slope had slid down and almost buried the path. As it was still a bit light out, Alice assessed the terrain and tried climbing over. But the slide was higher than it looked, so she tried to squeeze through the grass on the other side of the path instead. Then she heard the sound of beating wings.

A few moments later, tens, no hundreds, of butterflies or moths that must have been hiding in the grass until Alice disturbed them flew to the other side of the slide in an undisciplined but seemingly coordinated fashion. The sky was dark now, making it hard to tell their colors. All she could see was that each was the size of her palm. It all happened so suddenly that Alice could not help crying out. And right when she did, she heard a cat's meow, as well as what sounded like the call of a muntjac. The call was really close, seeming almost to come from the ground beneath her feet.

Alice, who had fallen back onto her butt, managed to free herself from the vines and stems she was tangled up in and get round the slide. The first thing she saw on the other side was Ohiyo emerging from the grass to greet her. Then her heart skipped a beat when she saw an adolescent, a youth with skin like mud, lying on the ground, apparently immobilized, pinned down by earth and rocks. There were tears in his terrified eyes.

An image resurfaced in Alice's mind, of one time when Dahu caught a muntjac. He and Thom had killed the beast with a gun, then taken turns carrying it down the mountain. They showed Alice a photo of the muntjac in the trap. It was still alive. The animal had a broken leg, and a look of despair, Alice sensed its desire to live. That night she refused to make dinner for them. She felt angry at the men for their nonchalant attitude, and because they had brought back the photo like a trophy or an interesting topic of conversation.

The young man now trapped under the slide had the same expression as that muntjac.

# 14. Alice

When Atile'i saw the woman appear before him, he remembered the Roaring Rite the Earth Sage had taught him. The Earth Sage said, if you encounter anything you are unable to understand, then roar with the strength that lies beside your beating heart and you will speak with the voice of your true self and even evil spirits will flee. Atile'i tried roaring now, but as soon as he opened his mouth and yelled his heart and leg began to ache, as if someone had taken a stone knife and minced his spirit into fish paste. That's how painful it was! So after yelling a few times Atile'i started to cry.

The Earth Sage said, "To let a single tear fall is to submit, to plead for help, to render all rituals inefficacious."

At first the woman seemed frightened by Atile'i's Roaring Rite, for she screamed and fell off the earthen mound. Then she scrambled back up again and embraced the animal that seemed so strange to Atile'i's eyes. Soon, maybe because she discovered Atile'i could not hurt her, the woman started examining him; and when she realized his leg was confined, a look of concern appeared on her face. After a while, she forced a smile, as if to offer him reassurance, and then she started helping him move the rocky earth off his leg. Maybe because of the pain, or maybe for some other mysterious reason, Atile'i's tears kept falling. He was like a sea turtle that has been stopped from going back where it belongs.

The woman was not the same as the white people Atile'i had imagined or seen in books. She had another kind of translucent skin, sort of like a jellyfish. The woman was not tall, and might even be a bit shorter than Atile'i. After freeing him, she kept talking and gesturing, but he could not understand a thing. The only thing he could be certain of was that the woman probably did not bear him ill. Her movements and tone of voice told him that. Atile'i tried to say a few words to her in reply, but she did not understand, either. Then, out of gratitude, he started to imitate the birdcall he had learned while lying there just now to take his mind off the pain. Atile'i pursed his lips and let air through his lips and throat to produce a sound that was at times resonant, at times warbling. This was the sound of thanksgiving. The woman looked at Atile'i with surprise, as if she had seen a bird that could speak a human tongue.

"A sound can fly over any land, like a wave on any sea," Atile'i remembered the Sea Sage saying. Without a doubt, the Sea Sage was truly wise.

Atile'i, too, remembered what happened after he dove into the ocean, afraid someone would discover him. His body was abnormally warm, the water relatively cold, so when he dove in the frigid seawater it initially felt scalding hot. He swam for his life, like a wounded barracuda spotted by a shark. He swam for he did not know how long, until his chest ached terribly and his spirit was ready to leap out of his throat. Then a great force flooded in from behind. Sensing the approach of a huge wave, he went promptly limp and let himself get tossed about. Atile'i clearly saw that the wave was pushing him toward land, and all around him were the strange things from the island. Underfoot and underarm, behind his back and before his eyes, Atile'i was wrapped up in a mixture of shore and sea, as if he was just another piece of the island.

Atile'i thought his spirit would depart when he hit land, but fortunately it remained in his body when the wave retreated. He hid inside a big rock. That rock was very strange: it was hollow, and around it were similar rocks, as if rocks also had the gift of imitating one another, just like people. He was shivering now, maybe because he had been soaking in the water too long. He had an instinctive desire to run toward dry land, assuming this was his only hope of survival. There was a group of people in the distance wearing strange clothes and carrying strange tools. Atile'i was careful to avoid them, doing his best to imitate the grass as he moved.

Inside a clump of grass, Atile'i had his first opportunity to size the place up. It was really peculiar: the land on one side was extremely high, and the land beyond the high land higher still, as if it led all the way up to the sky. The Earth Sage would never believe me if I told him. But was this Earth Sage's turf, too? Did he even know about the existence of such a large expanse of land?

Atile'i started to run toward the highland. He ran and ran, until he felt his body was not listening to him anymore. In the time it takes for a fish to get caught on the hook, he felt something press down upon his leg. Before he knew it he could no longer move.

"I'm caught! I am caught by many stones. Oh venerable Kabang, please save me," Atile'i muttered.

Atile'i could only lie helpless on his side, immobile. He remembered the way to dispel pain that the elders had taught him: imagine that you are a fish. Elders often said that of all the creatures the fish was the least afraid of pain, for a hooked fish can still strive mightily with a fisherman for a long time before its life passes away. If a person got hooked, he would likely submit in the blink of an eye.

"A man of Wayo Wayo only gives up when his blood stops flowing, just like a fish, for we are people of the sea," the Sea Sage had said.

Lying on the ground, Atile'i carefully observed this new world. In every respect, in its colors, scents and sounds, it was different from Wayo Wayo. Of course it was also different from the island on the sea. So this was what the world was like: you pass through something and come out the other side, and the world there is somewhat similar but not quite the same. Atile'i was pleased with himself for coming to this realization.

Then he heard the sound of the woman's footsteps. Then he saw the woman.

After releasing Atile'i from his earthly bondage, the woman kept repeating the same things over and over again to him. From her gestures, Atile'i guessed that she wanted him to stay put. Atile'i did not remain there in order to wait for her. In fact, he had no choice in the matter, because his leg was broken, and a person with a broken leg cannot go anywhere. Worse, a man with a broken leg could never become a good fisherman, and his diving would suffer as well.

"Never again will I have the chance to become a real Wayo Wayoan man," Atile'i thought, despairing like a gull caught in a *gawana*.

# 15. Dahu

Hafay felt a hot flash the moment the hail started coming in through the roof. Even her bones got goose bumps. It was the same feeling she'd had the night before the flood destroyed the village that year in Taipei. She looked over and those two foolish reporters were still shooting. Hafay had no time to think. She yelled for them to get upstairs immediately, but they still looked like they had no idea what was going on.

"Hurry up or it'll be too late," Hafay shouted, right before the wave hit.

Experience told her that the second wave is often the worst, so as soon as the first wave receded Hafay got them to run up to the road. Han picked up his camera, piggybacked Lily, and waded toward shore without looking back. Hafay followed close behind, and hard on her heels the wave was silently flooding in another time.

This time it was the sound of the wave that left people paralyzed.

Standing up on the road, or what was left of it now that most of the foundation had been scoured away, Hafay looked back just in time to witness one of the walls of the Seventh Sisid collapse, as if to the rhythm of the retreating wave.

"Oh Ina," Hafay murmured to the sea.

The year after the flood, Hafay's Ina took her back to the east coast. Instead of going back to the village, Ina decided to stay in town. She applied for a job in a massage parlor and rented a studio apartment. Every day when Hafay got up Ina would have breakfast ready for her. She would have just gotten off work, her hair looking exactly the same as when she'd left the night before.

Sometimes Hafay wondered whether people were right to say that you could choose your own life. Could you really? After losing her Ina, what else could Hafay do but follow in her footsteps? And if she had not spent those few years in that line of work, how could she possibly have saved so much money so quickly, enough to build the Seventh Sisid? Life is sometimes a trade-off. I give you something of mine in exchange for something of yours, or I borrow from the future to get what I don't have now. Sometimes after all the trading is done, you get back something you'd given up, Hafay sometimes thought.

Hafay did not shed a single tear when she saw the Seventh Sisid collapse, probably because she'd had a premonition that one day the house would have to be returned, most suitably to the sea.

That day, after helping Hafay clean up the things that had fallen out of the Seventh Sisid, Dahu drove Alice's car to school, charged the battery, drove back and parked it. Then he walked over and sat down by Hafay, handing her a lunchbox. In all this time, Hafay's eyes had not for a single instant left the place where her house had been.

Dahu asked: "You got a place to stay?"

Hafay shook her head.

"Stay with us then, for the time being. I've moved to a Bunun village down south in Tai-tung. The people in the village are building traditional houses. I've built one myself, but nobody's living in them yet. I can live in mine for now, and you and Umav can stay with my Uncle Anu. There's air con at his place, so it's more comfortable. If Alice comes back and doesn't have a place to stay, I'll invite her to come crash there, too," Dahu said, all in a rush.

Hafay shook her head and said, "I can go stay at an inn."

"Don't get on the bad side of your bank account, Hafay. Don't quarrel with your bread and butter. It'll take some time to rebuild, but maybe if you save some money the Seventh Sisid can be restored."

Hafay didn't say a word, or respond in any way.

"We're still alive, right?" Dahu loaded the things he had gathered into the backseat, then opened the door to the passenger side. Many years later, Hafay would recall that Dahu's gesture just meant so much to her, because at the time she was unable to decide anything for herself. She really needed someone to open the door for her.

They drove south along the coast. Hafay faced the driver's side, gazing past Dahu's melancholy profile through the window out to sea. Only now did she realize that the Trash Vortex or whatever it was called had pretty much covered the shoreline. The garbage glittered in the sunshine like it was encrusted with jewels. Dahu did not say anything to Hafay the entire way, while in the backseat his daughter Umav slept on Hafay's chaotic pile of luggage.

When they were almost at Deer County in Tai-tung, Hafay said, "At least I've still got the coffee machine." Dahu burst out laughing.

"Why're you going back to the village?" Hafay asked.

Dahu said, "I've been away a long time. I started out with a plan to go to the city and get an education, then after I graduated I just wanted to come back to the village to teach elementary school. I didn't expect to fall in love with my wife. She was the reason I left the village again." In a quiet voice, Dahu started telling Hafay about him and Millet, as the headlights probed the long, nearly straight highway ahead.

"I can make a bit more driving the taxi in Haven, but lately I've been thinking: Forget it, you know? The good thing about the village is that you're welcome there no matter when you go back, and no matter what kind of job you do you can always scrape by. As it happens I've got an uncle here, Uncle Anu. He went to the city when he was young to get himself a master's degree, just like me, and one year when he was back for a visit he heard there was this really nice piece of land that a consortium wanted to build a columbarium on. Uncle Anu managed to get a loan to buy the land. He borrowed some from friends and the rest from the bank. He does tours there at a place he calls the Forest Church. He teaches the city folk about the Bunun lifestyle, how we plant millet, how we hunt and build our houses. It's been a while now. I've been coming down and helping out every chance

I get. Now I'll just move back here for good. Besides, Umav has kids to play with in the village."

"You haven't mentioned this to Alice, have you?"

"Not yet. This is something I just decided recently."

Everything is just getting started, Hafay thought.

It was already evening when they got to the village. Dahu gently shook Umav awake, and friends in the village were making dinner for everyone, not just for Hafay and Dahu, but also for some tribespeople who'd just gotten back from cleaning up the beach.

Then a stocky middle-aged fellow with a childlike grin walked over and slapped Dahu on the back. Dahu introduced them: "Anu, Bunun." Dahu pointed at Hafay and said, "Hafay, Pangcah."

Anu was a talkative fellow. He got Hafay to listen to him when she was feeling depressed and did not want to listen to anything. He told her all about why he had founded the Forest Church, what problems he'd had, how much money he still owed, how many times the bank had tried to seize his house, and so on.

"My house almost got auctioned off quite a number of times."

"Then why didn't it?"

"Nobody's interested. Who would want to buy it, in this location? Only Bunun people would be willing to live here. Ha ha! It's rotten luck for the bank. I hear the loan officer that approved my mortgage lost his job!" he said, laughing, and Hafay could not help laughing along with him.

"There are only two kinds of people who would loan money to Anu: angels and fools," Dahu said.

Soon Anu was lying on the floor, drunk, and wouldn't budge. His friends and relatives all went home. Dahu took Hafay to the guest room, which had two single beds, one for Hafay and the other for Umav.

Hafay lay on the bed but just couldn't get to sleep, not expecting that Umav would also be having a sleepless night. Umav was sitting up in bed, watching the moonlight outside.

"Auntie Hafay, want to take a walk in the Forest Church?"

"The church? Right now?"

"Yeah, now."

"Do you have keys?"

Umav looked at Hafay, surprised. "How could there be keys to the forest?"

They walked to the end of the road, passed a mesa with a view of the river valley below, and came to stand in front of two towering trees. Umav said, "This is the gate." Hafay realized she had gotten it all wrong: the Forest Church was a tract of woodland without even so much as a fence around it. The two of them stood there as if they had turned into a couple of animals.

"I thought it was a real church."

"What do you mean, a real church? Are there false churches, too?"

"That's not what I meant . . ." Hafay said. "What's inside?"

"Walking trees," said Umav.

# 16. Hafay

"Once upon a time, there was a girl who always took her basket along when she went to work in the fields, but very mysteriously would never allow anyone to peek inside. But a nosy neighbor wondered why there was always a handsome young man helping the girl plow and plant when she was working. So the neighbor went behind the girl's back and told her Ina."

"What was the girl planting?"

"Millet, I guess."

"My dad says that you don't really have to plant millet; we can just scatter the seeds around."

"Probably where the girl was living they had to pick up stones and turn the soil and plant the seeds."

"I guess she would never admit that there was someone helping her."

"Good guess. You're so smart, Umav. The girl just denied everything. Her Ina had a funny feeling about her daughter's basket, and suspected it might have something to do with the handsome young man the nosy neighbor had told her about. One day the girl got sick. She tossed the basket by her pillow and lay in bed. Her curious Ina waited until she was fast asleep, then took off the cover and looked inside. She could hardly believe her eyes: inside the basket was a fish, two feet long and seven inches wide."

"How big is that?"

"This big." Hafay showed Umav with her hands, and Umav was obviously satisfied. "My dad has caught way bigger."

"The mother cooked and ate the fish, and then put the bones back in the basket. When the daughter woke up and discovered the fish was gone she went and asked her mother, 'Where's my fish, Ina?' Her Ina told her off, yelling, 'What an ungrateful daughter you are! The other day when we pounded *mochi* sticky rice there wasn't anything to go with it, and there you were hiding a great big fish from me. How dare you!'"

"The daughter must have been angry because her mother got her all wrong."

"Maybe she got angry at her Ina, or maybe there was some other reason, but in any event, the daughter was so sad when she heard what her Ina had done that she swallowed the bones in the basket and died. Turns out that handsome man was a fish in human form."

"Why not a handsome man in fish form?" Umav asked.

"That makes sense, too. My Ina told me the story, but I forgot to ask her why it wasn't the other way around. Umav, you're so bright."

Dahu couldn't stop chuckling. Pangcah and Bunun people are both fond of making up stories. When he was a kid Dahu asked his father: "Who did you hear the story from?"

"From the elders."

"Who did the elders hear the story from?"

"From even older elders."

"But the even older elders were children once, too, weren't they?"

"Yes, they were, Dahu."

"So they heard the story, too."

Dahu's father thought it over and said, "Dahu's right, even the oldest elders were children once. A story can take children places they've never been before and tell them about things that happened to folks even older than their elders."

Dahu had noticed that Umav was really paying attention when Hafay told her the story. She wasn't like that with other people. She really seemed to trust Hafay. The first day Hafay came to stay with them Dahu was a bit worried, but the next day when he heard Umav had taken her to the Forest Church in the middle of the night, his mind was set to rest. He knew the sacred trees there awakened fear, awe and caution, and that nobody who had seen those trees would want to end her life.

These past few days Dahu had gone back and forth between Deer County and Haven more times than he could count. The stench along the shoreline was getting worse, and it was especially stuffy there. The concrete wave-dispersal tetrapods piled along a long stretch of the east coast made the cleanup work all the more difficult. A few environmental groups with chapters operating in several local high schools and universities threw themselves into the coastal cleanup. It was heartwarming to see young people all along the way relaying the trash away, but there just weren't enough vehicles. It wasn't looking like the shore would return to its former self anytime soon.

Dahu's junior high school classmate Ali was a primary supervisor at a deep ocean water company. He came to the cleanup site to carry out an inspection wearing the latest model of respirator. "I'm telling you, it's not in the papers yet, but over ninety per cent of our pumps and pipes are devastated. The pipes are covered in trash from the vortex. We put an underwater camera down and it's not a pretty sight: the bottom's done for."

"Worse than the county government says?"

"Dahu, don't be so naive! How could the county government possibly tell the truth? Seriously, I'm worried that my boss is going to just leave the pipes in the Pacific and take the hell off."

"I can't say for anyone else, but I believe your boss has it in him, absolutely."

"Christ, the County Mayor is probably going to up and leave one of these days."

The sea once had the power to put fear in the hearts of the people living along the coast, and to change their fates, but now it had turned into a demented old man with some teeth missing. The wind blew up light plastic bags that had dried in the sun. They were like flowers, unbearably putrid flowers. Having lived all that time in Haven, Dahu always felt half-Pangcah himself, and now he couldn't help worrying about his Pangcah friends. How would they survive? And what would become of their long-imperiled fishing culture?

Ali picked up a section of hard plastic tubing that had probably floated around in the ocean for decades and said, "We can process glass bottles easily, but nobody knows what to do about these older plastic tubes. You know what? The past few years the government's poured tons of funding into reducing the amount of garbage in the vortex, but it's actually a scam. Think about it. Where is the trash supposed to be buried after it's been cleaned up? All the incinerators, landfills and advanced trash-sorting facilities on the island wouldn't have enough capacity to digest it all. You think Ilan and Taipei will welcome the garbage out of the goodness of their hearts? Dammit! Japan and China have been passing the buck, but garbage is fair, and now the ocean currents have broken the vortex up and everyone's getting what's coming to him."

On the last trip before dark, Dahu discovered that Alice's bright yellow car was not where he'd parked it. She must have taken it. Just then his cell phone rang, and sure enough it was Alice.

"Dahu, can you let me stay in your hunting hut?"

"Sure, but it hasn't been used in a long time. I hope it's still habitable."

"Great. Thank you, Dahu."

"You want to live there?"

"Well . . . sort of."

"It's not too comfortable."

"No, it'll be fine. I've got a tent and a full set of climbing gear. No need to worry about me. Oh yeah, how's Hafay?"

"She's fine, but the Seventh Sisid collapsed."

"I saw. The same thing will happen to the Sea House, I reckon."

"Yeah, maybe. When the time comes everything will collapse. Where are you now?"

"Close to your hut."

"Can I go over and help?"

"No, no help, I don't need any help. Dahu, listen to me, I want to be left alone for a while. I'll come and find you when I'm ready."

When Dahu got back to the village that evening, Umav told him that she'd taken Hafay to see the walking trees again in the morning. "It's different during the day." The walking trees was actually a stand of fig, phoebe and autumn maple trees, weeping fig trees in particular. The aerial roots of fig trees drop from the branches down to the ground and grow into prop roots. Villagers once used fig trees as border markers, only to discover that they could "up and walk."

"Come spring, I guarantee you're in for a surprise."

"You mean in the forest, right?"

"Yup."

"There'll be butterflies," Umav interrupted.

"Yes, there will. In winter, some different species of crow butterflies will gather here, and for a certain time after they pupate there'll be golden cocoons everywhere. Later they'll emerge from their cocoons and there'll be swarms of butterflies flying wing above wing. Ah! It's a moving sight to see."

"Really! I guess I'll come next year and see for myself."

"You can just settle down here. Our village could use an extra pair of hands. Lots of tourists are making the trip already. We've survived relying on this forest and that mountain."

Hafay didn't respond. Dahu felt he'd been a bit too forward in saying what he'd said, but it was too late to unsay it now.

Several days later, Dahu encountered Hafay as he was arranging things in the traditional house in front of the Forest Church. She couldn't get to sleep. So they started chatting while tying the corn up to dry by the window. After helping with the coastal cleanup for the past week, Dahu was exhausted. Hafay seemed to sense this and said: "You're beat, aren't you?"

"Yeah."

"People give off a certain smell when they're tired." She laid her hands on Dahu's shoulders and started to give him a massage.

"Do they? I've never heard that before."

"I'm a professional, you know! I used to work as a masseuse in Haven." The sound of the wind whistling through the Forest Church could be heard a long way off. The breeze on Dahu's back really relaxed his muscles. "I really studied the art of massage. Ina taught me, and so did other girls in the massage place. Your sense of touch can tell you a lot. Joints and tendons can feel like they are bubbling with vital energy, like there's some live animal running around in there. A person who's giving a massage uses her fingers, elbows and joints to apply pressure to those places and loosen them up. I kid you not, sometimes you'll see dark vapors escaping from a guy's body. But if you inhale them you'll have a terrible pallor the next day."

"Really? Sounds almost supernatural."

"It's true. Nothing supernatural about it."

"What were the customers like?" Dahu knew but asked anyway.

"All guys. They came for a hand job. The massage was just kind of on the way."

Dahu was surprised that Hafay would be so candid. Indeed, there were two kinds of masseuses. A few were real masseuses, but most were the other kind, and Millet was the other kind. It must be obvious to Hafay what he was thinking. Dahu blushed.

"*Aiya*, it's no big deal. It's just making money by doing another kind of labor, that's all."

"You're right." Dahu did not know how to respond, so he laughed and said, "Actually, I've been to a place like that." As soon as he had said it he felt he had said the wrong thing.

"You told me, that day, when we were driving. You mentioned Millet."

"I did? Ha! I told you about Millet?"

"Uhuh. Oh yeah, do you know what *Hafay* means in Pangcah?"

"Sure do. The first time I went to the Seventh Sisid, I thought, Hey, isn't that a coincidence? *Hafay* means millet."

Like the sound of some plant weeping, Hafay suddenly started to sing. She sang in Pangcah, improvising the lyrics up as she went along.

*Ignored, unseen, mislaid with ease, a tiny millet grain,*
*might fall away in the faintest breeze,*
*beneath the August rain.*
*You passed on by, you passed on out, my wristwatch read 6:10,*
*the time the grain was set to sprout,*
*interred, to live again.*

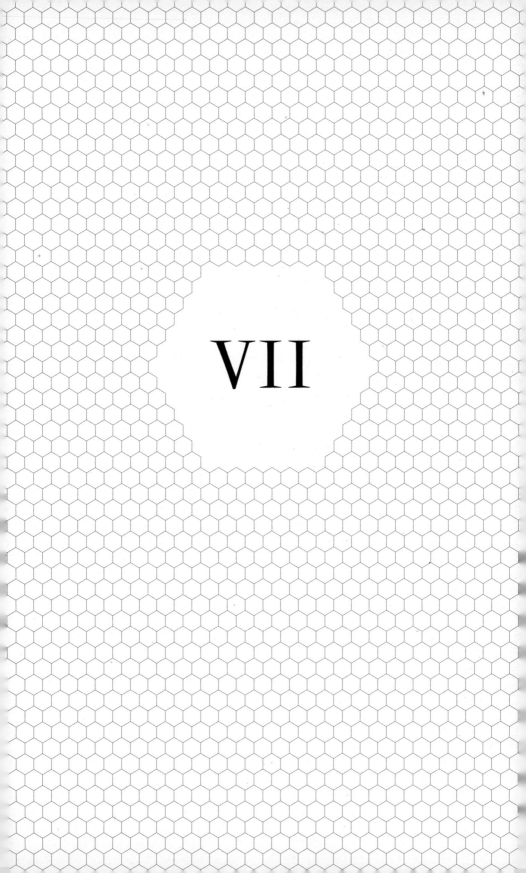

VII

# 17. The Story of Atile'i's Island

"My name is Lasu Kiyadimanu Atile'i," I said. "You can call me Atile'i."

"I'm called Alice." I guess that's what she said.

Alice has brought some food and a temporary house. It is a bit stuffy, but at least we don't get rained on. It's a bit like the house I built on the island of Gesi Gesi. She rubbed a strange-smelling ointment on my wound and told me to swallow some other remedies.

She lives in the wooden house, and I live in the temporary house. At first she wanted me to live in the wooden house, but since she saved my life, I cannot live in a nicer house than her. That's not the way of Wayo Wayo. At first she couldn't understand anything I said, but gradually we have come to recognize the scales and tails of speech, to realize the fish eyes of what the other is saying.

That strange black-and-white creature is called a "cat," and Alice calls her Ohiyo. I asked, "What does Ohiyo mean?" Alice released a torrent of words once she gathered what my question was, but it wasn't hard to guess that Ohiyo is what you say to greet someone in the morning.

"*Ohiyo.*" I try pronouncing the name, but the word feels awkward on my tongue. The cat just walks away when she hears me call.

"What about you? What do the people of Wayo Wayo say?" I think that's what she wants to ask. I have told her our island is called Wayo Wayo.

We say, "*i-Wagudoma-siliyamala.*"

"What does that mean?" she said, raising and lowering her shoulders; I gather that here as on Wayo Wayo this gesture means, "I don't understand."

I point at the distant sea and spread my arms to indicate that today the sea is calm. Today the sea appears holy and tranquil, like a sleeping animal or a dead whale. "It's very fair at sea today."

"*i-Wagudoma-siliyamala.*"

"*i-Wagudoma-siliyamala,*" she repeats, but these words are a bit hard on her tongue.

Alice seems unaccustomed to this kind of life. I often find she can't get to sleep at night. She has a strange box: you press it and it gathers part of the world inside, like an eye that can remember what it sees. She uses the box to hold the "reflections" of flowers, birds and bugs, which she then compares with "reflections" in her books. In those books are the "reflections" of the "reflections" she has seen. I wish I could draw a picture like that, a picture of a reflection that looks just like the real thing.

She's also brought things called "tables" and "chairs" and put them outside the wooden house. If the weather is nice she sits in a chair at a table and uses a "pen" (I finally understood that those twigs I drew with during my stay on the island of Gesi Gesi are called "pens") to write what appears to be words in a book. She always writes for a long time, and all the while her eyes are dreaming.

I asked her what she was writing and she said she was "writing a story."

"What are you writing a story for?"

"I am writing a story to save a life," she said, I guess.

She likes to look at the pictures on my skin and ask me what they mean. I've told her the story behind each picture, the story on my shoulder, the story on my back, the story on my elbow. But I don't know if she understands my stories or not. Some of the pictures on my body faded, so I've drawn new ones over them. The picture on the left side of my belly is of the day Alice saved me. I used the pen she gave to me to draw her reflection in my eyes when I was held fast in the earth. And the trees behind her, too. She looked sad when she saw the picture.

She's fed me things I've never eaten before. I was getting familiar with the alpine terrain, so when my leg got a bit better I tried to make the house a bit bigger with some wood. I put up an awning, so that even if it rains she can still write outdoors sitting under it.

Sometimes first thing in the morning Ohiyo brings back things like crabs or rats and puts them on the steps of the wooden house. I think she wants to offer tribute to Alice.

When Alice isn't writing she likes to talk to me. At first we did not know what the other was saying but gradually we got better and better at "sensing" meaning. She tells her stories and I tell mine, of Wayo Wayo, Rasula, my Yina, the Sea Sage and the Earth Sage, and the beached whales. I don't think it really matters if she understands me or not, because to Wayo Wayo islanders words can be smelled, touched, imagined and closely followed with your gut the way you follow an enormous fish.

I like to tell my stories and to hear Alice tell hers. I like the sound of her voice and the look on her face when she pets Ohiyo. Sometimes her voice reminds me of my Yina, other times of Rasula. So as long as the rain isn't too heavy, we sit together day after day in the morning, gazing at the sea. I tell her, "Let me tell you about Wayo Wayo, to let an image of Wayo Wayo grow in your mind."

Ours is an island of warriors, a place where dreams gather, a way station for shoals of migrating fish, a coordinate of the rising and setting sun, and a rest stop for water and for hope. Our island is woven out of coral and covered with the droppings of seabirds. Kabang has formed a small lake upon Wayo Wayo out of His tears, a lake we depend on to eke out our existence.

In the beginning, all things imitated one another: the island imitated the sea turtle, the trees imitated the clouds, and death imitated birth, so that everything was more or less the same. Originally our tribe lived deep in the ocean. We built a city in a trench, and Kabang gave us a kind of fluorescent shrimp to eat. In an underwater land of plenty, we didn't have a care in the world. But, being the cleverest race in the sea, we discovered that there were many things tastier to eat than shrimp, and we kept reproducing, feeding, migrating, expanding our city without restraint to satisfy our every whim, until we had almost driven away or annihilated all the other ocean races. Finally we roused Kabang to anger.

Kabang resolved to punish us. One night the undersea volcanos at the two ends of the ocean erupted, a great murky cloud engulfed our city, and our ancestors emerged upon the face of the deep. But just then a school of dosi dosi fish swam by, their scales glistening so brilliantly they blinded the eyes of almost all the ancestors. The blind did not know where to turn. The few tribesmen who had not gone blind were responsible for caring for those who were without sight. Among the sighted, the warrior Salinini speared a dosi dosi fish. He wanted to give it to the elders to eat, only to discover that every scale bore the unmistakable mark of Kabang. Only then did the people realize that they had angered Kabang, that this was His punishment, and that the only remaining recourse was to beg for His forgiveness. The brave Salinini resolved to swim alone to the Sea Gate at the extremity of rain and mist, for it was said that on the other side there was a True Isle, the abode of Kabang. Salinini wanted to go there and pray to Kabang, hoping to receive His mercy, that He might grant the people a new place to dwell.

Salinini swam for the time it takes for the sun to live and die a thousand times. His skin peeled, his hearing failed, and his back fin broke, but the rainbow was always in the distance. Finally, moved by Salinini's determination, the omniscient Kabang decided to give the people another chance. He said: *I can allow you an island, but your numbers must never exceed the trees growing thereupon. You will lose the ability to subsist in the sea for more than a short length of time, and you will be exiled from the vast, shoreless, open ocean. As prisoners on the island, you will know isolation and the fear of drowning. Once a friend, the sea will become a foe. It once gave but now it will take. Yet you must still rely on it, trust in it, worship it. Hearken, ye people, my song will turn to rain, my gaze to lightning, as my mind is all-pervading like the water of the sea. The words I utter will become the spirits of the deep. They will watch over you and edify you.*

Thereupon, our underwater ancestors waded out of the sea and onto Wayo Wayo, and these words of Kabang became the most sacred prayer in our Sea Rite.

One day, who knows how many years later, a gigantic bird arrived on the island. The bird began to preen itself and out of its feathers fell seven baby birds. Each of these baby birds became the leader of a tribe. The birds taught our ancestors the skills they would need to survive on land. When the birds left, they each left an eyeball behind, one for every tribe to guard and watch over. One stormy day, the seven eyes all split open at once. Two of those eyes hatched arms, two legs, one a head, one a torso and one an organ of increase. And the spawn of the seven eyes then combined into a swarthy giant of a man, a man with a sorrowful mien who called himself: the Sea Sage.

The Sea Sage was well-endowed: he never closed his eyes, not even while sleeping, like a fish. While diving he memorized the hills and dales of the seabed and the extent of the great kelp forest. He also familiarized himself with all the cracks in the rocks around Wayo Wayo where swimmers could breathe pockets of underwater air. He could even foretell the mood of the sea, knowing whether it would be fair or foul, in high spirits or low, and presage precipitation and ocean flow. Every day he made three tours of the island, declaring that he had to listen carefully to the news brought back by every seabird, every gust of wind and every little shell. He once said that every beached whale would leave behind valuable wisdom concerning the future and fate of the island. He knew that every stretch of sea and shore had its own unique aroma, shadow and glow, and since his knowledge came from the migrating ocean races, there was nowhere it did not reach. His incantations were like feathers, each one-of-a-kind and inimitable. The signals brought back by the waves were so faint that the Sea Sage would often stand at the shore like a parched tree, his sun-bleached hair sparkling. He refused to eat or drink, nor would he smile.

But sageship has never been inherited. Since the beginning it has been attained through initiation and instruction. The children of the Sea Sage cannot call their father Father, because the Sea Sage is of the island and no longer the head of a family or the father of children. The Earth Sage is the same. Each sage can choose any boy on the island and teach him everything he knows. Because any single boy might not get the chance to grow up, each sage chooses more than one disciple. My father is the Sea Sage, and to become the Sea Sage he had to receive a complete training from the previous Sea Sage. I received the Sea Sage's training along with my twin brother, and five other island boys. We learned everything there is to know about the sea.

My father is short a leg, but he has a keen inborn intelligence, and though many did not look well upon him he still found favor in the former Sea Sage's eyes. Knowing that he was disabled, he honed his swimming technique until his good leg was overgrown with barnacles. The Sea Sage used a whalerib as a staff, and even with just one leg, he was an unrivaled swimmer. It was as if that good leg of his was his tail fin.

It is said that in every generation, the incumbent Sea Sage receives a sea map from his predecessor, which he will hide straightaway under the skin of his back. This map is an accretion of wisdom, the revelation of Kabang. It alters with time to show the seasigns around the island moment by moment. But for the sea map to appear, the island people and the Sea Sage all have to suffer excruciating pain. When there are no fish to catch and the people face starvation, the Sea Sage will go somewhere alone to think up a way of tormenting himself, for only when his spirit approaches death will the sea map emerge and show the fishermen where to find the fish.

Every year when the shoals of migrating fish approach, the Sea Sage leads a flotilla of seven boats from the seven tribes of the island and presides over the Sea Rite. The Sea Sage floats facedown in the sea for a day and a night to commune with the ocean races and thank them for sacrificing themselves so that the people of Wayo Wayo might live. And the seven fishermen who represent the seven tribes take turns casting their nets, but are not allowed to haul up a single fish, to signify that they will keep the covenant against excess.

The Sea Sage is versed in all branches of sea lore, but most of the time he talks incoherently. It is as hard to get a grip on what he says as it is to grasp an ocean wave. Elders say that the first Sea Sage created the language of Wayo Wayo by imitating the sounds of seabirds. They say he could describe over a thousand kinds of waves, from finely pleated ripples to intermittent swells, from breakers smooth as blubber to surf like sparkling foam, from windblown rollers to impromptu undercurrents that flow when schools of fish swim past, and from wavelets born of the shallows to benthic volcanic tsunamis. Since the waves come in as many shapes and sizes as there are kinds of fish, and since seabird calls are beyond the ear of the common man, the difficulty of the language of waveshape and birdsong is extreme for most people. The only one who can make it comprehensible is the Earth Sage, the hunter, navigator and tamer of language.

When I was young, my father told me that, a long, long time ago, the Sea Sage and the Earth Sage were one and the same, until there came a day when the wife of the Sea Sage had twins. They squeezed out of her birth canal side by side, without priority. One was blue-eyed, while the other's eyes were dark brown. Though equally smart and alert, their talents differed. The Sea Sage knew that for the islanders to live well they had to attend to more than the signs of the sea, and that Kabang had for this reason given him two sons, neither subordinate to the other. The blue-eyed son inherited his father's untamed nature and sea lore, while the brown-eyed son declared that he had a method for turning sea into land: he had found an extremely hard transparent bottle (of a kind found everywhere on the island of Gesi Gesi, on which I later ran aground), actually three of them, and he filled these three bottles with pig innards, the pubic hair of virgins and a dash of the richest soil on the island. He brought the bottles to the shore and walked alone around the island ninety-nine times, and while he was walking the stars stopped moving and the sea stopped raging, yet the plants on the island grew ferociously. The Sea Sage announced: "Since the island is big enough and the creatures on the island have gone forth and multiplied, the people of Wayo Wayo shall covet nothing more." Having said this, he smashed the bottles into fragments the size of fish eyes. At the same time he laid down a law: as the habitable space on the island is limited, each family can only have one man-child and any second son has to leave alone in a *talawaka* on the hundred and eightieth full moon following his birth. He is not allowed to look back, not even if he is the son of a sage.

In addition to his linguistic gifts, the Earth Sage is also good at drawing.

His drawings all seem like things that really happened, or as if things that were really happening halted when he drew them. He is also a skilled house-builder. He taught Wayo Wayoans to use grass, mud and fish skin in the construction of their houses, and to stick the materials together with fish glue. To make fish glue, you simmer fish eyes, skin, bones and scales until the mixture turns the color of sap. Maybe because of the fish eyes, the joins of our houses glow by day and in the dark, reflecting the light of both sun and moon, as if there are spirits hidden within. Wood is only employed in a few spots, because it is simply too precious. The Earth Sage often reminds us that the island is small, and our treasure trees grow slow, so slow they are wiser than men. No man should be so rash as to cut them down to make something for his own use.

The word the Earth Sage uses most frequently is *gesi*. This word has many different meanings, but mainly it is used to describe what one does not understand. He often says *gesi gesi, gesi gesi*. He says there is *gesi* everywhere, and that there are things in the world that not even the Sea Sage and Earth Sage understand.

The day I left Wayo Wayo, the Earth Sage and the Sea Sage, my father—a prophet and a wise man—conducted together the rite of departure. For I am a second son, and second sons represent exploration, eternal immaturity and divine oblation.

I never expected to get grounded on Gesi Gesi, the name I gave to the floating island, meaning a place covered in incomprehensible things. I saw endless *gesi gesi* there, and even witnessed the formation of an island: black smoke burst forth from the sea, I smelled the reek of sulfur, and lava kept erupting for dozens of alternations of sun and moon. The boiling hot sea sizzled, and volcanic ash flew all around. Then lightning struck down through the clouds, and finally a new island floated above the waves.

In the name of Kabang, I swear: I saw the birth of an island with my own eyes.

I don't know how much time passed, but Gesi Gesi kept drifting until it neared your island. I discovered someone had landed on the floating island and immediately dove to get away. The sea brought me here to your island, where I was fortunate to meet you, my savior.

In those days I spent drifting around, I kept asking Kabang: Why am I the second son and my brother the elder one? Why should a pair of twins, born into this world only minutes apart, have fates so far apart? When my mother was carrying us, did that not already mean that we were "in this world together?" So where is there any distinguishing between a first and second son? I know there are no answers to these questions, for, as we say on Wayo Wayo, nobody knows where the fish swims in the vastness of the sea before it's caught upon the hook. I am a second son and have drifted here on Gesi Gesi, and these are things that cannot be changed.

# 18. The Story of Alice's Island

The kid is unlike anyone I've ever met. He's like a character out of a story, or a being from another world. His demeanor is at once novel and quaint. His leg isn't fully healed, so his mobility is limited. Most of the time he sits quietly on a rock and gazes at the sea in the distance. Sometimes he completely ignores me and falls into a most peculiar state, a combination of sighing, moaning and giggling. It takes me a while to cross the wall of language between us and figure out what he means. Mostly we rely on gestures and expressions to understand one another. I imagine that communicating in this way is always superficial, that what you can actually express to a person who speaks a completely different language is quite limited. I suddenly feel a loneliness more intense than mutual silence.

The kid says he's from an island called Wayo Wayo. I'm sure he told me why he left his island and drifted here with the Trash Vortex. He seems to think that the Trash Vortex is an island, too, and he calls it Gesi Gesi. But I don't get his explanation of the meaning of *gesi gesi* in his language.

Though I concentrate when he talks, I cannot comprehend his speech, so when he tells his stories and gets to the most critical moments, I have to keep leaping great ravines in order to keep up with him.

But when he said, "My name is Atile'i," I understood him right away.

\*    \*    \*

There was nobody there when I returned to where I'd asked Atile'i to wait for me that day. Just as I was about to give up looking, he suddenly walked out from behind a tree. It was as if he was part of the trunk. That gave me quite a fright! Apparently he was making sure I meant him no harm and that I'd not brought anyone else with me. I almost forgot that he was seriously wounded; even with an injured leg he seemed to have the ability to blend into the wilderness.

He also had an incredible tolerance for pain. I received some nursing training when I was younger and I knew immediately that his ankle might be dislocated, maybe broken in a few places. But when I returned, the dislocated joint had been put back in place. He must have gritted his teeth and readjusted it himself. Initially I was going to give him my arm and help him along all the way to Dahu's hunting hut, but he insisted on hobbling along on his own. He was like an injured beast, wary of his surroundings. I braced his leg with a makeshift splint and gave him some vitamins to restore his strength and some antibiotics to prevent infection.

Dahu's hut is really close to a piece of farmland Thom and I purchased. We used to go there on holidays to tend the garden and stay for dinner in the hut. After settling Atile'i in, I made another trip to the seashore to see what shape my house was in.

The sea is totally changed. From a distance it is still blue, or even multihued on account of the garbage. But having spent time with the sea on a daily basis I can feel its emotions. Now the sea seems to be made out of pain and misery.

While having a meal in town I saw that Ming had written a letter to the editor. He described this latest incident as "payback." "In media reports on the incident," he wrote, "the island seems to be a victim, as if the island is a person who has been wronged. There's never any mention of the fact that actually we contributed to the formation of the Trash Vortex. Considering the size of our island we made a pretty big contribution. In the past we avoided paying the inevitable price of development, and let more impoverished regions bear the cost for us, but now it's payback time: the sea has sent the bill for the interest."

I went to a hypermart to buy some rations and another, camping-style tent to store in the car. Before I knew it the sky was getting dark. By the time I hurried onto the mountain path I was losing my footing every few steps even with the flashlight. Just when I was starting to panic, a shadow flashed through the trees. My heart skipped a beat, but then I saw the shadow was limping: it was Atile'i. Atile'i turned and walked ahead, never letting himself out of my sight. The kid was showing me the way.

Atile'i's leg is gradually healing. One day when I was writing at my desk, Atile'i picked up a stone, sitting nonchalantly in the doorway. Suddenly all the muscles in his body tensed up and he hurtled the stone so hard it was like he was throwing part of his own body. He hit a green pigeon. I spent some time explaining to him that I have enough money for food and we don't have to kill birds, but he didn't really seem to get it. At night he's always alert to the symphony of mountain sounds, like a beast lying in wait for prey.

Sometimes he looks off in the distance like he's listening to the music of the spheres. Sometimes he adopts a strange pose, with his right hand palm up and his left leg slightly bent. I ask him what he's doing but he doesn't say a word. It's like he's turned himself into a tree.

Much to my amazement Atile'i can imitate the call of any bird near the hut, even ones he's never seen before. As long as he hears a birdcall seven or eight times he can do such a convincing imitation that he fools even the birds themselves. One time when he was sitting by the path he listened to the call of a crested thrush for all of a minute and imitated it at the top of his lungs, as if he'd turned into a being with a human body and the voice of a crested thrush, a voice that made all the lady crested thrushes fly down like they'd fallen in love with him.

A language that one group of people uses to communicate thoughts and intents sounds to another group like the calls of a screech owl or a muntjac. If we really tried learning birdsong the way we learn French or Russian, taking, say, two classes a day and keeping it up, would we eventually be able to talk with the birds? The very notion makes me all the more determined to learn the language of Wayo Wayo.

But language learning is long haul. One time I asked Atile'i where Wayo Wayo was, but he did not seem to understand. He opened the fingers of one hand and added the pinkie and ring finger of the other hand, as if to indicate a certain number. I hit upon the idea of giving him pen and paper and getting him to draw Wayo Wayo. He went into his own little world. I only expected a sketch, but he really put his heart into it.

Sometimes he draws with his fingers, sometimes with his teeth, sometimes even with his tears. When he finishes a picture he asks for another piece of paper. By now I can tell that he is going to piece the pictures together into a story. The first picture is of an old man doing the jellyfish float next to a few little boats. I can't tell what it means, but think I should go into town to buy him a sketchbook, so he doesn't have to keep drawing on his body. And this way I'll eventually have an illustrated anthology of the tales of Wayo Wayo.

Perhaps because I don't think he can completely understand me, I often feel like talking to him. It's like talking through an open window.

This is also an island, the island of Taiwan. In the olden days people called it Formosa. Look, this is an aerial view of Taiwan. You've probably never seen a photograph before, eh? Oh, that's right, maybe you saw lots of photographs on Gesi Gesi, all blurry because they'd been immersed in seawater. What's an aerial view? It's like a bird looking down at Taiwan from above the clouds. Look, there's ocean on this side of the island, and ocean on this side, this side and this side. It's surrounded by ocean on all four sides, so we call it an island. So actually, no matter which way people turn on an island, they're always facing the sea.

I don't know too much about science, but I learned some geography in school, and according to geographers the island of Taiwan only took on its present shape two to six million years ago. Do you have any idea how many years that is? It's a long, long time ago, yes? A long, long time ago. What's a geographer? I don't know if this will sound offensive, but I think a geographer is a bit like the Earth Sage on Wayo Wayo you were telling me about.

Strictly speaking, people like me are latecomers to Taiwan. We crossed the sea to get here a couple hundred years ago. A few years ago people were fond of saying that if you metaphorically compress the history of the world into a single day, humans only appear a few seconds before midnight. We now call the first people who lived on the island aborigines, and my two good friends Dahu and Hafay are both aborigines. Though they belong to different tribes, their ancestors came to the island a bit earlier than mine did.

And here's where you came onshore.

I moved here over ten years ago to teach at the local university. It's not that far from here. You see that house way down there? The one that has fallen over and been confiscated by the sea? My husband and son and I used to live there. As I said, I'm not from the east coast. I'm originally from a city in the north called Taipei. Before that, my mum and dad were both born on the west coast. In his youth my father went to work in a factory in Japan. His hometown is a place called Kuei-shan in the northwest, and my mum comes from Fang-yuan in central Taiwan. My mum believed in the sea goddess Matsu all her life. My father forfeited his inheritance after a falling-out with his family, so he had to go to Taipei to try to make a living on his own. And when the oyster field could no longer feed my mum's family, she had to take a part-time job in an industrial park that was kind of far from her home. She worked there for a while but then got laid off. In the end she, too, moved to Taipei. I don't actually know how my parents met. They never told me. My mum said that when they were young they moved around from place to place, like gypsies practically. They went wherever they could make a living.

My father and mother are both gone. I don't want to talk about how they passed away, and I don't want to talk about my brother, either. That'd only upset me. You know what I mean by "gone"? What do the Wayo Wayoans say when somebody dies? Dead, departed, passed away, gone to a better place? What? *Iwa kugi*?

(I start blowing up Toto's inflatable globe. This thing is ingenious. You just need to force enough air into it and it turns into a sphere. It's nearly to scale, and the words and colors on it glow in the dark. I blow and blow into the withered world until it's firm as a drum).

You see this ball? It's the Earth, the planet we live on. No, no, it's not just mine, it's yours and mine. Look, the place we live is like a star in the sky, it's just that we call the star we live on Earth. This ball is a scale model of the Earth. I bought it for my son. It even glows in the dark! That's because it has a special night-shine coating. Some things in this world glow, some don't. Some are like the moon, others like the sun. What do you say for the moon? *Nalusa*? And the sun? The other one, the one that appears during the day? *Yigasa*?

The place we're living on is actually just a small island. I sometimes feel that in a way the size of the island is not for us to decide. When my ancestors arrived on the island two hundred years ago, walking from here to here (I traced a line through the Central Mountain Range to the east coast with my finger) took months, and they risked their lives to make the trip. Maybe to some extent just like you were risking your life when you floated your way here. In fact, a lot of people came here in boats. I often think that if you stroll from town to town, from village to village, the island would get really big. When we were still dating I told Thom, "Maybe the island got the way it is today because the people living here wanted to be able to get anywhere on the island as quickly as possible."

The day you drifted here there was an earthquake and an extraordinary wave. Are there earthquakes on your island? When the earth shakes? There should be. There must be. Earthquakes are really common here. We have typhoons, too, and I'm worried that come typhoon season the Trash Vortex that brought you here might end up surrounding the entire island.

I would guess you're a teenager, fourteen or fifteen at the most? I had a child, too, and if he were still with us he'd be ten. I didn't want a child at first, because I didn't know what kind of future he would have to face. I didn't want him to have to inherit an island we've gone and messed up. But Thom and I still ended up having a child.

It's been raining a lot the past few years. Some places will get several hundred millimeters of precipitation in a single day when there's no typhoon. Summer's gotten extremely hot and long, and there's a shower almost every day. My friend Ming told me that some of his bird-watching friends have discovered that certain migratory birds can't even recognize the coastline anymore, because it's changing too fast. They hesitate before they land. It's in a sorry state, but this is our island home.

I also brought this to show you. Here. It's a digital photo frame. The things it displays are called photographs, and the photographs inside it are images of the past. Interesting, don't you think? These are my folks. And this is the place where they finally settled down in Taipei. It was called the Chung Hwa Market. We were really poor when I was little. My parents worked as hard as they could to send my brother and me through school. They thought that we'd do well in life if we got an education. My dad apprenticed in an electrical supply store. While he was out with the boss repairing air conditioners, my mother sold little egg-shaped sponge cakes in the market. My dad's boss let us a room on the third floor, probably about the size of this hut. My mother had us stay home and study instead of minding the cake stand, except on holidays. Both my brother and I really liked baking those cakes. You bake the one side, turn it over, then you bake the other. They smelled so good! I'll buy you some next time I go into town.

Look, this was my home in the Chung Hwa Market. We only had one bed. Mum, Dad, my brother and I all slept on the same bed. When I was a girl I often dreamed of leaving that home.

This is Thom, my husband, and this is our son, Toto. He was still an infant at the time.

Are there mountains on your island? The thing we're on right now is called a mountain, and that tall pointy place in the photo is a mountain.

This is a "true touch" topographical map. Try touching it. Doesn't it feel upraised, furry, wet? Some places feel hard. In the past you could just draw something pointy on a map and that was a mountain, but feel it now: that's what a mountain is supposed to feel like. Taiwan is a small island, but the mountains here are just incredible. My husband and son really loved mountain climbing. One day they went climbing and never came back.

My good friend Dahu found Thom's body a while ago, but my son has completely vanished, like a leaf blown into the forest, never to return. They only went for a visit, not expecting that the mountain would have them stay forever, I sometimes think.

Since then I've mostly been living alone in that house by the sea. At first we called it the Seaside House, but later the sea level rose and other people started calling it the Sea House. Now I call it Alice's Island.

To tell you the truth, I felt so much sadder losing my son than I did when my mother passed away. Your mother must be devastated. If my son were still here, he might be as tall as you in a few years. You know, I'm a second child, just like you. If you don't mind counting girls, that is.

Ah, not a cloud in the sky. It's been a long time since we've seen such a clear sky. The *Nalusa* is so beautiful and bright this evening. People on Wayo Wayo see the same *Nalusa*. Do you realize, Atile'i, that the *Nalusa* you see now is the same *Nalusa* you saw on Gesi Gesi?

Sometimes I talk and talk and I think he can understand everything I've said. It's not understanding in the linguistic sense, but in some other sense.

One morning he said, "*Ohiyo*, good morning." (I taught him how to say this). And I replied, "*i-Wagudoma-siliyamala*" (It's very fair at sea today). We've gotten used to using each other's language or mixing the two languages together.

In talking to Atile'i I've noticed that he often seems to repeat greeting queries. He keeps asking me, "*i-Wagudoma-silisaluga?*"—a question that may mean, "Is the weather fair at sea today?" to which the other person is supposed to reply "*i-Wagudoma-siliyamala*." At first I was puzzled, because we weren't going out to sea, so what did it matter if the weather at sea was fair or not. But you're still supposed to reply, "Very fair." Sometimes when the weather isn't fair at all, when it's raining and the waves are watching the island coldly from afar, Atile'i will still smile and say, "The weather at sea today is very fair."

Atile'i looked really happy that day, maybe because I gave him pen and paper of his own. He kept asking me, "Is the weather fair at sea today?" And I kept replying. Three minutes later, he asked again, for the sixth time. The seventh query came less than five minutes later.

I didn't mean to ignore him, but my mind was wandering. Not having received my reply, Atile'i looked humiliated, as if he'd been snubbed by his best friend. He had to confront me.

"You must reply: 'Very fair.'"

"But I already did."

"When someone asks, 'Is the weather fair at sea today?' And you hear. When you hear you must reply, 'Very fair.'"

"Even if it's *raining as hard as it is now*, you still have to reply in this way?"

"Yes."

"*Even if you don't feel like replying?*"

"Yes."

We both gazed out at the sea, which seemed to be slowly bringing rain. Every so often a breaker would come rolling in. Following a silence of ten waves, Atile'i asked me another time, "Is the weather fair at sea today?"

"Very fair," I replied and for the first time I realized I could ask him back. "Is the weather fair on your sea today?"

"Yes it is, *extremely fair*," Atile'i replied.

I don't know why, but right at that moment we both began to cry.

# 19. The Story of Dahu's Island

When I started to "categorize" all this trash I was amazed at all the strange, smashed-up stuff that turned up: the body panel of a scooter, a stroller, condoms, needles, bras, nylons, etc. I often wonder who the owners were and in what circumstances they threw these things out. I remember one time in the army I made a bet with a comrade that if I had the guts to wear a bra to bayonet practice he had to treat the whole company to drinks. Well, I really did it and we all laughed our heads off. That evening when I sneaked out to buy a midnight snack with a buddy, I scrunched up that pink lace bra and tossed it into the ocean. Sometimes I get this crazy idea it's floated back here with the Trash Vortex.

I find lots of people are misled by news reports into thinking that the only materials that won't decompose are plastics. My observation these past few days is that artificial fibers in general are also amazingly durable. And there are lots of things in plastic bags or styrofoam containers that are still particularly intact. I've found things like rings, glasses, watches and cell phones—these get sorted as "intact valuables." I hear someone even found gold! That's why there are so many outsiders on the beach these days: they think they can find treasures in the trash. But I'm more concerned about the residents of the tribal villages. They once depended on coastal planting and fishing to make a living, and now they can only get by picking through the trash on the beach. It's hard to escape an occupation, and once you're used to a certain lifestyle it's hard to change. That's what Millet told me, anyway.

I brought Millet here, too, when we were still together. We went for a few strolls along this exact same stretch of beach. This one time, one of her earrings fell out. We searched all over the beach, but instead of finding it we lost the other earring. I kissed one of her ringless ears and she squinted at me like a sleepy cat. I wonder if that pair of earrings is still somewhere on the beach.

Sometimes we also find living creatures trapped in the trash. Some fish seem to have survived in plastic bags for quite a long time. We discovered a nearly complete whale skeleton as well. What we find most often is dead sea turtles, ordinary green sea turtles as well as loggerheads and leatherbacks. The meat has usually been eaten, leaving only an empty shell behind. We notify the marine biologists, who come right away and measure the shells on the beach. These shells won't rot anytime soon: in the end all they'll do for these poor creatures is prove they once existed.

Each piece of trash that floated here seems to have brought a story with it from across the sea, because anything that's been thrown away has its own tale to tell.

For the past week, various experts have been gathering on the beach. There are specialists in ocean currents, littoral biology, plastics, etc. Today there was a team of trash experts from Germany who have reportedly come to "study" the trash we've sorted. They took samples, which had to be clearly labeled, indicating where each thing was found and how much it weighs. I hear one of the trash experts wrote a cultural history of Germany based on a landfill in the Ruhr. He recommended that the trash on the beach be sorted according to "function" not recycling value, because who knows? Maybe some day it might be an important source for the study of the cultural history of globalization.

Our public officials, it seems, authorized the team to take a certain quantity of samples while refusing to implement an overly fussy trash-sorting system. They need to get this taken care of before the upcoming election. Some of the higher-ups told us privately that all we have to do is sort the trash into recyclable valuables and worthless junk, then divide the junk into combustibles and noncombustibles, and to do it as quickly as possible. "Junk is junk even after you've sorted it. What good does it do to study this stuff?" they said.

Though "Restore the Shore, Formosa!" (the stupid slogan the government came up with to get everyone involved in the "beach cleanup") seems to be in full swing, I hear the expert assessment is that it'll take more than a century for the coast to return to normal. For myself, I doubt whether there is even such a thing as "normal" anymore. Does the Seventh Sisid count as part of "normal?"

You know Hai Lee, the writer of ocean literature? He often visits the area around the Seventh Sisid, right? The past few days he's been bringing students and volunteers to gather creatures that washed up dead on the beach. They've found shrimp, sea urchins, sea cucumbers, brittle stars, hermit crabs and true crabs. He says there are many species he's never seen before. I asked him whether the sea would return to normal someday, and he said there's no such thing as normal anymore: everything's changed.

I said that's not what my father taught me. My father said there were two things in this world that would never change: the mountains and the sea.

According to Bunun tradition, a man who doesn't know how to hunt is not a real man. The Atayal call us "shadows," because our hunting skills are so refined. But my father often said that the first thing to hunting isn't learning how to hunt but getting to know the mountains.

Father said that during the colonial era the Japanese kept forcing the Bunun to move around for fear we would unite against the authorities. They even forced us to cultivate rice, just to prevent us from getting to know the mountains. Once we got used to paddy agriculture, the status of a hunter plummeted, and the Bunun people knew the mountains less and less. And mountains will not protect a person who does not know them.

My father said that traditionally Bunun kids start young, learning diverse mountain lore until they are old enough to participate in the hunt. That's the year they undergo the ear-shooting ritual, which is like a qualifying examination to become a hunter.

I will always remember that year, the first time I was allowed to take part in the ear-shooting ritual. The elders put the targets in the ritual ground. There were six ears in all: at the top a pair of deer ears, in the middle a pair of roebuck ears, and at the bottom a goat ear and a wild boar ear. The goat ear was a furry little thing, so adorable. We stood so close that for a Bunun kid who had gotten trained in the use of a bow and arrow it should have been almost impossible to miss. My father was an ace marksman, both with a gun and with a bow. From the time I picked up a bow and arrow as a boy I was always told I had my father's shooting stance. The elders took turns carrying us kids to face the targets, and the arrows would pierce the ears with a thunk. They carried my brother out and his arrow hit an ear, a deer ear. Then it was my turn. I picked up the bow with supreme confidence and aimed, but in the instant I shot for some reason my bow sagged. I hit the goat ear instead!

The goat ear was so cute and tiny and I went and shot it.

Everyone was dumbfounded, and my father's face colored. Why? Because for the ear-shooting ritual you have to shoot either a deer ear or a roebuck ear. If you miss and shoot a wild boar ear it means you'll get scared whenever you see a boar. And a boy who shoots a goat ear will always walk along the brink of a cliff, just like a mountain goat.

I shot the goat ear. My father wouldn't talk to me for what seemed like forever. I thought he was mad at me. Only later did I realize he was actually worried for me.

My father is a *Lavian,* the captain of a hunting party. Our hunting ground is huge. We pile *badan* around it. See those piles of reeds over there? They mark our territory. Though I'm my father's son, the title of *Lavian* is not hereditary. Whether a young hunter can become *Lavian* or not depends on many things—hunting, cooperation and leadership skills, and much else. Only the best young hunter has a chance to become *Lavian.* Although I had shot the goat ear, I still performed the best in the hunting ground. But I sensed that my father remained very worried. He thought that shooting the goat ear was bad luck that would come back and haunt me.

One time we tried to round up a large boar infamous for its repeated getaways. It had killed a number of hunting dogs, and once it even managed to escape after taking a couple of my father's bullets. My father said it was *Hanito,* an evil spirit, and that you shouldn't look it in the eyes when you shot it or you would become enthralled.

The *Lavian* that time was my father, as always. Before dawn, the party assembled and formed a ring in an open field and waited for my father to sprinkle wine and sing.

"Tell me what has come before my gun?" my father sang.

"All the deer have come before my gun," sang the other hunters.

"Tell me what has come before my gun?" my father sang.

"All the boar have come before my gun," sang the other hunters.

Our guns overflowed with the smell of liquor. On the way to the hunting ground, I overheard my father whisper to my uncle that he'd seen a sign in a dream, but somehow he'd forgotten it after the wine sprinkling ceremony. My uncle reassured him, saying that people forget dreams all the time. Besides, not having a dream or forgetting one is no reason to leave the hunting party.

That time we carried out *Mabusau,* a hunting technique. First the *Lavian* judges where the boar is hiding and lets the dogs drive it out. Then the hunters fan out to surround it. At about five in the morning, when the sky had just gone light, the dogs caught a whiff of the boar and started barking like crazy. My father saw something rustling in the grass from far away and knew it was a huge boar, maybe that *Hanito* of a boar. He guessed which way the beast had fled and assigned pursuit routes to each of the hunters. I got the left-most route, because I was still a child of these hills with everything to learn. I ran and ran, listening to the dogs barking and the grass rustling as the scent and shade of every tree went swooshing by. Then I tripped and fell, head over heels. I picked up my gun, got up and ran, pressing down on my knife with my hand to keep it from slapping against my thigh.

I don't know why, but after I got up I couldn't hear anything at all: the forest had gone completely quiet, as if the world had been silent from the very beginning. I stopped to check which way the wind was blowing, what direction the distant grass was swaying in, when suddenly a huge shadow swept past up ahead, moving fast as wind. I took a deep breath and went after it, running so swiftly I was almost holding my heart in my hands. I don't know how long I had run when that shadow stopped dead, turned, and bellowed at me.

I was scared stiff. It was like watching a video that appears silent until it starts playing with the volume turned up all the way. Standing before me was a man. He was staring at me, his hair flying vinelike in the wind.

The man began to speak . . . if it can even be counted as speaking. His mouth didn't move in the least, but I heard him loud and clear: "Child, you are fated never to catch a boar, never to become a good hunter."

"What can I do then?"

"What can you do?" he asked me back. I discovered his eyes weren't like human eyes. They were more like compound eyes composed of countless single eyes, the eyes of clouds, mountains, streams, meadowlarks and muntjacs, all arranged together. As I gazed, each little eye seemed to contain a different scene, and those scenes arranged to form a vast panorama the likes of which I had never seen.

"What can you do?"

The question echoed back on a gust of wind, and I found myself standing over a sheer cliff, just like a mountain goat. It was like I was standing on an island. The distant sky was the color of a ginger lily, with dark green trees and a creek below.

I only found out later that the whole hunting party had been looking all over for me because something had happened to my father. My uncle's gun misfired and shot my father in the right eye, rupturing his eyeball and ripping a hole in his head. Father did not die right away. On the third day he actually managed to take out his breathing tube and summon my brother and me to his bedside. He asked me, "Where did you go that day?"

"I don't know."

"He was found by a cliff, just standing there like he was dreaming," my elder brother explained.

My father pointed at my brother. "You must learn to be a Bunun hunter." Then he pointed at me and said, "You cannot be a hunter anymore, not after shooting the goat ear."

"What should I do then?" I asked.

"Become a man who knows the mountains." Father's voice became very far away, and the blood from the wound to his right eye started seeping through the gauze again. He started losing consciousness. My elder brother pushed the button by the bed and the nurse rushed to find the doctor. My father held on in a kind of stupor for only seven more days before leaving us.

I didn't tell him I'd met a man with peculiar eyes. I thought there wasn't any need. Now my father's eyes were shut for ever.

After that, every time I went hunting I was found standing in a daze at the edge of a cliff. People avoided taking me along. Luckily I did well at school, and ultimately I even went to a university on the west coast. By the way, have you ever seen this hat of mine? I really like it. Those are bamboo partridge feathers on top. When my father named me, he caught a bamboo partridge, fed me the meat and kept the feathers for me as a memento. This might well be my most precious possession.

After Millet left, I started coming back to the village now and again to help Anu operate the Forest Church. Maybe I'm slowly getting to know the mountains. Now I just feel we have to make sure mountains like this don't disappear, mountains without potholed roads or tunnels, mountains where goats and boars and deer can run wild.

It's been blazing hot the past few days. Yesterday, looking up at the mountain from the coastal highway, I saw many trees that seemed scorched by the fiery Foehn wind. One time my father took us swimming at the seashore. "When the sea is sick, the mountains will be sick, too," he said, squeezing my little willy between his fingers.

# 20. The Story of Hafay's Island

I opened the Seventh Sisid because I wanted to have a dwelling with windows on all four sides. Because I'm afraid of houses without windows.

Dwelling places are really important to the Pangcah aborigines, because we think houses are for spirits to inhabit. Me and Ina drifted into the city, spent so long living there, but all the houses we lived in were haphazard, more like shacks. So the first thought I had when I made some money was to build a house of my very own, right by the seashore.

I remember Alice and Thom started building the Seaside House just when I broke the soil on the Seventh Sisid, so our houses were twins. Their house was really special, like nothing I'd ever seen before: it had solar panels on it, and the shape of it was unprecedented in these parts. I didn't have relatives or friends in the local Pangcah village, but when I was building the house everyone still came out to help. Remember? When it was finished we held a *mitsumod*. You were there, weren't you? You even helped me slaughter a pig Ah Jung's family raised. Time sure flies.

Would you mind if I ask you about Millet? Ahem. I mention her because hearing you talk about her reminds me that I used to do the same kind of job. Maybe I understand how Millet felt, more or less. Besides, maybe at the same time as I was working she was doing the rounds in a place with little rooms somewhere else. You know? The worst part about the job is when you're standing in the doorway, about to knock, and you don't have any idea what kind of man is waiting for you on the other side. You can't refuse, even if you don't like him, even if he's disgusting. You knock, the door opens, and you've got to spend an hour with a stranger.

I had a close friend at work at that time. Her name was Nai. She told me, try pretending you're a real masseuse, not someone doing "dirty" work. Every guy who comes here *must* have some aches and pains. So when you massage a customer, ask him what needs special attention, where you should press harder, and when you massage those places it's like . . . it feels like there's something alive inside. Nai said that if you give those places a serious rub, the customer might initially say it hurts but eventually he'll relax. Some guys go to sleep, others open up and start confiding in you. If you show him some tenderness a customer usually won't be too demanding, because lust will have been replaced with something else.

But there are all sorts of difficult customers, and some are sick with you-know-what and they're not too happy if you don't want to touch them or let them touch you. Some guys really make a scene. Sometimes when you've done half the massage, the wife or girlfriend will call and you pretend you're not overhearing, but it's really awkward. Some customers who haven't been able to come when time's up will try to pay half price and leave. Some will toss the money on the counter downstairs and jump into a cab. And when the bookkeeper counts it there's not enough. And other customers will even make harassing phone calls.

When I was doing you-know-what with the guys, I would turn off the lights and the TV. The room would get real dark, and I'd imagine I was on a small, deserted island somewhere.

I often thought: If I ever make enough money I've got to move someplace that's sunny and bright.

Nai always told me, whatever you do, don't fall for a customer. She told me for my own good, and for her own good, too. But there was one time when I almost did. I still remember the way his back looked. He had broad shoulders, with a long, tapering line from his neck to his waist, like this boy I knew in elementary school. He often came exhausted, with numerous knots or clots in his energy flow. I had to struggle to work them out. He hardly ever spoke, but you could sense his breathing was labored. Even though I almost never talked to him, I felt he wasn't a happy guy.

When it was time, I would turn off the light and tell him, "Mister, you can lay on your back now." He would turn over quietly, and I would sit by the bed with my back to him, holding his thing and relieving him. Sometimes he would gently touch my back with his big hands. Maybe you don't believe me but a woman's body can sense the emotion in someone's touch. Even when you just lay a hand on someone or someone lays a hand on you, you sometimes get a sense of what the other person has on his mind, though you're not real clear what it is. It's kind of elusive, whatever it is that's communicated through the skin. It's hard to describe, but you know it when you feel it. You can sometimes tell whether another person loves you or not, just by touch.

He visited almost every other week, and he always asked for me. I came to recognize his scent and physique. He wasn't like most guys who go to a place like that. I mean . . . most guys want to get their rocks off, whether they're young soldiers or middle-aged married men. Many of them start pawing you right after you go in because they've paid their money. But he wasn't like that, for some reason. He was always very gentlemanly, and regarded me as a masseuse except when I "relieved" him. Lots of times he didn't even ejaculate. The alarm would go off and he'd wipe himself down with a hot towel, say thank you, and leave.

He kept coming for about half a year I reckon. It sounds funny but in the last few months I started pretending that I had just gone for dinner with him, or for a stroll at the seashore, or that he'd just gotten off work and was so beat he'd just collapsed facedown on the bed as soon as he came in the door, and I would walk over and give him a massage without a word. I would imagine scenes like this. Sometimes I would even stare at his long pale back and imagine him suddenly turning over and saying something like, "You look great today," in that deep voice of his, like it was nothing special.

Of course, nothing of the sort ever happened. I hardly ever said a thing to him face to face, and all he would say to me was thank you. Then he'd put on his hat and leave, not looking up.

The only time we ever talked was this one time I started singing along with the MTV channel. After I was done, when he was putting on his clothes he asked me whether I liked singing. I said I did. From then on every time he visited he brought me a CD, all English songs I'd never heard before. He said they were all popular songs and that I could learn these songs since I had such a great voice. I can still sing all of them now, because he was the one who gave me the CDs. I even remember the names of the singers. Those singers were really good. It was like each of them had a magic trick only he or she could do.

Just like Nai said, any guy who comes here is someone else's husband, boyfriend or dad, so whatever you do, better not get any illusions. But Nai fell in love with a customer who later became her boyfriend, all the same. And I started to look forward to that man's visits, counting the days until he'd come see me again. I never asked him what his name was or what he did for a living. During the day I put my earphones on and listened to those CDs he gave me until I fell asleep.

He stopped coming in November of that year. The last time he appeared was the last day of October. I didn't have his cell phone number or any other way to reach him. All I remember is his back, and all I have are the CDs he gave me.

When I was massaging the bodies of strange men in those dark little rooms, the rooms you entered when your number was called, I would often wonder what was going on in the next room. I didn't even know what was going on next door. The wallpaper in the room I usually used was a picture of the seashore, but it was the sea in Greece not here. It was a sea I'd never visited. Anyway, it was just wallpaper the renovator had stuck up for no special reason. You could only see it clearly with the light on, but if you did that you'd discover damp rot in a lot of places. A big sheet of it had peeled away from the wall, and the sea didn't look the least bit real. It looked the most real when you turned the light down low. In those days, I was living right by the sea, but I rarely went to the shore, because I was sleeping days and working nights.

I'll always remember Ina's expression when she looked out to sea through the train window on our trip back to the east coast. She patted my head and tapped on the windowpane, murmuring things to me about the sea as the Pangcah people know it.

She said that the original ancestor of our village was the sky god, who lived in Arapanapanayan in the south. By the fourth generation the sky god had six great-grandchildren, the youngest of whom was a girl named Tiyamacan. The sea god took a liking to Tiyamacan, but she was not willing to marry him and hid herself from him wherever she could. The sea god became angry and raised a flood. That sea god would not take no for an answer.

Tiyamacan's Ina, Madapidap, missed her daughter very much. She turned into a seabird and flew up and down the coast calling out to her daughter. Her father Keseng climbed the mountain until he found a spot with a view of the sea and turned into a snakebark tree fern. Later on, her eldest brother Tadi'Afo, who had fled into the mountains during the Deluge, became the progenitor of another tribe. Her second brother Dadakiyolo went to the west and became the progenitor of the aboriginal people there. The third son Apotok went south and became the ancestor of some communities away down south. Lalakan and Doci, the fourth and the fifth children, sat in a long wooden mortar and floated on the floodwaters to the summit of Mount Cilangasan. The two of them had no choice but to become husband and wife and continue the family line.

At first, brother and sister kept having bestial offspring, a serpent, a turtle, a lizard and a mountain frog, but no human children. The brother and sister—no, the husband and wife—felt very, very sad. One day they received the sun god's blessing and had three normal daughters and a son. They gave them the sun's surname. I can't really remember the details, but the long and the short of it is that one of these kids ended up moving to our village and becoming our ancestor.

Ina said, people will always run around trying to find a place to call home—a place they like and where they can make a living. If you live on this side of the mountain a landslide might force you to the other side. If you live on the plains, other people might force you into the mountains. If you live on an island sometimes you might be able to go to another island. I think Ina knew what she was talking about.

At the end of the year I calculated how much money I'd saved and realized I already had enough to buy a piece of land and start building the Seventh Sisid. I finally left the business a year later.

It was hard at first. I had no one to help me, and I had to figure out lots of things on my own. And I discovered something really interesting: when I opened, many people came once and never returned. Guess why? You got it, they were all my old customers. Maybe they weren't used to seeing me somewhere sunny and bright.

I sometimes thought that he'd come in someday, order a cup of *salama* coffee or something, and sit at the Lighthouse, without me being able to recognize him, because whatever he did he wouldn't take off his shirt to show me his back. After all, just like I said, I only remember his back. I know every mole and polyp on his back, and the color of his skin. But all I know is his back.

If he had come in, I would have sung the songs on the CDs for him. I would have stood behind him and sung those songs for him.

# VIII

# 21. Through the Mountain

Detlef Boldt looked down at the island from the plane. It's been more than thirty years, he thought.

More than three decades before, when he was a feisty young man, he had participated in the biggest TBM (tunnel boring machine) design the world had ever seen. TBM was a game-changer in tunneling technology, offering an alternative to the traditional drilling and blasting method. Detlef had made a short trip to the island to attend a specialist meeting as a TBM consultant. He did not meet too many people during his short stay, and he only let his old colleague Jung-hsiang Li know he was coming back. He just wanted to enjoy a quiet trip with Sara. Yet the trip was not purely for pleasure, or at least Sara didn't think it was.

Sara was a marine biologist with an enduring interest in Norway's coastal biomes; it was off the coast of Norway that she'd met Detlef. Detlef had been invited to consult on a private methane ice DIP (development investment project). Several of his best students, all specialists in drilling techniques, were on the project team; naturally they asked their old teacher to come on board.

The survey boat Detlef was on was operating in waters just off the continental shelf where Sara happened to be leading a protest against a whaling vessel. Detlef, taking a none-of-my-business attitude, watched the situation unfold with detachment. He was a man who believed in professional competence, and appeared rather condescending, as if he were standing in judgment over the protesters.

The protest boat wasn't large. The "Don't Massacre the Giants of the Sea" banner they were holding up flapped in the frigid wind, and with Sara's red hair billowing out in front, it was really an arresting sight. Whether by accident or design, the whaling ship changed course and ended up scraping the protest boat. It was just a scrape, but the difference in tonnage was so great that the protest boat couldn't absorb the impact without tipping. The protesters fell into the water, and, because it was so close by, the survey boat offered emergency assistance. Luckily, the protesters were wearing life jackets. They all seemed to know very well how to survive in such a situation, which gave Detlef the impression that the protesters had let the boat go over on purpose. Then, when the redhead, soaking wet, was being helped onto the ambulance, she gave Detlef an unwitting glance, which gave him the "irrefutable" (a term that cropped up frequently in his technical reports) sense that something had hit him.

Detlef came up with some excuse to visit Sara in hospital, and soon they went on a date to the seashore. As they looked out across the seemingly icy waters of the Norwegian Sea, the lights in the distance were like flickering embers. The couple talked about everything under the sun: from the ecological consequences of methane ice extraction, the whaling industry and changes in coastal shellfish ecology to poetry; Sara used to share her enthusiasm for Keats and Yeats.

One time they got into a disagreement about whether Norway should continue whaling. Sara said, "The reason you think it's no big deal is because you've never seen a minke whale bleed to death right before your eyes."

"But many whalers are whalers because that's what their forebears have always done."

"Yeah, but aren't there lots of whalers whose forebears weren't whalers. I mean, can't people's occupations change? Can't tradition change?"

"Perhaps," Detlef said. "But you're also against methane ice mining."

"I am," said Sara.

"But it's a resource. The exploitation of this resource isn't going to hurt anyone."

"Not going to hurt *anyone*? Depends on your definition of 'anyone.' Methane ice is different from petroleum. As you well know, scientists now believe that it forms when gas migrates from deep within the crust along faults until it precipitates or crystalizes upon contact with ice-cold polar seawater. Which is to say that methane ice deposits are actually part of the ocean floor. We really don't understand how much damage extraction might do to the Arctic region. It could well alter fragile landforms and microclimates, couldn't it? Maybe no people will die, but other life-forms won't be able to adapt to such dramatic environmental change."

"But if we don't continue to develop, how will humanity survive?"

"Why not ask how other life-forms will survive if there are too many people? If the population of Homo sapiens were controlled, then we wouldn't have to extract so much from the environment, would we?"

"I think," said Detlef, "that as long as we can keep developing new ways of feeding even more people, as occurred during the Green Revolution, that means that the world can support 'this many people.' It's our generation's responsibility to feed all the people who are alive in the world."

"But in fact," said Sara, "there's mounting evidence now indicating that we can't afford to support 'this many people,' and that if everyone lived the way you and I do we'd need three earths. They calculated the ecological footprint at the end of the last century. But the reality is that wealth never reaches the poor, and they're the ones who have the most mouths to feed. This issue cannot be solved politically or technically, by another Green Revolution. The rich and powerful are already entrenched, and they don't really care about the people who go hungry."

"With all due respect, Sara, isn't the lifestyle you personally lead quite comfortable?"

"I do all I can to avoid unnecessary waste. Better to do what you can than not try at all."

Detlef pondered the unnecessary waste in his own lifestyle.

"Lots of people," Sara continued, "say that feelings aren't part of the scientific enterprise, but actually all scientists can do as scientists is try to determine what's true and what isn't. They can't tell us what the right choices are. I want to be a person who can offer the decision-makers better choices instead of avoiding all these thorny ethical issues by invoking 'professional neutrality' or some such hypocrisy. As long as the human population stops growing, and we change our way of life, there'll be no need to extract methane ice." Sara's red hair was swelling in the ocean breeze, like the only flaming thing in a pale blue fog.

"Do you know why this place is called Storegga?" Sara tried to clear the air by changing the subject.

Detlef shook his head.

"In Norwegian it means 'the Great Edge.' Have you heard of the Storegga Slide? It happened thousands of years ago, and in the past few years it's happened again. For the past several decades, with the acceleration of global warming, hydrates in the shelf frost layer have been melting and bubbles forming. The resulting crystal decomposition has increased sedimentary instability, causing a massive slide of a layer two hundred and fifty meters high and several hundred kilometers wide, practically half the distance from Norway to Greenland. It's changed the whole coastal ecology. Geologists initially argued that this sort of slide occurs once every hundred thousand years, in synchrony with the Ice Age cycle. You think it'll be a hundred thousand years before it happens again?"

"Hard to say."

"Right, it's hard to say." Sara gathered her windblown hair and said, "Probability theory isn't much use for the prediction of this kind of catastrophe, because there are only two outcomes: either it happens or it doesn't. To me, if the shelf frost collapses again someday, I wouldn't want it to be because people have been digging around in the earth. If it happens naturally, I won't have anything to complain about, because it's none of my business and out of my control. Whatever happens, I just don't want it to be because of us. We're everywhere! Why do people reproduce to the point that we cover the entire planet? Enough already! I don't have a child and won't consider having one, either, so I'm not thinking about these issues for the sake of my own offspring."

Detlef gazed at Sara's eyebrows, which were just as fiery red as her hair, and at her brown eyes beneath. The signals were clear: he was enchanted by those eyes. He wanted to deny it, but the truth was irrefutable.

Actually, Sara had been paying attention to the Trash Vortex for quite some time, ever since oceanologists started observing and arguing about it at the end of the twentieth century. She applied to Norway's National Science Academy for a grant to study the potential impact of the vortex on Taiwan's coastal terrain, but as the grant was still under review when the edge of the vortex hit the east coast, Sara decided to pay her own way. What hurt the sea hurt her personally. Now Detlef had an excuse for a return visit: it was only logical that he would take Sara to an island he'd been to himself many years before.

Jung-hsiang Li picked them up at the airport. He was one of the engineers that had participated in the same tunneling project and the only one who knew about Detlef's visit. When they first met Li had just gotten married. Now he was a man with a hoarse voice, thinning hair and a bit of a bulge, features which made him look older than his actual age. Back in the day, they had many e-mail discussions about the project in the year before Detlef actually came to Taiwan. They drew up a checklist for the superhard quartz-rich sandstone in the area and considered how to cope with crumbly strata and excessive groundwater inflows. Detlef's final assessment was that the difficulties involved in digging the tunnel shouldn't be insuperable, but it might not be worth the time and money: it was a cost-benefit issue. Jung-hsiang Li took the official line: the tunnel is feasible no matter what.

Detlef knew what this meant. On any project engineers like him were just moles. If he couldn't get the job done he could get lost. But not even considering his remuneration, Detlef wanted to know as a mechanical designer whether a TBM could drill through the quartz-rich Szeleng sandstone along the route, which contained so much quartz it was basically quartzite. It had a Mohs hardness of between 6 and 7, when steel was only 5! The young Detlef was very confident. Except that the structure of the actual rock stratum might not be quite as "regular" as they imagined from the samples. They had the geological report on a trial borehole several dozen meters deep, but that was just scratching the surface for such a big mountain as this. The actual texture of the heart of the mountain was anyone's guess. They would just have to improvise. But Detlef didn't care about any of that. He embraced the challenge. Besides, why not give it a try when someone was providing the funding?

Except that groundwater inflows might be even scarier than the sandstone. If they penetrated a water-saturated layer during the drilling process, the groundwater would start gushing out, propelling massive amounts of muck at the TBM and causing machinery breakdowns or triggering cave-ins. As a preventative measure, Detlef recommended the addition of a chain-style conveyor as a way of getting the inflows out of the way. After all, any damage to the machine would compromise mechanical smoothness.

The factory team custom-built two 11.74-meter diameter hard-rock double-shielded TBMs. Even assembling such huge machines was an enormous undertaking that took several months all told. During that time, the most interesting time of day for Detlef was checking his e-mail for progress updates.

Not surprisingly, there were setbacks when the machine was put into operation. The rock was so hard that the cutters kept developing abnormal wear and tear, and if they were not replaced immediately the diameter of the borehole would shrink. Like a cat trying desperately to get its head into a hollow, the TBM would keep trying to nibble away at the face of the rock; once the outer shield got wedged in there, the machine could only wait helplessly for the workers to come to the rescue. According to the data Detlef received, during the worst of it the cutters had to be changed every 2.3 meters. Moreover, the inflows were much more serious than anticipated, causing frequent shutdowns even with the conveyor.

When Detlef saw the photographs of the site he had to admit that he had been overly optimistic. Detlef felt a bit depressed, while at the other end of the e-mail Jung-hsiang Li was still bursting with confidence. Engineers like Jung-hsiang Li, and the whole Taiwanese project team in fact, showed an amazing determination to "see the tunnel through." Detlef fairly admired them for it, but at the same time, inexplicably, it frightened him.

Driving through the tunnel decades later, Detlef lowered the window to get an exact sense of the wind, temperature and artificial lighting inside. At the time, the workers had spent over a decade in a dark, dank cave that was cold in winter and muggy in summer. And the engineering team was up against Tertiary sedimentary rock, interorogenic fold and thrust belts, interstitial water trapped in the earth for tens of thousands of years, strike-slip faults, local normal faults, and eleven folded structures of varying dimensions. The tunnel was a great triumph, wasn't it? Or had it all been an unnecessary waste? Detlef wanted to find a chance to ask Jung-hsiang Li how he felt about it now.

When he was younger Detlef would have described it as a triumph, no question about it. But these past few years he was not so sure. Now he often told his classes that each mountain had its own unique "heart." "According to the data we had at the time," he would say, "the infrastructural authority had dug fifty-nine trial boreholes, seven trial trenches and conducted twelve seismic profiles. It was a large-scale geological survey, but as a way of plumbing the heart of such a huge mountain as this it was all just speculative 'dream interpretation.'"

Detlef would play footage of groundwater flooding the tunnel as a lecture supplement. That always made a big impression: with over seven hundred liters per second of groundwater flowing in, it was almost as if the mountain had resolved to get rid of the people who were probing its heart, for once and for all.

"You don't get drowned 'inside' a mountain every day, now do you?" Detlef tapped the hollow-sounding lectern with his digital pointer. These new lecterns felt none too stable when he leaned on them. The solid wood lecterns they used to have were extremely heavy. It was always like this now: no attention to detail.

"My job is to design a tool that will bore through the 'heart' of a mountain." Detlef looked his students in the eyes one by one. "But now I sometimes have my doubts. I wonder whether we shouldn't just go around, especially when it's a hill with a particularly complicated core. Going through a mountain to get from place to place as quickly as possible is one way of life, while going around is another. We thought we were making a scientific judgment, but actually we were making a lifestyle choice."

Hearing such an accomplished professor express such sentiments, students were often speechless.

"Saving time apparently reduces certain costs, but actually the government had to put all that money into the project in the first place. Sometimes when you calculate the net effect it's not necessarily worth it."

"In that case, you're out of work," a smart alec would sometimes comment.

"Maybe I'd change occupation," Detlef would reply. "Maybe I'd work as a dairy farmer or something like that. My father was a dairy farmer. We should all be able to think of another way to make a living, right?" He was sometimes not willing to admit how much he'd been influenced by Sara in saying such things.

One time Sara brought up an issue he had never considered before. For such a colossal undertaking, putting large numbers of personnel to work in a hellish environment, the technical difficulty of the project was not the only issue. The subtleties of human psychology seemed more important. Did the agency in charge of the project factor in the pressure put in one way or another on the people involved in its implementation? Were the workers, though unsung, given a hero's reward? Or did they make just barely enough to put food on the table?

Detlef sighed. "But on any project engineers like us are nothing more than moles. If I don't drill, someone else will," Professor Boldt said, both to the students sitting below and to Sara.

Detlef would never forget what had brought him to Taiwan in the first place: after the TBM on the westbound tunnel had gotten stuck for the tenth time they'd determined that the cause might be muck flooding the body of the machine. Jung-hsiang Li and his elder brother Jung-chin filled him in on the details of the disastrous turn of events in the car. Jung-hsiang was newly married, Jung-chin single, but they were both outstanding tunneling engineers. They even looked alike: they both had single-fold eyelids and thinning hair, were of medium height and wore dark brown square-frame sunglasses and the same style of work coat.

"Another dozen or so concrete reinforcement rings buckled, groundwater was gushing in again from the side, there were constant localized collapses, and the TBM started making a deafening thudding sound. We sent some people forward to spray concrete into the groundwater outlet, but the water pressure was too great. Must have been ten minutes later when we had the first power outage, which probably lasted a minute. When the power came back on there were rocks falling, and even small rocks hitting the ground caused quite an echo. I immediately ordered an evacuation. *Aye*, it was total chaos in there," Jung-hsiang said.

"Then I heard two pops in quick succession, like fractures in the bedrock. That scared the hell out of me. Not really able to see where I was going, I fell against the lowest rung of the TBM and gashed my calf. I picked myself up and sprinted toward the entrance. We barely made it out alive. There were successive collapses, and within twenty-four hours all the work we'd done had vanished," said Jung-chin Li.

"Might have been a water-resistant layer above the hard rock stratum, formed by millions of years of ground stress. If so, the high-pressure water seam burst when the TBM breached it, causing the collapse," said Jung-hsiang. Listening to the brothers' explanation, Detlef tried to imagine what had happened in the "heart" of the mountain and what damage the TBM had likely sustained.

"Thank God we made it out alive."

"You can say that again," said Jung-chin. "If you believe in God."

People who have never visited the heart of a mountain will never know how complicated and capricious it can be. In the cave, the quartz-rich bedrock sparkled in the lamplight, and the water trickling through the fissures in the rock still seemed to Detlef like miniwaterfalls, just like little unexplored alternate universes. The geologists on the project were busy collecting samples while the engineering personnel were measuring, calculating and extrapolating the data from the cave-in. A space half as tall as a grown man was strewn with muck, cables, twisted steel bars, tools and scattered pieces of machinery. Detlef rubbed the abrasive rock, more solid than steel, his heart pounding. The site had been cleared, exposing the end of the TBM. The mammoth machine, so uncannily familiar, was as helpless as a weird insect caught in congealed sap. A strange sentiment welled up inside him, a sense of failure mixed with melancholy. Quite unprofessionally, he even wondered whether he was damaging something, or about to disturb something.

But this feeling was fleeting. Detlef was a technical person, and the training he had received was not to feel moral doubt or indulge his imagination, but to assess the current situation and recommend the most advantageous and quickest possible resolution. He scrutinized the damage to the TBM while communicating through an interpreter with the engineering personnel on the surface and his comrades in the tunnel. They were discussing viable salvages.

Just then, from deep in the mountain, there was a huge noise, a noise Detlef had never heard before in his entire life. It could only be described as a voice in a dream.

All the personnel fell silent, and there was nothing but the sound of running water. Everyone appeared confused, out of breath. It might have been anywhere from a few seconds to half a minute when the lights went out. "Power's out again!" Detlef heard Jung-hsiang Li shout something, as if to tell everyone to keep it down. The workers were evidently well-trained, as nobody fled in panic and everyone quieted down. The men in the tunnel had everything under control except their panting, which made them sound like countless furtive beasts lying in ambush in the darkness. It was a darkness nobody had ever experienced before, an absolute darkness. Then, from the heart of the mountain, they heard the same sound for the second time, as if some enormous entity had stamped its right foot and now its left, with a third stomp following close behind. It sounded like someone was walking step by step toward the cave. No, maybe he was walking away.

"*Zou!*" Walk! No, run! Detlef understood at least this one Mandarin word, and he along with all the other personnel started fleeing toward the cave entrance the second Jung-hsiang Li gave the order to evacuate. They made it there safe, but were scared out of their wits. Some leaned against the wall; others knelt on the ground. There hadn't really been another cave-in, but that didn't make any difference to any of them, because there had been such a strange, oppressive air, such a distinctly hostile atmosphere in the cave just now. Everyone had felt it.

Detlef knew from the accident report that the blackout lasted for less than a minute before the backup power came on. But everyone who'd been in the tunnel that day felt that more than ten minutes was more like it. Was the discrepancy just psychological, subjective? Detlef kept wondering as he remembered the incident. Jung-hsiang Li said that because the outage was brief, and since it was an isolated incident, the higher-ups simply censored the record to avoid trouble. Detlef would have done the same had he been the person in charge. But then what exactly was that sound? There was nothing about it in the report, of course, not a word. Detlef asked Li whether the two cave-ins he'd been in had sounded the same.

"Totally different. In a cave-in you hear loose rocks colliding or a fracture in the solid rock. The sound we heard that time . . . well, you know as well as me. It sounded like a giant footstep."

A giant footstep. Just what Detlef had been thinking.

Extricating the TBM turned out not to be all that difficult, but soon after there was another serious collapse and the situation became even more complicated. Detlef estimated that fixing the TBM would cost almost the same as buying a new one. He spent a week writing up the report, predicting that the repair would take at least thirty-eight months. After intensive consultations, the infrastructural authority decided to dismantle the TBM and continue along the same section of tunnel with the drill and blast method.

Detlef would never forget. It was at the end of 1997. Hong Kong had just been returned to China, and Christmas was a few days away. It wasn't raining the day Detlef left the office of the construction authority for his hotel in Taipei, but a clammy, pale-blue fog filled the air. There were huge Christmas trees everywhere. Though there are few Christians in Taiwan, the islanders seemed surprisingly keen on the holiday.

The first time Detlef related his experience to Sara, sitting in a café in Berlin, he asked her, half-seriously: "We both thought it sounded like footsteps, but how could there be such a sound in that tunnel?"

"Who knows?" Sara thought her answer sounded too flippant, and didn't want to leave it at that. "Well, I've been studying the ocean for twenty years, and I've discovered that the sea in every different place has its own distinctive sounds. You can hear them if you listen carefully: wind over the water, waves crashing against the rocks, fish jumping and slapping the surface. There are sounds like this in the mountains, I'd bet. There are sounds the ocean makes we still don't recognize, and the same must be true in the mountains. Let's say a tree goes extinct. Nobody's ever going to hear what the wind blowing through its branches sounds like. If you think along those lines, you might say the footstep you heard that day was one of those mountain sounds we don't know about, at least not yet."

Detlef knew exactly what she meant, and even felt she'd read his mind. Actually, Detlef's hearing was abnormally keen, which is why he had gotten interested in tunneling years before. But he still wasn't prepared to let it go at that. "But don't you think that's too anthropomorphic?" he asked.

"Anthropomorphic? Why can't we be anthropomorphic?" Sara laughed, causing Detlef's heart to tighten.

"You sound more a poet than a scientist."

"I am a poet, as well as a scientist," Sara said. "But I enjoy being a poet more."

Sara's ear, like a shy little animal hiding in a thicket, peeked through her fiery hair.

The car was nearing the end of the tunnel. They passed the last mural design and distance marker. With "1 km" to go, there was already light beaming into the tunnel in the distance.

"It's incredible! To think that we could tunnel through such a mountain," said Detlef.

"Yeah," said Jung-hsiang Li. Detlef couldn't tell whether there was pride in his voice, or some other emotion. "You remember that time I went to pick you up in the car and told you I'd just gotten married? Now my eldest daughter is already married with children."

"Fifteen years just to dig this one tunnel," said Detlef. "Seriously, do you think fifteen years was worth it to shave an hour off the trip for all these people all these years?"

"Was it worth it? I don't know. I've never thought about it. My job is to dig, not to assess whether it's worth it or not."

"But now the heart of the mountain has been hollowed out," Sara said.

"What?"

"Oh, it's not important," said Sara. "I was just thinking that it was such a beautiful mountain and now its heart is hollow." They were now using ambient lighting in the tunnel. Lighting technology had improved by leaps and bounds the past couple of years, and the retrofit had only been completed the previous year. It now looked like there was a series of skylights on the ceiling of the tunnel spilling natural light down from heaven the whole way. The moment the car left the tunnel, the natural light took over. The weather when they'd entered was fair, so they didn't expect an overcast sky when they came out the other side.

Then, in an almost imperceptible voice, Jung-hsiang Li said, "To my elder brother it was most definitely not worth it." Jung-hsiang had mentioned his brother's passing. What he had not said was that two of his brother's colleagues were buried during one drill and blast, crushed to death in a shower of rock. Jung-chin had escaped death, but he couldn't shake depression. They were his friends. From then on he just went through the motions, working like a machine. One day after the road went through, the neighbors discovered he'd committed suicide. He'd hermetically sealed every crack in the room and left the gas on. It was like a cave inside.

"Actually, this is only the second time I've been through this tunnel since it opened," Jung-hsiang Li said, matter-of-factly, looking in the rearview mirror, as if he had just seen his brother's face.

"Get ready for a view of the sea."

# 22. A Rainstorm's Coming

Atile'i drank from the cup Alice offered him and said, "This water tastes of scorched earth."

Alice could not understand what he was saying, but assuming he was asking the name of the beverage, she said, "It's called coffee. This is *salama* coffee, Hafay's signature blend. I learned how to make it from her."

Communication proceeded slowly. They had to go back to square one to relearn how to refer to everything. There were new things, and new names for old things. It was difficult for both Alice and Atile'i. But Alice realized that there can gradually be dialogue, even between languages that are quite far apart. Sometimes one doesn't have to use language as it's commonly defined. For instance, Atile'i would use his speaking flute to help him express himself or his emotions when Alice didn't understand what he meant. Atile'i would play the flute with feeling and Alice would understand immediately. One time Atile'i was describing the beauty of his lover Rasula, "so beautiful that she can soothe anyone's *salikaba*," but Alice could not figure out what he meant until he played a short melody on the flute, utterly absorbed. "So beautiful that she can soothe anyone's soul, right? *Salikaba* means soul, doesn't it?" As if that was just what Atile'i, playing on the speaking flute, had said.

Ten days earlier, Alice would have doubted the reliability of flutesong translation, but now she would say, "I can understand almost everything Atile'i's trying to say with the speaking flute." It was like an interlanguage between them, helping familiarize them with basic words, like *"salikaba"* and "soul," and rules of usage. It was like some little elf that would fly over and whisper what Atile'i wanted to say in her ear.

Atile'i treasured his speaking flute because it was a gift from Rasula. The *kiki'a* wine she'd made was gone, but he hadn't lost the speaking flute, because he'd used a fine rope to hang it around his neck. The flute was wooden and about ten centimeters long. It was played horizontally like a transverse flute, except that the finger holes were in two parallel rows. The body of the instrument was so small that Atile'i could almost play it without his hands, by holding it in his mouth.

Maybe because Alice had a gift for languages, she could understand at least thirty, maybe forty, percent of what Atile'i was saying. Of course, "speaking" was still difficult, for the two languages were totally different phonetically. Alice slowly went from using her own language exclusively to being able to mix in some Wayo Wayoan words, which Atile'i found reassuring. It wasn't like he needed to be reassured about Alice. He knew from the beginning that this woman meant him no harm. This was just the consolation of language. After all, he had once thought he might die here, in a world full of bizarre and unfamiliar things, without ever hearing another person speak his native tongue again. Being able to hear someone speak broken Wayo Wayoan now made him very happy.

Sometimes it was hard to tell from his expression alone whether or not Atile'i was listening or understanding. He often looked off into the distance muttering something to himself. Later she understood that the mantra he kept repeating meant, "The fish will always come."

The fish will always come, as will the rain. The average rainfall seemed to be increasing, and it was falling more and more violently with each passing year. Alice was especially inclined to think of Toto on rainy days or when she saw a faraway look in Atile'i's eyes. Atile'i appeared to be five or six years older than Toto, because he said he had lived through a hundred and eighty moons before going to sea. Though it was hard to know how long he had spent at sea, there was still something childish in the expressions that he wore on his weathered dark-brown face.

Apart from Ohiyo, Alice had finally found someone she was willing to open up to about how much she missed Toto. Perhaps it was because Atile'i wouldn't understand the details of what she was saying that Alice felt more free to speak her mind. Even though they would never admit it, the people around Alice had all gone from sympathetic and patient to bored and sick and tired of hearing her talk about Toto. The very sight of her put people on alert. Oh no, here she comes again, they seemed to say to themselves.

Language might increase the distance of a story, making it seem even further away, but Atile'i was sensitive enough to realize that Alice really missed her son. That was the way it was, no doubt about it. He didn't have to understand her story to intuit how she felt. When Alice mentioned for the umpteenth time what it had been like with Toto around, Atile'i recalled something the Sea Sage had once said and related it to Alice: *"Ina'e kasi ka mona'e lulala, i'a sudoma."*

Alice had already learned some of the words: *mona'e* meant ocean, *lulala* was flower, and *sudoma* beach. But she still didn't understand the meaning of the whole sentence. She spent quite some time querying Atile'i before she felt she probably understood what it meant. Maybe it could be translated like this: *No beach, no matter what the island, can hold the waves.*

This was a maxim and an admonition. It would undoubtedly also count as a truth, even under scientific examination. Waves could not stay on a beach. There was often a fine line between proverbial wisdom and stating the obvious, between a truth and a truism, Alice thought.

"Only whales can be kept on the beach," Atile'i said. The islanders believe that whales sacrifice themselves for the sake of all the folks who are unable to go fishing. When sea creatures use the land to kill themselves, their spirits soar up to the clouds; when land creatures drown themselves in the sea, their spirits turn into jellyfish. These were the rules of the spirit realm, taught to Atile'i by the horde of second sons he'd met on the sea.

"Sometimes death is payback. At other times, it's just farewell, not owing anyone anything. As the days are long and the sea is deep, in the end the *salikaba* (Alice now had the word memorized) will betray the flesh, for the flesh is weak."

Maybe because Alice tended to translate literally from Wayo Wayoan to Mandarin she always felt that the young Atile'i's speech was overly poetic and a bit unreal. He made the pain that everyone had to suffer sound so beautiful. A kid Atile'i's age should not be saying things like that. But in another sense, Alice thought about all Atile'i had experienced at sea, far more than she herself had experienced anywhere. Maybe the soul that resided in his young body was more complicated than the one that dwelt in hers.

Alice started taking Atile'i to draw water in the morning. Atile'i was curious about everything he saw along the way. The first time he saw a waterfall, he fell down to his knees, his eyes brimming over. He said this was something the Sea Sage had prayed for his whole life long: "How wonderful it would be to have such a mighty spring on Wayo Wayo. The sea is so big, but there's not a drop to drink. That is the punishment of Kabang."

Alice wanted to tell him that nobody could punish anyone else. She gave him a long explanation, but couldn't be sure he understood.

Aside from drawing water, Alice also had to gather wild food plants. She had learned a lot by going to the Seventh Sisid, because Hafay would use plants Pangcah people often ate as ingredients in the meals she prepared. Things like *kakurot* (wild bitter gourd) to go with steamed fish. And you can combine *sukuy* (gac) with the snails you can catch anywhere and make a broth. Violet wood-sorrel can be pickled and served as a side dish. Rattan shoots make a great soup, while cassava can substitute for rice. Hafay also taught Alice how to make a pot out of a betel leaf and cook with it. You put the water and ingredients in the "pot" and toss in stones so hot from the fire that they make the water boil. Hafay said this was "stone bowl hot pot," Pangcah style.

Atile'i had an outstanding ability to recognize plants. Usually he could remember something after Alice had picked it a single time. Soon he took over Alice's job of foraging up in the hills. Sometimes when she got up in the morning, she would find the basket full of a day's worth of vegetables.

Alice couldn't resist giving him field guides to read. Atile'i was really interested in the pictures, which looked just like the real thing. He was learning the names of different species at the same time as he was getting more and more familiar with a foreign language. At first he only learned the practical plants, the wild vegetables or herbs, but soon he knew almost all the birds, insects and reptiles, too. He could tell Alice at a glance that up ahead there were three emerald doves, eleven lesser scimitar babblers, seventy-nine Japanese white-eyes and a yellow-mouthed screech owl, with its eyes closed. Oh wait, there's also a red-banded snake.

He quickly realized that the wild ferns, both cross-the-ditch and lady fern, that carpeted the mountains weren't poisonous. They were edible, and could be eaten raw as you walked along. Soon the gash on Atile'i's calf formed a scab, and the sore at the corner of his mouth was much improved. He picked breadfruits and wild raspberries and stored them in the cellar he'd dug to keep them cool and fresh. Alice was amazed. Atile'i knew a whole lot more about survival than she did. Sometimes she felt that the mountain knew Atile'i right from the start. He plucked buds and drank dew as he went along, as natural as a babbler in the woods nibbling on raspberries.

Once in a while, Alice walked down alone and drove into town to buy food. She would arrange to meet Dahu, Umav and Hafay along the way, and would always see the ruins of the Sea House, now almost completely inundated, and the endless seashore, still in a shambles even after several months of clearance. She got the latest news update about the Trash Vortex from Dahu and Hafay: journalists had recently started calling it the "Primeval Plastic Soup," which sounded like a dish on a menu.

One time when she came down to town, Alice caught a talk show on TV while eating in a buffet. Some famous buckraker claimed he had seen a little dark fellow swim to shore out of the plastic soup and vanish into a grove. "If you don't believe me launch a search in the mountains. You'll find him," the buckraker averred.

"Nonsense," said the owner of the buffet. Alice knew it was not. Could someone have possibly seen Atile'i run into the hills? Thank God Atile'i had already changed into the clothes Alice had bought for him and could speak some Mandarin now. It would not be too hard to make up some story. Not to mention that the folks on this kind of show were all talk, no action. And to most viewers, it wasn't supposed to be informative; it was pure entertainment, the kind of program that gave people everything but the truth. Nobody would actually go looking, would they?

At first Dahu and Hafay urged Alice to come back and live by the sea, but Alice told them that she wanted to stay in the hut for the time being, so they didn't force the issue. Dahu had sorted out the stuff from the Sea House and packed it up. He was planning to take it up for her, only to meet with her adamant refusal. The situation was so awkward Dahu could only relent.

"I'm sure there's something going on at the hut," Dahu said privately to Hafay.

"You still don't know Alice after all these years? If she wanted us to know she would have told us already," Hafay said. "Anyway, maybe she's just being a bit paranoid."

"Yeah, you're probably right."

"But haven't you noticed that Alice's complexion looks so much better? Didn't she say it's been awhile since she stopped taking that whatchamacallit medication? I think it's less likely now that she'd go and do something stupid, so whatever's going on at least it seems to be doing her some good so far, right?"

"I hope you're right," said Dahu.

Indeed, every time Alice came down she was talking more about Ohiyo and less about Toto. But now Hafay, too, sensed that Ohiyo wasn't Alice's only companion at the hunting hut.

Alice found a quiet place by the highway and tossed a few things from the Sea House, leaving most of them in the car. She kept all of Toto's books and stationery, even though she knew that keeping these things would only cause her sorrow. It was like leaving a deadly weapon lying around. She discovered a bundle of letters in a manila envelope, all from Thom.

From seeing each other to living together to getting married, Alice knew that Thom had pushed himself to the limit for her sake. But she was unwilling to admit defeat and let him go. One time she really thought Thom wasn't coming back. Toto had come down with a cold, and as soon as he got better Thom told her he was preparing to climb Mount Kilimanjaro. Alice did not say anything the entire day. When they were drying the dinner dishes Thom leaned over and asked: "Are you angry?"

"No. What's there to be angry about?"

"I know you're angry. The Umbwe Route isn't that difficult. We'll have a professional guide."

"It has nothing to do with the difficulty or whether you've got a guide or not. Don't you get it?" Alice's tone suddenly hardened.

"I guess I just don't fucking get it!"

"If you don't get it you don't get it. Whatever you want, Thom! Go do whatever you fucking want!"

Alice knew that she was being unreasonable, but she had a good reason, though for now she did not have the courage to confront it. For a while after Thom left, Alice thought: This is it, he's gone for good. He'll continue his adventures on seas, on slopes and in beds far away from her. Two weeks later Alice received a picture postcard from Thom of a glacier on Mount Kilimanjaro. The handwriting on the back was so finely penned it seemed to be printed in some old-style English font. In writing, Thom was always affectionate, never angry:

> *Without you my life would be nothing but a grim expanse of ice, frigid, flat and gray. On days without you near me I'm as haplessly muddled as a butterfly released into an alien realm, feebly flapping its wings among unfamiliar plants at the wrong height.*

The last few lines were so Nabokov. Ah, but that was Thom. Toto and what remained of their love had been spun into a fragile thread, the only remaining tie between them. Thom did come back in the end. But if the conversation turned away from Toto, the two of them turned into silent snipers, each returning to his or her own trench. Sometimes Alice thought that she should have let it be, let him leave long before. How could such a man belong to her?

Toto and Thom had been out of contact for two days, but Alice still had not thought to call the police. It didn't occur to her that there might have been an accident. She assumed maybe Thom was just trying to avoid her. To do so, he might not scruple to conceive a crude missing person plot, and might even take her Toto away with him.

This suspicion only disappeared when Dahu found Thom's body. Thom's death gave her mourning an outlet, but also caused her soul, which she had been propping up with hate for many days, to collapse. Thom had always been this person in her life who might disappear at any moment; Alice had been preparing herself for the worst all that time. But what about Toto? Why was there still no sign of him?

Dahu, the rescue team and the coroner all supposed Thom must have fallen off the cliff and died. He had comminuted fractures all over his body. But the route on which they discovered Thom's body was totally different from the one he had registered at the backcountry office. The placement of the body did not really make sense, either. It was as if someone had dragged him into the secluded rock house at the base of the cliff. Or had the force of impact caused his body to ricochet right into the shelter? And was this the reason he'd eluded discovery?

Alice listened as Dahu discussed what might have happened with some other climbing buddies. She couldn't understand why they didn't mention Toto. Toto still hadn't been found, not even his backpack, but they didn't seem at all concerned. Of the two people in the world who cared about Toto, one was gone, leaving her all alone. She lifted the shroud, took a look at the shrunken corpse hidden beneath, and signed the cremation authorization form without hesitation. She sprinkled Thom's ashes in the water in front of the Sea House. Alice never thought to inform his family, because Thom had simply never given her their contact information; he hadn't even told his parents when Toto was born. Which made her suspect that Thom had been alone in the world all along; maybe he remained alone right to the end. How she once loved his body, and the spirit it contained. Now all that remained of him was ashes and dust.

One night, Alice asked Atile'i about funerals on Wayo Wayo.

Atile'i said that Wayo Wayoan funerals are usually held late at night, because the islanders believe that with the approach of day, the spirits follow the stars and fade away. The deceased is carried alone in a little boat toward the edge of the waters around Wayo Wayo. There is a boundary the living can never cross, not even when fishing, because of a powerful undercurrent. The relatives of the deceased ride in two boats, one to the left and one to the right, to steady the spirit craft. When they near the current that will carry the deceased off, the Sea Sage chants the psalm of farewell. If they see lights flickering in the distance it is time to let go. Then the craft departs, never to return, while the relatives of the departed sing heartily as they row back. If they do not get the timing right, the craft will sometimes turn round and they will, however reluctantly, have to throw stones at it to sink it. Otherwise the spirit of the dead will never rest in peace.

"You sing? You mean singing? Like this?" Alice hummed the first melody that came into her head.

"Yes, singing."

"Did you ever ask why you do that?"

"Because it's good for the deceased."

"Why is it for the good of the deceased?"

"Because our ancestors want us to sing."

"Is whatever the ancestors want you to do necessarily good?"

"Whatever the ancestors want us to do is necessarily good."

"I see," Alice said, perfunctorily. She suddenly realized that the melody she had just hummed was from a song Thom had sung for her in the campground in Copenhagen.

"You see." Atile'i fell silent a few moments, as if lost in thought. Then he said, "May the Sea bless you."

She had just decided to follow the route that they'd taken together, father and son. No doubt this youth standing in front of her would be an ideal helper and companion on her quest. She wanted to make the trip to the place where Thom died and Toto went missing, to see for herself, once and for all, what it was like and how she would feel when she got there.

"Can I hear that again?" Atile'i asked.

"What?"

"The song. You were just singing."

# 23. The Man with the Compound Eyes I

Nobody has ever seen the forest he now beholds, like a forest in a novel that has grown into a real wood. This is not to say that the forest is not immense, peaceful, dark and deep. It is indeed immense, peaceful, dark and deep, just a bit unreal.

The man, blond-haired and big-boned, looks back and encourages the boy behind him, saying, "We'll be fine. I know a path to the big cliff over there. I've climbed it many times. It's fantastic there, really incredible. You'll know what I mean after you climb it: everything looks different from up there. I've even seen long-armed scarabs up there."

Long-armed scarabs. This time I have to see them for myself, the gray-haired little boy thinks to himself. The man is carrying all the equipment so the boy can keep up. The boy's skin is fair, his eyes enchanting—brown at first sight but almost blue from a certain angle. He is a tight-lipped, determined little boy. The boy has not called for a stop for over four hours since breaking camp this morning. The man has been making a point of helping the boy regulate his breathing and pace himself as they march in single file along an almost unmarked trail. If the boy stops walking the man senses it immediately.

So far the boy has stopped three times along the way, because he is constantly checking for scat along the trail, and for scarab beetles feasting on the scat. If he sees any movement he stops, picks out the beetles and puts them in a ventilated jar, without using chemical agents to put the insects under. He just tightens the twist top lid. "Wait in here a bit." The boy taps the jar, not actually opening his mouth but adopting a benign expression apparently intended to reassure the beetles. "Don't be afraid, I mean you no harm." But obviously the scarab he has just caught doesn't understand. Seemingly bewildered, it flails its three pairs of legs, trying to climb up the side of the jar only to slide back down again.

The man and the boy start sweating. The forest is dark and extremely still. It is a deep-toned stillness. The two of them share the sound of one another's breathing. Just when the boy feels maybe they should rest a bit, the forest comes to an abrupt end and his eyes light up, as if someone has just flipped the sunlight switch.

As soon as the boy and the man see the cliff off to the one side, they immediately feel that the forest just now has been as real as real can be, and that the immense rock wall they now confront is fantasy. The man has seen so many of the world's wonders, and has climbed this cliff face before, but he is still deeply moved by it. He enjoys this feeling most of all, the feeling of awe inspired by a certain anticipated scene. Meanwhile, the boy is thinking that the insects in his jar once lived at a place like this. He does not have too many adjectives in his vocabulary yet. He notices his heart is pounding, and that he feels giddy.

"Isn't it great?" the man says to the boy. The boy does not respond. He is too thrilled to know how to respond, and at the same time starts to doubt himself.

"This cliff wasn't here originally. It was only because of an earthquake that the mountain allowed the cliff to appear." The man sees that the boy is wavering. "When I was ten years old, your grandfather took me free diving. You know, in the ocean, without a scuba tank, and he told me, only if you go to places nobody's ever been can you see the colors nobody's ever seen." The boy nods, though he does not completely understand what this means.

The man has not left the island this whole year. When he's found himself at a loose end he has taken the boy to the practice climbing wall. He's seen what a quick study the boy is indoors, and everyone who's seen him outdoors has been amazed. It's like the kid was born with a rock climbing certification. Every time someone praises the boy the man is thrilled, as if he himself has been praised, and maybe this is why many people who know the man feel he is an oversized kid himself. The man surveys the cliff, looks for a new route. This is his custom, *never to climb the same wall in the same way twice.* Even when he brings his son who has just turned ten along with him.

The boy starts to get out his equipment, arranging his things one by one. He puts on his climbing shoes, safety rope and helmet. The man traces out the route in his mind, takes a deep breath and finds the first toehold.

"I lead and you belay, all right? Watch where I climb. I'll keep my movements small, and choose rocks you're able to reach. Got it?"

The boy nods and asks, "Will the long-armed scarab be able to climb up, too?"

Surprised by the question the boy had sprung upon him, the man thinks it over and says, "Of course."

While the boy waits below, the man ascends slowly, finding the route in the pattern of the rock. He uses rock wedges to make anchors, clips a quickdraw onto each anchor, and hangs the lead rope into the quickdraw as a belay, all the while looking down to check up on the boy, who is craning his neck, trying to trace the route the man is taking. Then the boy starts climbing. Faintly feeling the boy's weight on the rope, the man has a wonderful sense of well-being.

"No problem, you can do it," the man says quietly, as if he's afraid to startle the cliff itself. The boy sometimes looks up at the vertical path shining above him, and at other times he looks at the cliff face all around him. He finds himself in an alien realm. He is on the verge of tears, though not because he is afraid. No, this seems like a completely new kind of crying the boy has never experienced before.

They finally make it to the top as dusk approaches. The man and the boy yawp euphorically into the valley. Though the boy doesn't usually speak, his call is loud and clear. Looking down from here, they can see the forest canopy, a green sea gently swaying. The sound reaches the top of the trees and startles a few birds, which dart up and dive back down into the sea.

They excitedly get the stove ready to brew tea and cook a vacuum-pack meal. Their secret trip is now half done. Actually, the point of the trip is not to climb the mountain. For the man, it is purely so that his ten-year-old son can experience the cliff. It's also a chance for a father and son, who've been drifting apart, to renew their relationship.

After the picnic, the man explains the signs in the stars, adding, "You can see a million times more stars up here than you can down on the plains. Maybe you're thinking, But aren't the stars there, no matter what? Sure they are, it's just a question of visibility. Visibility means how far you can see. You remember when we went to a wetland one time to see migratory birds? The sky was foggy, because there were fine particles floating in the air. I remember your mother saying that gazing at the stars these days is like wearing a pair of fogged-up glasses."

Only the man speaks. The boy never replies, as if he simply does not exist. The man has regretted his decision to come to the island, but now he's past the point of no return. He once dreamed about being an explorer. In his younger days, he cycled around Africa, piloted a sailboat across the Atlantic, ran an ultramarathon across the Sahara, and even took part in an interesting sleep experiment, spending fully half a year thirty meters underground. He followed his wife—his girlfriend at the time—here to Taiwan. At first everything was great: she accepted his sudden disappearances, which lasted from two weeks to a month. But after she became pregnant everything changed. The man remembers a time when he was totally willing to stay for the sake of the child, to build a home to raise his son in. And he had built it. Things were perfect then: the child was on the way, they were living in a unique house, and his wife was tender and affectionate again. Then he discovered that he still felt a longing to leave home.

Occasionally, when the man felt so physically restless he couldn't stand it anymore, he would leave the house and go climbing or leave the island on some adventure with his friends. His wife would say it was okay but would give him the silent treatment when he returned, like he was a stranger. Later on he would just come and go without saying anything. Sometimes he didn't know whether to stay or go. Maybe that's why he turned to the consolations of sex. With his outstanding appearance, he has had no trouble finding Taiwanese girls willing to go to bed with him. A couple of times he even slept with his wife's students. Though he regretted it after, sex has come to dominate his life, brutally and overpoweringly, a bit like a disgusting piece of gum sticking to the bottom of his shoe.

"But I feel like the stars I see up here are as real as the ones I saw as a boy. When I'm climbing it's like I'm a kid again. Maybe that's part of why I enjoy it so much." The man kept talking and talking, more like he was talking to himself than to the boy. He sighed and said, "Sometimes things haven't gone away, it's just that we just can't see them."

The night sky clouds over and the man takes a flashlight and goes looking with the boy for beetles in the grove by the edge of the cliff. They have not brought much equipment, so he improvises an insect lure by propping up another flashlight on the ground and shining it onto a white T-shirt. It isn't that effective, attracting only a few moths, but one of them is an erebus, a kind of butterfly with huge eye spots on its wings. The boy turns on the new electronic field guide he has brought along with him to show the man. The two of them are completely content.

"Tomorrow we'll go down the cliff and spend the night in the forest. I've asked some insect experts, and we should be able to find long-armed scarabs in the forest. Haven't you already found quite a few stag beetles? We can spend the day there, then hike down. I'll take you down another side of the mountain, a shortcut through the valley. It's fantastic; an awesome route. The forecast said there'd only be four days of sunny weather. Then it's supposed to start raining, and rain isn't good. We've got to get home before it rains."

The boy nods. The fact that he seldom speaks makes him appear older than his actual age. The boy picks up the flashlight and goes to look around the camp. First he chooses trees with the light, then focuses on a few of them and searches up and down. He finds five or six different kinds of stag beetles. He knows which species of stag beetle likes what kind of tree. He catches one of each and goes back to the tent, to make a detailed record of the species, the size and the time and place of discovery in his notebook. He immediately puts them in insect jars.

He goes to sleep shortly after he gets back into the tent. He dreams he is walking alone down a fern-lined forest path, toward a faint light way up ahead. He keeps going until he comes to a stream. There is a mob of Formosan sambar deer crossing the stream, their legs so delicate that even the moonlight would weigh them down. Yet they leap so nimbly they seem to play the stream like a piano. He chases them but the deer disappear, as if they've turned into a school of fish. On the other side of the stream, the boy faces a wood, but then he feels something behind him. He smells something moist, something very, very near.

Having gotten this far in the dream, the boy starts to wake up. He opens his eyes and discovers it's raining, and that the man isn't by his side. He guesses the man has gone out to do something. He waits with his eyes wide open. The rain patters on the flysheet, and droplets condense on the inside wall of the tent, indicating that it is much colder outside than in.

Two fewer days of sunny weather, the boy thinks.

The man still hasn't returned the following day. His shoes are gone, and so is some equipment. The boy puts on his raincoat and looks in vain for signs around the camp. The sullen rain clouds in the distance envelop the entire mountain in gloom, and the smells of rain and grass mingle. The rain will fall harder.

The boy thinks he should probably turn on the transmitter. But on the second day of the trip the man has asked him to turn it off, saying they couldn't be tracked because they were going to make a secret trip to the big cliff. Now that he's gone, the only way people will come rescue Dad or me is if I turn on the transmitter, thought the boy. But then he thought, Dad can free dive to a depth of two hundred meters and single-hand a sailboat across the Atlantic, and nothing could happen to a dad like that. If Dad comes back I'll get in big trouble.

This thought calms him down. He retreats back into the forward vestibule of the tent and starts fixing a meal. None too skilfully, he lights the camp stove, gets the food out of the backpack and chooses oatmeal. Less than twenty minutes later, he has everything ready. There is still four days' worth of food, and he can just drink rainwater when the water they've brought runs out, and he also knows where the water purification tablets are. No problem. The only thing he has to face is silence. Exactly, just silence. All by himself. The hardest part is being alone. Everything will be all right just as long as he doesn't get scared.

He spends the next day waiting, and by dusk the rain is falling harder and harder. Visibility is now almost nil. He feels colder and colder, because lots of things are soaked. He thinks about turning on the transmitter again, then reflects, If Dad still hasn't come back tomorrow I can turn on the transmitter then. What difference will half a day make? That evening the boy lies in the tent listening to his heartbeat, but actually his mind is far away. He is dreaming again, each new dream a sequel to the last.

The boy turns his head to look, and it turns out one of the sambar deer is behind him now, sniffing at him. He turns all the way around and finds himself facing the wet nose of the biggest deer. He retreats a few steps, and the deer turns and runs off, its tail flashing like a firefly. Running after it, the boy discovers he is running along a cliff, and the deer has turned into a goat. The goat runs into a forest that looks a lot like the one they went through on the way up to the cliff. At the end of the forest the goat stops and stands its ground. He now sees there is a mob of deer there, and also a tribe of goats. The boy cannot tell which deer and what goat he was just chasing.

The trees, deer and goats are all looking at the boy.

After a while the boy realizes there is a man standing behind the deer and the goats, lightly stroking one of the ears of one of the goats. The ear is pointy and furry, like it's heard many secrets.

"Where's my dad?" the boy asks.

That man motions with his chin. The boy looks. He discovers the mountains are now far away, and he is standing at the edge of that huge cliff, one step away from oblivion. The great waves of the green sea below billow out before him boundlessly.

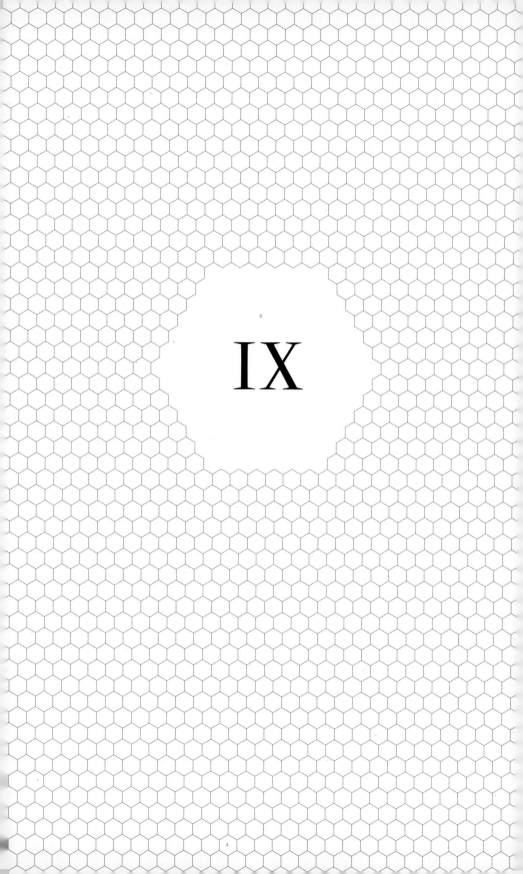

IX

# 24. The Coastal Highway

The first thing Sara thought of when she smelled that reeking beach was Professor Stewart's breath. He'd taught her English Colonial History; it was a smell of visceral decay. Never before had she seen such an exhausted, defenseless, vulnerable sea. Sara could not think of a better word for it than "exhausted."

In fact, she'd had the same feeling riding along in the car down the new highway, which had only been opened a few years before. Studying the map, she discovered that the old road had gone along the coast with the Pacific Ocean on one side and the mountains on the other, while the new road went straight through the most beautiful mountains on the island. They passed through quite a few tunnels that made Detlef marvel, What a technical achievement!

Detlef made a point of taking it slow. Jung-hsiang had lent them this Mitsubishi SUV, which gave them mobility. Once in a while, when the road curved back along the coast, the Pacific flashed in the distance, but it was not the deep blue sea they had looked forward to. With the trash floating on the water, the angle of the light reflecting off the surface kept changing, even causing a few resplendent rainbows to form. But when they got a chance to take a closer look they saw the seawater was a heavy, leaden color, not a true blue. And every once in a while, they could see the railway and the train. At dinner the night before, Jung-hsiang had mentioned that along many sections the track foundation had been scoured away, and that the authorities were looking into backing away toward the mountains again. In some places they would just have to dig. Jung-hsiang wanted Detlef's professional opinion on whether they could get through this range, and had asked him to attend to the terrain along the way.

"I'm afraid the main issue right now is the necessity of the project, not the technical challenge. It's about what kind of island you want," Detlef had replied.

Detlef and Sara stopped at Chung-teh to see the famous Clearwater Cliffs. The sea was battering the base of the soaring bluffs with various kinds of debris. Hordes of tourists were issuing continual exclamations of amazement as they admired the magnificent view from inside their cars. Sara was more than a little shaken by the scene. The cliff itself was glorious, but she couldn't get over how these tourists turned a blind eye to the sorry state the coast was in, regarding it as a mere spectacle. She turned on her paper-thin tablet and looked up this stretch of coastline on Wikipedia.

She had been on the island for two days, and only had brief impressions of the place, but she'd already noticed that the islanders were inured to breathing this air and were now trying to get used to the sight of this sea. The pristine Pacific Ocean as she had seen it in so many images had now vanished. Sara was reminded of a documentary series called *The World's Oceans* her father had played for her when she was in elementary school.

"Look, this is our Pacific. Isn't it sublime?" At the time Sara thought that the only sea of the Norwegian people was the Norwegian Sea, given by the grace of God. Her geography teacher had told them that due to the balmy North Atlantic Current, the Norwegian Sea was the only ocean in the Arctic that was navigable year round. "Our Norwegian Sea," he said. Sara still remembered the look in his eyes. But for her father, every sea was "*our* sea:" "*our* Indian Ocean," "*our* Atlantic," "*our* Pacific."

Sara's father had the same name as the first explorer to reach the South Pole. Many assumed he had changed his name because he loved adventure, but when he introduced himself he always stressed that it was the other way around, that he came to love the wandering life on account of his name. Between 1903 and 1906 the great Roald Amundsen had become the first explorer to sail through the Northwest Passage. He located the magnetic north pole along the way. But never in his wildest dreams could Amundsen have imagined that, after 2010, as a result of global warming, the land of ice and snow would gradually shrink and the Northwest Passage would be navigable year round, with no need to worry about which month was the melting season. It would have been like discovering Amazonia only to watch the rainforest shrink. Sara's father often felt that it was for the best that Amundsen the explorer was already dead, that he did not have to witness all this.

Sara's father had been an architect, but out of love for the sea he had abandoned his first career in the prime of life to become a fisherman. Because he was too often away, her mother had finally hardened her heart and left Sara at a friend's house in the harbor. Sara could not remember much about her, just like it's sometimes hard to remember when you made up your mind to do something. After the divorce, Amundsen kept taking his boat out into the fishing grounds every year to chase the shoals of smew, gadus, blue cod and herring, sometimes even all the way to the western edge of the North Atlantic. He'd heard that fishermen in search of cod had discovered the New World earlier than Columbus, but had kept it a secret in order to guard their fishing ground.

Most of Amundsen's companions did not see how sad he was after his wife's sudden departure, only noticed that he started bringing Sara on board with him more often. Little Sara's childhood was spent at sea. Maybe this was one of the main reasons why she would go on to have the talent and the confidence to become a marine ecologist many years later.

Amundsen insisted on hunting one whale a year, but only one. He usually only selected such titanic adversaries as fin whales or sperm whales to uphold his modest pride and dignity as a Norwegian fisherman. Fin whales are rorquals, and most people would assume that *rørhval,* the Norwegian word for rorqual, meant "groove whale," *rør* meaning "groove" and *hval* meaning "whale." This made sense, because the rorquals have throat grooves. But Amundsen often told people he thought this was wrong. He read *rør* as cognate with *rød,* meaning "red," because when a rorqual's throat grooves expand they fill with blood and appear red. For him, the true meaning of *rørhval* was a great red-bellied whale in the deep blue sea. And Amundsen found the idea of hunting such a whale irresistible.

The international community had put quite a lot of pressure on Norway's whalers, but Amundsen remained his old self. He would often tell people, "I hunt with a traditional harpoon, not with a whale gun or a bomb lance. It's like a struggle for survival. What's wrong with that? Not to mention that I only hunt one a year!" Amundsen practiced the art invented more than a thousand years ago by the Basques and improved by the Norwegians. When the lookout up in the crow's nest spotted a whale, the harpooners would row out in smaller boats, surround it and launch their harpoons into its back. A rope on each harpoon was attached to a big hollowed-out gourd, which increased drag and caused the fleeing whale to exhaust itself more quickly. When the whale started spouting blood, the harpooners would aim at its weak spot and end the life of a great spirit.

Some environmental protection organizations believed that the use of the harpoon was even crueler than modern weapons as it would cause the whale greater pain. Amundsen found this impossible to accept. "All life must feel pain in the face of death. To live without pain is to live without dignity. We venerate the whales and don't intend to kill them off, and I don't make them suffer on purpose. We put our lives on the line, in exchange for theirs. When I hunt a whale, it's either him or me. I don't condone the commercial hunt, any more than you. It's the commercial hunters who are driving the whales to extinction. You should be going after *them,* not us. Get it?"

Amundsen was a one-man army, with a truculent manner to match. Modern boats were so much faster than traditional ones, but Amundsen made a point of following the old ways. "At least, the whales that die by my hand die with dignity. They have a fighting chance, the chance to take my life." Sometimes, before Little Sara was old enough to understand, he would explain, "People are a link in the food chain, and hunting in moderation won't cause any species to disappear. Hunting whales made the old Scandinavian fishermen strong. This you must understand, my little Sara."

To his friends, Amundsen was a typical Norwegian, tough and cold.

Only Little Sara saw the weakness in him. He would often sit up at night in the cabin of his boat and pierce and yank at his skin with a fishhook. This process left twisting scars, which soon snaked all over his arms. People were always shocked by the sight when he rolled up his sleeves and set to work out at sea. One morning while they were eating breakfast, Little Sara surprised him by asking why he poked himself like that. He fell silent a minute, then replied, "To feel what the fish feel, my Little Sara."

Many years later, Amundsen would say that his whaling career ended the year he turned fifty. That year he and his friends were chasing a pair of fin whales. They fought them all the way across the north Atlantic until they ended up killing the eighteen-meter-long bull and releasing the even more massive cow, because they had agreed never to kill females. But when the cow was leaving it took a swipe at the boat with her tail, not only ripping a hole in the hull but also destroying the propulsion system. Regretfully, they had to leave the male, letting its colossal body sink into the sea. Adrift, Amundsen and his friends sent out distress signals as they tried to fix the leak. They had even jumped into the whaleboat, ready to abandon ship, when a Canadian fishing vessel rescued them, lowering a transport net and hauling them off to Newfoundland.

It was already late autumn. Amundsen decided to winter in Canada, taking some time out for a trip down the Mississippi. Renting a boat and navigating this river had been a boyhood dream of his, ever since he had seen a cartoon called *The Adventures of Tom Sawyer*. Tom and Huck, Tom and Huck, Amundsen sang as he steered the boat, feeling himself fortunate to enjoy this kind of nostalgic interlude.

Amundsen returned to Newfoundland in early spring and met up with his whaling buddies to reclaim the repaired boat. A Canadian seaman named Kent invited him to hunt seals in Labrador, his homeland and a major breeding ground for harp seals. Amundsen had hunted seals in Europe, and it was actually not that hard. As an adventure lover, Amundsen was lukewarm about the idea, but could not really refuse Kent's avid hospitality.

This was the season when pregnant seals congregated on the beach to give birth and nurse their pups. Amundsen and Kent and other hunters moored their boats along a floe and entered "the ice zone" on foot. The floe was dull and gray, making a fellow like Amundsen, who came from a land of ice and snow, feel right at home. The pod of seals was like a class of carefree kids on a field trip, looking around, enjoying the scenery.

On the way to the ice, Kent had filled Amundsen in on some basic seal lore. "Baby seals are called 'whitecoats' because they are covered in snow-white fur. Two weeks later when they start developing silver fur they're 'ragged-jackets.' Another nineteen or so days after that, when they've entirely molted, they turn into silver-gray 'beaters.' Actually, when seal fur was fashionable in Europe, 'whitecoat' fur was the kind favored by the rich ladies, but now it's against the law to hunt whitecoats. The government says we can only hunt the beaters. I just don't get it! What difference does it make? Either way, it's still killing a seal!"

"But I don't have a hunting gun. You'd have to help me borrow one."

"No problem."

The weapon Kent handed him the next day wasn't a gun. It was a special kind of club called a hakapik, about the length of a baseball bat but with a metal hammerhead and hook attachment on the one end.

"How do you use it?" Amundsen asked, doubtfully.

"You bludgeon the seal's head with it. *Bang,* it's dead. A good hunter can kill a seal with a single blow, then skin it," Kent said. "Let the games begin."

When the hunting party got close to the ice floe, the alert seals started to bark like crazy and flee en masse into the water. They could not move very fast on the ice, but once they made it into the water they were out of reach, out of range. But the seal pups ran very slowly, and some couldn't swim too well, either. Some, too scared even to dive in, were soon caught by the hunters. Watching from off to one side, Amundsen discovered that killing a seal with one blow wasn't easy, even for a big guy like him, mainly because the ice floe was swaying slightly and the seals would try to dodge. Most seals took quite a few hits, screaming and cowering, their heads all bloody, before they stopped resisting, by which time they were either badly injured or out cold. When a seal submitted, the hunter would turn the club the other way around, hook the animal's neck and drag it over to the boat.

The blood would drip down from the end of the club, as if the club itself had suffered a mortal wound.

As the seals could not attack, Amundsen could not bring himself to strike. To him, whaling in the olden days meant risking a life for a life. At least that's how he and his old-school comrades still hunted whales, out of a conviction that whaling was an important part of Scandinavian culture. This was different: the seals were weak and vulnerable creatures with big eyes and pathetic cries. Amundsen just did not know how to do this. It would be okay if I used a gun, he thought. For the first time in his life Amundsen felt that for the killer to use a different tool changed the meaning of the act.

The seals were skinned right at the boat. One hunter used a razor to slice the skin, starting from the gash on the seal's head, while another helped him slowly peel off the animal's skin, just like removing a pair of too-tight jeans. Seal blood kept welling up, flowing onto the ice. Without eyelids, the seals that hadn't made it off the ice all seemed to be staring at him, glassy-eyed. Amundsen was a man long accustomed to slaughter, but this sight chilled him.

"Why not wait until they're dead before skinning them?"

"It's quicker to peel the skin off when they're alive," said Kent, sensing the doubt in Amundsen's tone. "It's true many hunters don't check whether the seal's skull has been shattered. I always make sure the seal is dead, but I don't blame those who don't. Too slow, no dough, right?"

Then a seasoned hunter called Alfie caught two male seals, cut off their penises with a knife, but did not skin them.

Amundsen asked, "Who's buying seal penises?"

"An adult's fur isn't worth anything, but its dick is. Asians eat it. They think it's like Viagra, that if they eat it they'll have the sex drive of a seal. If seals want someone to blame they should blame those fools who eat seal dicks. Actually, seals don't have a very good sex drive, at least not compared with me," Kent quipped.

Amundsen said nothing on the way back. He did not blame Kent or the other hunters or himself. He did not think his faith in whaling was misplaced. He simply sensed he'd gone hollow somewhere inside. Kent saw the qualms, the hurt and the questioning look in Amundsen's eyes, and the self-reproach he too had once felt returned. He avoided his friend's eyes and patted him on the shoulder, saying, "Life's not easy for these hunters. They just scrape by. It's the middlemen who make all the money. Sealing is the only thing some of these guys can do. It's all they have. If you don't let them seal, they'll starve."

Something wavered somewhere deep in Amundsen's heart.

Amundsen went back to Norway several months later. He ate the pickled fish Sara prepared for him. The fish eyes had been gutted, and when Amundsen stared at the eye sockets, the swiveling eyes of those seals, so juvenile, like the eyes of schoolchildren, inadvertently returned. It wasn't "killing" the seals that had struck him, but the "way" the seals were killed. People had to kill to make a living. Like it or not, that could not change, just like it wasn't right or wrong for the Inuit people to kill seals for survival. But people weren't just killing seals for survival anymore, and, more importantly, the hunters clearly had the energy and the ability to check whether the seals were still suffering, but their hearts remained unmoved. It must have taken them long years of training to turn their hearts to stone. Men who had to hunt for food did not have hearts of stone. They were full of gratitude toward the hunted animal, just as the eyes of their womenfolk and children waiting eagerly at home were full of anticipation. But the sealing he had witnessed in Labrador was nothing like that. Everything had changed.

At the dinner table, knife and fork untouched, he related his sealing experience to Sara.

"You don't think it's right? Daddy?"

"I don't know. There are still lots of seals. But there used to be lots of whales, too, and people had no sympathy for them. They saw whales as disposable. Sometimes they killed massive numbers of whales, taking only the thickest strips of blubber and not bothering with the rest. Then there came a day when there were not many whales left in the sea. Lately I've started to feel that even if people could never kill the last whale or seal, even if there were always another, we should only take what we need to live and no more."

"So you think . . ."

"Recently, I keep thinking that this isn't about the survival of a species. It's about why we're never satisfied with what we need, why we always take a bit more."

"What about the penises? Where do they sell them?" Sara was intently remembering the penises she'd seen before, two of them belonging to classmates, one to a friend she'd met working part time. She had held their penises. They were warm to the touch, and gave her the sense that there was some living thing within.

"China, Hong Kong or Taiwan, I guess," Amundsen said, stirring the soft-cooked egg on his plate. "Sara, most of my fishing buddies have not completely turned their hearts to stone. Many have no other choice. But behind them are the corporate bosses. Counting their cash in comfy chairs in nice heated rooms, they never appear on the boat or on the ice, and their hearts never bleed."

Sara would always remember the look of sadness that appeared in her father's eyes. They were brimming with pathos, an expression she had never seen before on any other animal. Amundsen's eyes were flashing, like he had an insect's compound eyes. "Sara, I renounce my identity as a seafaring hunter. The time has come. I really feel I must relinquish my former identity. I have to try to make a change, or I will feel that I have lived my life in vain."

Amundsen kept his vow. That year he sold his boat and joined an international organization opposed to the slaughter of seals. He went back to Canada and threw himself into the antisealing movement. He also took part in commercial whaling protests in Norway. From then on, Amundsen gave people a big headache on both sides of the Atlantic.

When Sara saw the sea her father had always called "*our* Pacific," a thousand feelings thronged her heart.

Although the beach had been given a "temporary" cleanup, some of the trash from the vortex would wash onto the shore every day with the tide, as if the trash island out there wanted to unite with the island on which she was standing.

Because he had a prior arrangement, Jung-hsiang was going to have an old classmate who was now teaching at the U of D host Sara and Detlef. But then he decided another friend he'd met mountain climbing might be more suitable. "His name is Dahu and he's aboriginal. When you visit Taiwan, especially the east coast, the aboriginal people make the best guides."

Immediately after crossing the bridge over the last river before Haven, they saw a dark-skinned man with a red bandana waving at them. Sara had a profoundly good feeling about this stocky fellow with a mournful expression. There was an unaffected quality in his every movement.

"Sara, Detlef, so nice to meet you! I am Dahu."

Dahu got in the driver's seat. About half an hour later they were heading down the coast by the Sea House.

The sea they saw from there was in a different state, because as far as the eye could see across the gently curving bay they could barely make out the edge of the Trash Vortex.

"How are you handling it now?"

"Well, we start by sorting the trash on the beach. Five decomposition vats have been set up in the nearby wastepaper plant. Anything that will decompose is sent there for priority processing. The valuable trash is sent elsewhere for further sorting and recycling. Any live animals we find are sent to the local university for experts to study. You'll see we've got nine work stations, but to tell you the truth we don't have enough people to man them."

"What about the local townspeople and villagers?"

"Many of them are Pangcah. The word means 'people,' and it's what the Amis aboriginal people around here prefer to call themselves. Most of the Pangcah in Haven are involved in the recovery work. I'm afraid that this is it for this stretch of coast and for the fishing ground too. Part of the sea culture of the Pangcah people has been ruined. To Han Chinese people, all the pollution means is that there's no more money to make from the sea, but for the Pangcah it's different: the sea is their ancestor, and so many of their traditional stories are about the sea. Without ancestors, what's the point of being 'Pangcah'?"

"Are you Pangcah yourself?"

"No, I'm Bunun," Dahu said. "The word *bunun* means that we are the true 'people.'"

Sara completely understood. Every people in the world, in the beginning, felt that they were the only "true people."

For dinner they went to Dahu's house. There they met a girl and a woman. The girl, Umav—what a charming name!—was Dahu's daughter. But he only introduced the woman by name without indicating whether she was his wife. Sara felt that she seemed not to be. The relationship between Hafay and Dahu seemed like what was between her and Detlef, just not exactly. It was like an article without an explicit thesis. She was told that the dinner was made mainly with the wild vegetables that the Pangcah people often ate. But there wasn't any seafood. Umav and Hafay could not speak English, so Dahu did most of the talking.

"There's seafood in almost everything we eat, but there isn't any seafood for now. You know how it is."

"No worries. It's a wonderful, lavish feast! And when you think about it, who knows if there'll ever be seafood again? Maybe now's the time to go veg," Detlef said, laughing, and the others groaned and laughed along with him.

This island has already started to redeem itself, Sara thought.

# 25. The Mountain Path

Alice woke up in the night and hiked down the mountain with her flashlight. It was still drizzling. This was the eighteenth straight day of rain on the east coast. Apparently, some sections of road and railway in Tai-tung had been swamped by the sea, and some coastal villages in Ping-tung, the ones that suffered the most subsidence, had been evacuated.

The path wasn't that easy to make out, but Alice was moving right along. She was growing less afraid of the mountain as she became more familiar with every little path she could take to get down, and with the rate of growth of every plant, every clump of grass along the way. So this was what a mountain was like, the same as a person: the more you know, the less you fear. But even so, you still never know what it's thinking. And just like you never know what a person is going to do next, you never know what a mountain is going to do next, Alice thought.

Alice had mixed feelings when she reached the coast and stood at the shore, once so familiar but now so strange. Since this stretch of coastline was relatively populous, the preliminary cleanup had been finished, finally. But seawater does not stay in one place; the trash island was spread out over an expanse of sea larger than Taiwan itself, so that when the second wave washed in it crammed trash into every discernible gap. The Sea House was now about fifty meters from the high water line, when the water reached all the way up to the edge of the road and surrounded the house with debris. Now the tide would begin to ebb. Alice took off her T-shirt and put it in a waterproof bag, then put on her swimsuit and waded down the slope of the road, which hadn't subsided, at least not yet.

At first, the water only reached her calves, but soon it was too deep to stand and she stepped into nothing. Her body tensed up for a moment in the frigid water, then relaxed.

In the darkness the seawater was inky black. She'd never seen it this way before. The lights from the streetlamps danced on the waves like flashing threads weaving themselves into something people did not yet understand. Alice put on a diving mask, strapped on a mini Aqua-Lung and plunged. In the glare of her headlamp she saw myriad plastic objects floating in various poses, like the unknown organisms of an alien world.

Alice saw that the sea was two thirds of the way up the second floor when she swam near the Sea House. All the windows were broken, and a huge chunk of one wall had collapsed, along with most of the main wing. She could now see the situation inside the house from underwater. She "dove" in through an opening, found her room by memory and opened the door. It was a bit heavy due to the water pressure, but fortunately there was a hole at the base and she could still push it open. She swam down the hallway, finding Toto's door ajar. His room was full of trash swept in by the tide, and his things had been washed out into the hallway or were hidden among the debris. She looked up and there it was, the mountain map Toto and Thom had drawn on the ceiling, same as always. But now Alice saw another route she hadn't known about until now.

All this time, Alice had been trying to get Dahu to tell her where he'd found Thom's body, but Dahu refused. Perhaps he had some sort of understanding with the police, because they wouldn't say much, either, only the name of the mountain. They were evasive, claiming that the only person who knew the precise location was the one who discovered the body.

"It wasn't us who carried him down," said a fat cop who was handling the case.

When Thom and Toto first went missing Alice desperately wanted the rescue team to take her up. That was how she found out which route Thom had registered. But obviously Dahu had found the body along a different route, and though the two mountains were connected, Thom still didn't have the permit to climb that other mountain. So why did he die there?

Then, one day, when Alice was sitting in the hut writing, she suddenly remembered the ceiling in Toto's room.

Now she was looking up at the map on that very ceiling. At first she was a bit lost, but having studied a lot of maps lately she quickly found the route. As she had suspected, Thom, maybe together with Toto, had conspired an alternate route without her knowing. They didn't follow the route they'd registered at the backcountry office, the route along which the rescue team had naively searched. Actually, they took the route on the ceiling. Alice kept looking at the map, until she seemed to see a gate, a path, the sky, rocks, the source of a tiny spring, and rain.

Seawater. A mountain path.

The seawater was thick like sleep, and when Alice stepped out of it onto the shore she felt like a lonely whale that had snuck on shore. Her heart was broken like glass and sealed like a dead clam.

The next evening, Alice used a 3D projector to shine a map of the earth onto a piece of white paper stuck on the outside wall of the hunting hut. She told Atile'i, "This is called a 'map.' The place we live, Taiwan, or any place, can be drawn on a map like this, and you can use a map to tell other people how to get somewhere. So when you're somewhere unfamiliar you can still find the way." Alice saw confusion in Atile'i's eyes and added, "If you know how to read a map."

Alice used a laser pointer to indicate the position of Taiwan on the map and said, "This's the island we're on now. Can you point to the island where you come from? Wayo Wayo?" Atile'i smiled sadly.

"No, the earth, here." Atile'i pointed at the ground, grasped a clump of dirt, and said, "Not, there."

"Atile'i, you don't understand. The map is this earth of ours shrunk down and drawn on a piece of paper. See, the whole world has been shrunk down and shone onto this piece of paper." Alice felt there was something wrong with her explanation, but that was no big deal as Atile'i could not fully understand what she was saying in any case.

"The sea can also become a map?"

"I guess so. There are nautical maps." Alice pointed at a spot in the South Pacific and said, "I guess that Wayo Wayo is somewhere around here."

Alice shone the next map, this one a large-scale map of Taiwan's Central Mountain Range, showing contour lines and tortuous climbing routes. On it was a red route, which she had drawn from memory. It was the route on the ceiling, the path through the mountains that Thom and Toto had actually taken.

"We are here, and I want to go here. Do you understand? I want to go here." Alice kept tracing the route with the laser pointer until Atile'i nodded to show he understood.

"Are you," Alice pointed at Atile'i, "willing to go there with me? Come with me."

"Is it far?"

"It's not close, I don't think." Suddenly a giant silkworm moth flew over and stopped on the map, like a mark, or like a symbol, like an interjection. It opened the eyes on its wings and stared at her.

"Her?" Atile'i pointed at Ohiyo.

"Ohiyo will wait for me to come back, won't you, Ohiyo? You'll be here, waiting for us to return, right around here? Or you want to go stay with Dahu?" Ohiyo purred sweetly several times, to voice her protest. Obviously she wanted to be free to hang out in the mountains all by herself.

Alice had spent quite some time at the library going through all the climbing records for this route. She bought all the gear she thought she'd need, and got a pack for Atile'i and another tent. It wasn't like the one Atile'i had been sleeping in; it was a new design, superlight and ultradry. With its streamlined shape and airflow system, an invisible air current would form over the tent, reducing the impact of rain on the roof and keeping the inside dry. She wanted Atile'i to go with her partly because she didn't know who to send him to, but also because she knew she would have to rely on this kid to survive in the mountains. She selfishly assumed that since he'd evaded all the deathtraps on the ocean, he could probably help her get to the place marked in red on the map.

The red dot marked a lofty precipice. The folks at the professional alpine association said it was a route few people would take, because the only interesting thing on it was a huge cliff that appeared after the big quake. Newly formed, it was none too stable and might be dangerous. It wasn't like this was a traverse you'd have to take through the area; there wasn't even a trig point on the summit.

"Ma'am, if you're not going rock climbing, you'd have no reason to go there," a coach at the climbing club said.

Alice chose a day in the midst of about the only sunny spell they would likely enjoy in the next three months to set out. The weather forecast was for five or six days of fair skies, if they were lucky.

Alice set out toward the trail with Atile'i in tow. She deliberately took a detour that was not drawn on the map. She'd heard it would allow them to bypass the backcountry checkpoint. It went by an aboriginal village and a power plant along the left-hand side of the riverbed. It was a Sakizaya community that had been in the news quite often in the past few years. The Sakizaya villagers had been working on an eco-cultural tourism project, and everything was on the right track until a series of landslides forced them to suspend operations. But solo climbers still preferred this route up the river valley, which led into the Central Mountain Range.

The next day they were already deep in the mountains. The path traversed gorges and sheer drops, typically precipitous terrain for the island's canyon-cut eastern flank. Though Atile'i had been living with Alice all that time in the hunting hut, this was the first time he had really witnessed the mountains in this way. Several times, while observing the changing alpine mistscapes, he knelt down and placed his head on the ground and made the special Wayo Wayoan hand gesture that symbolized the adoration of the earth.

The pair kept walking at dawn of the third day when clouds blew in and it started raining in the shadow of the mountain. Soon the rain obscured the lie of the mountain, giving them the momentary impression they were on a modest suburban hill. As the sun's rays grew stronger in the afternoon, the peaks in the distance became hazily visible again, until the light penetrated the clouds and revealed the ridges between the peaks. Yet at lower altitudes fog and mist still concealed the valley, giving the set of summits in the distance the guise of an island floating in an ethereal sea of clouds. At the sight of this vista, Atile'i suddenly fell in love with the island, just like he had always loved Wayo Wayo.

"Mountains?" he asked, pointing in the distance.

"Yes."

"So many?"

"Yes."

"God is there?"

"What?"

"God is there?"

Is God there? Some Taiwan aboriginal myths involving mountains came to Alice's mind. The first Atayal ancestor was supposedly born on Mount Dabajian. The Tsou had fled to Jade Mountain after the Deluge. And the Bunun, too, had their own Holy Mountain. Almost all the tribes did. But was a holy mountain a god? Alice would rather describe it as a source of sustenance and as a refuge. The mountains had no particular place in the folk religion of her ancestors, the Han people of Taiwan, but belief in the communal Earth God was ubiquitous. So in a certain sense, at a certain point of time, the mountains had, loosely speaking, been "gods." Alice was reminded of slogans people had made up in response to the rash of land-slides that had been striking whenever a typhoon hit, sometimes burying whole aboriginal villages, sometimes swallowing vehicles, sometimes merely knocking roads out and leaving entire villages isolated. There'd been calls for a return to nature and a renewed respect for nature and even an appeal to "worship the mountain god again." But maybe it was already too late. Even if once the mountains had been divine, all the gods would have departed by now, Alice thought.

"God was there, but not anymore."

"God is there, in Wayo Wayo's sea. The mountain is small, but God is also there," Atile'i solemnly declared.

Unlike Kabang, Yayaku, the Wayo Wayoan mountain god, was a chas-tised deity. Wayo Wayoans believed that there were many other gods who were not quite as mighty as Kabang but who were in charge of fate and destiny, each in His own domain. The reason Yayaku had been punished was that one day when Kabang resolved to wipe out a certain kind of whale that had given offense, Yayaku astonishingly extended the hand of mercy. He created a kind of kelp that grew as high as a mountain, let those peerless whales hide inside, and exhorted them not to come out until after Kabang had calmed down. But Kabang finally found them when a playful whale calf snuck out of the seaweed grove. Kabang quaked with anger and unleashed His vengeance upon Yayaku. Yet at the same time, Kabang had realized it would be rash and improper to exterminate a kind of living creature, and thereupon He rescinded His fatal decree.

But Kabang was still contemplating how He should punish Yayaku, at once to put the minor god in his place and boost His own prestige. Kabang had given Wayo Wayo to the people, but over time the rocks on the island would become sand, and the sand would be blown away by the wind and carried away by the sea and the island would get smaller and smaller. Thus, Kabang resolved to oblige Yayaku to take on the form of a little bird and the quotidian task of collecting the grains of sand that blew away in the wind or floated away in the sea and replenishing the island with them. Because the waves never rested and the wind never tired, Yayaku never enjoyed a moment of respite. But Yayaku was industrious and managed, when the gods of sea and wind were not exerting themselves quite so much, to pile up a mountain. In possession of this mountain, the islanders could cut down a certain number of trees without fearing that Wayo Wayo might someday disappear. This was why the islanders worshiped Yayaku as the Mountain God.

"So your mountain god is a bird?"

"Yes."

"Wouldn't it just be too cute to have a little bird as the mountain god," Alice thought aloud, gazing at the youth standing before her. She couldn't fully understand him, but there was more to what he was saying than just the words. His expressions, gestures, tones and dynamics made him a natural storyteller. His body had been milled, polished, scarfed and forged, as if by magic, a magic that would make people believe that any story he might tell, no matter how absurd, bizarre and unbelievable it might seem, must have actually happened in real life.

"Adorable? No, Yayaku has no feeling. He is cold."

They kept finding their way, and at dawn on the fourth day, they could see some peaks in the distance that Alice recognized from the map. She knew they were approaching the "forest" on the map. But by this time Alice was starting to show fatigue, so they took even more frequent breaks. Alice taught Atile'i how to read a map while they were resting. The key concept, which Atile'i soon grasped, was the use of a sign to stand for some natural feature. The next step was determining orientation, allowing the mind to match the observed landscape and its corresponding representation on the map. Atile'i's ability in this respect greatly exceeded Alice's. The only thing he could not get was proportion. The ocean was clearly vast. How could such a small image serve as a surrogate?

They made a fire to cook a meal. Alice had brought many vacuum food packs, which you could just heat up and eat. This evening they had spaghetti with pesto sauce and hot coffee. Atile'i had gradually gotten used to the food the Taiwanese islanders ate.

"So, what did you eat most often at sea?" Alice asked.

"Fish."

"How'd you catch them?"

"I used things on Gesi Gesi to make a spear gun, and oyster shells as hooks."

"You ate them raw?"

"What?"

"You didn't use fire?"

"Fire? No."

"No fire. Oh, right, it would be too difficult to make a fire on the ocean. What about writing? Do the people of Wayo Wayo have writing?"

"Writing? Like this?"

"Yeah."

"Writing, we have not. The Earth Sage says, speech is everything."

"Too bad you don't have writing. There are many things that can only be expressed using the written word."

"No need. Wayo Wayo has no writing, but we can express things all the same."

"But how can you compose poems without writing?" Atile'i didn't answer, having failed to understand.

"What do you call the moon again?"

"*Nalusa.*"

"Oh, *kaga mi yiwa Nalusa,*" Alice said in Wayo Wayoan.

"Tonight there is a moon," Atile'i translated into Mandarin.

"Ah, indeed, your Mandarin is much improved, tonight there is a moon. And what's the sun again?"

"*Yigasa.*"

"*Yigasa,*" Alice repeated.

"*Yigasa* shines with its own light, which *Nalusa* borrows to be bright," said Atile'i, reciting the lyrics of a Wayo Wayoan nursery rhyme.

"*Yigasa* shines with its own light, which *Nalusa* borrows to be bright," Alice said. "*Aiya,* that's poetry." But Atile'i still didn't understand what poetry meant.

That evening, shortly after the two of them had gone to sleep, Atile'i woke up, immediately pulled Alice over, covered her mouth to signal silence, and motioned for her to leave via the rear opening. Atile'i sensed that something was out there, but Alice saw nothing except an expanse of silent gloom. Alice's blood and heartbeat were still sluggish, and because she had not slept enough her legs were still in a dreamland. Atile'i on the other hand was preternaturally alert. He gazed intently into the darkness.

Soon, in the shadows of the trees, he made out a looming form. It seemed to hesitate but was actually resolute. When it moved close to the tent, Alice felt as if a bucket of water had been dumped on her head. Now she was completely awake.

"Bear!"

The bear looked over toward the voice. It stood up on its hind legs like a man and craned its neck to catch the scent, revealing the pattern on its chest, like a crescent moon in the vast night sky of its body. Attracted by the smells, it hesitated before roughly "opening" the tent, spilling their food out on the ground. Then it tasted every item on the menu.

Alice and Atile'i tried to hold their breath. Alice wanted to leave while she still had the chance, but Atile'i felt they should stay put and kept a tight hold on Alice. Though it made Atile'i nervous, this bear before him was a magnificent, alert and tenacious animal, as beautiful as all the animals he had ever seen. Wayo Wayo did not have such animals, not even close. Atile'i was spellbound.

With dawn approaching, the bear stood up again, stomped on the tent, crushing it, and extended its snout and sniffed, looking much taller than a grown man. Alice was clasping Atile'i's hand, her hands cold as dew. The bear slowly retreated into the forest, and the forest opened up again, readmitting the shadow into its fold.

The bear hadn't made a sound, had given neither provocation nor pursuit. It had just rummaged around for things it wanted and returned to the forest. But Alice and Atile'i both seemed to have died and come back to life. They had scented something ancient, like the mountain itself but somehow not quite the same. Something divine. If it had wanted to, it could have taken their lives away.

Only now did Atile'i slowly turn to Alice and say, with the utmost care: "Clearly, God is there!"

# 26. The Man with the Compound Eyes II

When the man wakes up he doesn't feel the pain he would have expected. He's just had a dream in which he tried on a night of absolute night to "blind climb" his way down the mountain wall. Because all was darkness he had to use every cell in his skin to feel the texture of the cliff. It felt just like the first time he entered his wife's body. Both of them had experienced a subtle trembling, as if they were replenishing something in one another's souls.

Two-thirds of the way down, as a result of overexertion, his nails felt sore, his toes numb, and his eyes were stinging with sweat because he was not wearing a headband. But the more physically ill, the more intense the mental thrill—a paradox those who have never engaged in this kind of activity cannot understand. The man breathed deeply until little by little confidence returned to his fingertips.

But in the moment it did, his fingers parted from the face of the cliff. It was as if he suddenly switched perspectives and saw himself falling, getting smaller and smaller. The clouds and constellations dispersed, everything around him dissolved into darkness, and all that remained was void.

It was a dream, after all. Careful not to make a sound, the man walks out of the tent to the edge of the cliff. The cliff is not as absolutely dark as it was in the dream. But leaves, backs of tree frogs, bent stems and droplets of water in leafy hollows . . . are all gleaming in the moonlight, making the cliff appear darker than it actually is.

Why not try climbing down? No, my boy is in the tent. What if something happens?

Why not give it a try? No, I can't.

A blind climb? I can't!

Why not try it barehanded, with no gear?

These questions fascinate him, stirring the blood in his veins. At some point the man gets up, fastens the chalk bag to his waist, changes into his rock-climbing shoes, and starts slowly climbing down the rock he sees in front of him. All inhibitions have been overcome; nothing can stop him now.

In the darkness, the cliff is like a knife and a shadow, hard to grasp. The man has strained his senses and used up almost all his strength, only managing to get five meters down. It is still not too late to go back up. But the man does not go back . . . or, one should say, he doesn't go back up. He continues his descent, first feeling around with the tip of his toes, and then shifting his weight when he finds a new foothold. He tries to maintain three points of contact and to avoid overburdening his shoulders and fingers on either side. If you could see him in the darkness you would exclaim, What a superb climber! He is bold and focused, his body consummately trained and possessing a simian aplomb.

Right then, the man hears someone else on the cliff, and not that far away.

A climber can hear the faintest of sounds when he concentrates his attention. Everything is audible: fingers thrusting into the muck, fingertips slipping over moss. If there's food digesting in his gut or force being sent to his toetips he can hear it. But at this particular moment the man hears something else, the sound of breathing. Clearly there is another climber up there.

Another person blind climbing? On the same cliff?

That sound stokes his competitive streak. Unconsciously, his movements quicken. It is like a test of strength between the two men in the darkness.

The other makes haste, too, and his every move is conveyed through the rhythm of his breathing and the occasional faint rustling of his clothes. Neither needs to be told which of them is one step ahead, which of them is the swifter at finding the next toehold.

That's when the man's dreamscape reappears.

In a moment of carelessness, his foot slips and his movements suddenly accelerate. The force of the fall pulls his left hand away from the wall for a hundredth of a second. With the man's usual reaction speed, he should have enough time to grab hold of the rock again, but just at that moment, very unfortunately, something like an enormous beetle flies right into the bridge of his nose, momentarily dazing him and sapping his strength for a hundredth of a second. He starts falling. The clouds and constellations disperse, everything around him dissolves into darkness, and all that remains is void.

His shattered helmet lies on the ground. The pain is excruciating, as if every bone in his body has been snapped. This is not a dream. An irksome rain begins to fall. It should be falling on the grass where he is lying, but somehow it sounds as if it's falling into an abyssal lake.

He can only get his eyes halfway open, and, blurry-eyed, all he can see is a shadow kneeling by his side. The shadow says, "Broken, every bone." The man can't tell from his voice whether he is the blind climber just now, but from his smell there is no doubt about it.

"Am I dead?"

"Pretty much. Fall in a place like this and you'll be dead before anyone finds you."

This is absurd. It does not sound like the man has any intention of saving him.

"Can you help me?"

"No, I can't help anyone," comes the reply, impassive, unwavering, unhesitating.

In spite of his physical pain, the man is quite conscious, and his vision gradually clears. He notices his counterpart is looking at him, but when their eyes meet it is less like he is looking at someone else and more like he is looking at himself. He closes his eyes again but finds himself haunted by the other's eyes. What amazing eyes the fellow has, as if innumerable tiny ponds have converged into an immense lake.

How come it looks like he has compound eyes? How could a person have compound eyes? Am I seeing things? the man thinks to himself. The man with the compound eyes has no intention to help or leave. He is just looking at the man quietly.

Then, for some reason, drowsiness overwhelms him. He starts to yawn. At first he yawns once every half a minute, then once every fifteen seconds, then ten, then five, until he is yawning nonstop, with tears in his eyes. Then he passes out.

Later he wakes, not knowing how much time has passed. He still feels sore all over, but is now actually able to sit up, and then stand. He can move without difficulty, except that any time he moves an injured part of his body he feels a heart-wrenching agony. It is as if all that remains of this body of his is a leaden despair. Noticing that the man with the compound eyes is still there, he tries asking for help one more time.

"Doesn't matter if you don't save me, but my son is up there, on top of the cliff. I beg you, please save him."

"I can't save anyone," replies the man, impassive, unwavering, unhesitating. "Not to mention that there's nobody up there to save."

"Nonsense! My son is up there! I don't care who you are, but please, *please*, I'm begging you, you've got to do something!" The man doesn't know where he found the strength to shout.

"You know very well . . ." the man says, his innumerable ommatidia flickering, his compound eyes like an undertow that would suck you in, drag you down and drown you, ". . . there's nobody up there, *at all*. Nobody *at all*."

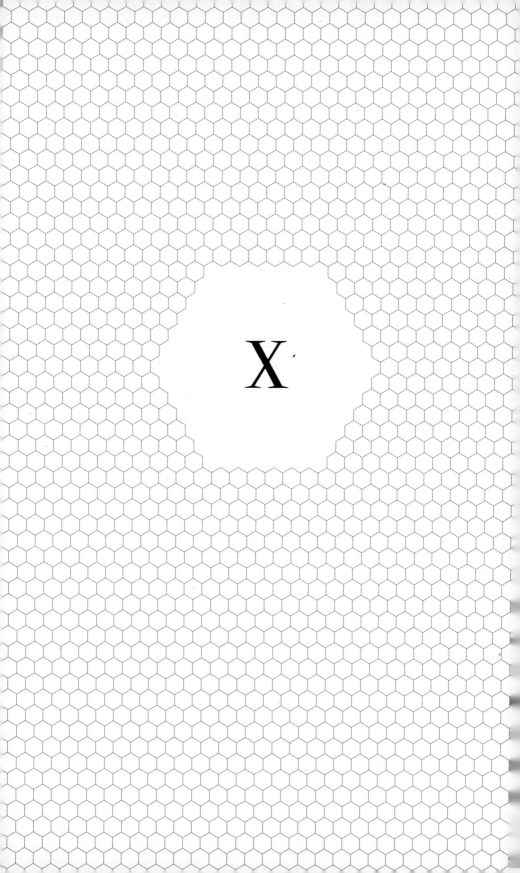

X

# 27. The Forest Cave

A dinner with too much millet wine had put them all in a mood of disoriented rapture. So when Umav suggested they go spend the night in the Forest Church, everyone agreed it was a great idea, including Detlef and Sara, who hadn't understood a word.

Standing in front of Heaven's Gate, a name Anu had given to the two massive weeping fig trees at the entrance to the Forest Church, everyone was shining his or her flashlight up and down the trees from various angles and listening to an intricate symphony, of the breeze blowing through the grove, owls hooting in the trees, muntjacs calling from mountains over yonder, insects chirping nigh, and Stone and Moon barking from time to time. Detlef and Sara still didn't know what was going on. Having no idea of the Forest Church, they'd assumed this would be a light evening stroll, not a hike through a primeval forest.

Then Anu, who'd looked drunk to begin with, walked to the front of the group, faced the "House of the Ancestors" to the one side of Heaven's Gate and began performing a libation. People who don't understand Bununese would on first hearing think it sounds like pieces of wood knocking together. It is a solid, seemingly rooted, arboreal language. His prayer complete, Anu took out the wine flask and shot glass he carried at the hip, poured the wine into the glass and sprinkled it on the ground. Then he poured another glass and passed it around so each could say a prayer in his or her own language and take a tiny sip of the wine. Dahu held Umav's hand and they recited a Bunun prayer. Hafay prayed in Pangcah, Detlef in German, and Sara in Norwegian.

"No problem, the forest can understand what everyone's saying," Anu said, immediately returning to his usual jocular self and lightening the somewhat solemn atmosphere a bit.

"There might be big brothers and sisters here, so you need to poke the grass with a stick as you go along," said Anu, his voice softening. "A big brother or sister is a poisonous snake. We mustn't just say 'snake.' That would be disrespectful." Then he turned his voice back up to its original volume and said, "Everyone follow me. Don't shine your flashlight in people's eyes, and listen to the footsteps of the person ahead." Dahu translated Anu's words into English for Detlef and Sara.

Anu took everyone down his favorite hunting path. Over ten years before a developer had wanted to buy the land and build a columbarium on it. To protect a forest in which the Bunun had always hunted, Anu tried getting a bank loan to buy the land. He got more than he bargained for. He had no head for money management and was soon drowning in debt. There were a few times when he was ready to give up and sell, but fortunately later on he got support from some aboriginal villagers and Han Chinese friends and was able to make ends meet. The past few years the forest had become a place for tourists to experience Bunun culture. Several years before, Anu's youngest son Lian had gone into the forest to check the village water supply, and maybe because he forgot to pray to the ancestral spirits or because his prayers were not pious enough, a fig branch that had cracked in a typhoon came crashing down just as poor Lian was passing by. Lian was no longer breathing by the time he was discovered that evening. Long estranged from his wife, raising his sons alone, Anu would go into the forest every day to seek solace. Anu did not blame the forest. It was only doing its duty, by growing, shedding leaves, dying, or by fatally crushing a Bunun youth who just happened to be walking underneath.

So Anu had a peculiar feeling whenever he regarded this particular stand of fig, phoebe and autumn maple trees. It was not something he could tell the people around him about. He always imagined that one of the aerial roots hanging down from one of the weeping figs was his son's avatar, a notion that fortified his resolution to guard the forest. When he took visitors on eco-cultural tours here, he would ask them to experience the forest one sense at a time. They would close their eyes and touch a tree root, lean on the tree and smell a wild mushroom, taste prickly ash leaves, and listen to a certain birdcall to judge how far away it was. It was as if by getting these people to do these things, at least a few of them would be able to smell, touch, hear or sense his son's spirit. To him, in some form or other, Lian was still alive.

He led the group before a giant boulder in the crushing embrace of a gnarled old tree that had perched on top of it, wrapping its twisted roots around it. Underneath the rock was a small cave where Bunun hunters waited out the rain. Dahu was himself a guide, and Hafay and Umav had been there many times. Anu said, "The cave knows everyone here but our guests." He wanted Detlef and Sara to go in and let the cave "get to know them."

There was space for two grown-ups in the cave, though for westerners of Detlef and Sara's height it was quite a squeeze. Dahu retold his joke about how being over 170 cm tall was a disability among the Bunun, adding that Detlef, who was close to 190 cm, must be severely height challenged. A man of this height would tend to get tripped or tied up by the vines and creepers as he runs through the forest, seriously limiting his pace.

"Actually, there's caves like this everywhere in the forest, some in rocks, some formed by rainstorms and rockslides. But don't ever take shelter in caves in trees and rocks above a certain altitude. Those caves tend to be bear dens. If the bear happens to come back and finds an uninvited guest, it'll catch you," Anu said, "and take you to the police station."

After this burst of banter, Anu let them rest there for the time it takes to have half a cigarette, then guided them to another place where he had tied a rope up a huge fig tree to a height of about two and a half stories. The forest floor was slippery from all the recent rain, and Anu kept reminding everyone to be a bit more careful.

Anu quite liked these two unassuming foreigners. Detlef had an academic background, but he didn't act like a big professor who would throw his weight around. He was like a worldly wise elder, while Sara was a person with the courage to try new things. Anu knew he'd have no trouble getting along with Sara from the moment she downed the first glass of millet wine he poured for her.

"Anyone who drinks his wine in one gulp, no matter how it tastes, is probably a friend," Anu's father had told him once when he was young.

There were no lights on anywhere nearby. Now Anu wanted the two of them to experience what it was like to travel the forest by night, so he advised everyone to turn off his flashlight and follow the person in front by holding hands or listening for the sound of breathing.

Which was why no one noticed when Hafay, who was last in line, stayed behind and ducked into the cave under the rock.

Hafay's heart was pounding the first time Umav brought her to the Forest Church. She felt she'd finally found a vessel that could contain her, a shell in which she could hide like a hermit crab. From then on, when no one was watching, Hafay would go into the forest by herself and crawl into the cave and rest like a bear in hibernation, thinking of nothing at all.

Though she was aboriginal, Hafay had pretty much spent her whole life in the city, and even after returning to the east coast she still passed most of her time in Haven. When she opened the Seventh Sisid, Pangcah friends invited her to join her age set, participate in the local Pangcah tribal order, and live there with them. But after taking part in a few age set activities, she still didn't feel like she fit in, no matter how friendly the people were, even when she was dancing. Sometimes she would run into former customers. So, to avoid embarrassment, Hafay started to withdraw from tribal village life.

But the first time she set foot in the Forest Church, the damp air and the smells of the roots and the grass made her feel that she was in her element. She liked the way the weeping figs survived by growing aerial roots that went down, down, down until they reunited with the earth and helped prop up the parent tree. She liked the scarred old trees even more. A split in the bark was sealed and healed by the tree's own sap. As if all pain would pass.

If Ina were still alive she would like it here.

Ina died because she just would not take her girlfriends' advice. After her life settled down again, Ina fell in love with another customer, assuming every guy was like Old Liao, who had loved her in his own way. Hafay did not get too worked up when she finally got the call from the madam at the massage parlor, maybe because she had already foreseen Ina's death when Ina dove into the creek and finally found Old Liao's body. Except this time Ina ended up dying underwater, as she had countless times in Hafay's dreams. The black flower of Ina's long hair bloomed forever, and Ina would never float back up again.

The girls in the massage parlor said that Ina had gone out with Big Tom. Nobody knew who Big Tom was, except that he was a new guy Ina was seeing. And nobody knew how or why she'd died. Only one thing was certain, that the money in Ina's account had all been withdrawn, and by Ina herself, so that the police had no leads, no way of pressing the investigation. Luckily Ina had opened another account for Hafay, so her life did not have to start from zero.

Now, under cover of darkness, hiding out for the time being in the cave, Hafay felt so much better. It was dark in here but not like in the little rooms in the massage parlor. This small cave insulated you from the sound outside, so when you first came in you heard your own heart beating as well as a slight ringing in your ears. Hafay had drunk quite a bit tonight, and she just needed to be by herself in the cave for a little while, for a brief respite from the rain.

Dahu noticed Hafay was not with the group when he was helping everyone rope climb up that humungous weeping fig. But he guessed she had gone into the cave for some alone time, something he often did himself. That cave was inviting. It made you want to crawl in and see what it was like. He decided to keep quiet so as not to disturb her. Whatever the forest was doing to her he did not need to interfere.

Anu was telling the two foreigners the tale of the *Vavakalun.* Over the past two decades he had told this story a thousand times at least. But every time Anu tried to tell it for the first time.

"In the old times, the Bunun people used to choose big rocks and trees as landmarks. One time the ancestors chose a big tree as a boundary marker. A while later they looked and thought, Hey, that's strange, that marker appears to have moved. And it doesn't look quite the same as it did before. Well, as soon as they paid attention they discovered that when this kind of fig tree is mature it dangles its aerial roots all the way down to the ground. Sometimes the parent tree dies but the aerial root survives and becomes a new tree. When it's been too long since the previous visit, the tribespeople might mistake the new tree for the old one. That's why we call it *Vavakalun*, meaning a walking tree."

Anu asked Detlef and Sara to touch the roots to see if they could "hear the tree sucking water out of the ground or dividing into two." They caressed the roots very obligingly. This kind of tree, with its twisting, branching roots, was totally new to them, because it was a species seldom seen in northern countries.

There in the darkness, feeling the root system of the tree on the boulder, Detlef had realized that one day the roots would crack the rock. There should be some kind of noise when the roots got inside the rock, and when it was finally split asunder there might be an earsplitting sound. Of course, as an engineer, Detlef had confidence in his own expertise, but he had never been so impressed as he was now by what the power of nature, so much greater than his own, was capable of. In this case, the forces involved were beyond calculation. Including the force exerted by the leaf-cutter ant that had just crawled onto the back of his hand.

Detlef searched in the darkness, and at some moment his eyes found hers and they gazed at one another a brief while.

The hike had not been that strenuous, but actually they'd been walking down a shadowy hunting path through a miniature tropical wilderness. Detlef had been noticing myriad tiny sounds along the way. He often said that he wasn't really good at anything, except that he had really good hearing. In this respect he had a gift. He had grown up in a cultivated family. His father was a business manager, his mother a middle-school teacher, and he, an only child, had always been academically inclined. With his exceptionally keen hearing, his favorite activity as a boy was to find something apparently silent and try to "dig" by pressing his ear close to it, trying to hear the subtle sound it was actually making. One time, late at night, he stole out into the garden and dug up an anthill in the flower patch until he was standing in a pit two meters deep. His parents were astonished when they got up the next morning and found a big hole in the garden and Detlef covered in dirt. But they did not scold him, they even let him keep digging wherever he wanted. He got in the habit of testing the terrain wherever he went, crouching down and touching the ground, or propping himself against a rocky outcrop.

Detlef remembered at nineteen years of age visiting a technical academy where he'd seen a model of Charles Wilson's Patented Stone-Cutting Machine. He was enthralled. Intimating power, it was a kind of metaphor for getting to the hearts of various things. To him, it was the ideal machine. Henceforth he took every course he could in geology and mechanics. For him, these two fields of knowledge had a single method and the same aim: "comprehend principles, overcome obstacles, bore to the core."

Detlef made a name for himself by making improvements to the TBM design. He had achieved some stature in the industry. But nothing in his entire career had made a deeper impression on him than the experience he'd had here on this island over twenty years before.

Everyone in that cave of a tunnel heard it. But what was that sound? He had been grasping at an answer all this time, but it eluded him still. Only after meeting Sara did he begin to think that maybe, just maybe he did not have to drill all the way through when there was a sound he did not understand, that some sounds could only exist if they were left alone, undrilled, intact.

And just now when he and Sara had squeezed into that small rock cave, his shoulder touching hers, it was like being in a dream. He felt he could hear, through the wall at the end of this little cave, the sound of the whole mountain.

Not surprisingly, the sound that a living forest or mountain makes is different from the sound of an eviscerated mountain. Detlef reached out and held Sara's hand, wanting to convey this thought to her.

\* \* \*

Sara was now feeling the roots of the tree with her other hand, wondering whether her widely traveled father had ever seen a tropical forest like this. On that trip he'd taken to the Mississippi, had he gone downstream into the warm South and encountered trees there like the one she was now seeing?

Actually, Sara never even got the chance to see her father's body. His friends had already cremated "their Amundsen" by the time she was informed of his death. He had died in his favorite place—on the ice—but in Canada not in Norway.

Sara could not say she had not begrudged Amundsen his absences. At least when she was an adolescent, she thought for the longest time that he loved the sea, the fish, the whales and, later on, even the seals more than he loved her. Her mother's departure had thrown Sara into a man's world, a world of gory slaughter and relentless pursuit that she always regarded with disgust. And when she found it hard getting accustomed to life at sea he never gave her a word of comfort, just let the sea torment her. The sea had separated her from her mother, and even if Sara had wanted to go looking for her, there was no easy way for her to get back to land. The only way she could punish her father was by looking away whenever he spoke to her, looking toward the sea instead.

Her father finally permitted her to start a life on land when she was fifteen, and from then on they lived separate lives, one at sea and the other on shore. He was always away, while she worked nonstop in her seaside lab learning science and getting to know a freedom she'd never enjoyed out on the open ocean. When she went into oceanography, she realized she understood the sea way better than her classmates. What the professors taught in class was just a way of talking about what she had lived through, and a way for her to revisit a girlhood spent at sea. Sometimes, pondering some issue in marine ecology, Sara could almost hear her father haranguing her from the ship's railing.

He would wire money into her account regularly, but hardly ever sent even a simple postcard. Soon after Sara obtained her Ph.D. she got a repu- tation for being fierce. When most professors were cozying up to the government, she was the "spear of knowledge" for protest organizations.

She was always able to pierce the criminal subterfuges of state agencies or capitalists hiding behind the letter of environmental protection regulations or pseudoknowledge, no matter what the issue: the exploitation of polar oil or methane ice or excessive whaling in the name of research. The literature reviews she did were so thorough that the scientists defending the capitalists always got beaten back, unable to hold their own against her. While most people described Sara as "fierce," only she knew about the emotional knots a traumatic childhood had tied in her soul.

When Sara's father was found, the hunters initially mistook him for a flayed beater. Obviously, he had been battered to death with a hakapik. His head had sustained multiple blows, leaving his face almost unrecognizable. All his teeth had been knocked out. As he was not found until several days after the fact, his arms and abdomen had been eaten away. Maybe the seals had come on shore and divvied him up. They didn't even leave his reproductive organs.

Amundsen himself was known for his fierceness in the environmental protection movement in his later years. He once blocked a Japanese whaling boat disguised as a scientific research vessel in the Antarctic for seven days, until his own craft got rammed so badly it lost propulsion. He had, quite illegally, pointed a gun at a group of sealers until they retreated. He spent the entire winter on the ice guarding the seals, until he was arrested and charged with criminal intimidation. His hair went completely white; his face, scoured by ice and snow, was covered in scars, while his beard, covered in salt crystals, was hard as baleen. Heart disease often made him wince, and people who saw him knit his brows thought he was unhappy. Only Amundsen knew that he had never felt more contented in his entire life than he did now.

His friends made a special point of presenting funeral invitations to minke whales, fin whales, sei whales, codfish and harp seals. None of them could come, of course, but his daughter Sara did attend the memorial service. A fellow she called Uncle Hank, an old friend of her father's, brought Sara his personal effects: a hunting gun, a harpoon, a pair of binoculars and the birthday presents he never remembered to send in time. His presents were all the same: a tiny, inch-long boat carved out of styrofoam floating in a deep blue sea inside a crystal box. There was a girl in the boat, with "Sara" written on her cute little dress. On the base of each box Amundsen wrote, in that distinctive flowing script of his that slanted like an ocean wave, "*our Pacific*," "*our Indian Ocean*," "*our Arctic Ocean*," "*our Norske-havet*," with the word "our" in bold and the date at the end.

"That's our village down there." Anu led everyone through another wood until they reached the edge and a wide-open vista appeared. Some lights were still twinkling in the village below, and in the distance the Laku Laku River was shimmering. "That's our village, and the mountain is our holy land, as well as our refrigerator."

By now Umav too had discovered that Hafay wasn't there. She kept looking back into the darkness to check whether Hafay had caught up. She pulled at Dahu's hand and said she wanted to go back. Dahu looked at his daughter in the darkness and found that at some point her expression had changed without him noticing, that she no longer had the eyes of a wounded bird.

"Let's not bother Auntie Hafay for now. She'll come out when she's ready," he said, bending down to whisper to his daughter.

"We'll sleep in traditional Bunun houses this evening, if you don't mind. See the two buildings made of bamboo and stone over there? They might not be that comfortable to you, but for the mountains this is a five-star hotel. Inside, you'll hear the sounds the mountain makes at night." After hearing Dahu's translation, Detlef and Sara said they liked the idea. Having lived on an oceangoing fishing boat, Sara didn't believe that there was any place in the world she couldn't take.

In a mellow mood from the wine, Anu pointed at the village and continued his explanation, saying, "We call it *Sazasa*, meaning a place where sugarcane grows tall and animals leap, a place where folks can thrive." Anu gestured toward a mountain on the other side of the Laku Laku River, then looked round and motioned toward another mountain on their side of the river and said, "My father said the Japanese forced us to leave our original village on that mountain over there and come live here by the river on the slope of this mountain. But it's all worked out for the best, because now we're closer to the sea. My dad used to take me hunting when I was little. We would follow the trail up that mountain all the way up to the summit and then go down to the sea on the other side. My dad told me, sea and mountain aren't the same. The sea washes everything clean. It even washes us clean, inside and out.

"It's just that the sea isn't the same as it used to be," Anu said.

# 28. The Cave Beneath

Exhausted from the past few days of hiking, Alice finally came down with a cold. She was trembling all over. The medicine in the first-aid kit had no effect, and soon she had sunk into a feverish state with hot flashes and cold shivers and times when she was half-comatose. Atile'i picked several kinds of herbal medicine with the knowledge he had gleaned from the field guides and cooked up a pot of medicinal broth. He collected dry sticks for a fire in order to save propane. Alice drank the broth and her vitality was actually somewhat restored.

"The mountain will cure you," Atile'i told Alice.

Alice was still determined to take advantage of the last half day of fair weather and make it through the forest to see the mighty cliff. Maybe it was the language barrier or maybe it was that he sensed her determination to get there, but Atile'i, now a powerfully built youth, decided to carry Alice, who was apparently delicate but actually hard as granite inside, through the forest on his back.

This was a typical mid-high altitude alpine forest: the forest floor was covered in layer upon layer of fallen leaves, and the tree trunks were tall and straight, and each cast its own shadow. Atile'i felt like he was walking on waves. It reminded him of the island of Gesi Gesi, as well as of everything on Wayo Wayo. Especially Rasula.

Now Atile'i was holding Alice's thighs, which were gripping him around the waist. He couldn't help it: he got an erection.

He remembered Rasula's *kiki'a* wine and that last night they'd spent together: the look in her eyes, the sound of her moans, and the smell of her body, her soft body, so totally different from Alice's but also so alike.

During this time, without anyone to teach him, Atile'i had as a matter of course come to understand certain things. Such as the reason his fellow islanders had established the custom of the "last night," when young maidens had the right to pull a second son into a thicket of grass: because that was his only opportunity to leave a seed behind on Wayo Wayo.

If any of the girls had gotten pregnant with his child, he hoped it was Rasula. He knew that if an island girl got pregnant, then that was that, and nobody would care whose seed it was. Wayo Wayo women did not calculate their ages in years; they only spoke of "the year I had the first child" or "the year I had my second." Which was why some Wayo Wayo women did not know how to respond when asked their age, because they were infertile. Such women did not bear the marks of time, and often lacked the protection of relatives. Atile'i hoped Rasula was expecting, so that there would be at least one person to take care of her. He knew it would be his elder brother Nale'ida, though. Nale'ida would be responsible for keeping Rasula's drying rack covered with fish, for this was the law of Wayo Wayo.

Of course, he had no way of knowing, because at this moment he happened to be on another island, an island who knows how far away from Wayo Wayo. And now he might never be able to ride Gesi Gesi again and find the way home.

At this thought, Atile'i felt that every step was taking him deep into the forest, so deep he might never find his way out.

Alice, riding on Atile'i's back, felt a strange consolation, as if Thom had finally come back to bear her up. She held the young man closer.

Alice knew that the lifestyle she'd been leading with Atile'i at the hunting hut seemed stable but in fact could change at any time. They could not stay there forever: it was too flimsy, might collapse in a typhoon. And Atile'i couldn't keep hiding there indefinitely. She had to make some decisions on his behalf, including whether to introduce him to other people, beginning at least with Dahu and Hafay. Perhaps he could be friends with Umav, like brother and sister. Who knows, maybe someday Atile'i might cease to be Wayo Wayoan and "go Taiwanese," Alice thought.

But Alice had her own issues to deal with. All this time at the hunting hut, it appeared she had just been quietly foraging, writing, getting on with her daily life, but actually she hated herself for not being able to live except in writing, except in a world in which she talked to herself.

Maybe I need to take a trip to the cliff myself, Alice had thought.

And as Atile'i carried her over the undulating forest floor, she suddenly remembered a time many years before on the way to the creek with Thom when they had caught a stag beetle with a lovely pair of mandibles. Delighted, she had brought it home to make a specimen of it, hoping to surprise Toto on his birthday. She used ether to put it under, pierced its exoskeleton with a size-three insect pin and placed it in one of the cells of a small insect specimen case. There were already two inmates: a giant Formosan stag beetle and a deep mountain stag beetle. The mandibles of this newest member of the collection were just so conspicuous. It was so beautiful, like a miniature deer.

One sleepless night, she went to get pen and paper out of the drawer only to be given a terrible fright. She jerked the drawer open, spilling out the contents.

It turned out that the newest member of the collection, still pinned in its cell, was slowly rowing its three pairs of legs, like it was in a swimming pool. Maybe because the dose of ether was too small, that bug, brimming with life, had only gone into a temporary coma. Now it was resurrected. Its neighbors were still peacefully impaled, while this tiny deer kept pacing the void, unable to go anywhere.

Do insects feel pain? Maybe when their relatives or family members are gone, they are oblivious, but when pierced with a size-three insect pin are they really as senseless as we imagine them to be?

As Atile'i carried Alice through the forest, each of them was giving off a distinctive smell, because of memory. The olfactorily acute forest critters noticed. The damp, long-settled leaves were silent, but the freshly fallen leaves sounded like brittle bones. Atile'i snapped the bones of the forest floor with every step. It was raining now, the raindrops falling gently, and when Atile'i looked up he thought he could see the end of every thread of rain.

They finally managed to get through the forest to the base of the massive cliff before nightfall. It was like a wall, a giant creature. All the winds in the world had to stop before it, and the forest could only look up in wonder.

Atile'i let Alice down and wiped his sweaty, shining face. Alice pulled out the raincoat stashed in her windbreaker and put on her rain hat, wrapping herself in a small, yellow world. She was calmer than she had expected. So here it is, she thought. Here it was.

Since it was already dark, Alice and Atile'i had to stay another night in the mountains. And because the bear had destroyed the tent, they had to search all over for a place to get out of the rain, finally finding a hollow beneath the cliff. It was not deep, but if you crouched down you could pack a few people in there with you. The ceiling was higher on one side than the other, and at the low end the hollow was apparently connected to another cave, though Alice could not see for sure in the dark. She remembered the people in the alpine association telling her that the cliff never used to exist, that it only appeared after the earthquake due to fault displacement.

The mountain was split asunder, the cliff made manifest. This was the destination on the map. Was this where Dahu had found Thom's body?

Alice stared at Atile'i from behind. He was making a fire to brew tea. In the flickering light, his shadow on the wall beside her was sometimes . as big as Thom, sometimes as small as Toto. She caressed Atile'i's shadow on the stone wall of the hollow embedded in the base of the cliff, murmuring, "So this is where you've been, all this time." Now, in full possession of her faculties, Alice finally realized that all is shadow. But even a shadow is enough. Even a shadow of a shadow is enough.

Atile'i, having finished making the fire, was sitting quietly watching the rain outside. The rain suddenly became surprisingly heavy, and rainwater started flowing in and down toward the nether reaches of the hollow, whence it trickled away. It was as if there was a river running through the cave straight toward the heart of the mountain, destination unknown.

"How is the weather at sea today?" asked Atile'i, calmly.

Alice did a double take for a few seconds before replying, in a voice as fine as drizzle, "Very fair."

# 29. The Man with the Compound Eyes III

The man sits up, but the pain forces him to lie back down. Then he yawns a big yawn, whether due to sorrow or some other emotion he does not know. It is as if the world of men has become too tedious and he would prefer eternal sleep.

After the yawn, the man is pleasantly surprised to discover that the pain has subsided somewhat. The man stops stifling his urge to yawn, and the yawns come fast and furious, like they are lining up, waiting for the man to exhale them. In less than a minute he yawns a grand total of thirteen times.

"Not as painful as you might imagine, is it?"

The man knows most of the bones in his body are broken, that it's the kind of compound fracture that can never be reset. He has sustained many serious fractures in his life, and knows what it feels like, as if the feeling has been etched in his memory. But this time he does not actually feel any pain.

"Strange, it doesn't hurt." The man quickly alerts to what this lack of pain implies. "So, I'm dead?"

"How many yawns?"

"Fifteen." The man has miscounted. It's actually been thirteen.

"Then, by the regular definition, you're dead."

The man does not understand what "by the regular definition" is supposed to mean. He props himself up, stands up, and walks away from the cliff, looking up anxiously. "But my son is still up there."

The man with the compound eyes shakes his head, as if perplexed by the man's inability to understand, and says, "He's not up there. You can say he's up there all you want, but in fact he isn't. You know it well."

I know it, I know it not, I know it, I know it not, I know it, I know it not, I know it, I know it not . . . Incensed, he ignores the man with the compound eyes and tries to climb up the cliff by himself, but finds he cannot. He seems to retain a physical existence, but cannot operate his body as he pleases. More precisely, he can't climb. He seems to be limited to a single plane of movement, as if he's gone flat. So this is what death is like.

"You can't go up, not anymore," the man with the compound eyes confirms, his reply impassive, unwavering, unhesitating.

He knows the man is right, he cannot go up, so he sighs a sigh so heavy and so cold that it seems to cover the plants around him with a film of frost. But he is still worried about his son. He is so anxious he gets up to try over and over again.

The man with the compound eyes does not stop him, only waits until he tires himself out and sits down dejectedly on the ground. In despair he looks at the man with the compound eyes, as if to use every last ounce of strength to appeal for assistance, but all he sees is the man's compound eyes, which seem to change from moment to moment in hallucinatory permutations and combinations. And the scene in each of the tiny ommatidia that compose every compound eye is completely different with each passing instant. Watching carefully, the man's mind is helplessly mesmerized by the instantaneous images playing in each ommatidium: could be an erupting undersea volcano, might be a falcon's-eye view of a landscape, perhaps just a leaf about to fall. Each seems to be playing a kind of documentary.

The man points at the ground and says, "Sit down and have a chat, all right? If you're not in any hurry."

"What's the hurry, if I'm dead?" The man sits down resignedly.

"So, how much do you know about memory?"

The man is a bit taken aback by the pop question. "It's just what you remember, isn't it?"

"Sort of. I'll give you a crash course. Generally speaking, human memory can be divided into declarative memory and nondeclarative memory. Declarative memory can be reported, for instance in speech or in writing. And nondeclarative memory is, roughly, what you call the subconscious mind. It's the memories a person might not even know he has. This is not to say that it can't be reported, just that usually it is not reported, because you don't even know about it. Do you follow?"

The man nods, but he does not know why he has to sit here, listening to this stuff.

"Well, these two kinds of memory can be subdivided into three basic types: episodic, semantic and procedural. Remember your son still couldn't speak until the age of three? Then one day, when he was looking at an insect specimen, he blurted out a complete sentence, didn't he?"

The man nods again, but is baffled: how can this man possibly know such personal minutiae? At this, he realizes he is not too certain about the timing. When exactly did the event take place? Was Toto three or four? He couldn't have been older than five.

"This is an event, an episode in your life, and you can report it, so it's a declarative, episodic memory. Here's another example: you remember your wife's and son's birthdays, don't you?"

"Of course I remember."

"Well, that's semantic memory or factual memory. Even if you forgot something like this you could still look it up, right? It's on their ID cards, and even if you misremember, there's still a 'mismemory,' right? Basically, if there's not been any mistake, their birthdays are recorded the same everywhere, because they're facts. And people have a way of confirming the facts. In the world people have constructed for themselves you can usually look up a fact like that. You still with me?" The man nods.

"But episodic memory is different. The details you remember about any event must be different from the details your wife remembers. Right? For instance, for when you and your wife met for the first time, what exactly did you say to her in the forest? Each of you remembers different details, that's for sure. You almost ended up getting into a fight over it on many different occasions, didn't you? You were both remembering different parts of the same episode."

The man lowers his head and thinks about it. "I get it. What about procedural memory?"

"You've climbed this rock wall many times before, haven't you? If I asked you to look up at the cliff could you more or less make out the routes you traveled?"

I suppose I could, the man thinks, but he isn't too sure. The man revisits the climbs in his mind. The second time a seasoned rock climber takes a certain route some details from the first time will come back to him.

As if continuing the man's line of thought, the man with the compound eyes says, "Right. Certain details will occur to you the moment your fingers touch the stone, details you normally couldn't remember no matter how hard you tried. Sometimes it might even cross your mind that there's a cleft in a certain rock as you climb. Am I right?"

He looks at the man with the compound eyes in amazement.

"People's minds are continually weaving the threads of memory together without anyone being aware of it. Sometimes not even you know what you might remember. Even if you climbed this rock wall a hundred times you probably wouldn't bother remembering the position of every rock and foothold, but your body would remember as a matter of course. If someone moved a certain rock, your fingers and toes would tell you the next time you climbed."

The man looks in the man's eyes and seems to see a familiar scene in one of the fine ommatidia. Though overall, the man's head is no bigger than an average person's head, nor are his eyes bigger than an average person's eyes, there were at least tens of thousands of ommatidia in each of his compound eyes, each so tiny as to be invisible to the naked eye. But if so, the man wonders, how can he be sure of what he is seeing?

"When it comes to memory, people are no different from any other animal. I'm not kidding. You probably won't believe it, but actually even a sea hare has memory. Eric Richard Kandel, a scientist famous for his research on memory, started out experimenting with sea hares. Fortunately, he survived the Kristallnacht, the first systematic Nazi attack on the Jews, or he wouldn't have had the chance to study memory. In a certain sense, maybe it was because Kandel had a profound understanding of what it's like to have something etched in memory that he was driven to try to understand it."

The man with the compound eyes said, "Animals like sea hares may not have much episodic or semantic memory, but animals with developed brains have episodic, semantic and procedural memory, just like people. Migratory birds remember the seacoast, whales remember the boat that harpooned them, and seal pups that manage to avoid annihilation will remember the murderous coat-clad, club-carrying creature that chased them. I kid you not, they'll never forget. But only human beings have invented a tool to record memory."

The man with the compound eyes reaches down and takes out a pencil he has stuck in a pocket on his pant leg. The pen is broken in two, but there is no doubt it can still write.

"Writing."

As he says this there are two dull rolls of distant thunder. Dark clouds are shrouding the sky. A change in the weather.

"There was thunder just now: this is a fact. And it's a fact that we're talking. But if there's no one to record what just happened in writing, the evidence of its occurrence will only be found in the episodic, semantic and procedural memory of two people, you and me. But if you represented these memories in writing, you would discover that the mind adds massive amounts of material anytime it weaves an episodic memory. In this way, the world reconstructed in writing approximates even more closely what you call 'the realm of nature.' It's an organism."

The man with the compound eyes reaches into a rotten log on the ground nearby and, as if performing a magic trick, pulls out a pale, rough thing like the larva of some beetle.

"But the world that people perceive is too partial, too narrow. Sometimes, you consciously, all too consciously, only remember what you want to. Many apparently authentic episodic memories are partly fabricated. Sometimes things that have never happened anywhere in the world can be vividly 'represented' in the mind, again by virtue of the imagination. Many people have diseased brains, and some of them even mistake one thing for another, like the man who took his wife for a hat."

The man with the compound eyes gazes off into the distance. How strange that even though compound eyes do not focus like human eyes, he can still tell where the man is looking. "Similarly, as I was just saying, it's not just humans who have the ability to remember. And of course it's not only Homo sapiens who have the ability to make things up. But only you people can turn the contents of their minds into writing, that's for sure. This larva I'm holding will never be able to recount the memory it will have of being a pupa in a cocoon."

The man discovers that at some point the larva in the man's hand has pupated, covering itself in a brown cocoon.

"So what you mean to say is that . . ." The man cannot finish his sentence. He falls into a stupor, maybe a state that people who have just died all experience.

"Your wife's writing kept your son alive," said the man with the compound eyes, looking the man straight in the eyes. "You remember that summer? That snake? That afternoon? You lost the life you'd born and raised. It was your wife who kept the diary, did all the things only your son would have done, bought the things he would have needed when he reached a certain age and read the field guides she imagined he would have found interesting. She went out into the wilderness and collected specimens, then rendered possession of them unto your son. And in order to protect her, or rather in order to protect her 'brain,' the people around her went along with her memories, at least with the memories she was willing to acknowledge. And for this reason, at the opposite extremes of life and death, your wife and your son have enjoyed a kind of symbiotic coexistence."

The man feels something flashing in front of his eyes, fleetingly. Someone puts out the light of his life. Someone has extinguished something.

"In fact, since then your son has only existed in her writing and daily activities, and you have been an accessory. You two have been the bearers of a traumatic memory, and its authors."

The man sighs. Clearly, something leaves his body at that moment. "So my son's later existence is meaningless?"

"Not exactly. At least for a certain period of time, by a kind of tacit understanding, he lived between you and your wife, didn't he? He lived, like a chain. He didn't die by the regular definition, only he wasn't alive anymore. No other creature can share experience like this. Only human beings can, through writing, experience something separately together."

The man with the compound eyes looks into the man's glimmering eyes as they start to dim: this is a sign that he has reached fourteen and a half yawns.

"But at the end of the day memory and imagination have to be archived separately, just as waves must always leave the beach. Because otherwise, people couldn't go on living," the man said. "This is the price humanity must pay for being the only species with the ability to record memory in writing."

The man discovers that the chrysalis in the man's hand has begun to writhe, as if being trapped inside the cocoon is quite painful and it wants to end the pain.

"In all honesty, I don't envy you the possession of this power over memory, nor do I admire you. Because humans are usually completely unconcerned with the memories of other creatures. Human existence involves the wilful destruction of the existential memories of other creatures and of your own memories as well. No life can survive without other lives, without the ecological memories other living creatures have, memories of the environments in which they live. People don't realize they need to rely on the memories of other organisms to survive. You think that flowers bloom in colorful profusion just to please your eyes. That a wild boar exists just to provide meat for your table. That a fish takes the bait just for your sake. That only you can mourn. That a stone falling into a gorge is of no significance. That a sambar deer, its head bent low to sip at a creek, is not a revelation . . . When in fact the finest movement of any organism represents a change in an ecosystem." The man with the compound eyes takes a deep sigh and says: "But if you were any different you wouldn't be human."

"And who are you, then?" The man uses the remaining fraction of his final breath to spit this question out, and it is as if a chorus of a million voices asks it.

"Who am I? Who am I indeed?" The cocoon in the man's hand is throbbing violently now, like an emerging galaxy in the agony of formation. His eyes are flashing, almost as if they contain flecks of quartz. But if you looked carefully, you would see that they are not really flashing, that some of the ommatidia are wet with tears, tears so exceedingly fine they are harder to perceive than the point of a pin.

Pointing at his own eyes, the man with the compound eyes says, "The only reason for my existence is that I can merely observe, not intervene."

XI

# 30. The Man with the Compound Eyes IV

The boy resolves to climb down the cliff.

He attaches the safety rope and slowly starts climbing down. Because he is light, the boy does not feel the weight of his body at first, but soon he feels his strength deplete. He's never imagined his body is this heavy. He looks up, and all he can see is an endless stone wall. He has to wipe the sweat on his brow away with his arm, so it doesn't sting his beautiful brown eyes, which from a certain angle look a bit blue.

When he is about halfway down, the boy's foot slips. In a moment of panic he plummets. Luckily he returns to the wall, but by this point his energy is drained, and he can go no further, neither up nor down. At first his body feels hot, and the sweat keeps dripping down, but soon his motionless body feels the chill of the wind. He shivers.

Stuck there, the boy realizes his hearing is now keener than normal. In addition to the sound of the wind blowing, the leaves falling and insects beating their wings, he seems to hear his father talking to another man at the base of the cliff. He cannot understand most of what they are saying, but when he hears the other man say, "He didn't die by the regular definition, only he wasn't alive anymore," he suddenly feels his body grow light. No, better to say that his original *sense of weight* disappears.

He cocks his head to one side, as if in contemplation, and decides to climb back up instead of continuing down. He is surprised to find that for some reason when he starts ascending he feels light as a feather, hollow in the middle.

The boy reaches the top of the cliff, walks into the tent, and opens his backpack. Inside is the pocket in which he keeps his insect specimen bottles. He takes them out, walks outside, opens them and dumps out the beetles, one by one. Initially the beetles are terrified. They all play dead, lying motionless on the ground, legs curled up. Then the boy turns the beetles over, one at a time. Several minutes later, a few of them tentatively crawl a short distance, then open their elytra to reveal transparent wings so thin as to be almost invisible. And then they flutter off.

*Flap flap, flap flap, flap flap . . .*

The boy stands at the edge of the cliff. The beetles are now mere specks in his beautiful eyes, but their elytra can still be discerned. "Such beautiful insects!" says the boy in a singsong voice. Just then, a huge beetle with charming green and yellow mottling on its elytra stops on a rock in front of him. "A long-armed scarab! A male long-armed scarab!" calls the elated boy.

"Look at that long pair of arms! See how large its elytra are!"

But from that moment on, he feels everything start to get "blurry," not "blurry" in the regular, visual sense but a kind of blurriness that people could never imagine. It is as if he is transforming into a leaf, an insect, a birdcall, a drop of water, a pinch of lichen, or even a rock.

*Flap flap, flap flap, flap flap . . .*

It is as if there's never been such a boy who climbed that massive cliff in that incredible scene, which is now, once again, received into one of the ommatidia, far smaller than pinpoints, of the man with the compound eyes, along with the panorama of all scenery. No scene now remains, except in memory.

# 31. End of the Road

Dahu kept calling but couldn't reach Alice at the cell he'd given her. So the morning he woke up in the Forest Church, he decided to drive up the coast to the Sea House, to make sure Alice was all right. Reaching the shore, he saw that the volunteer cleanup team had started the day's work. Maybe it was a false impression, but the Sea House seemed to be sinking even further into the sea. He saw a man and woman, like a mother and son, facing the Sea House and pointing at things. Dahu went over and asked and they turned out to be the writer Kee's widow and son.

"My mother just wanted to come by and see the old lot, and to check whether Professor Shih is all right," the son said.

"She's moved already, for her own safety," Dahu said.

The writer's widow seemed filled with regret as she said, "We used to plant vegetables here, looking out to sea. Who would have thought it would end up underwater?"

Dahu resolved to take a trip to the hunting hut, even though it might make Alice angry. When he got there, he was even more convinced that there was someone else living at the hut besides Alice, because there was a tent outside the hut, and a fixed-frame awning had been added on to the hut itself. He also discovered a kind of food cellar, and there were books and drawings scattered around the room. He could tell right away that some of the drawings, wild, and incredibly imaginative, were not from

Alice's hand. So that was why he could never get through to her: Alice had not even taken her cell along. The cell was off and it was being used as a paperweight for those drawings instead. Dahu was going to take the phone with him, but on second thought decided to just set the phone with the solar cell up, turn on the transmitter, and leave Alice a note. This way, Dahu could still get in touch with Alice after she got back. And once she picked up the phone, he would also be able to track her no matter where she went.

But Dahu was still determined to form a rescue team to go into the mountains to find her. He did not know whether Alice really needed rescuing, but he tried to plan for the worst. That's what his wilderness experience had taught him to do.

Right then, Atile'i was carrying Alice back down the mountain. Alice saw Dahu from far off and had Atile'i let her down so that they would not be seen. They hid until Dahu left; only then did Atile'i carry the debilitated Alice to the hut. The first thing Alice did was to turn on the phone and give Dahu a call.

"You're back! I was at the hut just now but I didn't see you. I was about to form a search party," Dahu said, greatly relieved.

"I'm fine. Nothing's wrong. No need to form any party."

"Is there someone there with you? Where've you been these past few days?"

"Uh . . ." Alice wasn't going to tell him, at least not yet. "I'll explain it to you some other time."

After hanging up, Alice looked everywhere for Ohiyo before finally finding her in the straw basket Atile'i had woven, her forepaws covering her eyes and her body curled up into a perfect ball, as if nothing had disturbed her rest.

For whatever reason, when she was looking at Ohiyo fast asleep, Alice suddenly got the urge to write, and she did not want to waste a minute. She sat back down in her Writing Pavilion underneath the awning, got out the notebook, and continued writing the novel she'd never been able to finish.

Atile'i could not help saying, "You're sick. Why not . . . rest?"

"I want to do some writing."

"What about?"

"Something that apparently happened, but maybe never actually did," Alice said.

Sara took up residence in the tribal village of Sazasa starting the evening she stayed in the Bunun house in the Forest Church. She got up early every day and went to different sections of seashore to observe, take notes and write up her new research proposal. Detlef served as her chauffeur and occasionally went up into the hills to hunt or down into the fields to plant millet or sorghum with some of the villagers. The two of them were getting more and more acquainted with, but at the same time depressed about, the condition the coastline was in. Every day, Sara persisted in measuring the sea temperature at several specific sites. She'd discovered that the average temperature was 1.6°C higher than the previous record.

"This means that a continuous increase in rainfall is likely," Sara said to Detlef.

"And the water pollution?"

"Awful. I guess only a few invertebrates will survive, and just barely. Dissolved oxygen levels are also down, and the plastic items exposed to the sun will keep releasing toxins into the sea, like a witch poisoning the water night and day. Look, the sea's all discolored."

Detlef looked and the sea was indeed a blotchy patchwork of red and brown. "The shallows are covered in algae."

Detlef and Sara had fallen in love with the island. But now the happy-go-lucky people living in this relatively poor part of the island had lost even the right to go out to sea.

After Dahu confirmed that Alice was safe and sound, he kept up his coastal cleanup work and his Forest Church work with Anu. Alice would answer when Dahu called. When he went by the Sea House he would sometimes see Alice out and about, and occasionally Detlef and Sara would be there too. Sara was quite intrigued by this woman who'd been living in a hunting hut in the hills ever since her house had gotten inundated. But though Alice was willing to exchange pleasantries, it seemed there was a window in her heart that was always shut. No matter how Dahu tested the waters, Alice remained unwilling to reveal the identity of the person who was living with her at the hut. "Give me some time," Alice said.

Hafay was busy serving villagers and tourists *salama* coffee, and Umav was responsible for telling travelers various Pangcah and Bunun tales. She was enjoying herself, and was becoming more of a young lady every day. She'd grown bangs, and used a hair band to gather up her hair, revealing the moles on her ear lobes.

That's how they passed the winter.

Spring had just arrived, and Detlef and Sara had to leave because Detlef had to give a guest lecture at a university back home. One evening, a few of them were sitting around shooting the breeze, and Hafay recommended Detlef and Sara take a trip south before they left. "It would be a shame if Sara never got the chance to observe the sea down the coast." The plan quickly took shape: they decided to go in two vehicles, with Dahu and Anu driving. Alice was also invited, but as usual she made up an excuse and declined to go.

"The millet will ripen when it's time," Hafay said, to comfort Dahu.

When the car reached the entrance of the village, Dahu rolled down the window and said in Bunun to an old fellow crouching at the side of the road: "*Mikua dihanin?*" (What's the weather like today?)

"*Na hudanan,*" the elder replied. (It's going to rain).

Actually, it had been raining incessantly since last year, far more than predicted. Rain now seemed to be the only weather, from drizzle and occasional sunshiny rain to afternoon thundershowers and sudden downpours. "We're drowning!" was the mood of the entire island. There was a deluge of reports of floods and landslides, along with a concomitant economic downturn. The malaise had lasted over a year and had contrib- uted to the low voter turnout—less than fifty percent!—in the election at the end of the previous year. The islanders no longer believed any politician could get them out of this mess.

"How can one mudskipper lead a school of mudskippers out of the mire?" wrote Alice's cynical friend Ming in a letter to the editor.

One day at dawn Alice was finally done revising. She'd completed two works of fiction, a novel and a short story. Atile'i already had a vague idea of what "fiction" was. It was like he'd always imagined there was a story behind everything he did not understand on Gesi Gesi. When Alice told Atile'i she was done, Atile'i asked: "What's the name of it?"

"The long one or the short one?"

"The long one."

"*The Man with the Compound Eyes.*"

"And the short one?"

"It's also called, 'The Man with the Compound Eyes.'"

That afternoon, Atile'i insisted on taking Alice somewhere. Alice was initially quite surprised, and extremely apprehensive, because she was still unwilling for Atile'i to be seen in public, lest he get hurt. When they were almost at the coast, Atile'i led Alice into a wood to the right, through which there was no distinct path to be seen. It would originally have been on slope land, but what with recent terrestrial transformations it was now surprisingly close to the shoreline. Various kinds of garbage that had not been (and might never be) cleared were piled up at the edge of the wood. Atile'i had something to show her. He lifted up what seemed to be a huge sheet of scrap canvas, to reveal something astonishing underneath.

It was a boat.

All this time, Atile'i had been sneaking down at night while Alice was asleep and coming here to build a boat. But it was not a *talawaka* this time. It was made out of several kinds of wood from the mountains and some garbage collected at the beach. The basic construction of the hull reminded Alice of the traditional balangays of the Tao people of Orchid Island, only with a rain awning. Atile'i explained, "I saw the boat in a book. I learned how."

How had the youth before her managed to construct a seemingly well-formed plank canoe with only crude tools and a few pictures in a book to consult?

"I can read books." It was true. Atile'i had gone through many books since he started reading on Gesi Gesi, even though he never understood the writing. He had his own way of reading.

Alice wished Atile'i would stay, but as he would not give a definite answer, Alice knew that he was determined to go.

"I heard Rasula's voice. And there were two. Every evening," Atile'i said. "But lately there's only one left. Wayo Wayoans ... belong at sea. I ... must find Rasula."

With heavy steps, they walked wordlessly back to the hunting hut. They did not sleep the whole night through. By morning, Alice had prepared two full suitcases of things she imagined one should take along on a journey across the sea. Atile'i smiled and reduced the gear to a single suitcase. He asked Alice for a fistful of pens.

"If I die soon, my spirit ... might never leave. If I live long, I can ... draw pictures on my skin." He took off the green polo shirt that Alice had bought him, and his chest, arms, belly, and even the parts of the back he could twist his arms to reach, were covered in the stories of their life together on the island: Ohiyo, water flowing into the sea at the river mouth on a rainy day, alpine birds, and even Toto. He drew Toto's tiny form on a huge, apparently boundless cliff that extended from his hips to his shoulder blades. Alice could not understand how he had managed to do it.

Alice couldn't resist caressing his dark, youthful body, which was going forth to meet death a second time. Finally, her tears started to fall, and she cried and cried like the rainy season you can never drive away.

Dahu drove Detlef and Sara, Anu, Hafay and Umav. Heading south, they saw a sea that had flooded the rocky coastal terrace terrain. They saw a sea that had forced the tribal villagers of Laeno to move inland. It was like they were on an inspection tour. They witnessed how the great ocean had dumped back all the trash people had dumped into it, and how the mountains had buried the hollows people had dug into the mountains to build roads thinking there would always be roads here.

Dahu was about to turn onto a county highway that had been pushed through by the local government about seven or eight years before. Local politicians claimed that the rationale for the road was improving transportation in remote areas and completing the ring road around the island. Later it was demonstrated that the road had been built for the sole purpose of conveying nuclear waste to a small southern village for dumping. It had absolutely nothing to do with making life more convenient for the local villagers.

The night before, they had stopped at a noodle shop in a small seaside village for some food and rest. Anu ordered two hundred dumplings in one go. Dahu told them about the route they would take the next morning. "I went there nine years ago, before the county highway was completed. Let's not take the highway all the way. I want to take you guys along the old hiking trail. You'll see the most sublime coastal scenery. In the beginning, it was the trail the aboriginal people on this side of the mountain took when they wanted to deal with the aboriginal people on the other side of the mountain. I think we should leave at dawn, to make it there for daybreak."

Right then the television in the little noodle shop was broadcasting one of those tireless talk shows. The topic this evening was castaways in the Bermuda Triangle. At one point they were talking about the Gulf of Mexico, where about twenty years before the fishery had collapsed because of an oil spill and where six months ago a squid boat that hadn't been able to catch a thing had rescued a dark-skinned girl with charred red hair. The girl was thought to have been drifting for at least a month. She was very weak, and only managed to regain consciousness for a few minutes upon receiving medical assistance, during which time she kept muttering, "Atile'i! Atile'i!" Language experts believed this was very likely a word of supplication in her language. The girl was put on life support. She slipped back into a coma, but her brain activity only ceased when doctors performed a Caesarean and removed the fetus she was carrying from her abdomen.

"It's a miracle." Hafay and Dahu both realized that the leggy anchorwoman with the heavy makeup was actually Lily, the lady from the day the Trash Vortex hit. The ex-anchorwoman on this channel got sacked after the tsunami incident; who knows how Lily had gotten promoted to the post? The infant was vigorous, the report continued, despite an unfortunate congenital defect: its legs were joined together, like a cetacean tail fin.

Sara had Dahu translate the news for her. Nobody knew whether to be sad or happy for the child. Umav said, "Sweet! Fused legs will make it easier to swim."

They could be sure there would be no good news in the weather forecast, because the earliest typhoon of the year was in the offing, and at the beginning of March already. It would very likely advance toward the east coast. Experts predicted that the storm would break up the Trash Vortex and cause it to surround the whole island. Moreover, the typhoon had a well-developed cloud structure and would bring a considerable amount of rain.

By the wee hours of the morning, Dahu and the other travelers were on the road again. In the darkness, the two cars were flooded with a multilingual torrent. But soon Dahu had to slow down and stop because of reduced visibility up ahead.

"I can't see the road," Dahu said.

The road had disappeared.

Because of the haze, they could not see the shape of the sun when it appeared on the horizon. Initially all they could see was the space immediately in front of the headlights. Gradually it got light enough for them to see where the road should have been: the road had been engulfed by the rising sea. Maybe it was too remote for there to be any reports on it, or maybe they had not been paying attention to the news. In any case, this unnecessary road, rarely traveled except for transporting nuclear waste, had now sunk beneath the waves, just like that.

As if the ocean is where they'd taken the road to get to, the band of travelers stood and gazed out across the vast Pacific at a listless sunrise, at the end of the road.

Dahu, Hafay, Umav, Anu, Detlef and Sara all got out of the cars and stood at the edge of the road that led into the sea, speechless. And the resolute Pacific kept delivering wave after distant wave.

Having set out a bit earlier than Dahu and Anu and the others, Alice was now helping Atile'i slowly push his boat into the sea. Alice cocked her head and looked at Atile'i, wondering whether all of this had really happened or if it had been a figment of her imagination. Had she really spent the past while living with a youth who had come here across the Pacific on a floating island of garbage?

The sea was indistinct in the darkness, like a grainy old photograph. It was as if there was finally something to grasp hold of out there in the void. Alice sat in Atile'i's boat. Staring out into the distance, they were both preoccupied. Time passed slowly, and Atile'i didn't show any sign of rowing. It wasn't until a flock of gulls flew past that Atile'i finally spoke. "Alice, can you pray for me?"

"Sure. But to whom should I pray?"

"Anyone. Kabang, or your god, or to the ocean."

"Will my prayer make any difference?"

"Maybe not. The Sea Sage . . . my father says that you never know what will happen in the face of the sea, for the sea taketh away and the sea suddenly giveth another day. This is why we must pray." Atile'i slipped into Wayo Wayoan halfway through, leaving Alice a bit in the dark as to what he was on about.


Dahu and the others sat down like there was a beach at the end of the road. They did not want to leave too soon, even though they were certain there was no going on to the old trail. Dahu was rambling on about the time he'd hiked it many years before. He talked and talked, his voice trailing off until not even he could hear it anymore. Umav kicked at the waves. Sara took samples of seawater. Detlef was recording the scene with his video camera. Anu just took off his clothes and jumped in for a swim.

Dahu noticed Hafay was wearing sandals today instead of boots, exposing her extra toes. He felt that each extra toe was like an adorable millet sprout.

Hafay started to sing. They all stopped what they were doing the moment they heard her voice. Even the sea seemed to cease slapping at the shore. All that remained in the world was her song.

First she sang a Pangcah ballad, then an air she'd composed herself, then an English folk anthem from many years before. This was a song she had learned from a CD that man had given her. She had memorized every verse of every song on those CDs, even though she had no idea what the lyrics meant.

> Oh, where have you been, my blue-eyed son?
> Oh, where have you been, my darling young one?
> I've stumbled on the side of twelve misty mountains,
> I've walked and I've crawled on six crooked highways,
> I've stepped in the middle of seven sad forests,
> I've been out in front of a dozen dead oceans,
> I've been ten thousand miles in the mouth of a graveyard,
> And it's a hard, and it's a hard, it's a hard, and it's a hard,
> And it's a hard rain's a-gonna fall.

> Oh, what did you see, my blue-eyed son?
> Oh, what did you see, my darling young one?
> I saw a newborn baby with wild wolves all around it,
> I saw a highway of diamonds with nobody on it,
> I saw a black branch with blood that kept drippin',
> I saw a room full of men with their hammers a-bleedin',
> I saw a white ladder all covered with water,
> I saw ten thousand talkers whose tongues were all broken,
> I saw guns and sharp swords in the hands of young children,
> And it's a hard, and it's a hard, it's a hard, it's a hard,
> And it's a hard rain's a-gonna fall.

This was a song from such a long time ago. But even Dahu, who had heard Hafay sing a lot of songs before, felt like Hafay's voice replenished something inside his empty soul. Even Anu, who did not understand a word, felt like he was responsible for the sorrow in the song. Even Detlef, who had really been to the heart of a mountain, felt like something had been hollowed out and a cavern had appeared, a cavern so deep and vast it could never be reinforced. And even Umav, who was just a girl who did not yet know the ways of the world, felt that a hard rain was really going to fall.

Her red hair flying like a flag, Sara was stunned by Hafay's voice. The raindrops in Hafay's song seemed to shatter in the gale, making the rain seem much heavier than it actually was. Sara and Hafay exchanged a glance, and then Sara took over the lead, with Hafay singing harmony:

> *And what did you hear, my blue-eyed son?*
> *And what did you hear, my darling young one?*
> *I heard the sound of a thunder, it roared out a warnin',*
> *I heard the roar of a wave that could drown the whole world,*
> *I heard one hundred drummers whose hands were a-blazin',*
> *I heard ten thousand whisperin' and nobody listenin',*
> *I heard one person starve, I heard many people laughin',*
> *I heard the song of a poet who died in the gutter,*
> *I heard the sound of a clown who cried in the alley,*
> *And it's a hard, and it's a hard, it's a hard, it's a hard,*
> *And it's a hard rain's a-gonna fall.*

> *Oh, who did you meet, my blue-eyed son?*
> *Who did you meet, my darling young one?*
> *I met a young child beside a dead pony,*
> *I met a white man who walked a black dog,*
> *I met a young woman whose body was burning,*
> *I met a young girl, she gave me a rainbow,*
> *I met one man who was wounded in love,*
> *I met another man who was wounded with hatred,*
> *And it's a hard, it's a hard, it's a hard, it's a hard,*
> *It's a hard rain's a-gonna fall.*

Just then the Wayo Wayo islanders were waking up. They had the impression that last night's wind had been particularly strong. As a matter of fact, the night wind on Wayo Wayo was always strong, but what the islanders did not know was that every night for the past several hundred years, Wayo Wayo had been losing a hand's worth of surface area and moving north one ten-thousandth of the length of a sand worm. And that this morning, a silent flotilla was monitoring some remote area of the great ocean and lining up like a firing squad. Each crewman stood at his post, gazing toward the horizon. Before long a beam of light leapt up into the sky, flew level for several thousand kilometers, then dove. Just getting up, the Wayo Wayoans thought a massive shooting star had crashed into the sea.

The beam of light plunged beneath the waves and kept boring its way down into an abyssal trench. Never seen before by man, the trench was home to bizarre creatures who could have come from outer space. Suddenly, every creature in the entire ocean heard a deafening sound, like no sound that had ever been heard before, as if some mighty being were departing. A great gash opened up deep in the trench, and a shock wave was transmitted toward the two ends, raising a tsunami of unprecedented power. Of iron will, that wave pushed another piece of the Trash Vortex toward Wayo Wayo. In three minutes and thirty-two seconds, it would, like a gargantuan carpenter's plane, peel away everything on the island, the living and the nonliving, into the sea.

On the island, only the Sea Sage and Earth Sage anticipated the event. The day before they had appealed to Kabang without receiving any reply.

"Why does Kabang not respond?" the Sea Sage and Earth Sage were deliberating.

"I don't think he ever will."

"Shall we warn the islanders?"

"Would it make any difference?"

The two of them fell silent for a while. The Sea Sage murmured, "I really want to know Kabang's reason. I just wish I knew why." The wrinkles on his face were so deep that his features seemed to be caving in.

"As you know, Kabang needs no reason for anything, even if His will is for Wayo Wayo to quietly abide in some small corner of the world," said the Sea Sage.

"Even if His will is for Wayo Wayo to quietly abide in some small corner of the world," said the Earth Sage. In unison, they repeated, "Even if His will is for Wayo Wayo to quietly abide in some small corner of the world."

At the approach of the great garbage tsunami, the two Sages were sitting at either end of the island, one of them facing the sea, the other facing away, both watching everything happen with their eyes wide open. The Sea

Sage's eyes began to bleed from overexertion, while the Earth Sage grasped the ground until the joints of his fingers shattered. When the wave smacked into the island, their bodies were instantly ripped apart, and even though they were both firm of will, they couldn't help howling in agony. Everything on the island—the houses, the shell walls, the *talawaka*, the beautiful eyes, the woeful calluses, the salt-heavy hair, and all the stories about the sea—was consigned to oblivion in a heartbeat.

At the same time, as if they'd all hearkened unto an epiphany, the sperm whale avatars of the second sons of Wayo Wayo silently assembled into a cetacean rank and file of head to fluke and fin to fin and started cleaving the waves, hastening toward a certain end. Day and night they swam, with no time to change into spirits after dark, with no time at all to rest. The pod passed through the Tropic of Capricorn, through the eyes of three newly formed typhoons, through cold seas and warm, heading straight for land.

One morning a week later, a pod of several hundred sperm whales would be discovered beached on the shores of Valparaíso, Chile, with grim eyes, cracked skin and crushed ribs—ribs crushed by their own weight. Tears would track the cheeks of creatures that did not normally shed tears. Villagers would try at high tide to push some of the whales back into the sea, but the whales, obstinate and resolute, would swim right back on shore.

Cetaceanologists from around the world would rush to Chile in the shortest possible time, because this pod of sperm whales would be entirely male, quite an odd occurrence. Even more surprisingly, one of the whales would be a giant of almost twenty meters in length, a one-of-a-kind in this day and age. As experts would indicate, precocious puberty induced by overfishing had sharply reduced sperm whale body size. Based on recent records, they'd assumed there were no more such truly massive sperm whales left anywhere in the world.

Till the end of their days, the experts who would gather on the Chilean beach would tell one story over and over again: the experience of watching a host of giant creatures die. Blood would trickle out of the mouths of the huge whales, noxious air would spray in huge quantities out of their left nostrils—their blowholes, located on top of their snouts—and their tails would flail in agony. As if they wanted to force memory from their brains, they would hammer the sand with their heads, leaving huge pits on the beach and making a heavy, hopeless monotone that would pass clear on through to the other side of Chile's coastal mountains, giving the farmers working in the fields pain of the chest.

Aside from the pounding, the beached whales would not make any other sound. Reminiscing in later days, the experts would all claim that they had heard the call of the whales when they beached. They would try to imitate the call in Mandarin, English, German, Klon, Galician, Dhivehi. Some language prodigy would even try in the dead languages of Manx and Eyak. But nobody would be able to imitate it accurately . . . for each would feel a terrible pain in the throat, like choking on a fishbone.

Then Valparaíso would shudder like an injured whale, as whale by whale by whale by whale by whale by whale would breathe its last upon the beach. The ones that would die first would bloat up under the oppressive sun, decompose and suddenly explode one after another. Their innards would go flying through the humid, stuffy air and spray down like rain on the cetaceanologists, the fishermen and the children who would have come to gather whale bones. The smell, a putridness no one would have ever smelled before, would make one and all pass out or crouch down and start vomiting.

And by the time they would recover their wits, the entire pod would have already expired, leaving the experts to tally the dead: in total there would be three hundred and sixty-five whales. A Swiss cetaceanologist in his seventies named Andreas would kneel down and weep, would actually weep himself to death. His mortal cries would touch the hearts of everyone on the beach, and everyone would join in and cry along with him. Their tears would drip onto the beach, soon to be recovered by the rising tide.

But the concentration of salt in the sea would not thereby increase, not in the least.

It was right at sunrise that Wayo Wayo was engulfed by the tsunami. Atile'i was facing away from the island, playing on the speaking flute as he rowed into the fragmented Trash Vortex, never looking back. The tune he played was incomprehensibly tender and ineffably anguished. After seeing Atile'i off, Alice swam back to the roof of the Sea House, stood on a broken solar panel, and tried to find Atile'i on the horizon. As the prow and the rain tarp were both made of materials from the vortex, camouflaging the craft and allowing it to proceed by stealth through a sea of trash, Alice looked for quite some time before she spotted him. His silhouette had become small as a gull's. Soon Alice started to sing, maybe for Atile'i, maybe for herself. It is one of the songs Thom had sung for her toward the sea the evening she first met him. She still remembered him telling her about the Dano–Swedish War of 1808–1809 and the artillery battery at Charlottenlund Fort, a relic of that conflict.

"This shore really saw war. The cannons really fired their balls. Soldiers really died on this beach. And boats really sank in that sea. This here is no ornamental cannon." He told her he'd lived in a cave over thirty meters underground, piloted a sloop across the Atlantic, and was now preparing for the challenges of rock and mountain climbing. Then they made love. Thom's penis penetrated deep inside her body, shining like a torch. In that little tent, she looked over his shoulder and saw the world aglow. In a certain instant, gazing into his pale blue eyes, she seemed to see a million worlds.

> *Oh, what'll you do now, my blue-eyed son?*
> *Oh, what'll you do now, my darling young one?*
> *I'm a-goin' back out 'fore the rain starts a-fallin',*
> *I'll walk to the depths of the deepest black forest,*
> *Then I'll stand on the ocean until I start sinkin',*
> *But I'll know my song well before I start singin',*
> *And it's a hard, it's a hard, it's a hard, it's a hard,*
> *It's a hard rain's a-gonna fall.*

"May the sea bless you," Alice says in a voice much smaller than the point of a pin. The youth has left, has entered the sea. And at this moment the weather on the sea is anything but fair: as rain clouds gather in the distance, Alice can tell that a storm is coming, the likes of which none of the islanders, who have weathered innumerable storms in their time, has ever seen before.

Alice swims back to the shore. The cleanup crew is already there. People run over to offer help when they see her there soaking wet, but Alice just walks in the direction of the hunting hut, keeping her head lowered so they will not be able to get a good look at her face. Now she is walking alone up toward the path through the loveless and pitiless forest. She met Atile'i for the first time along that path; she used to take it with Thom to get water from the stream. She walks and walks, and the moisture on the stalks of grass gradually soaks through her shoes and wets her toes, slowly gets into her eyes. Suddenly Alice feels something furry brush past her leg.

Ohiyo. It's Ohiyo.

Alice is happy she still has someone to say *Ohiyo* to. Without Alice noticing, Ohiyo has grown into a beautiful adult cat. Alice has to do something for this little survivor.

The cat raises her amazing little head, opens her eyes, one blue and the other brown, and, responding to Alice's call, looks right back at her.

## About the Author

Wu Ming-Yi was born in 1971 in Taiwan, where he still lives. A writer, artist, professor, and environmental activist, he has been teaching literature and creative writing at National Dong Hwa University since 2000 and is now a professor in the Department of Chinese. Wu is the author of two books of nature writing, the second of which, *The Way of Butterflies,* was awarded the China Times Open Book Award in 2003. His debut novel, *Routes in the Dream,* was named one of the ten best Chinese-language novels of the year by *Asian Weekly* magazine. *The Man with the Compound Eyes* is his first book to be translated into English.

## About the Translator

Darryl Sterk has translated numerous short stories from Taiwan for *The Chinese Pen Quarterly,* and now teaches translation in the Graduate Program in Translation and Interpretation at National Taiwan University.